KNIGHT'S DAWN

Book One of the Red Pavilions

Kim Hunter

www.orbitbooks.co.uk

An *Orbit* Book

First published in Great Britain by Orbit 2001
This edition published by Orbit 2002
Reprinted 2003 (twice)

Copyright © Kim Hunter 2001

The moral right of the author has been asserted.

A CIP catalogue record for this book is available from the British Library

ISBN 1 84149 090 3

Typeset in Revival 555 by
Palimpsest Book Production Limited,
Polmont, Stirlingshire
Printed in Great Britain by
Mackays of Chatham plc, Chatham, Kent

Orbit
An imprint of
Time Warner Books UK
Brettenham House
Lancaster Place
London WC2E 7EN

To Pete, a man of wild and wonderful
ideas, and of generous spirit

Chapter One

'Wake up, wake up, someone is near!'

The knight wearily opened his eyelids. There was a dead snake near his foot, with a bloody cudgel next to it. A raven hopped around the snake and stick, yelling at him.

The light hurt his eyes. A pale white sun glared down on the knight from the heavens. He was on a hillside, a slope, on which there had been a great battle. All his muscles ached from the fighting. He felt utterly fatigued. It was all very hazy to him now, blurred and warped. He tried to recall what he had been doing in this battle and who the armies were.

If he allowed his mind to look back he could see the battle in full bloody murder. Around him he beheld a great heaving mess of men, armies rolling one over the other, multitudes of men tumbling like waves of water into hordes of other men. They hacked with battleaxes, thrust with swords and spears, beat each other with maces. Weapon points entered flesh through seams and chinks in armour. Arrows thudded into the chests of knights, penetrating breastplates as if they were paper. Heads and torsos were split asunder. Skulls were battered and crushed by warhammers. There was fire and blood and the bright flashes of a hundred thousand blades, lance heads, pike tips.

'There he is! Do you see him? Down by the tree line.'

The vision of the past washed away and the knight's eyes were clear once again. He stared at the area indicated by the raven. There was a horseman down there, wrapped from head to foot, swathed in calico dyed with indigo, only his eyes exposed. The man was a obviously a lone hunter. He rode his piebald steed with his knees only, leaving his hands free. On his left wrist was a hawk wearing trailing scarlet jesses. There were golden bells on its ankles. In the hunter's right hand was a small black crossbow, with a bolt in the breech.

'I see him,' said the knight, not considering why he was talking to a bird. There was too much other strangeness in the air to worry about things perhaps unthreatening. 'I shall keep him in view.'

In his mind's ear he now heard the shrieks of wounded and dying men on the hillside around him. Some cried for a physician, some for their mothers, some for their comrades. The cries were pitiful to hear. There was the yell of a decapitated head, as it continued its shout of terror even after leaving the shoulders of its owner. There was the clashing of steel on steel, thousandfold, ringing through the surrounding hills. Screams, groans, death rattles. It was a cacophony which filled the knight's head. The bullroarers and the trumpets. The animal-skin drums and the log-drums. The whistles and bladderpipes and ox-horns. To the ears of the animals in the woodlands and valleys, this deafening discord must have sounded like the end of the world. Especially when their own kind were being slaughtered: the noise of screaming horses as they are disembowelled by the lances of knights, or limb-lopped by foot-soldiers, is something no creature ever forgets.

'See,' said the raven, 'the hunter views his quarry.'

A purple heron flew overhead and the hunter released his hawk. The raptor shot skyward, after the heron which had now swerved in flight. There were few signs of panic in the fleeing prey. Only the leisurely flapping of the great wings and the harpoon head stretched a little further forward.

At that moment, while all eyes were on the hawk and the heron, a black boar broke cover. It rushed at the hunter's steed from the flank. The horse's eyes rolled and it whinnied in fright, rearing to the right. The hunter steadied his mount with his knees and took careful aim with the crossbow. There was a *thwunk* and the bolt struck the boar in the brain. The beast's legs folded under it and it rolled, crashing into a thicket, dead as a rock. The hunter then looked up to see the heron plummeting from the sky, the hawk having stooped and struck.

'We should go and speak with this man,' said the raven.

For the first time the knight turned his attention to the talking bird.

'Who are you? *What* are you? Did you come to feed upon the dead?'

'Dead? What dead?' asked the bird.

The knight looked about him quickly and then remembered. It had all taken place in his mind. Yet he knew there had been a battle. Looking down at himself he saw that he was wounded in a number of places. They were not serious cuts or abrasions, but they were fresh. His uniform was filthy and in tatters and he wore the remnants of bloodstained armour. He was caked in sweat and dust. His throat was parched: choked with the same dust that decorated his clothes. From his belt hung an empty black-and-silver scabbard, twisted and bent. Stitched on the leather of the scabbard in silver-wire thread were the words, *Kutrama and Sintra*. The knight was suddenly bewildered. Who was he? What was his name? Why was he lying on this hot hillside, talking to a raven who was looking at him as if he were a corpse?

'Why do you stare at me like that?'

The bird said, 'A crow can look at a king.'

'Well, I don't like it. If you want to end up on a gibbet, just keep on doing it.'

'Irritable beggar, aren't we? No need to get annoyed. I was just looking at your eyes. They're blue. I've never seen eyes that colour before. Everyone around here has brown eyes.'

The knight, who had been unaware of the colour of his eyes, touched his eyelids.

They turned away from each other to stare at the hunter, who was now gathering up the carcass of the boar and strapping it to the rump of his mount. His hawk was enjoying the brains of the heron, where the hunter had cracked its skull with a rock. This was the raptor's reward for a clean kill. The hunter then sat on a rock and began plucking the heron, purple feathers flying over his shoulders. As the knight descended, the raven hopping on behind, the hunter had finished cleaning and gutting the heron and was preparing a wood fire on which to roast it.

There was a beck nearby. The knight went straight to this and began scooping up the water to drink: clear water, but not sparkling. It was midday, the sun horizontally overhead, but the warmth from it was weak.

The knight was then aware that the hunter was speaking to him.

'Are you in need of assistance?'

The hunter's voice was confident, firm, but not very deep.

He looked and sounded like a slimly-built youth and his delicate movements offended the knight's masculinity. Dark-brown eyes stared at him from a band of flesh beneath the swathes of blue calico. There was enquiry there, if not concern.

'Where am I?' asked the knight. 'Has there been a battle here?'

The hunter said, 'Your eyes – they're blue.'

'Does that matter?'

The hunter shrugged and delivered answers which were crisp and to the point. 'You are just south of the Ancient Forest, near the petrified pools of Yan. To my knowledge there has been no battle hereabouts for over a century.'

'But, that can't be true. Look at me!' He opened his arms and invited inspection. 'I am wounded. My uniform is in shreds.'

'I cannot account for your condition. There has been no battle here. What is your name? From what country are you? This is not a time to be wandering Guthrum alone. There are brigands and bandits abroad, and the queen's soldiers are suspicious of lone travellers. They have licence to execute strangers found roaming the countryside. If you do not end up with a broken skull, you might be hanged from gallows such as those you see on that hill.'

The knight looked up. In the distance, beyond the stream, was a triple-gallows, with several corpses hanging from it. As the soldier stared at this place of execution, seemingly miles from any village, town or city, he noticed that few of the hanged figures had hands on the ends of their arms.

'Guthrum,' murmured the knight, grasping at the word and inspecting it closely. 'That name should probably mean something to me, but it doesn't. And as for my own name, I can't remember it. Do I even have a name? I feel I am in some kind of dream, or nightmare. I know nothing about myself.'

'Perhaps you are mad?' suggested the hunter, matter-of-factly.

'No, no. I do not *feel* mad.'

'Madmen never do. To whom were you speaking, as you were coming down the hill? To yourself?'

'Why, no,' the knight turned and pointed to the raven, hopping on some stones in the stream. 'To that bird. It speaks as well as you or me. Raven, say something to the hunter.'

The raven simply sipped at the running water with its beak. It looked like any of the other birds in the area. There was no comprehension in its demeanour or its eyes.

The hunter nodded slowly. 'I think you are mad.' He pointed to the roasted heron carcass, part of which he had already eaten. 'You may have some of that if you're hungry. Then I must be on my way.'

'Wait!' said the knight, quickly. 'Where are you going?'

'Why, back to Zamerkand of course. I would rather return home before nightfall. If this countryside is dangerous during the day, it is ten times worse at night. There are bears and wolves to contend with, not to mention—'

'Take me with you,' pleaded the knight. 'I have no weapon with which to defend myself and I don't know the way. I can assist you if you are attacked. Forgive me, but you do not look strong enough to defend yourself against enemies on the road.'

The eyes hardened. 'Did you see me kill the boar?'

'Hunting is a different matter. It takes more than a sharp eye to kill a human. You need the strength of will.'

'Strength of will? A moment ago it was my physique that was important – now it's whether I have the stomach for killing. You really should make up your mind what it is about me that you find lacking.' The hunter stared hard for a few moments, then nodded. 'You may follow my horse. I can't take you up behind me because, as you see, I am carrying a wild boar.'

The knight felt inclined to argue that his life was more precious than a boar's carcass, but the hunter had already swung himself back into his saddle. The hawk had taken to the air again, but the hunter whirled a silver lure around his head, on a long piece of cord, and the hawk came down to his wrist. Then the hunter set off at a leisurely pace, his palfrey high-stepping through the woods, the ground being spongy with thick moss. The knight, weary though he was, trotted on behind chewing on a drumstick. At one point the raven flew down from a branch and landed on his shoulder, to whisper in his ear, 'You're mad, you are. Fancy talking to a black bird.'

The bird then flew away, leaving the knight bemused and angry, wondering whether indeed the raven was right.

During the journey the hunter stopped once to treat the knight's wounds with herbs and healing plants. The cuts were fairly superficial, but there was still a danger of infection. Deep inside him was a bitterness, a hatred for something he could not explain to himself. These feelings were like dark shadows in his soul, but he did not know what was casting them.

In the forest, great spiders' webs joined high oak branches with the ground. The soldier inadvertently ran through these, getting his face and hands gummed with the sticky threads. When they left the woods and began crossing boggy ground, there were clusters and knots of snakes in every peat hag: far too many to be natural. Every so often they came across another gallows, with hanged people dangling from the bar.

In most cases the hands were missing, though some fresh corpses were intact. The knight wanted to ask the hunter about this, but could not catch his breath enough to be able to hold a conversation.

After three hours of travelling, when the clouds were pink islands in the evening sky, the two men crested a ridge. The knight found himself looking down on an immense walled city with turrets and towers rising as thick as spears from an army of closely-packed warriors. Zamerkand.

There were flags and banners fluttering from every pinnacle. Dark, triangular windows peppered these spires and the wind blew through them and played melodies as if they were holes in a flute. Domes and cupolas crowned every other one of the tall columns, upon which the weak evening sunlight glittered with malevolent sheen.

The knight's aerial view revealed that within this massive fortification of tall spiky buildings were several palaces, parks, gardens and courtyards. Fountains showered expansive lawns, around which were myrtle hedges, shrubberies and spinneys of conifers and deciduous trees. There were bright lakes and moats that flashed in the evening light. Moreover, a whole town existed within the city walls, with houses, cobbled streets, stalls and cattle pens.

Around the city were at least a hundred large tents – sandstone-red in colour.

An arched stone tunnel ran from one side of the city, across the open wooded countryside, its terminus out of sight beyond the hilly downs and woodland sweeps. The hunter explained that beneath this fortified tunnel lay a canal, straight as a silver arrow, which connected the city with the sea. Along this canal went trading barges, protected from attack by six-foot-thick walls, to meet with ships coming and going from a natural harbour on the Cerulean Sea. Trade with countries like Uan Muhuggiag, across the blue water, was brisk and profitable. It kept the citizens of Zamerkand reasonably wealthy, even during times of siege, when the countryside was ravaged by fighting.

'What a wonderful place,' said the knight, pausing to drink in this magnificent scene. He looked around him, at the silhouettes of several gallows on the neighbouring ridges, and down before the city gates at what appeared at a distance to be severed heads stuck on sharpened stakes. 'Unlike the countryside in which it resides.'

'Ah, as to that,' said the hunter, having alighted, 'you must understand that HoulluoH is dying. His grip on the world has slipped, and people are fearful. But all will be well soon. Things will right themselves once the new King Magus is in command.'

'King Magus?' queried the knight.

The hunter placed a slim hand on the knight's shoulder, which made the tall, dark stranger to this land feel uneasy.

'You really are a newcomer, aren't you? Guthrum, my friend, is a region of many wizards, the greatest of which is the King Magus. It is he who ensures that those who have the power of magic do not abuse it. He maintains a balance in the land, between good and evil, nature and supernature, magicians and ordinary folk.'

'Do the wizards have blue eyes?' asked the knight, hopefully, wondering if he had special powers.

'My dear friend, *no* one in Guthrum has blue eyes.'

The knight shrugged off the over-friendly hand from his shoulder.

'I am not your dear friend and would prefer it,' he said, 'if you did not touch me in that manner.'

There was a twinkling in the eyes of the other, who appeared to be smiling beneath the mask of blue calico. The knight knew he was being mocked, but could not do anything since he was in debt to this person.

'As you wish, soldier, but you may be in need of a friend in these troubled times, here in Guthrum.'

Soldier? That was as good a name as any. He had no other. Until his memory returned and he knew his identity he would call himself *Soldier*. It was a manly name, if nothing else.

'I can take care of myself,' he said. 'Don't you worry about me.'

Soldier stared down at the castle again. In the ruddy light of the dying sun, blood-scarlet in contrast to the whiteness of its midday face, he could see the red pavilions surrounding the city. He estimated that each pavilion would probably accommodate eighty to a hundred men and there were around a hundred pavilions. Ten thousand men. Each one of the pavilions had a pennon flying from the tip of the centre pole. These pennons bore a symbol but the distance was too great to identify them. When he asked the hunter he was told they were animal symbols – boars, eagles, falcons, cats, dogs – which denoted a company of men. Each pavilion was an entity unto itself and loyal in the first place to its commander. In battle it was the honour of the pavilion which was foremost in the minds of the soldiers. Men lived, fought and died for the pavilion and nothing was permitted to smirch its honour.

'Who are in the pavilions?' he asked. 'Do they guard some visiting royal or noble?'

'Mercenary soldiers,' replied the hunter. 'Troops from the land of Carthaga. Queen Vanda uses them to supplement her own army, when she is forced to wage war. Actually the

Carthagans do the brunt of the fighting, while the Guthrumites usually end up supporting *them*. They have special qualities. They are brilliant warriors – brave, selfless, disciplined, dedicated to their duty – they've been in the pay of Guthrum for centuries now and are intensely loyal to us. Each soldier serves twenty years then returns to Carthaga. He can keep his whole extended family on his pay while he is a serving soldier and he receives a huge bonus for completing his time.'

'Why are they outside the city walls?'

The hunter shrugged. 'It's the way it has always been. They never enter the city. Perhaps at one time they were not wholly trustworthy? It has become tradition now. The Guthrumite imperial guards are responsible for policing inside the city and for protecting the royal family. Carthagans protect the city from attack by outside hostile forces. If a larger army is required, then the citizens are armed and put in the field.'

Soldier and the hunter then descended from the ridge, with the raven somewhere around in the gathering gloom. As they approached the city Soldier could see that the Carthagans were a squat, broad-shouldered people. They were swarthy, with flat faces and square frames. He and the hunter were not stopped or accosted while they passed through the red pavilions. Soldier assumed this was because they were only two and hardly a threat to an army of ten thousand tough, battle-hardened warriors.

Soldier decided it would be a different story when they reached the gates of the city, decorated with an avenue of heads on stakes.

They walked through this ghastly gauntlet. Matted hair hung over eye-sockets picked clean by the birds. Tongues, also attacked by birds and insects, hung from between swollen lips. Noses and cheeks were pitted by the weather and other agents of destruction.

'Help me,' whispered one particularly gruesome skull as Soldier passed it by. 'Help me, please!'

Soldier turned and stared at the head, startled by the voice, only to see the stalking raven squatting inside, staring out through one of the empty eyesockets.

'Fooled you,' murmured the raven, in a satisfied tone. 'Fancy a bit of dinner? Plenty here.'

With that the black bird left the back of the skull and began pecking at the rotting flesh.

'You're disgusting,' said Soldier, curling his bottom lip.

The hunter said, 'Were you speaking to me?'

'No, no,' replied Soldier, wearily, 'just to the raven. You know? My madness? I am a lunatic after all.'

'Just so,' said the hunter. 'Come, we must enter the city before the gates are locked for the night. Otherwise we might have to share the hospitality of one of these pavilions. Good fighting men the Carthagans might be, but they are also among the legions of the sweaty and unwashed. Their favourite fare is wild-oat porridge dried in the sun, cut into slabs and fried in goat's lard. If you want to sleep with the stink of axle grease in your nostrils and breakfast on oats fried in animal fat, that's fine, but I rather look forward to a supper of fish and almonds, followed by a night in clean sheets bearing the fragrance of sandalwood.'

'You would,' muttered Soldier, under his breath, 'but I doubt I'll see better fare than fried porridge.'

Chapter Two

There was a good deal of traffic going through and milling around the outer gate at this time of the evening. It was the hour of the day when those whose work took them beyond the city's walls came back inside for protection during the night hours. There were coaches and horsemen, peasants with ox-carts, dog-carts and hand-carts, and lone men and women on foot, some carrying the implements of their trade: scythes, axes, saws, hammers. Many of the vehicles were piled high with faggots and wood. Others with animal fodder or vegetables. The way through the gate was ankle-deep in dung and though Soldier attempted to tread carefully, his leggings were soiled almost to the knee shortly after joining the queue. The whole area stank and the flies were large and bothersome.

Soldier assumed that they would be stopped by the outer guards on the gate and questioned, but they hardly even glanced at the hunter and himself. Once inside the outer ward however, it was an entirely different matter. They were almost pounced upon by four burly men in uniform and led to a gatehouse tower. The hunter was taken inside, while Soldier was made to wait. It was growing dark now and the lamp-lighters were abroad. There were brands in iron cages on the walls round about and these were being torched. Soldier felt it must be a wealthy place to have street lighting and was duly impressed by all the activity.

The hunter's mount stood tethered to a post nearby, looking mournfully at the door through which her master had vanished. On its back was the boar the hunter had shot with his crossbow earlier in the day. Soldier was now extremely hungry and the thought of the boar roasting on a spit played havoc with his imagination. He wondered if the hunter would invite him to a meal, now that they were inside the city.

'All right,' said a guard, coming out and beckoning to Soldier, 'in you go.'

Soldier stepped inside the tower to find himself immediately in a room where a scrivener in a grey robe sat at a desk. The man was elderly, with a wall eye and a rather sour look on his face. He was also quite ugly, being bloated and puffy-looking, with a poor complexion and some kind of rash on his neck.

'Name?' said the man in a bored voice, his quill pen poised above a great leather-bound book.

Soldier looked about him, bewildered. There did not seem to be another door in the room, yet the hunter was nowhere to be seen.

'Where did the hunter go?' he asked.

The scrivener looked up with his one good eye, impatiently.

'Stranger,' he said, in a quiet patronising tone, 'I would like to get this over with as quickly as possible, so that I can get back to my soup, which is cooling on the table by the window. Soup is not my favourite fare, but it is one of the only meals I can digest in comfort these days, since all my teeth are gone and my gums are somewhat diseased. If you do not reply within three seconds, I shall have you thrown outside the city walls where you will spend the night – or not – depending on how soon the wolves get to you, most of whom, I am jealous to be so informed, still retain a full set of fangs.'

'Soldier,' said Soldier, quickly.

'What?'

'My name – my name is Soldier.'

The scrivener scratched away in his book, his left eyebrow raised and his tongue-tip sticking out of the corner of his mouth.

'Soldier,' he repeated. 'Nothing more? Not "Soldier from Kandun" or "Soldier of Tyern"? Usually when one's name is one's trade, a town or a city follows. "Smith of Blandaine," for example . . .'

'Just Soldier.'

'Then my next question is, where are you from, Soldier?'

'From – from the Ancient Forest.'

The scrivener looked up from beneath his brows, his wall eye disconcerting Soldier.

'The Ancient Forest? That region is uninhabited. What is more, you do not look like a local, like one of us, so to speak. You seem to be a foreigner and a very strange one at that. Blue eyes? I never heard of such a thing, not even amongst the beast-people beyond the water margin. You'll have to do better than that, Soldier.'

'Look,' he blurted, 'the truth is I don't know who I am or where I'm from. I woke today on a hillside just beyond the Ancient Forest. I feel as if I've been in a great battle – I'm sure I have. But the hunter who brought me here said there had been no battle in that region for years. I don't under-stand what's happened to me, but I mean no harm to anyone in Guthrum. I simply need a safe place to sleep until my memory returns and I can put my life in order.'

'Ah, yes, the hunter. You have money?'

'Money?' the soldier felt in his tattered pockets, around his belt for a purse, and came up empty. 'No, no money.'

The scrivener put down his pen and smiled. It was a horrible expression, even worse than his scowl.

'Then how do you expect to live?'

'I thought – that is, I hadn't really thought. But I'm willing to work. I'll eat scraps for the time being. I'll fight with the dogs for bones under the table. It doesn't matter. What I need is time – time to recover my wits.'

The scrivener suddenly and surprisingly shrugged. 'As you will. I understand you clutched the hem of the hunter's garment and craved hospitality? In which case we can't refuse you shelter, that person being a citizen of this state. You may have to sleep in the street, but that's up to you and your fortunes.' The scrivener pointed the goose-feather quill at Soldier as if it were a weapon. 'But stay out of trouble. You're lucky you were not caught and hung in the countryside. Am I understood?'

'Perfectly. I will be the model citizen.'

'You will not be a citizen at all, since you are an outlander. But you will be *good* or you will be *dead*.'

'Yes, yes, you have my word.'

With that the scrivener called the guard. Alarmingly, Soldier was marched away towards a half-lit shack standing not far from the tower. He had thought he would be released immediately, but it seemed there were other procedures to go through. The shack turned out to be a blacksmith's forge, with a great furnace making the place unbearably hot. There a tall, skinny man, whose skin was pitted with black scars from flying red hot iron filings, fitted an iron collar around Soldier's throat and sealed it with a rivet.

Soldier yelled, as the pain of the hot rivet bit into his neck.

The smith grunted.

Still wincing, Soldier asked, 'Are you from Blandaine?'

The smith stared. 'Yes, how do you know?'

'Because I have heard that people from that town are unfeeling bastards.'

The smith's eyes hardened. 'You be careful, stranger. When the time comes, it'll be me who takes that collar from your neck. My mother was a gentle woman, but I have inherited all my character from my father, who was one of the queen's torturers. The best at his trade, so I'm told.'

The guard laughed, and said, 'Come on, stranger. On your way now. If I were you I'd make my way down to the canal district, where you'll find the rest of the riff-raff.'

'How long do I have to wear this thing?'

'A month at the most.'

Once the iron collar was in place Soldier was allowed to go. He realised he had been given the collar so that he could easily be identified. People would know he was a stranger and be wary of him. He would be under observation, by the local residents, during all hours. If he turned out to be a thief, or worse, he would be banished from the city. These precautions seemed very reasonable to Soldier, even if he did feel a little bitter at being subjected to them. In dark times people protected themselves against infiltrators from the wildernesses.

His new iron torc was uncomfortable at first. It chafed his neck. But he knew he would soon get used to it.

Soldier made his way through the dimly-lit cobbled streets, not really knowing where he was going. Eventually he came across a canal, which he followed to a network of moored barges. The canals were fed from the water in the moat, which in turn received an inflow of water from the natural system of rivers and lakes beyond the city walls. He was now in the centre of the city. He went towards a quay. There he saw a sight that shocked him to the core.

The bloated body of a woman was floating in the water, caught up in the mooring rope of a small barge. Just as Soldier spotted her, someone came up from below decks and saw her too.

'Bloody corpses!' Soldier heard the bargee's words quite clearly. 'They stink in this weather . . .'

The bargee took a boat-hook and prised the cadaver away from his mooring line with as much passion as if it were the carcass of some animal. The white limbs and naked torso of the victim of some horrible violence — her head was split down through her nose and upper jaw — then went floating off on the current of the canal. The bargee grunted in satisfaction, before going below again. There had been no compassion in the bargee, only irritation that a lump of flesh had snagged on his boat. Soldier was appalled by the lack of sympathy shown by the bargee and the horrible nature of the woman's wounds.

'What is this place I have come to?' he asked himself.

Sitting on the edge of a quay and contemplating his shadow on the water below, Soldier thought about his life. It amounted to only twelve hours. He had been born at noon, so far as his memory told him, and it was now around midnight. He knew nothing about himself. In his mind he clung onto those aspects of his short life which meant something to him. The hunter, for example. That they should have met on the edge of the forest was pure coincidence, yet Soldier felt that the hunter knew more about him than he had revealed. Soldier believed the hunter's interest in him went deeper than just a casual meeting and acquaintance. And where had he gone? The hunter had simply disappeared into thin air, taking his horse, hawk and boar with him.

'He's probably roasting a pork joint over a log fire now,' said Soldier.

'Wrong. The meat is already cooked and fit to be devoured. The hunter is just this minute eating the hog's head apple. You know, the one they put in the pig's mouth when they roast him? In his other hand is a jug of ale. I bet you'd like both, wouldn't you? Unfortunately, all you're likely to get tonight is a pie crust washed down with some of that canal water.'

Soldier turned to see the raven perched on the edge of the wharf, a piece of pie at its feet.

'Where have you been?' Soldier asked.

'Oh, here, there and everywhere. Aren't you going to thank me for the bit of pie? I've eaten my share. This bit's for you.'

Soldier reached out and gobbled down a piece of crust half the size of a man's hand.

'Can you get any more?' he asked. 'I'm still very hungry.'

'Are we friends?'

'Do we have to be? Can't you remain a figment of my imagination?'

'Not if I'm going to steal real food for you.'

Soldier nodded. 'I see your point. All right, we're friends. Does that make you happy?'

'Not deliriously, but we need each other. What would you like me to fetch you now? A piece of pork crackling?'

Soldier closed his eyes. 'Oh, yes – yes, yes, yes.'

'Well, if I don't return, you'll know I've got a crossbow bolt up my arse. Nice necklace, by the way. Pearls would have suited you better.'

The bird flew off, into the night, leaving Soldier fingering his metal collar.

People were beginning to gather now, around the storage houses alongside the canals. Some of these huts were empty and it was to these that the homeless gravitated, presumably to find shelter for the night. Soldier was looked on with mild suspicion as they drifted by him. He sat on the quay, minding his own business, not speaking to anyone. There were ragged women with urchins in tow. There were men who looked spent and wasted. There were the drinkers and the hemp-smokers and the gambling addicts. There were those who had fallen on hard times because of luck, and those who had brought hard times upon themselves. None of them approached Soldier directly and he did not feel confident enough to speak to anyone either.

A short while later the raven came back with meat in its beak. For the next hour the raven fed Soldier as if it were one of its own fledglings. Then he fell asleep on the quay. Fortunately it was a warm night, so he did not suffer any exposure. The following morning he wandered the city, the raven on his shoulder, finding the market-place. There he breakfasted on cabbage and kale stalks which he found in the gutters.

It was in the market that he first saw his reflection in a copper mirror. The face, with its patchy black beard, was a stranger to him. He thought it looked tired but tough, with an unblemished complexion not pocked or scarred in any way. Indeed, he looked a soldier. His hair was dark and cut unfashionably short, seemingly by a barber lacking in skill. He guessed his age to be around thirty years. Beyond that, his reflection told him nothing about himself. He remained a mystery to his own eyes.

He began begging for his food. There was a hostility amongst the people which quickly emerged. Soldier was kicked and beaten, sent on his way with bruises and all but broken bones. He was shocked too, by the level of apathy he found in the citizens. They did not seem to care about anything at all. Several times he came across bodies, in alleys or floating down the canals, with signs of violence on them. Clearly murder was rife, and he feared being blamed for one of these deaths. It is easy to point the finger at a stranger and yell, 'Assassin!' There was a high level of corruption too, with bribes freely passing between citizens and figures of authority. This Guthrum was a dangerous place for anyone who had no friends and did not know the unwritten rules which kept men alive in such times.

It was on one of his forays around the market-place, begging amongst the stalls, that he met Spagg.

Soldier stared at the stall in front of him in amazement. Displayed there were severed hands, some of them stuffed with herbs and with candles stitched between the index and forefinger. Others were in their naked state. They had all been drained of blood. The dried ones looked brown and grizzled, and in some of these the sinews and tendons had shrunk so that the hand now resembled a claw of some giant raptor.

'Can I help you friend?' asked the warty-faced individual behind the stall. 'Do you wish to purchase my wares?' He looked into Soldier's face. 'Do you wish to sell those blue eyes? They're rare in Guthrum. Unique, even. I could get quite a bit for those eyes, if we preserved 'em in good gin.'

Soldier stared at the man who wore a leather apron and skull cap.

'I need the eyes. They're the only pair I've got. And I can't buy anything. I can't afford anything. Can't you see I'm poor? What are they for, anyway?'

The individual chuckled. 'You don't know me? Ah, the iron collar. You're a stranger. Well, I'm Spagg, and these, my friend, are hands-of-glory. The hands of hanged men and women. Ownership of one of these will unlock doors to a fortune. You don't need money now. Just promise me some of your future earnings, so to speak, and I'll let you have one on tick.'

Soldier remembered all the handless corpses hanging from the gallows out in the countryside.

'You cut them from bodies?'

Spagg said proudly, 'I have the only licence for hanged men's hands. Got it from the queen's own chancellor. I'm the only seller of this kind of merchandise inside the city walls. You won't find better quality anywhere. Ask anyone.' He picked up one of the hands, a rather battered looking specimen, and presented it to Soldier. 'Grisly objects, I can hear you saying, under your breath. But this macabre-looking item can make you invisible, my friend. If you light the candle, made from the hand's own fat, you can freeze your enemies into immobility. A useful tool for a man whose business takes place late at night or in the small hours of the morning.'

Soldier shook his head. 'You see this collar? If I'm found to be a thief, I'll be expelled from Zamerkand.'

'But with one of these,' smiled Spagg, 'you can come back in again without being seen.'

'If you believe in such things.'

Spagg carefully put the hideous extremity back in its place on the top of the stall.

'Ah, there's the rub, friend. You have to believe in it for it to work. Many's the customer who has come back to me and said, "Spagg, this here hand-of-glory don't work." And I say to 'em, the reason is, friend, you got to *make* it work. You got to put your faith in it, believe in it, or it's just another chopped-off bit of body, ain't it? Now, what about a straight swap? This genuine hanged man's hand, for that bent old black leather scabbard with its silver tip and band.' Spagg pointed to the buckled sword sheath on Soldier's belt.

Soldier clutched his sheath. 'No – no, this stays with me.'

Spagg shook his head and clucked. 'You won't get nowhere in life by bein' so possessive, friend. Look at you. You're close to starving . . .' his eyes suddenly narrowed and he looked to be deep in thought. Then he said, 'Here's a thing. What about you come to work for me? I can't pay you much, but you'll get one good meal a day out of it, at least. What say?'

'What would I have to do?'

'Why, you go out and collect the hands for me, while I stay here and sell 'em. Whenever I do the collectin' meself, I have to close the stall. This way you could keep me supplied and I could be here all the time to do the selling.'

Soldier said, 'It wouldn't be because collecting the hands is dangerous work?'

Spagg, a knotty-looking man with a shapeless ribcage and pointed shoulders, did his best to looked shocked.

'Me? Scared to go out? Why, you'll not find a braver knight within these five miles square. It's not about that, it's about business. I need to be here, to do the sellin'.'

'Why don't you leave the stall to me, and then you'll be free to do the collecting?'

'And trust a stranger with my money?' This time he was genuinely shocked. 'You must have worms in the brain. Listen, iron collar, I've made you an offer. Do you want to take me up on it, or not? No more arguments, mind.'

'How much then?'

Spagg shook his head in disgust. 'I've never met a man so close to starvin' to death who had time to haggle and bargain with his patron. I'll look after you, don't you worry.'

'How much?'

'Two spinza a hand. The left hand's more valuable than the right, but I'll pay five spinza for a pair, but they've got to match, mind. I don't pay anythin' for hands with thumbs missing. If they was thieves before they was murderers, then more than likely they'll have had their thumbs chopped off. Tattoos is fine, 'specially if they're black arts ones – you know, skulls and magic symbols and such. Some of my customers like to collect ones with different tattoos. Scars? Well, if they're interesting marks. No badly mutilated ones. Any questions?'

'Do I have the use of a horse?'

'Horse?' cried Spagg, the look of disgust almost a perma-nent expression now. 'You get a donkey and like it.'

Thus Soldier went to work for Spagg, the hand-of-glory merchant. Spagg's donkey proved to be an ugly and obsti-nate beast, older than the mountains and often harder to move. It was a gruesome trade, but Soldier was prepared to accept almost anything to provide himself with food.

Chapter Three

Spagg gave Soldier a wooden baton with a crudely-carved weasel on one end. This symbol was a market-trader's credentials. When Soldier was stopped by the imperial guard, or when he wanted to leave or enter Zamerkand, he had to produce the baton to prove his right to move freely as the employee of a citizen. The iron collar remained always a great burden and restriction. City guards continually stopped and searched him. Ordinary citizens kept him at bay with hostile glares and narrowed eyes. He was made to feel aware that he was permitted to stay in the city on sufferance.

The first time Soldier went outside he found he was quite looking forward to entering the open countryside again. The city was claustrophobic, the atmosphere inside smoky and smelly. Every street in the city was engrimed with faeces from dogs, cats, livestock and birds. Every wall, door and window bore the sooty traces of smoke. Once through the gates the air seemed cleaner and brighter. He breathed deeply as the donkey beneath him ambled along. The raven came with him, for company. Soldier was getting used to having the bird around.

'Raven, how is that you have human speech?' asked the Soldier, as the sky opened up before them. It was a hazy day, the pale sun hanging in the sky like a paper disc. 'You must have helped a wizard at some time.'

'No,' replied the raven. 'In fact it's the opposite. I stole from a witch.'

'And she rewarded you with speech?'

'No, she changed me from a human into a bird. I was a thief, running the streets of the city. When Clegnose caught me stealing from her house, she transformed me into a raven. Then the old cow died, leaving me trapped in the form of a bird. I don't mind. It's easier to find food this way.'

'You can never become a boy again?'

'Only the witch who cast the spell can remove it.'

'I've noticed that you don't often reveal the fact that you have the power of speech.'

The raven ruffled its feathers. 'Why would I, not being a fool? Only problems lie in wait for the raven which goes around bragging it can speak. There are those who would cage me and use me to earn money for them as a curiosity. There are those who would kill me, thinking me a demon.'

'Why choose me?' asked Soldier. 'I might be one of those two kinds of men.'

'You? You are as much a curiosity as I am, with your blue eyes and no name. You have just as many problems.'

'I suppose you're right,' sighed Soldier.

The donkey was carrying him up a slope now, about two miles beyond the city. It was a grassy hill with smooth granite rocks occasionally rising above the turf, like whales breaking the surface of the sea. Soldier could see a gallows on the crest of the hill, with a hanged figure dangling from a rope. This was his destination, but it seemed he could not get any nearer to it, no matter how hard he tried. After a while Soldier realised that the problem was not one of magic, but one of perspective. The gallows were so tall, the hanged man so large, that Soldier had been further away than he realised. When he reached the corpse he saw that the victim was at least nine feet tall. Not only that, the man had extremities disproportionate even to this large body. The cadaver's hands and feet were quite huge.

The corpse was in about its third day and therefore relatively fresh.

'About the same time a hare should be hung before jugging it,' said the raven. 'Three-day-old flesh is sometimes as tasty to humans as it is to birds.'

'You stay away from this corpse,' warned Soldier. 'I don't think I could stomach watching you pick at his eyes.'

'He hasn't got any,' pointed out the raven. 'Nor a few other parts as well.'

Soldier stared and saw that a particular item of the body had already been cut from its roots.

'Well, let's get on with it.'

Soldier opened the bag of tools he had been given by Spagg and took out a pruning saw. He then began the grisly task of sawing off the giant's right hand. It was a slow business, for the body kept swaying back and forth. To reach the hand Soldier found he had to sit on the giant's right foot, like a child sits on a playground swing. Even so, try as he might he could not get through the thick bone with the saw, and finished up hacking through it with a hand-axe from the bag. Spagg had asked him only to use an axe in an emergency, because it spoiled the look of the goods on display. However, this was definitely an emergency. Soldier was getting hot and thirsty, and this one set of hands was taking up much of his day. He had hoped to return with a whole sackful by the time the evening came around.

Finally, both hands had been removed, just as some troops came riding by.

'What d'you think you're up to?' asked the sergeant-at-arms.

'Official business,' said Soldier, producing his baton. 'I work for Spagg, the hand-of-glory merchant.'

The sergeant wrinkled his nose. 'That flea-bitten cur? All right then, but don't hang about here all day. A rogue Hannack has been been seen in the district.'

'A Hannack?'

'You don't know who the Hannacks are?' said the sergeant and his men laughed. 'You *will* know, if any of them find you, especially with that beard you seem to love so much.'

'What does that mean?'

The sergeant said, 'You notice me and my men have smooth shiny chins? There's a reason for that. Hannacks don't fight so hard when a man's clean-shaven. You still look puzzled. Well, you'll find out. Tell that whoreson Spagg to employ someone with a bit of nonce in future. Idiots like you should not be wandering about out here. Not that it matters. One blue-eyed stranger more or less makes no difference to me.'

With that the sergeant-at-arms called his troops to follow him and they rode back towards the city.

Soldier spent the remainder of the day gathering more hands from various corpses. Not as many as he would have liked, but then the giant had taken up a good deal of his time and energy. Towards evening the sun turned to blood again. As the donkey was plodding along, back down a track towards the castle, a figure appeared on horseback to the west. Soldier saw the horseman ride to the top of a ridge, where he sat and stared at the hand-gatherer on his slow-moving donkey.

'Hannack,' said the raven. 'Now you're for it!'

Soldier bristled with annoyance. 'People keep telling me that, but who or what in Guthrum is a *Hannack*?'

At that moment the bareback rider spurred his horse and came charging down the ridge towards Soldier. Soldier noticed that the Hannack was riding a wild horse, hairier and stockier than those mounts used by Guthrumite troops. The rider himself looked just as savage as his mount. He appeared naked, but strangely his skin was loose on his body. It seemed wrinkled and folded, and it rippled in the wind. In the warrior's left hand was a warhammer, one side blunt, the other side spiked. His expression was formed into a brutal mask: his battle face. He handled his mount with accomplished ease, as if the beast were joined to him at the thighs and shared the same brain.

His head was startlingly bald.

'Here he comes,' cried the raven, 'wearing the skin of a defeated enemy.'

So that's what it is, thought Soldier, a cape of human skin.

'What does he want from me?' cried Soldier. 'I'm obviously very poor.'

'Your chin,' replied the raven. 'He wants your lower jaw, Soldier.'

Warriors were warriors, but there were those who tried to look handsome and bold, and those who tried to look as fearsome as possible. Hannacks were obviously into the more gory side of war.

The city below was agonisingly close. The red pavilions of the Carthagans even closer. Soldier attempted to spur the donkey on to greater speeds than the languid step it had been giving him until now. The donkey was not used to such treatment. When riders kicked it in the ribs it was inclined to stop and fume at the mistreatment. It did so now. Soldier yelled at it, kicking harder. It grew mental roots from its hooves and prepared to lock itself to the earth.

Soldier leaped from the animal's back and with his tools in one fist and sack of severed hands in the other, he began running down towards the gates. There were guards there who stared at him, being run down by a savage horseman, but they made no effort to send out help. They simply watched, with horrified interest, as the thundering hooves of the Hannack's mount gained on Soldier. Some of the Carthagans had come out of their pavilions and were pointing and gesticulating, yelling for their comrades to come and watch the single combat. One of them cried that it was not so much a combat as a murder. They were convinced the Hannack would kill the dark-haired man with the thick black beard.

Soldier's breath came out in short bursts. He knew he was not going to make it through the gates. Nowhere near. He dropped the sack of hands and reached into the bag of tools. There he grasped the hand-axe he had used to chop the extremities from the giant's arms. With this weapon in his grasp he took a firm stance and waited for the horseman. There was the thought in his mind that he was a hardened veteran of war. He should know what to do in these circumstances. And indeed, he did. He could not go for the man with a small weapon. He had to hit the mount, wound it, bring it down and the man with it.

The Hannack bore down on him with ferocious intent. There was no savage glee or joy-of-battle in his face: only concentrated sense of purpose. Soldier could see this fierce lone warrior was set on killing him.

As the speed of the Hannack's charger increased, the warrior's second skin flapped in the wind. He looked like some horrible dead man, risen from the grave. Soldier set his feet squarely on the ground and swung his hand-axe back and forth, ready to deliver a blow. His fear was now gone and had been replaced by a coolness. What remained was a keen series of thoughts, assessing the situation as it progressed. Yes, he knew he had always been a soldier, for though his memory had gone the skills of his trade remained.

'Well done, friend,' yelled one of the guards at the gate in admiration. 'It would have been useless to run.'

The Hannack was almost upon him. Soldier swung sideways with the little axe, aiming for the horse's outstretched nose. The Hannack was lightning fast and swerved to protect his mount. Soldier's swing carried through, missing his original target, but striking the Hannack's thigh. There came a yell of pain from the attacking warrior, who turned on his mount to a position where he could strike down. However, Soldier's left arm went up to protect his vulnerable temple. This left the lower part of Soldier's face as the only real target. For reasons of his own the Hannack stayed his hand, did not smash his warhammer into Soldier's hairy jaw. Instead, the frustrated warrior tried for Soldier's right shoulder.

He missed, because at that moment the donkey, either terrified by the fracas, or simply enraged by all this unnecessary activity, charged past the steed's flank and lashed out with his hind hooves. He struck the Hannack's mount on the rump. The horse shied and bolted forwards, causing the Hannack clutch at the reins. In doing so the warrior dropped his warhammer. Soldier immediately picked up this weapon, longer than the hand-axe and far more deadly, and began wielding it himself. The horseman saw that he had to arm himself again and drew a broadbladed sword slung from the side of his charger. As he did so, he found himself in a storm of arrows, which were now coming from the direction of the nearest red pavilion. Carthagan archers had fetched their weapons and were raining missiles down on the Hannack. One struck him in the shoulder. He pulled it out, gave Soldier a frustrated, if not longing look, and then rode off towards the hill country to the north.

Soldier breathed a sigh of relief as he watched the dust clouds fly from the horse's hooves in the blood-red light of the dying sun.

He patted the donkey on the rump. 'You saved my skin there, old fellah. Extra hay for you tonight.'

'An extra something for your other helper?' suggested the raven, who had flown back again. 'I was going to fly at the face of that Hannack, but the donkey got in the way.'

'Oh, I'm certain you were,' said Soldier, sarcastically.

'No, really, I was.'

'Let's forget it, shall we?'

Soldier wrapped the Hannack's warhammer in a piece of sacking. He would keep this prize. It might come in useful to him later, since his empty scabbard attested to the fact that his own sword was lost. Soldier then led the donkey towards the city gates. On the way he expressed his appreciation to the stocky Carthagan archers, who had assisted him.

'I owe you my life,' Soldier shouted.

One of the archers shook his head.

'Courage needs assistance from time to time. You are no Guthrumite, for otherwise you would have fled the Hannack.'

Soldier went over to this short, square, narrow-eyed man. His chest was bare and the muscles stood so proud of his form they might have been embossed by a sculptor used to working in bronze. Soldier was quite envious of his physique, yet he was only one of hundreds of others with similar physical qualities.

'You don't think much of Guthrumites then?'

The other replied. 'They make fine cooks and clerks.'

'But not fighters.'

'There have been some, but not many.'

'Tell me,' said Soldier, 'what did the Hannack want of me? He seemed so anxious for the kill.'

The Carthagan stroked his chin and smiled. 'Your beard.'

Soldier saw that the other man was clean shaven, like most people he had met within the castle too.

'What about my beard? You can't take another man's chin fuzz. What would you do with it?'

'He wanted your mandible. Didn't you notice he avoided smashing in your face? That's because he didn't want to damage your lower jaw bone. Hannacks are all as bald as boulders in a stream. They take the bearded mandibles of their enemies and wear them on their heads, to cover their hairless pates. He might have skinned you too, if you hadn't been so close to the castle. Just because he was wearing the skin of one enemy, does not mean he wouldn't take a spare. You're very lucky, friend.'

Soldier left the Carthagan and went to the gates. There the Guthrumite guards underlined the Carthagan's words, telling him he was a lucky so-and-so. Soldier was more inclined to think that his skill as a fighter had more to do with it than luck.

When he got through the gate he was again pounced on by four guards of the inner ward, who viewed his iron collar with distaste. When he produced Spagg's baton they sneered.

'The hand-seller. Is that what's in the sack?' asked one of the guards, a tall fellow with a thin nose.

'Yes, the hands of hanged people.'

Soldier opened the sack so that the guard could peer inside.

'What's that?' cried the tall, thin man, pointing. 'There's a big one in there.' He reached in and pulled out the giant's hand.

'By Theg,' said an older guard, 'that's the hand of Jankin the giant. Has he been hung then?'

'He *was* hung,' sniggered another of the guards. 'Very well hung, so I'm told. That was the reason Queen Vanda ordered his neck to be stretched. He impregnated one of her plain cousins, so I heard the captain say.'

The fourth guard added thoughtfully, 'The old maids of this castle are going to be bit upset about Jankin being hanged. The story is that Jankin serviced a good many spinsters and very satisfied they was too, he being so well-endowed. There'll be weeping and wailing in certain lonely quarters once the news of this gets around.'

'There was another thing missing from his body,' Soldier said. 'His penis.'

'Ho! Some old witch has had that,' cried the thin guard. 'She'll sell it on, once she's breathed a bit of life into it.'

'Or, if she's very ugly, she'll keep it for herself,' said one of his friends.

The guards all laughed uproariously and told Soldier he could go on his way.

Spagg was less enthusiastic when presented with the large pair of hands.

'How am I goin' to find room on my stall for Jankin's great mitts?' he asked, holding up the monstrous appendages. 'You've chopped 'em. Look at the stumps! Bah! They're like two slabs of pale meat. And there's no character to 'em,' he quite rightly pointed out. 'There's no tattoos, no scars, no hard gristly bits or misshapen warts. The hands of a clerk's got more interest in 'em than these. At least a clerk's usually got a pen callus on the writing hand. These have got no blemishes at all. Why, they're as soft and smooth as a baby's bottom. Look at the perfect shape of the moons on the nails! The cuticles. Everythin's trimmed and neatly filed. Them's *manicured* fingernails. Jankin couldn't have done a hard day's work in his life.'

'From what I hear,' said Soldier, 'he had no need to.'

'You mean his bedroom antics? I suppose those widders and old maids paid him, did they? What a way to earn a living, eh? Plying your trade between white cotton sheets.'

'I heard it was the silk ones that were his downfall.'

Spagg nodded, holding the pair of hands up to the light. 'Ah well, maybe if I distress 'em a bit, with a hammer and some chisels. Make 'em look as if they've been through terrible times? Tricks of the trade, Soldier. Can't just give up on 'em, just 'cause they *look* brand new, can you? We'll knock a bit of character into 'em.'

Soldier said, 'Isn't that cheating?'

Spagg looked up quickly with a frown on his forehead.

'When you buys things in a market, you take risks. You don't find honest men in places like this – only in shops, what charge more money for the same goods. You buy cheap, you takes a risk is what I say.'

Spagg paid Soldier for his work and told him he could have the rest of the evening off.

Gratefully, Soldier took the donkey to its stall and gave it some hay.

'I owe you my life, fellah,' he said, patting its nose. 'You are the prince of donkeys.'

Now that he had some money in his purse, Soldier went

looking for accommodation. However, at every boarding house or inn he received the same rejection. It seemed no one wanted a stranger to the city, a man who wore the iron collar, in their house. Some hardly opened the door before slamming it in his face, not even listening to what he had to say. Others threatened him. It seemed a hopeless task. In the end, as night was coming on, he went back to Spagg.

The merchant was just in the process of gathering his hands from the stall: little ones, big ones, red ones, pale ones, black ones, copper ones, hands with twisted thumbs, hands with missing fingers, hands with no nails, hands with tattoos, skinless hands, hands with webbing between the joints, hands of every description, all bearing the obvious signs of preserving fluid. Spagg picked them up and placed them carefully, even lovingly, on top of each other, like stacking books, before wrapping them in sackcloth and placing them in leather saddlebags.

'Can I stay with you?' pleaded Soldier. 'You must have a place for a bed where you live? If I stay on the streets I'll be robbed. There are footpads, cutthroats and cutpurses everywhere. They're more numerous than cockroaches once the sun goes down. I've got to sleep some time and they'll be on me as soon as I close my eyes.'

'Use that new warhammer to beat 'em off,' replied the unmoved hand-seller, nodding at the weapon which was now stuck in Soldier's belt. 'The story of you sending that Hannack back to the hills is spreading over Zamerkand faster than flies can breed. The night-people'll be scared stiff of you.'

'Be reasonable. I can't fight in my sleep. Some rascal will tap me on the temple and I'll quit this world, reputation or no.'

'Not my fault, not my business,' replied Spagg, loading the

last of his gear on a cart. All around him the other market traders were in the process of leaving the great square. Soon it would be empty of everyone except Soldier. 'Why don't you sleep on the guildhall steps,' said his employer, 'then you'll be bright and early for work tomorrow morning. I need to you help me put some dirt under Jankin's fingernails, and chip and crack 'em a bit. The only thing they've touched in the last few years is the breasts and fannies of the female gentry . . .'

'Why won't you take me home with you?'

'Because my lover wouldn't like it – we value our privacy.'

Soldier stared at the hand-of-glory merchant. He was a small, squat man. His torso had a shrivelled look to it, while his arms and legs were thin and gangly. His greying hair was stiff with dirt and looked as if it had been cut with a blunt instrument. His feet were large, his ears were large, his nose was large. His skin was pockmarked with the ravages of the pox and there was a horrid hairy mole on the point of his chin. In short, he was an ugly brute.

'You have a lover?' said Soldier, and before he could help it he had added, 'She must be very unfussy.'

Spagg raised his eyebrows. 'We're not all as fond of peaches-and-cream as Jankin was, you know. Anyways, you can chunter on all night, you ain't comin' home with me.' He started to walk towards the stall where the donkey was stabled and then turned and said in a generous tone, 'You could try a woman called Uthellen. Lives at number 133 West Gate Street. She sometimes takes in lodgers, even suspicious ones like you.'

Soldier saw he wasn't going to get anywhere with Spagg and left the square to seek this Uthellen woman's house. Nightwatchmen came out of the recesses in the castle walls to light the faggots in their cages. Street people had already started fires on corners and in alleys, to keep themselves warm during the night. Even these low-life individuals stared suspiciously at the man wearing the iron collar, indicating with their eyes that he would be wise not to stop and try to share the comfort of their fires with them.

As was usual, he came across one or two bodies on his search for the house. One was lying in an alley, its head beaten to a bloody pulp and looking like a watermelon which had been squashed by the wheels of a cart. The other was hacked into several pieces, the bits scattered over the road outside a tavern. The watch had obviously not yet found the remains of either of these ugly signs of violence. It reminded him that this was a city where death was cheap and very often nasty. His hand never left the warhammer. He found the weapon a great comfort when shadows flitted within alleys.

Finally, in the light of the faggot torches, he found a house with the number 133 painted on it in crude figures. There had been no 133 West Gate Street, and Soldier had assumed that Spagg must have got the names mixed up.

It was a green door in an alley so narrow he had to slip up it sideways to prevent grazing his shoulders. The alley snaked up through houses on a hill at the back of the city. There were no windows through which Soldier could peer and get some idea of the occupants, but it did not look a very salubrious set of residences. He simply had to knock on the door of 133 and hope to get a welcoming reception. The knocker on the thick wooden portal was a demon's claw clutching an iron ball. It invited use. He listened at the door first and thought he could hear faint grunts, or perhaps moans and groans going on behind it. Maybe the lady was sick? Perhaps that's why she took in unsavoury lodgers, because being ill she could not work and needed the money desperately? At least someone was home.

He knocked hard.

Nothing.

He knocked even harder.

Still nothing.

He knocked harder still.

Nothing, nothing, nothing.

He used the warhammer, thumping loudly enough on the wooden portal to awaken the dead.

The door flew open and an enormous, sturdy woman filled the opening to the house. She was tucking a grimy blouse into the waistband of her even grimier skirt. Huge breasts weighed down the blouse front. Huge muscles bulged the blouse sleeves. Huge legs stood firm as tree trunks in the doorway. Soldier had obviously interrupted something, though his brain reeled drunkenly at the awful possibilities.

'WHAT?' she roared.

Soldier took a step backwards, to be out of reach of the stench of her foul breath.

'I – Spagg told me – that is, do you have a room for rent?'

The woman's jowls were red with anger.

'Room? There's only one room in this hovel, and that's got me in it and – for a very short time – a little friend. There's no space left for a cockroach, let alone a grown man.' She peered more closely at his neck. 'You've got an iron collar. Get out of here, before I call the watch!'

'But Spagg said . . .' cried Soldier, desperately.

'I don't know any Spagg.'

The door was slammed shut. Soldier could hear bolts slamming into their sockets. That was that.

Soldier walked back to West Gate Street, despair in his

heart. Still he could not find 133. At that moment the raven landed on his shoulder, making him jump.

'Don't do that,' he said. 'What do you want?'

'It's not what I want – it's you who needs something. I've been watching you. I heard what Spagg said. You're barking at the wrong door, Soldier.'

Soldier was puzzled. 'What do you mean?

'Look down at your feet.'

Soldier did so and saw nothing but the cobbled street.

'I see stone,' he said.

'And?'

Soldier used his powers of observation a little more.

'And iron grids, every hundred yards.'

'Bravo! Precisely. The openings to the sewers below the city streets. Each of them are numbered.'

Dawn came up in Soldier's sluggish brain. 'Not a house number – the number of a sewer?'

'Bravo. Now, off you go. The one you want is by the south wall.'

The raven flew off, up towards the turrets and towers, with their flapping banners and flags.

Soldier tramped along the street until he reached the south wall of the city. There he found the grid marked 133. He lifted it and climbed down the iron ladder, trying to ignore the stink of the air below. The first few yards were dark, but once he had reached the tunnel where the muck flowed in a sluggish stream down the centre, he noticed faint lights. There were people down either side of the river of sewage.

Soldier stood on the narrow ledge and said, 'Uthellen? Is there a woman called Uthellen here?'

A woman with a young boy sitting in the light of a cheap tallow candle looked up quickly. There was fear in her face.

When she saw she was being observed she looked down again, just as swiftly, and pretended to be doing something with the boy's shoes – taking them off – or putting them on.

'Are you Uthellen?' called Soldier again.

This time there was no sign that the woman had recognised the name. She continued fussing with the boy's feet. Soldier climbed down on to the ledge and made his way towards her.

Soldier decided that the woman would have been very attractive, if it were not for her rags and grime. She had a small, oval-shaped face set with deep, brown eyes. Her hair too was probably a chestnut colour under the dirt. The boy with her looked weak and sickly. His limbs were as thin and knobbly as sticks and his complexion was pale. There were dark rings around his eyes and the hair on his head was thin and patchy. Two eyes, bright as fiery coals, burned with intensity in his face. Was that with fever, or with some inner strength?

Soldier made his way to the pair, over grumbling bodies, until he reached the woman's side.

She looked up. There was still dread in her eyes.

Soldier said in a low voice, so that others could not hear, 'I mean no harm to you, woman. My name is Soldier. Spagg, the hand-seller, said you might find me somewhere to sleep. I actually asked him if there was someone who would rent me a room, but I see that like me, you have no dwelling.'

'Oh, Spagg?' There was some relief in her voice and the look of terror faded a little, though it did not vanish completely. 'I'm – I'm sorry. There is someone who would . . . but never mind that. You are a stranger to the city. I see that by your collar. So, they will not give you room to sleep? I have this space,' she said, indicating the stone bank of the sewer. 'I rent it from the Lady of the Sewers, who is responsible to the Queen's Chancellor for the good running of the city's sewers.'

'Ah, so it doesn't come free?'

'Nothing comes free in Guthrum,' she said. 'You have been here a *very* short time if you haven't learned that. The Chancellor has his finger in every pie.'

Soldier was surprised. 'Chancellors are usually rich men – why would this Queen's Chancellor bother with renting sewer space?'

'Have you ever asked yourself *how* chancellors become so wealthy?'

Soldier thought about it and nodded. 'You have a point. In that case, may I share this spot with you? I have good coin to pay rent.'

At these words several people in the half-darkness around them shuffled as if paying attention.

'All I need is a place to sleep,' he added. 'Nothing more, nothing less. If you and the boy could find it in your hearts to help a man with the iron collar of a stranger, I should be eternally grateful.'

She grimaced, ruefully. 'Of course you may share my space, but now you have told everyone you have money, one of us will have to remain awake at all times. If we all three fall asleep at once, they'll rob us blind – won't you?' The last two words were shouted for the benefit of the listeners. Grins and nods came from the beggars, thieves and vagabonds sharing the sewer. There were no protests. They knew what they were and what they knew what they would do given the chance.

'I'm sorry,' said Soldier. 'I have a lot to learn, obviously. You sleep first. I'll stay awake and count the stars.'

'Stars?' said the boy, opening his mouth for the first time

and staring up at the curved black ceiling of the sewer. 'What stars?'

'In here,' replied the Soldier, smiling and tapping his head. 'The bright stars of the open fields and woodlands.' He sighed. 'They are with me always, even in places like this.'

Chapter Four

There was a part of the extensive city grounds which did not have the stink of dogs or the filth of the streets. Here there were pleasant bowers and alcoves, beautiful thickets of small-leafed lime trees and green mazes of myrtle and hibiscus hedges. Painted statues and ornamented seats were everywhere, while fountains served expansive camomile lawns and clusters of yew shrubs. Lakes full of exotic fish, bearing glittering jade lizards on their banks, were scattered around. Deer and other wildlife wandered between these drinking places, decorating the landscape with their animated forms.

Everywhere one looked there were swathes of colour: the white sweep of a gathering of lilies, a flush of red roses or tight-bulbed tulips, a shady bank dusted with the hazy blue flax in bloom. These were the gardens on which two palaces stood: the Palace of Birds and the Palace of Wildflowers.

Queen Vanda lived in the Palace of Birds.

At first glance it might seem as if this building's beautiful architecture had been fashioned from plaster bricks in the shape of birds. However, closer inspection would reveal that these were actual birds, frozen in a variety of actions –

perched, flying, eating, alighting, swimming — birds with beaks open, birds with beaks closed, birds with smooth feathers, birds with ruffled feathers. They were once warm, live creatures that had been turned to stone, then used in the making of arches, turrets, towers, pillars, window-frames, ledges, portals, and all the other necessary and decorative features which go into the making of a palace fit for a queen and empress.

It was, however, a house of sadness.

Queen Vanda, like her sister, Princess Layana, who lived in the nearby smaller Palace of Wildflowers, dwelt much of her time in a terrible twilight world on the borderlands of madness. Thus the walls of both palaces were padded with silk brocade stuffed with goosedown. It was said that ten thousand wild geese had died to provide the padding which helped to prevent either sister from braining herself on the stone walls of their respective homes.

The parents of the sisters, the old queen and her consort, had died when the children were young. The royal offspring had been in the care of their nanny since birth, and she, poor soul, had crept unknown into senility at the time of the old queen's death. No records had been kept. The queen had been uninterested in her daughters. She had consigned the girls to the nursery where they were cherished and kept from all society by their doting and jealous nanny.

Since reason had left the old woman in whose care the royal children had been left, there was no discovering their exact ages. One day she said it was Vanda who was the oldest, the next Layana, then changed her mind the following morning. It was Humbold, then only a clerk in the civic library, who set about discovering which of the two children was the elder. His keen inquiry led him to the conclusion that it was Vanda who was five years of age and Layana who was four years and three months. Once Vanda became queen, at the age of twelve, she rewarded Humbold with several promotions for his research.

There were times when the queen was quite lucid and rational, but there were also times when her reason flew out of her like a startled bird from its nest and the dark shadow of lunacy clouded her thinking and her actions. This morning was one of those days when her thoughts were clear and she called for her chancellor to attend her in her bedchamber.

'How is your majesty this morning?' asked the chancellor, warily, on entering the queen's boudoir. 'I trust you slept well?'

The queen was sitting up in bed, the satin sheets covering only her legs. She was robed in a pale peach silk gown which emphasised the thinness of her form beneath it. Her ribs showed through like a furrowed field. Her elbows were sharp points halfway down the mandarin sleeves. Her collarbones made silk arches around the neck of the robe.

'No, I had nightmares as usual. I dreamt I was being torn apart by witches and eaten alive. It was horrible. Each part of me was a conscious living creature with a mind of its own, so that when the witches ate my liver, my heart watched in great sorrow and agony, seeing its body-mate torn apart and devoured by these wretched hags . . .'

As the queen spoke her expression changed. She began to look more and more haggard and distressed. Chancellor Humbold stopped the flow with a sharp, 'How terrible for you, your majesty . . .'

Humbold was not much concerned by the queen's grisly dreams, but for him to retain his position it was necessary that she be lucid for at least part of the time. If it ever emerged that she had lapsed into complete, irretrievable, howling madness, the queendom would collapse completely and he would be robbed of the power he now wielded. While she was seen as partially able, there would be no revolution. Rulers were entitled to run slightly mad in any case: they were products of inbreeding, even incest. Queendoms however, like chickens, required heads. Without a functioning queen – even a cruel one – chaos and disorder would prevail. Murder would be the order of the day and the streets would run with blood. Hated chancellors would be dragged from their beds and hung from tower flagpoles.

Humbold was the true ruler of the queendom. There had once been an empire, but that had been lost by Queen Vanda's mother, though the trappings were still in place – the Imperial Guard and other such institutions. There was still great wealth in the queendom, from the imperial era, but once-conquered neighbouring countries no longer paid tribute to Guthrum. It was a static wealth. The empire had withered, but the city state of Zamerkand still flourished.

There were old scores to settle however. Many of the tribes around and about saw themselves as victims of the old empire, and now that the mighty had fallen were eager to crush it completely. The cry of 'Barbarians at the gates' was expected to be heard at any time, now and in the future. Only the mercenaries, the Carthagans, stood in the way of Guthrum's utter destruction. A sacked and burning city, its population slaughtered to man, woman and child, was in the mind's eye of every citizen. Guthrum was living on the edge of a precipice. Queen Vanda's fortune paid for the foreign troops to guard Zamerkand's walls, but the queen's wealth was not bottomless and one day would run out. Then the Hannacks would come, and the clans of beast-people from the North – the Horse-people and the Wild-dog-people – and coast raiders would sweep in from the Cerulean Sea. Guthrum would be devoured by fire and sword and its people consigned to death or slavery.

'What are the duties of the day?' asked the queen, getting out of her bed. There was a fountain in the middle of her room. She allowed her attendant maid-servants to strip her and wash her in its waters, oblivious of the presence of the chancellor, who it has to be said was slightly revolted by the sight of her gaunt, careworn body. 'Do we hold court?'

'There are petitions for your majesty to hear. To save your majesty time I have weeded out the unnecessary ones . . .'

She looked up as a maid-servant wrapped her wet body round with orange-coloured cotton towels.

'Surely I should hear them all? Surely I should be the one to decide whether or not they are necessary?'

Humbold smiled. 'Forgive me, your majesty. I have taken the liberty of whittling them down to fifty. There were originally seven-hundred-and-ten. I'm sure your majesty would be too exhausted to hear such a number of suits.'

The queen raised her eyebrows as she was being dressed.

'That many? You're quite right. Even fifty sounds a tiring number. You are forgiven for usurping my power, Humbold, this time. Next time, however, you must tell me beforehand how many there are and I shall decide whether you whittle them down to a manageable number.'

'Your majesty is quite right.'

Most of the fifty supplicants were bearing false suits, all invented by Humbold himself. In this way he kept a buffer between the citizens and the queen. Four hundred of the original seven hundred and ten involved complaints against the chancellor himself. He could not have such things coming to the ear of the queen. Those not of his own making which he had allowed through the filter were minor quarrels between neighbours – someone's pig had eaten someone's vegetable patch – and nothing at all to do with the way Humbold ruled the castle city state.

'Has anything unusual happened recently?' asked the queen. 'While I was – asleep.'

While you were in the thrall of your ugly lunacy, thought Humbold, screaming fit to bring down the walls of the castle.

'No, not really . . . oh, yes, there was a stranger – he came to the city with one of our hunters. Apparently the hunter found him on a hill. The man was convinced he had been involved in a battle just prior to meeting the hunter. Indeed, he looked like a soldier, though his uniform was in rags and his sword sheath was empty of a weapon.'

'Why do you mention this trivial account to me?'

'Why?' frowned the chancellor. 'I don't know. There's something about the way this man was found – or found himself – that is troublesome to me. Just a feeling, nothing more. The manner of his coming worries me. I sense more importance in it than just happenchance. I fear this stranger, who calls himself Soldier, may be bad for us. But I'm not entirely sure. I feel it best to keep him under observation before executing him.'

The queen, now dressed in regal fashion, in great swathes of light cotton with silk trimmings, started.

'Is he out to destroy us, do you think?'

Humbold raised the palms of his hands. 'It's just a feeling, your majesty, and I am having the man closely watched. If he remains within these walls I intend to invoke an old law of Zamerkand. I found it the other day, in one of the books in your library. It states that a stranger requesting hospitality must be given such, but for one lunar month only, after which if he has not left the city the Lord of Thieftakers, our highest judge, may have him arrested and put to death.'

The queen said, 'Are you sure you didn't just write that law yourself?'

Humbold smiled. 'Your majesty jests.'

'And you think this is necessary, to have the stranger put to death? Perhaps your feelings are mistaken? What if he is some kind of messiah, come to save us from destruction?'

'That's why I have allowed him to live for a while. If he is such then he will reveal himself before the month is out. However, if he has nothing to offer us, or is simply a lost stranger, then we can dispose of him. No, no, your majesty, if this man is any sort of threat to us I will have him executed after the full moon has passed.'

'As you will, Chancellor Humbold; now what of the rest of the day?'

'I am afraid, your majesty, that we have rebellious elements in our midst.'

'Traitors?' She breathed the word.

'A traitor. Fear not, your majesty. I have had the man concerned arrested. He was preaching sedition in the taverns of the city. This is one Frinstin, Keeper of the Towers . . .'

'Frinstin? He speaks against me?'

'There are several witnesses. They shall be called at the trial.'

Vanda stared as if into a room of darkness. 'Trial? There will be no trial. Execute him.'

Humbold altered his facial muscles a little into something that might, in some quarters, be recognised as a smile. 'But, you may require proof, your majesty.'

'I need no proof, Chancellor Humbold. Your word is good enough, is it not? You have heard the case against him?'

'Indeed I have.'

'Then cut off his head, today.'

A nod from the chancellor. 'And his successor?'

'I leave that to you, Humbold.'

'As you wish, your majesty.'

Later, the queen was in her throne room, ready to hear supplicants and make judgements. Humbold, as ever, was by her side, gently guiding her. He was subtle, had to be, for she was not an unintelligent person. Long hours of studying his queen had enabled Humbold to make just the right noises at the right times. He knew just when and where to intervene and when to stay silent. Sometimes he remained aloof even when he wished the judgement to go the other way, knowing that in this particular instance, on this particular subject, it was better to take a small defeat than risk losing the confidence of the queen.

Two people entered the throne room and bowed very low before the monarch. She acknowledged their presence and waved them away as if she were wafting cool air on her hot brow. The two went off into one corner to speak quietly with each other.

They were rich and powerful personages, these two. One was short and muscular, with a broad face and high forehead. Her name was Qintara and she was the Lady of the Ladders.

The other was tall and thin, with a narrow nose, a small mouth and a generally pinched look about him. His eyes were piercing and glinted like flints. He surveyed the room as the other talked in a low voice.

This was Maldrake, Lord of the Locks.

Both Qintara and Maldrake belonged to Chancellor Humbold, of course. They were his creatures. There were many taxes on the citizens of Zamerkand, which kept its residents safe from raiders and other warring states, and gave them their secure trading canal to the sea. They paid dearly for their protection. There was a tax on steps and stairs, collected by the Lady of the Ladders. It was she who assessed how many steps went to a citizen's room, or trading place, or house. If you lived above the stench of the dung-covered streets, in a high tower, then you had to be able to afford it. There was a tax on locks, collected by the Lord of the Locks. The larger and more complex the lock, the more a person had to protect, and therefore the more tax he could afford to pay.

There were in turn, a Keeper of the Chimneys; the Lady of the Sewers; the Lady of the Doors; Keeper of all Gates; and so on. The same principles of tax applied to all: those who could afford conveniences could afford to pay tax. Controlling much of this wealth was the devious Humbold, who had over the years managed to fill most of the posts in the city with sycophants, and so took a percentage of all taxes paid to the queen.

There were not many who resisted Humbold now. Frinstin had been one of them, but he was the least powerful, the least important of them all.

Marshal Crushkite, Warlord of the Guthrum Army, was one who hated and opposed Chancellor Humbold whenever he got the chance. The standing army of Guthrum – the Carthagan mercenaries aside – was not large, but it was well-armed and very loyal to its officers. Humbold had to fawn in front of its senior officers, especially Crushkite, and he loathed them all. The marshal strode into the throne room now, tall and aristocratic, a thoroughly military bearing, his head a shock of lion-mane hair, his expression disdainful, his manner arrogant. He crossed to the queen and gave her a sharp bow. The queen smiled. Crushkite, broad-shouldered, narrow-waisted and handsome in his fiftieth year, was one of her favourites. The fact that he had the brain of an ass had always escaped the queen's notice.

Not so that of Humbold. It was his one source of comfort.

'Marshal Crushkite,' murmured Humbold, as the warlord passed him by, 'you have heard of this stranger we have in our midst. He calls himself "Soldier". Don't you think that's rather impertinent, since he belongs to no army?'

Crushkite turned his baleful eyes on the man he considered to be lower than worms.

'A man who's been a soldier is always a soldier, Humbug, dontcha know that? Training, discipline, loyalty to a regiment – they never leave a man. I've seen 'im. Might have to execute him, but that's neither here nor there, he's got a fine, straight figure. Spine like a spear. Not like you limp daffodils who've never marched anywhere except to your wardrobes. Got a battle-look in his eye, too. Officer material if ever I saw it.'

'Captain Kaff doesn't seem to think so,' Humbold offered, craftily, attempting to drive in wedges.

'Captain Kaff doesn't have to agree with my opinion in private matters: he simply has to obey orders in military matters. Good day to you, Humbug.'

Humbug! The chancellor bristled as he smiled. Humbug!

Crushkite was not Humbold's only problem. There was the Lord of the Royal Purse, Quidquod, keeper of the queen's personal fortune, a man who was incorruptible, could not be bribed, could not be swayed by rhetoric. He was old, incredibly intelligent, and could destroy Humbold with a few words in the queen's ear, if any proof of embezzlement ever fell into his hands.

There were one or two minor personages feared by Humbold, but gradually he was whittling these down.

'Humbold,' called the queen, after having had a short conversation with Quidquod, 'the Lord of the Royal Purse seems to differ with you over the matter of Frinstin. He feels that perhaps you are being a little hasty.'

Humbold simmered internally, but smiled on the outside.

'Has he more information? How tragic. It may be too late, your majesty . . .'

'Not so,' replied the crusty, grim-faced counter of the royal coin, 'I received a message from Frinstin this morning and acted on it straight away.' Quidquod bowed solemnly to the queen. 'I took the liberty of postponing the execution.'

'Quite right, Quidquod. If you have evidence which speaks of Frinstin's innocence, then we must discuss it before he has his head lopped from his shoulders. Both of you be in my inner chambers before noon. We'll take the matter further.'

Quidquod bowed.

Humbold bowed.

Humbold felt a rage go sweeping through him, reaching to the very depths of his soul.

Chapter Five

Soldier was awakened by the sound of beautiful singing. He did not understand the words – they could have been birdsongs for all the intelligence they imparted – but there was no denying the quality of the tone. He was aware, as he opened his eyes, of shadows scuttling away along the banks of the sewer. Sitting up quickly he realised the straps on his belt purse had been half-severed. He had been in the process of being robbed when the singing woke him.

Turning to Uthellen, Soldier said, 'A simple shake and a warning would have been enough.'

'Enough for what?' She too was stretching and rubbing her eyes.

'Enough to alert me. There's was no need to sing, even though you have a wonderful voice.'

She blinked at him. The boy was awake too, staring.

'Sing?' she repeated. 'What are you talking about?'

The boy pointed with a bony finger. 'It was that. The sword sheath.'

Soldier looked down at the scabbard strapped to his side. 'This? What do you mean?'

The boy said, 'I heard it, before you woke. It sang in the language of the wizards. It sang in the voice of a castrato,

'*Awake, awake, oh warrior mine,*
Before you're slain by thieving swine.'

The Soldier grasped and inspected the scabbard with *Kutrama and Sintra* stitched into its leather.

'Are you mad, child? Scabbards don't sing. Perhaps someone was throwing his voice.'

'No, it was the scabbard.'

Soldier frowned and stared hard at the boy.

'What do *you* know of the language of wizards?'

Uthellen suddenly came to life and clutched her child to her breast. 'Nothing – he knows nothing. We all fell asleep and someone woke us.' Desperately she called out into the darkness, 'I thank you, whoever it was, for giving us a warning.'

With that she began to gather what belongings she had and seemed to be preparing to leave.

'Where are you going?' asked Soldier. 'It's still night.'

'It's almost dawn. The boy and I should leave now.'

Soldier shrugged and reached into his purse. 'Here,' he said. 'Here's the money I promised.'

She took it with a gracious thank you, and before very long Soldier was alone on the ledge. He was a little puzzled as to why Uthellen and the nameless boy had left so soon. She seemed to go into a panic when her son started to speak of wizards. Of course, it was not good policy to take the name of wizards in vain, but there had been nothing of that sort. It was the mere mention of them that put her into disquiet. Soldier didn't understand it at all. And the boy had been so convinced it was the scabbard which had warned them of the robbers!

Soldier could not get to the bottom of it. He resolved to

speak again with Uthellen, that night. But when he returned after a day of sawing off the hands of murderers and bandits, she was not there. One of the other sewer residents told him she would not be back. She came to offer her apologies, said the man, and left her promise that you could have her ledge. Soldier was surprised, but there was little he could do about it. He simply took her place and paid the rent when the collector came to demand it.

'Do you charge the rats as well?' asked Soldier of the rent collector. 'They spend their days down here, as well as their nights.'

The rent collector, a little man with narrow shoulders, shook his head.

'You'll be in a deal of trouble, friend, if you mock Her Majesty's officers. I'll 'ave you danglin' from the battlements by your thumbs, any more lip. I may look weak and puny to you, but there's a cartload o' soldiers outside would love to kick you from here to there and back again. Get my meanin'?'

'There's not a lot of meaning to get, but as a stranger here I should probably watch my tongue.'

'Absolutely, friend.'

The time passed swiftly. Before he knew it, Soldier had been in the castle a month. By day he worked for Spagg and at night he slept in the sewer. It was not much of a life, but it was all he had at the present time. There was some idea that he might progress by degrees, but to where or what he still had no clue. Then the hour came when he was arrested.

He was standing by Spagg's stall at the time, helping to persuade passers-by into purchasing hands-of-glory.

'Want to make yourself invisible?' he called. 'Do all those naughty things you've always wanted to do, without fear of being seen or caught? Men, get into the ladies' public baths without being noticed! Women, follow that two-timing husband of yours and catch him with his pants down! Come on, buy a hand-of-glory, dirt cheap on Wednesdays, Fridays and the queen's unofficial birthday. Waxed-and-wicked fingers guaranteed to light first time. Makes a fine glow to read or sew by, without the added extra cloak of invisibility. A must for professional burglars and grave-robbers . . .'

Six castle guards led by a captain came from a corner of the market square and made straight for Spagg's stall.

'Uh, oh, what have you done this time?' Soldier asked Spagg.

The stallholder was already creeping away, distancing himself from his assistant.

'Not me,' he muttered. 'You.'

It was execution day. Murderers, rapists and child molesters were hung outside the walls of the city, but traitors were decapitated within. In a courtyard near the Lord of Thieftaker's office they were cutting off heads. One could hear the sound of the axe chinking past the block as each head rolled. Occasionally there was a scream cut short by a thumping sound as a head fell onto the boards of the executioner's platform. It was not difficult to imagine the bright-bladed sword raised high above the quivering neck, then flashing down.

The soldiers had come to add to the number of victims in the Lord of Thieftaker's yard.

At first Soldier thought they'd come to take his collar off, thinking he had earned the right to citizenship after a month of wearing the uncomfortable iron ring. However when the captain shouted on the march, he knew he was mistaken.

'The stranger known as "Soldier" is hereby under arrest,

having been sentenced to death by the queen for remaining within these city walls for one lunar month without authority or invitation. Take him!' This last order was directed at his guards.

Soldier felt something flare within him. It came from that corner of his mind where guilt and hatred dwelt side by side. He leapt back with great alacrity, reaching down for his sword.

Of course, there was no sword to draw. However, the Hannack's warhammer was still in his belt. He drew this and crouched like a cornered rat, ready to deal death to those who would take him and execute him. Soldier was not about to spend the remainder of his days on a gibbet, without first putting up a fight. The square suddenly came to life. Citizens began erupting from nearby buildings – the inns, bawdy-houses and the guildhall – and those already in the square began to crowd round, sensing a battle to the death.

The officer had drawn his sword and his men began to hem Soldier in with their spears.

'No need for that. You can't get away,' said the captain. 'Innocent people will get hurt.'

'Never mind us innocents, let's see a good fight!' roared a voice from the crowd. 'Let's see some gore and guts!'

A great cheer went up. Some ragged children who had previously been playing kick-ball with an unfortunate live rat were beginning to force their way to the front, squeezing through the legs of the adults. Donkeys and other livestock were raising a din from the pens in the east corner of the square. A dog had stopped in its tracks and stood there, wondering what on earth was happening in the usually quiet market-place.

Soldier struck out and hit the head of a guard, who went sprawling back into the crowd with a dent in his helmet. The man tried to struggle to his feet, helped by cheering onlookers, but only succeeded in staggering a few paces before his knees buckled and he passed out. His spear rattled on the cobblestones.

The remaining five guards stabbed with their weapons, infuriated that first blood had gone to their adversary. Soldier's warhammer clattered along the line of spears, like a child's stick along iron railings, jarring the guards. He ducked and weaved under their efforts to pin him. His acrobatics delighted the spectators, who shouted encouragement. Once the warhammer came down on the foot of a guard who went in too close and put him out of the action. Another time the deadly spike on the back of the hammer went through the empty hand of this wounded man's nearest comrade. Soldier yelled in triumph, screaming that victory was his. He flailed his warhammer around his head, yelling into the face of his opponents, his features a mask of hatred. The guards backed away under this furious onslaught, looking to their leader for support.

The captain remained calm and unimpressed.

'If I call for another troop, they will surely finish you where you stand,' he told Soldier. 'If you give in now you will at least get the chance to be heard.'

Voices shrieked from the heart of the crowd,

'Don't do it!'

'Fight to the death, stranger.'

'Don't let them take you alive!'

But Soldier realised these were just vultures, these people who wanted to see him take on the Guthrum guard. They lived humdrum lives here in the city and they wanted a bit of a thrill. He was nothing more than a circus act to them. Bear-baiting, cock-fighting, iron-glove-boxing. These were the sports that excited these people. Once he was lying bleeding, with a crushed skull, on the cobbles they would laugh and go back to eat their sandwiches of bloody cow meat covered in spicy sauce and talk about matching fighting dogs against each other.

The captain was right. Even if he won and put all the guards out of action, the blood-lust of the crowd would be up. He was still a stranger here. The mob would tear him to pieces and think nothing of it. They would be doing their duty by the queen. The market-place was now packed with people. There was no escape. He was doomed whether he fought or not.

Something landed on his shoulder and a voice in his ear whispered, 'Give it up. I'll get you out later.'

Then there was a flutter of black wings and the raven was gone again.

'Ahhhh, dark magic,' yelled a spectator. 'See, the black bird of death landed on his shoulder!'

'It spoke to him,' shrieked another. 'I heard it!'

Soldier let the warhammer fall to his feet and held his hands high in the air.

'I surrender,' he murmured.

One of the guards, a man with an angry red face, was about to run him through, but his officer sharply admonished him.

'Do that and it'll be your last act, corporal. This man is to go before the Lord of Thieftakers for proper sentencing.'

'I can understand,' said Soldier, nodding to the frustrated corporal. 'I wounded his friends.'

The captain lashed Soldier viciously about the face with his chain mail glove, leaving a red smear from temple to chin.

'And that's enough out of you, too, scum. You are not required to understand anything. Speak only when you're spoken to.'

Fury flared within Soldier. He almost struck the captain and thereby ended his life there and then.

Those guards who had received minor wounds to foot and hand let their comrades dress them. The others fitted a milk churn yoke across Soldier's shoulders and tied his hands to it. Then they hobbled his legs with a short rope. It amused them to have him trotting in little spurts to keep up with them, as they began to cross the square. The people parted to form an avenue. A moment ago they were with him, while he was fighting the guards. Now that he had been humiliated by his enemies the fickle mob turned against him. They jeered, yelling insults and obscenities, calling his mother a harlot, his sister a strumpet and labelling his brother and father as bastards. Since he had none of these relations, or at any rate did not know them, their taunts did not bother him in the least.

The crowd could see that Soldier was not biting on their bait. This annoyed them and they began then to pelt him with rotten vegetables and offal. The captain let this target practice go on until a flying pig's intestine missed its mark and wrapped itself around the throat of one of his guards, then he ordered the crowd back.

'I'll flay every damn one of you,' roared the captain. 'I'll come back here with a troop of horse-soldiers and clear this square, or have the cobbles running with blood! I'll show you cattle-slaughterers what *carnage* really is.'

The gentle citizens of Zamerkand wisely ceased their sport. They knew how far to go and when to stop. They let the captain leave the square with his captive and soon the place was humming with business once again.

Soldier was taken to a keep in the north part of the castle. There he was dragged before a white-haired, dignified-looking man whose portrait half-filled the wall behind his huge desk. He was too important to look up when Soldier was finally standing before him. In fact he continued to write in a large ledger for another thirty minutes, sipping occasionally on a steaming beverage contained by an onyx beaker. Even if he was curious his eyes did not drift upwards to look at the prisoner. Only once he had used a salt shaker as a blotter did he place his goose-feather quill on its stand and look up into Soldier's eyes.

'This is the stranger, the one they call the Soldier?'

'Just "Soldier",' said Soldier.

He felt an agonizing, stinging pain on the back of his neck as he was again struck by the chain mail glove.

'Quiet, prisoner,' said the captain. 'Speak again and I'll cut off your thumbs.'

'I will decide whether there is any cutting to be done, Captain Kaff,' said the dignitary. 'You may have recently been made the Captain of the Imperial Guard, but I am in charge in here.'

There was an offensive pause before the answer came.

'Yes, my lord.' The tone was sneering.

'You are getting above yourself, Kaff. Do not rely too much on your friendship with Chancellor Humbold. Chancellors have been known to fall, and once they do, it is into my hands that they fall. There's a thin line between a man who holds a powerful position in the court and a traitor. It's the queen who decides where the line is drawn and on which side a man is standing.'

There was only a brief hesitation this time, before the answer came back in a more civil tongue, 'Yes, my lord.'

'That's better, Kaff. Much better. One day I'll take you on a tour of the rooms below this one. It's hot down there, very hot. Stifling, in fact. Even now you should be able to feel the warmth rising through the floor from the coke furnaces below, where we heat the branding-irons and red-hot anus-pokers. If you listen very hard you may be able to hear the squeaking of the racks. You won't hear the screams, of course, for the first thing we do is tear out a prisoner's tongue. Silent screams – the mouth wide open, the eyes starting from the head, but with no sound coming out – that is what we aspire to in the room below this one.'

This speech, Soldier knew, was as much for his benefit as the captain's. He was meant to be intimidated. He was meant to be terrified of what was going to happen to him. Soldier knew now that he was in the presence of the Lord of Thieftakers, head of magistrates, judges, lawyers and the watchmen who policed the streets of the city.

The Lord of Thieftakers now rubbed the sides of his nose with both hands before proceeding.

'You have been here a lunar month?' he asked Soldier.

'Yes, my lord.'

'And you have made no attempt to leave, now that your statutory month is up?'

'I didn't know I *had* to leave. No one told me.'

The Lord shook his head. 'Ignorance of the law is no excuse.'

'Surely *some*one should have told me, my lord?'

'Someone should have, but they didn't, and so here you are before me, awaiting my sentence. Well, I have no choice but to sentence you to death.' He looked at a sundial on the windowsill of his room where the sun came through. 'Normally I would have you beheaded, but the executioner has almost finished for the day. Instead, you will be taken from here and disembowelled and your innards fried in a copper bowl while you still live. Once you are dead the rest of your remains will be placed in a gibbet cage. Said gibbet to hang outside the city gates where the rooks and crows may cleanse your bones. That is all. Do you have anything to say?'

'I would prefer to wait for the next set of beheadings.'

'Anything else?' asked the lord, in deadpan voice.

'Wait,' said Soldier, desperately. 'Surely there's something I can do? An appeal to the queen, asking for mercy. There must be some way . . .'

The Lord of Thieftakers raised an eyebrow.

'Hasn't the captain explained it to you?'

'No – no, my lord. The captain has said nothing.'

The lord sighed. 'In that case, *I* shall have to, won't I? One. Your death sentence may be revoked if a Guthrum citizen with either wealth, business or land comes to plead your cause and stand surety. Two. If a lone wolf appears before the city gates under the next night's moon. Three. If a maid of Guthrum agrees to take you to husband. That's it.' To the captain the lord said, 'Take him back to the market-place. See if anyone wishes to stand surety, or if some fool girl wants to marry him. If neither happens, then take him to the tower and slice open his belly!'

'But a wolf might come,' argued Soldier.

The captain smiled. 'All wolves are slaughtered on sight by the Carthagans who ring the city walls.'

Soldier remained silent at this news. He had to rely on Spagg to get him off. Or if he could see Uthellen, on the way, he would plead with her to marry him. She was poor and in need of a man's protection. All was not yet lost.

The captain, who let it be known afterwards that he felt this was all a waste of time, led Soldier back towards the market-place, to where Spagg was back at his stall. The hand-seller was in none too good a mood. Having left his stall unattended, Soldier had allowed some of the hands to be stolen before Spagg could get back to his wares.

Spagg was very sorry, he said, but he couldn't stand surety for Soldier.

'What?' cried the condemned man. 'What are you saying? I've worked for you for these past few weeks. Haven't we been friends?'

Spagg shrugged. 'Firstly, if you ran away they would take my business from me. It's the business that's the surety, not me.'

'I won't run away,' promised Soldier, desperately.

'Secondly,' replied Spagg, ignoring this interruption, 'someone wants you dead. Someone with a bit of power, other-wise you wouldn't be in this fix. I'm not going to cross a pow-erful man for someone I've only just met. I hope the behead-ing is quick, for your sake.'

'It's not a beheading. It's a disembowelling,' said Soldier.

Spagg winced and then shrugged, turning away, leaving Soldier feeling wretched. Soldier then appealed to anyone in the crowd who had any sense of kindness to stand surety for him.

'You'll probably steal the teeth out of my head,' one man shouted back, 'the minute I fall asleep.'

'What did I say?' said Captain Kaff, after a few minutes of further barracking. 'A waste of time.'

At that moment Soldier spotted Uthellen in the crowd. He waved to her.

'Marry me, or I die,' he cried to her. 'Please, Uthellen . . .'

Her face looked stricken, but she did not come forward.

One of the crowd explained why. 'She has a child – she's no maid – you need to marry a virgin to save yourself.'

'Oh,' said Soldier. He raised his voice again. 'Is there no one . . .?'

Peals of laughter went up. 'In *this* crowd? You must be joking. Any woman here is waiting for a customer.'

'No, no, please.' Soldier was getting desperate. 'There must be a maid-servant, out shopping for her mistress? Does anyone want me? I have this magical scabbard to offer.' He held up the empty sword sheath for all to see.

The leather-caps and dirty-aprons around him hooted, their stinking breath hitting him in the face.

'I'll work hard for you. I'll protect you . . .' more peals of laughter. 'I'll even love you.'

'Oooowww, that's temptin',' said a bulky woman with greasy matted hair and a warty face. 'I ain't bin loved since I don't know when. An' I've bin a maid since I was forty-two.'

The crowd hooted again.

Captain Kaff said, 'You've had more men up your skirts than a rat's got fleas. No serious takers? Right, that's it, I'm not hanging around here all day, smelling cattle dung. Let's go, Soldier.'

Soldier, now in the depths of despair, was led from the market-place, to his last destination. Spagg shouted after the captain, 'When you cut 'im up, for the gibbet, let me have his eyes. I'll split the profit with you.'

The captain shook his head in disbelief. 'You see what kind of people they are?' he said to Soldier. 'They're filth. They'd sell their own children for a stew if the price was right. That man was your former employer and now all he cares about is making a small profit out of your remains.'

'If that's the way they are,' replied Soldier, 'that's the way they've been made by the world they live in. Who's responsible for that?'

'They are what they are,' replied the captain. 'You can't make ambergris from pond scum.'

As the guards were hurrying him through the cobbled streets they had to pause for a sedan chair to cross their path. The chair was carried by four naked men: slaves by the look of them, since they did not appear to be Guthrumites. Behind the gauze curtain was the silhouette of a slim woman. Suddenly there came a call from within and the carriers halted.

The captain of the guard looked on, as puzzled as Soldier himself, as the gauze curtain was slowly opened by a delicate hand. Then they could see the occupant of the sedan chair. Her profile was quite beautiful. What could be seen of her radiant features, half-hidden by a white silken hood, were lovely to behold, with high cheekbones and eyes as dark as blackthorn sloes. She had black hair, which was pinned up, revealing a pale slender neck. The skin on that throat, and on her cheeks and brow, was fair and unblemished. Wafting from her direction came the fragrance of attar of roses mingled with sandalwood.

He knew that it was impossible, but Soldier could not shake the idea that he had met this woman before somewhere.

The lady, never once moving her head to turn her eyes fully on the guards and their prisoner, called softly for the captain to attend to her words. He stepped forward, went to the side of her chair, and listened to what she had to say. Soldier could hear nothing of what passed between them. Then the captain was dismissed and the curtain was dropped. The sedan chair carriers raised the lady aloft and were about to depart with her when Soldier cried out on impulse.

'Lady! Marry me! Or I die a horrible death!'

Immediately he was punched and kicked by the guards around him, including the captain.

Amazingly, however, the chair was lowered again, the curtain was opened.

This time the lady turned her head to stare. She looked directly into his eyes and no doubt observed their unique colour. Now Soldier saw that the other side of her face, hidden from him until now, was hideously disfigured. She gave him a fleeting, distorted smile, from which no warmth could come through that rippled flesh. Again she called the captain, who went to her side, and a whispered command left Kaff looking white and shaken. Then the sedan chair was again raised and was whisked away down a side-alley. The captain stood transfixed for a moment, staring in its wake, then he returned to shake his head at Soldier.

'I don't know whether you're the luckiest man alive — or the most unfortunate.'

'She agreed?' cried Soldier, elated. 'She will marry me?'

'So she says.'

'Who is she?'

'That, my poor friend, is Princess Layana, sister of Queen Vanda, of Guthrum. Your wedding will take place at the Palace of Wildflowers in three days' time.'

'A princess!' cried Soldier.

'An ugly princess,' muttered the captain, wanting no one but Soldier to hear this perfidy. 'A mad princess.'

'What do you mean? Is this why you called me unfortunate?'

'Indeed it is,' said Kaff. 'You have escaped one painful death for another. Princess Layana is violently insane. She has already brutally murdered two husbands, one with nail scissors, the other with a long darning needle. Watch out for your eyes and always keep your pants buttoned tight.'

'But — husbands? Is she not a maid?'

'She is still a virgin, despite the two husbands. One got dead drunk at his wedding. That same night he was attacked by his deranged bride bearing nail scissors and woke up without his manhood. He bled to death in sheets which had turned from crisp white to sodden red overnight. The second husband was warned not to enter the princess's boudoir during her bouts of madness. Unable to contain his lust he secretly arranged a rendezvous in a rooftop garden and had his eyes winkled from his head. In his blindness he stumbled over the battlements of the palace and fell to his death.'

'At least I live for a while longer,' Soldier told the captain.

'Make no mistake about it. She will destroy you, as she has others.' Kaff paused before he said in a faraway voice, 'It is such a great pity for her that she doesn't see what is before her eyes.'

There was something in the captain's tone which caught Soldier's attention. He stared into Kaff's stricken eyes. In there, he saw another kind of madness.

Soldier sighed. 'You're in love with her yourself.'

The metal glove lashed out yet one more time, splitting Soldier's lip. Blood ran from the corner of his mouth.

Kaff said, 'You're not married to her yet – don't become too insolent, stranger. You might have an accident on the way to the wedding. Wouldn't *that* be tragic?'

Soldier stared into Kaff's face and realised that now he had made a *real* enemy.

Chapter Six

Soldier was taken to a house near the Palace of Wildflowers and handed over to a man-servant of the princess.

'What lovely eyes,' said the eunuch. 'You've got a summer sky in your head, haven't you?'

Soldier's iron collar was removed by a blacksmith brought in for the purpose then dismissed. Fortunately it was not the man who had put the collar on.

In the centre of the hollow-squared house was a beautiful courtyard, trimmed with bushes of entwined rosemary and lavender, and studded with medlar trees. Lyre-birds fluttered on the mosaic paths and strutted between sprays of pure-white lilies, pecking at the brown fruit from the medlars. Doves decorated the statues of gods and wild beasts. Soft music came from ivory horns projecting from the fresco which lined the walls. Clouds of colourful butterflies drifted from corner to corner, purely decorative, while hardworking imperial blue dragonflies kept the surface of the water free from invading mosquitoes. Forming the centre of the courtyard was an oblong pool with fluorspar steps leading down into its pink water and a fountain which seemed to spray rose petals that somehow dissolved into pink-crystal liquid drops before falling gently onto the waters of the bath.

Guards stood and watched, smirking and nudging each other, while Soldier was stripped and bathed in the pink water by the man-servant with soft hands and pallid skin.

'I can do that,' said Soldier, as the man lovingly soaped his body. 'I'd rather do it myself.'

The man-servant, who said his name was Ofao, smiled a secret smile.

'You don't have a choice, sir. This is my work. I have been told to bathe you, smear you with perfumed oils, powder your bottom, and make you generally presentable.'

'You keep your damn hands off my bottom,' growled Soldier. 'or so help me I swear I'll cut off your manhood.'

Another secret smile from Ofao. 'I'm afraid that's already been done, sir.'

Once Soldier had been bathed, given a shave and haircut, and wrapped in a light cotton gown, he was left to reflect on the change in his fortunes.

That evening the stars were out in great bunches, like sparkling grapes on vines. He sat in a soft chair on the roof of the house, staring at the Palace of Wildflowers nearby. Why had she done it? He was nothing to her. Yet he knew he had met the princess somewhere before, though he could not say where. It was another of those terrible puzzles which haunted him.

'You'll go blind.'

'Wha . . .' Soldier looked wildly about him.

'Too much thinking. It sends you blind. It's all right, it's only me,' said a deep black shadow from the darkness of the rooftop. 'I told you I'd come and get you out. I can pick locks you know, with my beak. It's a talent.'

'Oh.' Soldier relaxed. 'It's you, raven. Well you're a bit late. I'm no longer a prisoner.'

'No?' said the raven, hopping out onto the white marble parapet before Soldier's eyes. 'Then what are all those guards doing, in and around the house? Are they there to read you bedtime stories?'

Soldier shifted his weight, uncomfortably. 'Well, in three days time I'll be free, once I'm married.'

'You have faith in that, do you?'

'So, what do you suggest?'

The bird wiped its beak once or twice on the stonework of the parapet, as if he were sharpening it.

'Sorry, just been eating goat's guts. Can't get the stuff off your beak afterwards. Now, where were we? Oh, yes, suggestions. Well, I'm not here for that, am I? I'm here to be told what to do. You decide if you want to escape and I'll help you do it. If you want to stay here and be wed to a lunatic with a face like a well-used cart track, then I'll go along with that too.'

'You watch your tongue.'

'How do you know ravens have got tongues?'

'I might just find out in a minute.'

The bird made no reply to this.

Soldier then asked it, 'This singing scabbard I have. Why didn't it warn me about the imperial guards in the market square? It warned me of the thieves down in the sewers.'

The raven was silent for a moment, then it replied, 'You didn't need warning. You saw the guards coming.'

'Oh, so you think it only warns me when I have no knowledge I'm being approached.'

'Maybe – probably – yes.'

Soldier clasped his hands together and nodded. 'That makes sense.'

'You smell nice,' remarked the raven.

Soldier looked down at himself. 'I've had a bath – I've *been* bathed.'

'You look nice too, without that beard. You have boyish features. Perhaps that's what attracted Princess Layana. Your handsome face?'

'Perhaps.' He rose from his seat. 'Now, I'm going to get some sleep. Are you hanging around? Or have you got somewhere to go?'

'No, no – I've already eaten – I think I'll stay here the night. Don't you worry about me.'

'I shan't,' muttered Soldier, then an idea came to him. 'Look, I want to get in touch with that woman again – Uthellen – the one with the peculiar child. Can you go and find her for me? Scour the streets from the sky. Make yourself useful.'

'What do you want a woman for – you're betrothed.'

'This has nothing to do with anything like that. I want to help the woman. She helped me when no one else would. My intended would understand that.'

The raven had to have the last word however.

'It is strange though, that she agreed to marry you, isn't it? She must have *some* motive.'

'You've already said – my handsome features.'

'That was to goad you into some sort of sensible thought on the subject. You don't really believe she's fallen in love with you at first sight, do you?'

Soldier did not answer. He agreed with the raven. It was an odd situation. Why *did* she wish to marry him?

* * *

The wedding itself revealed nothing more than Soldier already knew. A priest was in attendance, but that was not to marry the pair. He was there to help with the signing of documents. In fact it was quite a drab affair, which the princess did not even attend in person. Layana sent one of her maid-servants to stand for her. The raven had told Soldier he must take three objects with him: fish, fowl and flower. The first represented the oceans of the earth, the second the skies above the planet and the third the lands of the world. He offered these symbols to the bride. If she, or her representative, accepted them, the pair were married in the eyes of the gods and confirmed that by Deed of Matrimony.

On the third day Soldier was escorted to the Palace of Wildflowers. There were no trumpets, no flutes, no sweet marrying music. There were no guests. There was no bunting, no decorations, no visible sign it was a wedding.

Soldier had taken gifts along with him. The first was the home of a pretty mollusc with long thin spines running down two sides: a comb shell from some exotic sea, a decoration prised out of the brickwork of the house he was living in. To represent the sky he had a black feather plucked (with permission) from the raven's tail. A dark-green oleander wand, with pink bloom still attached, completed the three objects, appropriate because it grew wild almost everywhere.

'What happened to all the guests?' he asked a guard, afterwards, when the hall was empty but for the two of them and the priest. 'I thought the queen would be here, at her sister's wedding.'

'Since the bride hasn't even bothered to come, you can't expect her relations and friends to be there, can you?'

At that moment a messenger arrived and announced he was from Princess Layana.

'About time,' said Soldier, hands on hips. 'Well, out with it, man. When am I to see my wife?'

'The princess states she does not want to see you,' answered the messenger. 'Not now, not ever. You are free to go about your business in the castle, but you must stay away from Princess Layana. It's for your own good. Her previous husbands met with, er, fatal accidents. She would prefer you did not meet with the same kind of misfortune.'

Soldier was surprised to find a bolt of disappointment go through him. He had only seen his wife once, when she had stared at him from the confines of her sedan chair, but he now found within him an enormous attraction to her. Yes, she was unsightly, even perhaps grotesque when viewed from one side, but he had never been a man to trust appearances. It came as a shock to learn he was not even to meet his wife again, let alone make love to her as a husband should. Any fanciful thoughts he had of winning her love flew out of the window.

'Is this true? Do I not get to see my bride?' cried Soldier. 'What kind of marriage is this?'

The messenger, a courtier of sorts, was stern with Soldier.

'The queen's sister has saved your life, stranger. What more could you ask for? Are you not grateful to the princess? Her finer feelings could not allow you to die, once you had made supplication to her. Yet here you are, whining about the number of guests and the lack of cake and ale at your feast.'

The number of guests? There were not any. Cake and ale? There had been nothing to eat or drink.

It was true. He had his life. But human nature is such that now he had it, it seemed a trivial thing. He wanted more. He wanted the wealth and position he had thought came with being the husband of a princess. He wanted the princess herself, in his bed, loving him. He wanted a home, this simple little palace, a place to put his feet under the table. Perhaps a few hunting dogs? A trained falcon? One or two servants?

Was that too much to ask?

The messenger thought it might be.

'I would settle for your life – even that might not be yours for very much longer. The new Captain of the Imperial Guard, Kaff, does not think kindly of you, stranger. He is rising in power every day. If I were you I would slink into obscurity and stay there until they carry you away in a box.'

Subsequent to this good advice, Soldier was given a purse containing a sum of money and was then thrown out into the street.

Soldier roamed the streets, looking for Uthellen. He was married now and intended to stay faithful to his new wife, but he could not forget Uthellen. It had seemed to him that she was afraid of someone, or something. Had she managed to get herself onto the wrong side of the law? Or perhaps she had upset one of the chancellor's minor officials in some way? Whatever it was, it caused her to scuttle away from him if she saw him first, because he came across her again in one of the three long narrow streets that ran parallel to each other the length of the city, some five miles of ground. She immediately clutched her deformed child to her side and ducked into a sidestreet. When he ran to this point, she was gone.

'If she doesn't want to see me, then I have to respect that,' Soldier told the raven. 'Unless it's because she thinks I mean her harm, which I don't, of course.'

'Who knows the mind of a woman?' replied the raven, preening his feathers. 'They're such vain creatures.'

When evening came Soldier decided to go to an inn for the night. There was no reason why he should not spend some of his wife's wedding present. He found a large inn with a room and a comfortable bed, then spent the evening eating roast chicken and getting drunk on ale. Since he had money he was willing to spend he gathered about him several tradesmen. There was a cobbler at his elbow, and a wheelwright, and a butcher, and one or two other aspiring gentlefolk from the market fringe. Halfway through the evening he was far gone enough to share his personal and domestic problems with the whole tavern.

'Who does she think she is?' he cried, drunkenly. 'Just because she's a princess doesn't make her someone special.'

'Er, excuse me, but I think it does,' said the cobbler

'Who asked you?' snarled Soldier. 'You'll get no more ale from me. Not you, or your friends. What's more, I could knock your block off with one punch.'

The cobbler thought differently, but to make sure he enlisted the services of his friends the wheelwright and the butcher, and between them they threw Soldier out of the inn. He landed, sprawling, on the hard cobbles of the alley. The cool night air sobered him somewhat. Picking himself up, he staggered down the alley towards one of the three main streets. He was too befuddled to notice that someone else had slipped out of the inn behind him and was stalking him silently along the alley.

'My father placed a wager, upon a young grey mare . . .' sang Soldier, weaving back and forth across the alley and using the walls as resting points on his journey.

The sound of his voice cloaked the stealthy steps of the man who rapidly came up behind him. Something held in the hand of the stalker flashed in the moonlight: a short blade of sorts. At that moment a voice sang out, clear and sweet, into the night airs of the city street.

Soldier stopped his own song in mid-line.

'Wha . . .'

Soldier's brain was not sodden enough to forget the tone of that voice, even if he did not understand the words. The scabbard! A warning! He swung round just as the would-be assassin lunged at his back with the curved dagger. Soldier swung an arm across, parrying the blow. His clouded brain cleared instantly. Next he lashed out with his foot, catching the attacker on the shin. The man howled in pain and this time used the dagger to slash with, slicing through the fabric of Soldier's jerkin, the one put on his back by Ofao.

'You bastard,' cried Soldier. 'I'll get you for that!'

Before the other man could settle himself for a murderous blow, Soldier struck him hard on the chin with his fist. The assassin fell backwards onto the stone alleyway, his dagger flying out of his fist and skittering over the flints. Soldier then brought a boot down on the offending wrist and heard a satisfying crack. His attacker yelled and rolled out of the way of any further kicks. Soon he was on his feet and running, down the alley back towards the inn, with Soldier swaying on his feet, watching him through narrowed eyes.

'I have enemies,' muttered Soldier, picking up the curved-blade dagger and thrusting it into his belt. 'Someone wants me dead.'

'Kaff, no doubt,' said a voice at his shoulder.

The raven.

'Why aren't you around when I need you?' grumbled Soldier. 'You could have warned me a lot earlier than this bent and battered piece of leather-and-metal hanging from my belt.'

'I've only just got here.'

The drunkenness returning, Soldier staggered to a wall and leaned against it.

'Why does this scabbard sing in a language I don't understand? What's the use of that? If I hadn't swung round by instinct, I'd be dead by now.'

'It sings in the tongues of wizards,' replied the bird.

'The boy said that. But why?'

The raven shook its head. 'Ever thought that it might be because it *belonged* to a wizard? I don't know where you got it, but if the owner ever catches up with you, you'll be joining me in the animal kingdom. I hope he turns you into a nice fat worm, so that we can be together always – me on the outside, you on the inside.'

Soldier shook his head to try to clear it. 'Why are you with me?' he asked. 'I wonder about it.'

'You saved me from a snake,' replied the raven. 'A serpent was about to swallow me whole when you beat it to death with a stick. You saved my life. I owe it to you.'

'I don't remember that.'

'On the hillside, where you thought the battle was.'

Soldier said, 'I must have been asleep.'

'It was while you were waking up.'

'I still don't remember.'

The raven snorted. 'You don't remember much at all, do you?'

Soldier let this pass. 'Did you find the woman and the boy?' he asked.

'That's why I came to get you. They're on their way out of the city. The woman is afraid of something.'

Soldier blinked and looked around him at the shadows cast by the moonlight. 'So am I. Someone tried to kill me here.

You say Kaff was probably behind it? I think you're right, raven. In which case I had better get out of Zamerkand too, before I'm murdered in my sleep.'

'Your *drunken* sleep.'

'Never mind the wise talk, let's find Uthellen.'

The raven flew ahead, stopping every so often for Soldier to catch up to him. They wound their way through the city streets, avoiding watchmen. Finally they came to the north gate. Ahead of him, Soldier could see the woman and the child, hurrying along as if they were being pursued.

Soldier caught up with them. 'Wait – I'm coming with you,' he said.

Uthellen turned in alarm. She looked up into his face.

'Why do you want to do that? Leave us alone. You're causing us trouble.'

'I don't mean to. I have to get out of the city. People are trying to kill me. I want to find somewhere to rest for a while, in peace and quiet.'

She clutched the witchboy to her breast. 'You're spying on me. You're a wizard, or a wizard's agent. Go away. Leave us alone. We won't harm you.'

He took one of her hands in his own. 'I swear to you,' he said, 'I'm no wizard, nor wizard's spy. I'm a simple soldier, who woke on the hillside and found himself with no memory. It's true I have this scabbard, which appears to be magical, but I don't know where I got it or from whom.'

'You talk with that jackdaw, I've seen you.'

'Please,' replied the bird, '*raven*. My mother wouldn't have a jackdaw in the house. They steal things.'

'Mother,' said the awkward child, detaching himself from her clutches, 'I think we should take Soldier with us. I trust him. Let him come with us.'

She looked worried. But clearly her son's words had a profound affect on her. Staring into Soldier's eyes, she said, 'They worry me.'

'They're just eyes,' said Soldier. 'Nothing more. I come from a different race to Guthrumites, that's all.'

'Different as well from the Carthagans and every other people I know.'

Soldier shrugged. 'Perhaps I'm from across the sea? I seem to know there are people with dark skins over there. There are images in my mind which are just there, like pictures hanging on a wall. I know there are a tall stately people with long black hair and dusky bodies.'

'But not blue eyes.'

'No, but perhaps they are from another place?'

Again the boy interrupted. 'Mother, we must leave, but we should take Soldier with us.'

She sighed. 'All right, we travel together.'

'And trust each other?' said Soldier.

'I have no choice,' she replied.

'Now that's settled,' said the raven, laconically. 'Let's get on.'

They were stopped at the gate, but it was pure boredom on the part of the guards. They were in the middle of their night duty and the world was peaceful. They questioned the three, assuming they were a family, and asked them why they were leaving the city at three in the morning. Soldier said they were going out to gather mushrooms, to sell in the market.

'We have to be out early, to gather them before the sun comes up and blemishes their caps.'

'On you go then,' muttered one of the guards, 'bring us back a couple for our breakfast. I like fried mushrooms. No funny ones mind. Just your plain wood or field mushroom, with a nice velvety-brown underside. Nothing with red spots or white gills. A friend of mine was dead in half an hour, just from licking his fingers after pickin' the wrong kind.'

The other guard said, 'They say a death cap can kill you just by seeping into your pores. You don't even have to put it into your mouth.'

The first guard shuddered. 'On second thoughts, I'll stick to eggs and bacon. You don't find destroying chickens or death pigs, do you?'

Uthellen, Soldier and the boy slipped out into the night. They made their way towards the distant forest. It was dangerous anywhere outside the city, but at least in the forest there was plenty of cover, lots of places to hide from potential enemies. There were wild boars and wolves in the forest, but though any boar might charge them if cornered, wolves tended to avoid contact with humans. Soldier knew there were lots of myths about wolves attacking humans, but there was very little truth in them. In his experience, locked somewhere in the recesses of his mind, wolves were only really dangerous if they sensed their human prey was sick or feeble in some way, and they – the wolves – were starving to the point of madness. Wolves were not stupid. Better to run down a wild boar than tackle a human being.

They reached the forest without incident. It was getting light as they entered the pale of the trees. They had to battle their way through huge webs built by giant spiders, which blocked every path. There were stagnant pools and rotten trees everywhere, and carcasses of dead animals and birds. Carrion creatures infested the area, feeding from the corrupt flesh of their own kind.

'Better stick to the edge,' said Soldier. 'We don't want to get lost straight away.'

'It's all right,' said the witchboy, leading them into the thick undergrowth. 'I know every part of the forest.'

'You've been here before?'

'We've not been out of the city before, have we Mother?'

Uthellen didn't answer, but Soldier took her silence to mean yes.

'Then how do you know your way?' he asked the boy, beginning to get worried as they went deeper into the gloom of the trees.

'It's all in here,' replied the boy, enigmatically, tapping his head. 'Trust me, just as I trust *you*.'

They found a mossy bank by a little brook with a waterfall that gushed from a rocky outcrop. There were plants and wildflowers growing in amongst the lichen of the outcrop's cracks. Great trees shouldered each other around the small glade, letting in narrow sheets of light. Here there was a pretty pink campion flower, there some mauve herb robert. Frogs and newts swam in the small pool at the bottom of the tumbling waterfall. A grass snake slithered away, under a stone, one of the shy creatures of the forest. Butterflies and dragonflies decorated the air above the sparkling waters.

'This is a beautiful place,' marvelled Soldier. 'How is it that the rest of the forest is in a state of decay, while here it's clean and fresh?'

'There are small pockets which escape corruption,' said Uthellen. 'We're lucky my son knows of them.'

Soldier then set about making a shelter for them. He still had the assassin's dagger in his belt and he used this to cut some staves to form the frame for a bivouac. He covered the frame with moss and leaves, making a small apartment for himself and a bigger one for the other two.

When the watery-pale sun arrived, they were ready for it.

There just remained the problem of food. Soldier went out, following the brook away from the scent of their camp, to set snares for wild creatures. He made a fishing line from some twine unravelled from Uthellen's belt and a hook from one of her metal hairgrips. With this makeshift angling tool he left the boy happily fishing in the brook ahead of the falls, while he set his springy willow traps at the watering places of wild animals. By the time evening came he had caught a hare, while Uthellen's boy had managed to hook a rainbow trout.

'We can eat like royalty,' he said to Uthellen.

The boy looked up from his task of cleaning the trout. 'You *are* royalty,' he said.

Soldier thought about this. 'I suppose I am,' he said at length. 'I'm the husband of the queen's sister. But she doesn't acknowledge me. She's not interested in me as a man. She merely took pity on me as a human being. Princess Layana married me to stop me from being tortured by the Lord of Thieftakers.'

'You don't know that,' said the boy. 'Maybe she's protecting you against her madness, by not letting you into her house. Perhaps she secretly cares for you.'

Soldier studied the boy carefully in the light of the campfire. His stick-thin limbs appeared quite dark in the dancing shadows thrown by the flames. They protruded from a scrawny body which would have any observer thinking the child was consumptive. His face was gaunt and elf-like, with narrow inquisitive eyes and a long thin nose. The hair on his head stood as erect as the bristles on a brush. He was clearly a peculiar looking individual. But with his last remark he had revealed that his insight was very incisive for someone of his age.

'Just how old are you, boy?' asked Soldier.

'Eight,' replied the child proudly, as children do when they think they have reached a superior level and expect to be praised for their wisdom, 'and a half.'

'Well, that's quite a speech for an eight-year-old, but of course you're quite wrong. The princess has only seen me once. People don't fall in love at a single glance.'

The boy stared at Soldier. 'You did.'

This observation really made Soldier sit up. He said to Uthellen, 'This boy is remarkable.' To Soldier's surprise she looked frightened at these words. She moved closer to her child as if to protect him from Soldier. Perhaps it was Soldier's imagination, but even the dark trees circling their camp seemed to shuffle forward as if to come to her assistance, should she cry out for it.

'No – no – most children of his age say things like that. They don't know what they're talking about really.'

The boy whom Soldier had, in his own mind, labelled the 'witchboy' looked up into his mother's face.

'You can trust him, Mother. Don't worry. Soldier has come from another place. He won't hurt us.'

'Of course I won't hurt you,' said Soldier. 'Do you think I would cause you harm, Uthellen?'

Uthellen continued to look scared and hugged her child to her breast.

'Tell him our secret, mother. He needs to know. If we are to share our exile with him, then he must be told.'

'No,' she whispered. 'He could be a spy. Who knows what form . . .' here she stopped abruptly and shuddered.

'What form?' Soldier was bewildered by all this cryptic talk. 'You've lost me, I'm afraid – both of you.'

The boy then began whispering with urgent tones in his

mother's ear. For a while Uthellen continued to shake her head, but finally she broke down and sobbed. Soldier let her cry for a while, then assured her again he meant no harm to her.

'If you think I'm some kind of demon in disguise, well, there's no way of proving that I'm not.'

'Tell him, Mother.'

This was by way of a command from the boy, rather than a request.

'All right,' said Uthellen, quietly. 'But Soldier, you must swear an oath never to reveal what I'm about to reveal to you. It would put my child and myself in great danger.'

Soldier was a little ruffled by these words.

'I'm not sure I even want to know, if that's the case. I've got enough burdens to carry with my own troubles. I don't know who I am. I don't know where I come from. I don't know why I'm here. I'm a stranger in a hostile land. It may be the result of some accident, but I feel I have some purpose here, but what it is or how I find out seems to be an insurmountable task. If you're going to add to the load I have to carry, I'd as soon as not know your secret.'

'Perhaps,' said the boy, mysteriously, 'you have come to Guthrum – to our world – to seek some kind of redemption? If this is so, you must seek it with all your might and soul, for it won't come looking for you. You must grasp all that is offered, in the hope of finding some kernel of understanding within.'

'This boy is exceptional,' cried Soldier. 'What is he, some kind of priest?'

Uthellen drew a deep breath and the shadows moved in even closer.

'He is the son of a very powerful wizard,' she replied.

'A wizard?' Soldier stared at the boy. 'Then why does he look so sickly?'

The child gave him a cold and emotionless smile which chilled Soldier to the bone. In that smile he saw the strangeness of the creature before him. This was no mortal, with a mortal's feelings and thoughts. This was a being of another make-up, a creature incomprehensible to human view. The boy might as well have been an intelligent wolf, or a knowing serpent, for all that Soldier knew about what was in his heart and mind. This boy was of a different race to that of men and women.

'Wizards are not strong in their youth,' replied the boy. 'They're weak and puny, the prey of men. That's why there's so few of us. We die of disease, we are killed out of fear. In the beginning we have to develop our minds at the expense of our bodies. We do not have a *natural* ability to employ magic, that comes with patient learning – just as the knowledge of such subjects as science, philosophy and mathematics comes to men and women. You would not expect your own son to be born with vast learning. You would send him to a teacher who would tutor him.' The child paused for a moment, then added, 'Later the flesh will cover my bones, but for now I must starve my body of the energy my mind needs to develop its powers. I must use all the potency I can produce in sharpening my thoughts and intellect. When I am worthy of a name I shall be given one – a wizard's name – until then I shall live – or die – in anonymity.'

'Whose child is he?' asked Soldier, anxious to keep the boy in the third person. 'Are you really his mother?'

Uthellen explained to him the nature of the world at that time.

'You have come to us from the outside,' she said, 'and

you're not familiar with what is happening to Guthrum and the world at large. You have seen the weak, pale sun. You have seen the hanged men, the stagnant lakes, the lethargy and corruption which festers within the walls of the city. For some time now we have been on the brink of war with our neighbours. There are horrible murders committed without compunction.'

'Why is this?'

Uthellen sighed. 'To explain that, I must tell you how things are here. Guthrum is a country surrounded by mountain ranges, beyond which are forces of great evil. The greatest of these ranges is the one to the east, where on seven of the tallest peaks sit our gods, one on each.'

'These gods,' said Soldier, 'they keep the evil at bay?'

'Not so much the gods, who are simply there because they are part of the unnatural world around us. This wickedness is held back by the vigilance of a fraternity of magi. The King Magus provides spiritual and moral guidance to this fraternity. He is responsible for a balance of good and evil in the world.'

Soldier was sceptical. 'The King Magus, I take it, has supernatural powers?'

'Of course,' said Uthellen. 'He resides in the western mountains. The King Magus at present is a wizard called HoulluoH, who has been ill for the last fifty years. He's dying of old age – it's rumoured he has seen seven hundred years of our history – but wizards live long and in consequence take a long time to die. HoulluoH's strength has all but gone, and the nameless evil from beyond the mountains is seeping through and poisoning the minds of the people of Guthrum.'

'This sounds like a good excuse for lawlessness and chaos

to me,' said Soldier. 'I don't believe in the presence of "nameless evil" – only in the evil that mankind fosters.'

The boy interrupted their conversation now, with his own views. 'Perhaps, Soldier, you come from a place where pure evil does not exist, where it is only generated in the hearts and minds of mortals greedy for wealth and power. Here there are forces which are difficult to control. Yes, there are men, and wizards, and all manner of creatures who perpetrate their own kind of evil, but there is also the distilled essence of evil which comes from living in a world where nature and supernature live so close to one another that they often merge. Magic and the ordinary meld into an indivisible one. There are blurred lines here, boundaries which are crossed by beings from both sides. Here, Soldier, you will find the unexpected.'

'So,' said Soldier, still unconvinced by this explanation, 'the depravity I saw within the walls of Zamerkand and the decay of the natural world at large, all this is due to one sick and dying wizard?'

'Not just to that,' replied the boy. 'Some of it is due in part to my wicked progenitor, who was banished by Queen Vanda's father, the old king of Guthrum, at the request of the King Magus, my uncle HoulluoH. The old king's family has, for his pains, been rewarded with spasmodic purple madness, which visits at odd times. No one knows where OmmullummO is now, but wherever it is his mind reaches out and corrupts all it touches. OmmullummO, my father, never got over the fact that his older brother HoulluoH was instated as King Magus. Jealousy gnawed at the mind of OmmullummO until he finally turned rogue wizard, opposed to a world in balance. My father no longer believes in symmetry, only in pure evil. He wished the world to be flooded with corruption, and must still wish it, since once a wizard has turned rogue he is lost to iniquity forever.'

'Where is your father now?'

'No one knows – perhaps a long way away.'

'Yet his magic still reaches us?'

'Those who take the wrong path find power at the end in great abundance, for there are few who have used it.'

Chapter Seven

Soldier woke in the middle of the night covered in small creatures which had their teeth buried in his arteries. He leapt
up, yelling, and tried to fend off the invaders. They were not
so easily dislodged from their task. Soldier shouted for assistance. Uthellen and the boy woke at his second cry. In the
glow from the embers of the camp-fire they saw his plight.
The boy took a stick and began beating the parasites, small
beings about two and a half inches in length, of human appearance. They clung on with their teeth and when one was severed
by Soldier's blade, its head remained with its jaws gripping
Soldier's flesh, while its wriggling torso fell to the forest floor.
Soldier had to squeeze the head to open its jaws, so that he
could remove it.

On inspection, Soldier found his skin covered in bite marks.

'What are they?' he cried.

'Drots,' replied Uthellen, still striking the furious little
figures. 'Blood-sucking fairies.'

The fairies began to suffer severe loss of numbers under
the onslaught of Uthellen's and the boy's blows. Eventually
the small creatures began to fall away, flying into the darkness

with their wings humming loudly. Soldier could tell the vicious little beings were angry by the sound they made. One of them, having been stunned by the boy's stick, was disorientated and whacked into a tree at great speed. It gave out a terrible shriek, before dropping at Soldier's feet and buzzing there, thrashing with its arms and legs, until it finally died and lay still. Soldier, now free of the creatures, picked it up and studied it in the light from the glowing charcoal.

'It's like a tiny human,' he marvelled. He pressed the jaws again, revealing the serrated teeth inside the fairy's mouth, two of them longer than the others. 'Except for these.' Then he saw a bloated one, wriggling on the edge of the fire. It was mortally wounded and in great pain. He trod on it swiftly to put it out of its suffering. The drot burst, showering the embers with Soldier's blood, making the flames sizzle.

Soldier's head suddenly began to swim and he felt a little weak and woozy.

'I don't feel so good,' he said, his manhood suffering from the confession. 'I've come over a bit faint.'

'Loss of blood,' said Uthellen. 'You'd better lie down while I warm up some hare soup for you. You'll be all right with some rest. In the meantime, my son will gather up some blackthorn branches and make a protective barrier to keep out such creatures as these.'

Soldier sank gratefully to the ground.

'Why haven't I met these drots before?' he asked, his voice a little shaky.

'You only find them in forests,' Uthellen replied. 'They infest these particular woods in great numbers. Mostly they feed on the blood of cattle, but they like the blood of mortals a lot. They say it's rich in goodness, because of the variety of foodstuffs eaten by human beings.'

'Why didn't they bite you too?' asked Soldier, a little resent-ful of being picked out as a sole victim.

'They wouldn't suck the blood of a wizard's son – it would kill them. And I think I was sleeping too close to the fire for their comfort. I kept waking up very hot and intending to move, but was too sleepy to do it.'

Soldier said, 'You could have warned me.'

'We forgot. It's been a long day. It just never crossed my mind that we would be attacked by drots.'

'Is there anything else you'd like to warn me about?'

The boy, now dragging thorn branches and placing them in a circle around the camp, said, 'There's a giant boar some-where in these woods, but we can't worry about him.'

'Why can't we?'

'Because we don't know where he is. If he attacks, we'll just have to do what we can to protect ourselves. He preys on travellers in this forest. The boar kills them, leaves them to rot for a few days like jugged hare, then returns when the flesh is soft and putrid to eat his fill, as a scavenger feeds on a decomposing carcass. He has a name too.'

Even though Soldier had been amongst the Guthrumites and Carthagans for only a short while he knew instinctively that if the boar had a name it was more than just an ordinary beast. Just as a sword with a name is a unique weapon, so a wild animal with a name is also exceptional. This boar had to be the bastard son of a god, or a creation of the gods. Such a creature might terrorise a whole town or city for many years, until someone came along and killed themselves into the annals of history by slaughtering the beast and becoming a hero.

'What's the name of this boar?'

'He is called Garnash. They say he weighs a black ton and his tusks are like sabres.'

'So, we have a giant boar for company.'

At that moment there was a howl from the distant forested hills above their camp.

'And wolves, of course,' added Uthellen. 'There's the wolves.'

'Of course there are,' grumbled Soldier, sarcastically. 'And the odd rogue Hannack roaming the countryside, looking for a bearded mandible to hack off and use as a wig.'

'Oh no,' Uthellen assured him, 'a Hannack would never come in here – his horse wouldn't like the thorn bushes.'

'Well that's something, I suppose. Now, can we get some sleep? I'm feeling fatigued by all this.'

Soldier lay there, trying to get back to sleep again, but there seemed to be all manner of things out in the darkness, pressing to reach his vulnerable form. In the distant hills the wolves raised their heads to the moon and let their throats sing. He listened to their night noise. After a while Soldier began to recognise a repeated sound. It was as if they were calling out a single word, though the meaning was lost in the hollow of the howl. Howls are smooth, flowing sounds, mellow in the utterance, and from a great distance they are difficult to interpret. Soldier had the feeling the wolves were calling a name – his real name – but maddeningly he could not quite hear the syllables.

'They know who I am,' he said, mournfully to himself, 'but I can't make out what they're saying.'

'I can't understand what word it is they're howling either, or I would tell you.'

'Uthellen?' said Soldier. 'Are you still awake?'

She came to him then and snuggled down beside him. He could smell her hair, which had been washed with some kind of forest herb, letting out a fragrance which tested sorely his resolve to remain celibate for his wife. Still, he turned his back on her.

An owl hooted derisively.

'Do you find me repulsive?' said Uthellen. 'Am I simply a woman from the sewers?'

He sat up now, the same owl hooting its scorn. 'I find you extremely attractive. That's why I have to turn away. Uthellen, you know I am married . . .'

She said in a disappointed tone, 'But your wife does not love you. She has sent you away. And your marriage is not yet consummated.'

'Still, I cannot. I know it's stupid. Most men would give their right hands to sleep with a woman such as you. A week ago I would have been one of them. But there's been a union of two people and I am one of them. It's part of who I am. I can't put that aside and forget it ever happened. Also I have to be in love with a woman in order to make love with her, otherwise the act means nothing to me. I'm sorry.'

She pulled him down beside her and wrapped her arms around him, hugging him tightly.

'And you are not in love with me?' asked Uthellen, refusing to let him go. 'You hate me?'

'I don't hate you, I'm very fond of you – I shall be like a brother to you – but not a lover.'

The owl hooted so much Soldier thought it must fall off its branch. Soldier gritted his teeth. He really was very fond of Uthellen and could have loved her easily, if another had not come along. But that other person *had* come along and now there was an iron door between Soldier and other women.

He got up, thoroughly miserable, and went and sat on a great root beneath a tree. In the moonlight, forest fairies, smaller than the drots, came to him. They covered him in swarms: transparent wings humming, tiny eyes glowing, hot little fingers pinching him with sharp nails. When he did not respond to their pinches they bit him lightly all over his skin, inflaming his lust. The faster Soldier brushed them off, the more they swarmed over him. He gave up. With his passion swimming Soldier went back to bed and tried to get some sleep. All that came to him were images of himself and Uthellen, rolling on the mossy ground amongst the roots of an old grandfather hornbeam, making love in high and furious fashion.

When morning came Soldier had found little sleep, but he had not broken his vow of renunciation. He had remained true to his lady and tired though he was this was a source of comfort to him.

Uthellen rose before the boy was awake. 'I'm sorry,' she said. 'I should not have tempted you in the night hours. Please forgive me. Something – something got into me. I think it might have been a residue of the boy's father. From time to time I am driven to wickedness by those traces of him which remain in me.'

'There is nothing essentially wicked in wanting to make love to someone,' replied Soldier. 'But I am greatly interested in the father of the boy. OmmullummO is still abroad somewhere in Guthrum?'

Uthellen nodded. 'Or one of its bordering countries.'

'Then how did – how did you become pregnant by him?' asked Soldier. 'Did you meet him before he was banished?'

'No. He was able to project his lust into a youth, who then seduced me. Wizards can obtain vicarious gratification from making love to women through a surrogate male. After we had finished our passionate meeting the poor youth collapsed and withered away. He became like a puffball sucked dry of any moisture: a husk with simply nothing but dust inside.'

'And through this one mating, you became pregnant with the boy?'

'Wizards are potent creatures. You must remember to keep my secret, however. His father wishes him dead. Most children of such unhallowed unions are killed by their wizard fathers before they reach the age of seven. They're a threat to their elders, being young and pure of spirit. Their minds are not yet corrupted by ambition and the craving for power, or by any other worldly desire.'

'But one or two reach adulthood?' Soldier said.

'Of course, that's how supernature plans these things, otherwise there would be no new wizards. Just as in the natural world two or three newly-hatched turtles out of fifty manage to reach the sea, after running the gauntlet of gulls and other birds, so one or two wizards' offspring make it past the year of seven. Again, like the turtles, of that generation of three perhaps a single one will survive being eaten by the monsters of the ocean – the sharks and other predators – to reach adulthood.'

Soldier marvelled at these things. 'So, you have managed to keep your son alive, despite being hunted by – by *what* exactly?'

'By the agents of his father: rats, spiders, beetles and other small creatures that infest dark places.'

At this moment the boy himself woke up. He rose and began collecting wood and leaves. These he put on the fire. Soon there was a blaze going from the embers. It warmed the sheltered and shaded glade. The boy then cut a gourd from a nearby climbing plant and hollowed it out with the Soldier's knife. This he filled with water from the pool, then, nestling it in some hot stones which kept the gourd from the actual flames of the fire, he managed to heat some water to a tepid temperature.

'He's a good lad,' said Soldier. 'Look at the way he did those chores, without being asked.'

'He's my son,' said Uthellen, proudly.

Soldier noticed marks on the boy's ankles. They were like inflamed handprints. He asked Uthellen what they were.

'They're the handprints of the witch who acted as midwife during his birth. I have burn marks from her hands too, around my thighs and on my stomach. And before you ask, I went to a witch rather than an ordinary midwife because I knew I was giving birth to a wizard's son. The birth of such a child is very difficult. They are always in an awkward position in the womb, a kind of defensive crouch, ready to ward off any attack. The witch had to break his bones to get him out of the womb, that's why his arms and legs look a bit peculiar. Once he is fully grown, he can straighten them with magic.'

'Broke his bones?' cried Soldier, appalled at the thought.

'It happens in ordinary births, too, where the baby is trying to come out sideways.'

'I never knew. How did you know you were giving birth to a boy? It could have been a girl.'

'Wizards don't have daughters, only sons.'

Later, while Soldier was making himself a bow and arrows, he asked the boy, 'Have you ever been attacked by rats or spiders?'

'Rats, yes. Once by a snake – a blind cave racer.'

'What did they do?'

'They tried to tear open my throat, so that I would choke · or bleed to death.'

Soldier raised his eyebrows. 'Yet you escaped injury.'

'I killed them all,' said the boy, his dark eyes flashing with menace. 'When I was a baby, still in my cradle, I strangled one rat and bit the head off another.'

'I can believe it,' replied Soldier, a chill going through him as he studied the youngster. 'Look, I'm going hunting. I'll be gone an hour, then I want you to call me. Can you do that? I don't think I'll get lost, but just in case I would like to be guided to the camp by the sound of your voice.'

'All right,' said the boy, once again a compliant child, ready to the bidding of an adult. 'I'll shriek like a magpie.'

Soldier was dubious about this. 'What if there are real magpies shrieking their heads off? I might be confused and try to go in all directions.'

'Magpies don't come into this wood. Not this deep. No birds, except perhaps owls, come in here.'

'If you say so.'

Soldier left, carrying his bow and a spear he had made with a sharp flintstone and a staff. By noting which side of the tree moss grew on, he managed to keep in one direction, moving stealthily through the undergrowth. Once or twice he attempted to kill some small creatures – a polecat, a tree marten – but missed each time. The animals of the forest might fall for his clever snares made of supple saplings, but they were too quick for his hunting skills. He was not very adept with the bow, especially since his arrows had no flights. In the end he decided to return to camp empty-handed. Soldier waited for the boy's cries to guide him into the camp.

A call came from the boy, somewhat earlier than expected. A shriek from a distant place. Soldier realised he must have wandered further than he thought from the camp, for the sound was very faint. He tried calling back, but the boy had chosen his tone well. Soldier's deep, low voice was lost in the ferny brakes after a few yards. It needed a high penetrating shriek to carry through the woods. Soldier gave up trying to tell the boy he had heard him and travelled as quickly as he could in the direction of the sounds.

As he was passing through one glade where the sunlight shafted through and picked out small red flowers like drops of blood amongst the star moss, Soldier got the distinct feeling he was being stalked. He turned quickly, looking in all directions, but was faced only with the wooden pillars of the forest, the canopy above and the undergrowth beneath. Soldier listened intently, trying to pick up any sounds of breaking twigs or the drumming of hooves on hardened earth.

Nothing.

No sound, no scent, no sight of any follower.

Yet he knew he was being hunted. He had set out from camp to hunt, but now he was the prey. What would go after a man in the daylight? Not the wolves. They might attack a lone disabled or sick traveller at night, but not a healthy man in the light hours. A bear? Unlikely. Bears tended to avoid humans. The only thing Soldier could think of was that he was being tracked by Garnash, the wild boar. There was nothing else, man excluded, which might set out after a human hunter.

He looked down at his weapons. If the boar was after him he was in deep trouble. All he had was the bow and a makeshift spear.

'But if I killed this Garnash,' he told himself, 'I would not need to worry about Kaff or people like him. I would be a slayer of magical beasts. Behold, they would say, the marvellous hunter, slayer of Garnash!'

He cut a vine and spliced the ends, then made a noose from it. The other end he tied to a thick bough some thirty feet off the ground. When Garnash felt something round his leg, or his neck, he would instinctively run headlong to free himself from it: that was the nature of beasts. In doing so he would simply tighten the noose of the thick vine and entrap himself. Soldier intended to remain up the tree until Garnash had exhausted himself by running around, perhaps getting entangled in other trees. Then he would simply climb down and stab the great creature in the heart with his spear, finishing the job with the dagger he had in his waistband. There was no danger involved, should things go wrong, for Soldier would be high up in the branches of a great tree.

All the while these plans and preparations were taking place there were the calls from camp, but he had to kill Garnash before he returned to the boy and Uthellen. Wouldn't they be surprised? Soldier wondered whether the knife he had would be big enough to cut off the head of the boar, so that he would have proof of his kill? It was something he could worry about later.

Soldier climbed the tree and sat in the fork, his hand on the vine. Down below he could see the patch of leaves which hid the noose under them.

He waited.

And waited.

Dusk began to fall.

Eventually he heard a sniffing and snorting sound, not too loud, coming from the undergrowth. Certainly there was some kind of wild pig, a hog of some sort down there, but whether it was Garnash or not there was no way of telling. Then some leaves of bushes parted and a great creature entered the gloaming of the clearing, slipping along like a huge dark shadow.

It was a monstrous black boar. Soldier's heart missed a beat on first seeing this beast. Indeed it was a giant, with a great bristled belly which hung in the dust. Its head was as large as a curled-up man and the back of its neck, and its shoulders, were ridged with rolls of skin. Soldier could see thick wedges of dead flies which had been trapped in these creases in the animal's flesh and pulped there. Its snout was flat against its face with two caverns which were its nostrils. A black ruff of coarse hair fringed its lower jaw like a man's beard, and two massive yellow tusks curled out and away on either side of the creature. Set above the crumpled snout were two glaring, intelligent but utterly merciless eyes. This was a vicious creature which would have no compunction in charging down anything on the earth and goring it with those tusks.

It lumbered forward, sniffing the air, and then to Soldier's absolute horror, it stood up on two legs.

Soldier gagged with fear at that point, seeing this monster with its pizzle erect, its pinky-dark underside revealed, staring around the glade as it stood some twelve feet tall. It scoured the undergrowth around it with those cold, callous eyes, looking for signs of its prey. Soldier was frozen to the fork of the tree wondering what on earth had possessed him to take on this formidable enemy.

One step, two steps, three steps. Awkwardly the beast went forward, still turning that great dome of a head this way and that, sniffing and staring. Drool dripped, splattering, from its jaws as it opened its mouth to reveal a thick row of blackened teeth strung between its long tusks.

It sniffed hard again.

Then it looked upwards, at the tree fork where Soldier crouched, and after a few seconds the jaws went lopsided into a position which might have been described as a grin had it not been on the face of a beast. Garnash had spotted his quarry, hiding from him in the tree above, and did not seem too disconcerted.

Down went the huge brute on all fours now. It raced to the other side of the clearing. Then it charged, head down, to butt the trunk of the tree. There was the terrific thump of an inch-thick skull with a ton of weight behind it smacking the bole of a tree. The earth shuddered and a quiver went through the world. Soldier clung on for dear life. The tree was a great oak, very solid, very mature, yet it shook like a sapling on its roots as if it had been struck by a mobile mountain.

Rotten branches fell, acorns showered the glade, the roots squealed and creaked. How Soldier managed to hang on to the trunk and remain aloft was a miracle. He was as vulnerable as a bird's nest balanced in the fork of a twig.

At that moment Soldier saw that the creature had one hind leg in the patch of leaves which hid the noose. He jerked quickly on the vine. The loop tightened around the haunch of the great brute. It let out a terrible scream of anger, and charged away into the brush.

For a moment or two Soldier thought his plan had worked. This feeling fled the instant the vine reach its end and was taut around the boar's leg. Garnash kept going. The tree did not hold him. It began to lean. Roots started to tear from the soil on the far side. Gradually the grunting boar tore the huge tree loose from its anchor. Soldier clung on desperately. When the oak was at forty-five degrees, he fell. He dropped stone-like onto the hard backbone of Garnash. Reaching to steady his fall he clutched at a bunch of bristles like long needles on the boar's back. They were wrenched from their roots. Garnash let out a terrible scream which seemed to explode in Soldier's head.

Soldier then began running, terrified out of his wits.

Garnash saw him and started out after him. The tree acted

as a hold on the leash. The giant boar, still screaming its anger, continued to heave. Finally, just as the oak came crashing down all the way now to the forest floor, the vine snapped. Garnash lumbered after his prey. But Soldier had a head start on the boar. His feet flew, spurred by terror. He went through brake, leaping over streams, around between tree trunks. He ran until he saw the glow of a camp-fire in the darkening green and finally, gasping for breath he stumbled into the camp.

'Quickly,' he gasped, 'get up a tree – Garnash is after me.'

The boy and Uthellen did not move. They stared in amazement at Soldier. He looked down at himself, expecting to see a leg missing, or at least an arm. There was nothing wrong with him except that he was covered in red mud from head to foot.

'Did you hear what I said,' he cried, frustrated by their inactivity. The boar's just behind me! Look,' he held up the long coarse bristles he had torn from the boar's back, 'here's my proof. Now, quickly, quickly.'

Still they did not move and eventually the boy said, 'Garnash won't come in here.'

'Why? How can you be so sure?'

'Because of the fire,' answered Uthellen. 'Garnash, like most wild beasts, is terrified of fire.'

Solder felt drained. He allowed himself to relax. What they were saying made sense. It was doubtful the giant boar would risk coming so near to man's greatest weapon. The smell of woodsmoke alone was enough to send any normal animal into a panic. But Garnash was no ordinary beast. Perhaps fire meant no more to him than it did to a human?

'Are you sure?' he blurted at Uthellen.

'Do you think I would be standing here if I weren't?'

Still shaking, Soldier went and sat down beside the fire. His flight had taken all the last of his energy. He lay back, his head on the turf, and fell asleep. Later he was vaguely aware of being woken and fed with some rabbit stew. Then he was allowed to sleep until morning came.

He awoke to the distant sound of trumpets and the rattle of drums.

'Something's happening in Zamerkand,' said Uthellen. 'There's a lot of activity.'

'We can hear them from here?' Soldier said.

'The wind is from the south, carrying the sound over the plain.'

'What could be occurring?'

The boy, who seemed more interested than his mother in what was going on, said, 'War. Those are war trumpets.'

Soldier sat up and shook his head. He went down to the stream with the far-off blare of trumpets still in his ears. There he bathed, before returning to the camp-fire where there was wild fare to be had. He drank cool water and ate. Then he took up the matter of the distant trumpets with the boy again.

'You say it's war?'

'Probably with the beast-people, or the Hannacks of Da-tichett,' replied the boy. 'I'd guess they were going after the Horse-people and the Wild-dog-people. Animal-headed people from the northern country of Falyum. They've been causing trouble up in the passes lately, threatening to muster and descend upon the castle. If they manage to stop quarrelling amongst themselves and join forces they're a considerable foe. Fortunately for the Guthrumites the Falyum clans squabble all the time amongst themselves, up in the passes of the mountains. Unwittingly they perform a function for the Guthrumites, just by acting as a buffer between themselves and outlanders – outsiders.'

'What's wrong with outsiders? I'm a stranger myself.'

The boy shrugged. 'It's the way they are.'

Soldier asked the question, 'The Horse-people and the Dog-people? Are they barbarians?'

'You could say that. One of them is responsible for destroying the beauty of the queen's sister, your wife. Princess Layana. She was savaged by the Wild-dog-man, Vau. Those twisted scars you see on her face are from the teeth of Vau.'

A sudden and fierce rage swept through Soldier.

'She was bitten by someone? I thought it had occurred in a fire of sorts. How did it happen?'

'Princess Layana was out hunting with her hawk, riding her favourite palfrey, when she and her small escort happened upon a raiding party. One of the Dog-men leapt at her and buried his teeth in the right side of her face. They had to prise apart Vau's jaws with the blade of a sword in order to release the princess. In their concern for the princess, Vau, though badly wounded, was allowed to escape. Your wife has never fully recovered from the attack. That is aside from her madness, which has another cause.'

Inflamed by the story, Soldier got to his feet.

He said with venom in his tone, 'I must join this war. I have to find the Dog-man, Vau, and kill him. This has become my business at last.'

Chapter Eight

At the time Soldier was making his dramatic pronouncement to a startled audience of two, Princess Layana was rising from her bed. Her boudoir was a room in the tulip-bud cupola of the Green Tower. On the palace walls below her four windows, covered with white-iron grills to prevent her from jumping to her death in moments of suicidal madness, the trumpeters and drummers were making sounds of war. In between their blaring and rattling, doves and pigeons cooed on the rooftops. The two sets of sounds were incongruous: symbols of war and peace, side by side, competing for attention.

Layana's bedroom, like that of her sister's in the Palace of Birds, was padded with soft materials. The door to her bedroom was always locked from the outside by her servants. This too was to do with her insanity. It prevented her from wandering in the night hours, when the guards and maid-servants were less alert than during the day. Today she was sane, and would be for two or three weeks, since she had just had a bout of the terrible sickness that afflicted her mind. There was always a respite between attacks of madness. These were not kind to her, because they lulled her into false hopes.

The longer they went on, the more she hoped that such a calm period of sanity would be permanent. But eventually, or sooner, the madness returned, ravaged her mind and soul, and left her feeling weak, drained and sickened by what she had done, or might have done, while under the influence of involuntary violence.

Still wearing her chiffon nightdress she went to the window of the green tower. On reaching it there was a flurry of white, fan-tailed doves, which roosted on the sill outside. The birds took to the air noisily. She was not sorry to see them leave. Their cooing was so monotonous early in the day.

'Such a beautiful morning,' murmured Layana, staring out at a clear blue sky. 'May it last forever.'

Then the trumpets blared again, and the kettle drums rattled, and now some whirling bullroarers moaned.

Layana suddenly recalled that she was now married to a man she did not know.

Had it been out of pity? Or were there some feelings in her breast for this Soldier? Layana was confused. It would have been trite to say she did not know her own mind. Her mind was *not* her own much of the time. Yet she had never before allowed her emotions to dictate to her. Her first two husbands – may they rest in some kind of peace – were not chosen out of love, but for their stable characters. She had hoped at the time they would be strong enough to contain her wild excesses of mindless violence with the strength of their personalities.

How wrong she had been about that!

But Soldier was different.

Contrary to the belief of Kaff, the queen, and others, her first encounter with Soldier had not been in the street, she in her sedan chair, and he in chains. Her first meeting with him had been while she had been roaming the forested hills in the south, secretly hunting.

Between her bouts of madness, and during daylight hours only, Layana was given the relative freedom of Zamerkand. The queen accepted that if her sister's madness came upon her at that time there were slaves, guards, or chair carriers, who could restrain her and take her back to the Palace of Wildflowers. However, unknown to her sister, and to the grief and fear of her servants who kept such things secret from the queen, Layana sometimes gave her chaperons the slip.

On these occasions she would make her way to a black-smith named Butro-batan, whom she had befriended in her childhood, when taking her palfrey to be shod.

Butro-batan was a big, ugly man with enormous arms and a head which sat right on his shoulders without a neck to turn it. When he did have to look at something either side of him, he turned his whole upper body. The skin on his face and shoulders was pitted with small burn marks where the sparks from hammered white-hot iron had sprayed him. He was a man of fierce temper whose strength frightened those who knew him, although no one could recall if he had ever actually used his fists on another man. On the other hand, he was as gentle with great plough horses as if he were shoeing kittens. The young princess, on first taking her mount to be shod by Butro-batan, had been the same age as his daughter when the child had been killed by a crowd of terrified people near a horse trough.

The blacksmith's daughter had died foaming at the mouth. A frightened mob had stoned her to death thinking she was possessed by a demon. Somehow, the heat of the forge, around which the child used to play, had caused her to be subject to fits. One of these came upon her while she was unaccompanied in the market-place and those around her had panicked. The blacksmith missed his daughter, sorely, and of course felt guilty. He always wondered if in some way he had been responsible for her death and there were burn marks from red-hot irons on his forearm where he had punished himself for his negligence.

Butro-batan was always ready for the princess. He kept a horse and hunting hawk for her in a stable at the back of his forge, along with weapons and clothes. The blacksmith was in the process of making the princess a beautiful suit of light armour, since she had expressed a desire to wander even further abroad, and he wished to give her the best protection he could offer. Butro-batan knew he would be put to death if the queen ever knew that he was assisting her younger sister in throwing off the restraints that royalty and madness imposed, but he did not care. Butro-batan was past worrying about such inevitable things as death.

Thus it happened that while the princess was on one of these illicit hunting trips, swathed in cottons to disguise her female form, she had come across the soldier. She had seen him wake on the hillside and look about him in a bemused way. For a while he seemed to be talking to himself and staring over the landscape. Eventually the soldier had come down to her, ragged, bloody, dazed, and with an empty scabbard dangling from his belt.

'Youth,' he had said, 'where is the battle?'

'What battle?' she had replied.

He certainly *looked* as if he had been fighting. Not only was this indicated by his outward appearance, but by the obvious weariness in his spirit. His blue eyes had enchanted her. She still wondered if there was witchcraft in them. Was she under a spell, or was she at last in the throes of a romance? She did not really believe the latter was possible. Princess Layana had been told by others that she had a cold heart, that she could never love anyone but herself. Over time she had come to believe this statement.

'You are just like your father,' her old nanny, now dead, used to say to her. 'A heart of ice. Keep it frozen, my little one, and you'll never be hurt.'

She believed her old nanny. She believed her father had been a cold man. There were stories that Layana's mother had spent her life going from one wild affaire to another, looking for the warmth and affection she was never given in her marriage. Captain of the guard, corporal of the watch, musician, poet, cleric, clerk – it had made no difference to the old queen – she had bedded all. The embittered husband and consort, seeing himself as victim, had forsworn women in general.

As if that were not enough, Layana was now hideously scarred, from her encounter with the Dog-man, Vau.

Now she was not only inadequate, she was ugly, and she had no doubt Soldier would find comfort from her madness in the arms of other women.

'He will not stay in the bed of a witch,' she had told her maid-servant and confidante, Drissila, immediately after the wedding, 'even if she is a princess and he a pauper. So I shall not allow him here in the first place. I shall reject him from the outset, preserve my pride and his life, for it's entirely possible I shall attempt to kill him in my madness.'

The dark-haired Drissila was at that time combing the hair of her princess with the spiny seashell Soldier had brought as one of his wedding gifts. She was standing behind her mistress, who was sitting in an ornate wooden chair. The maid-servant's image in the silver hand-mirror waved nature's comb at Layana.

'I think that's a good idea. He's a handsome man, but those eyes of his make me shudder. Such a strange blue. You would think him capable of murder! Perhaps it would be you who wouldn't rise in the morning, after your wedding night?'

'You think he looks like a murderer? I think he looks like an angel.'

'That's because you're besotted with his devil-may-care attitude, my lady. Oh, he's a suave, swashbuckling soldier all right, but there's something else about him. Something very, very dangerous, if you ask me. You're blind to his real personality.' Drissila had sniffed at this point. 'If you want my opinion, my lady, I'd say throw him on the rubbish pile with the other two, before we're all murdered in our beds.'

'I think he looks vulnerable. You really think he's dangerous?'

Drissila had been quite adamant about this point, which she spoke about with absolute confidence. She had stopped combing the princess's tresses and had stared her mistress in the eyes.

'There's something deadly in him. He seems defenceless and guileless, but I can sense something deeply dangerous about him. He's a rogue soldier, my lady, who's been through some dreadful experience which has caused him to seek his fortune in a world where he's a stranger. Hazardous adventurers are pushed from behind, as well as pulled from the front. He's done something dreadful in his past. He's capable of doing something dreadful in the future. We'd be best to keep him away from us.'

The fact that he was a dangerous man did not detract from him in Layana's eyes. In fact it made him more desirable.

Some women were attracted by such character. Yet, she felt she was chasing after rainbows. Soldier had married her to save his life, nothing more.

'Who could love an ugly harpy like me?' she had sighed, turning her face a little to study the twisted eye, the raked cheek with its crimped furrows of flesh, the torn corner of the mouth. 'Such repulsive looks would be enough to turn the stomach of a mortuary physician.'

'Never mind your face, you have a beautiful heart,' her devoted maid-servant had told her. 'That's more important.'

'Not when the madness is on me,' Layana had replied.

This conversation had taken place several days previously. Now the princess waited for Drissila and her other maid-servants to come to her boudoir. In the meantime, she watched the activities of the world outside her palace.

The window of her room in the tall tower was high enough for her to witness the Carthagan troops mustering beyond the castle gates. War was in the air. The banners, the standards, the martial music proclaimed it. The red pavilions were being struck, poles and ochre coverings were being stacked and folded. Not all the Carthagans would be marching north. Half would stay to guard the city gates from any counter-attack by the beast-people of Falyum. Suddenly Layana stiffened as she saw a figure coming down from the forested regions. Soldier! He was making his way towards the Carthagan mustering ground.

'Oh, what is he doing?' asked Layana of herself. 'I thought he was safely in the city somewhere.'

The sound of the door to the room being opened captured Layana's attention.

It was Ofao. He looked around the door, staring into her face, seeking, she knew, the signs of ill-humour.

'I'm all right, Ofao,' she said. 'I'm fine today.'

He stepped warily into the room.

'I'm so pleased, my lady.' Then he was suddenly concerned and solicitous. 'But you look so pale? Are you ill? Why are you standing by that open window in just a flimsy night-dress? You'll catch your death, my lady.'

'I have just seen my husband.'

Ofao whirled, looking around the room.

'No,' she said, 'not in here. He's outside the city walls. Look,' she pointed through the window. 'See how he strides towards that Carthagan captain. What is it he's carrying? A wooden spear? A bow? Can he be thinking of joining the Carthagans in their campaign?'

'It certainly looks like it, my lady. There is determination in his step and in his face,' murmured Ofao. Then he added in a wistful tone, 'Isn't he a fine figure of a man?'

Layana narrowed her eyes at her man-servant.

'You forget yourself, Ofao. He's my husband.'

'Yes, my lady, of course he is. And – anyway – he's not interested in other men – not in that way.'

'Well, I'm grateful for the information,' she said. 'Does that mean you've attempted to seduce him?'

'No, no, my lady. One can tell, without doing that.'

Layana was silent for a moment. Then she said, 'Sing to me, Ofao, to calm me. My feelings are in turmoil.'

Ofao opened his mouth and began to sing a song in the high notes of a talented castrato. He sang sweeter than any bird. Layana closed her eyes and let the notes carry her to some place beyond the oppressive world, a place where new husbands joined the army to fight and uselessly die in battles which had no real meaning and served no purpose beyond themselves.

Chapter Nine

'What do you think you're doing?'

The question was asked by the raven who had just flown down to Soldier's shoulder.

'I'm going to join the army.'

'Slow down, slow down. Why'd you want to do that? You're not a Carthagan.'

'Because I'm not getting anywhere like this. I need to advance my position, obtain more status in this country. No one takes me seriously. I need respect. The only way to obtain what I want is to progress upwards, through the hierarchy. I'm a soldier. The best way to get on is join the army. That's what I'm doing.'

The raven clicked its tongue. 'They'll treat you as spear fodder. They always send the raw recruits into the teeth of the enemy front line. You'll go down in the first wave of casualties. How will that advance your position?'

'I'll survive. I intend asking to join the Forlorn Hope anyway. That's the only way to get on quickly in the army.'

The Forlorn Hope was a group of volunteers who went first into the battle. They took the brunt of the first shock wave

of any charge. They were suicide troops, always in the vanguard of an attack. Those who survived the battle were given
an automatic promotion to the next rank, or sometimes they
skipped a rank and went higher still. It was all or nothing,
since a huge percentage of the Forlorn Hope always lay dead
on the battlefield after any confrontation.

Soldier brushed away the raven and went up to an officer
who was supervising the striking of pavilions.

He said, 'I wish to join the Carthagan army.'

The officer, a lieutenant who just happened to be a woman,
looked him up and down. Carthagan men were short of
stature, but very stocky. The women of that race however
were on average a head taller than the males and of slimmer
build. This lieutenant seemed wiry-strong and had sword-
scars on her brow, just below the rim of her leather-and-metal
helmet. Like the warriors she led, she wore an armoured
breastplate and metal epaulettes to protect her shoulders, but
nothing else. There were no shin guards or arm guards. On
her feet were leather sandals.

'You're not even a Carthagan,' she sneered. 'And you intend
to fight with those weapons?'

Soldier was conscious that he was carrying his wooden spear
and his bow. He had left the dagger with Uthellen and the
boy, in the forest, for he knew they would need some kind of
tool and weapon. He wished now that he had killed the giant
wild boar, Garnash, and had come to them as a hero, so that
he would have some credibility as a warrior. He tried to think
of what to say next.

He said, dubiously, 'I think I could get hold of a warhammer, if it's still there. The Lord of Thieftakers has it.' A
spark of hope went through Soldier. 'Some of your warriors
saw me take it from a mounted Hannack, just a few weeks

ago, right here on the plain where your pavilions are pitched.'

'What's the Lord of Thieftakers doing with it then?'

'It was taken from me when I was arrested. But I have been freed without charge now. I – I'm Princess Layana's husband.'

Some light came into the lieutenant's eyes. 'Oh, you're that fellow, are you? Of course, the blue eyes. I should have remembered. Well, even so, being the husband of royalty doesn't make you a good fighter. The Hannack thing – that could have been sheer luck – probably was. A foot-soldier against a mounted Hannack? I would bet on the Hannack every time.'

'Nevertheless,' began Soldier, desperately, 'I'm a battle-hardened veteran.'

'From which battles?'

Miserably Soldier replied, 'I can't remember.'

The lieutenant shook her head. 'Look at that spear! It looks like some cave dweller made it. It doesn't even have a metal point. What's that stuff you've tied around the haft?'

Once again Soldier was reminded that he had not come here as a hero, the defeater of the great Garnash.

'It's hair – bristles from the back of a boar.'

'What boar?'

Some of the troops who were busy folding the pavilion covering looked up at this point. They seemed interested in the answer.

'Garnash, the giant boar,' said Soldier. 'I tried to kill him, but failed.'

The lieutenant's eyes opened wide. 'You hunted Garnash and lived?'

'Well, yes, I *lived*, but I failed in my attempt to kill him.'

A sergeant said, 'How did you get the hair?'

'Wrenched it from his back, while I was riding him,' replied Soldier. 'I was clinging on to it when it came away in my hand.'

'You *rode* Garnash?' cried the lieutenant. Then her expression changed. 'You're lying. You must be.'

Soldier's eyes turned to blue steel for a moment. 'I do not lie about such things as exploits,' he said, his tone even and dangerous. 'A man who has only his honour left to call his own needs to retain the truth, or he is totally impoverished. A judge can lie. He has his status to protect him. A prince can lie, he has his wealth and position. A serving soldier can lie, for he has a large family, his regiment, to support him. A traveller, a stranger with an empty purse, cannot lie, or he has nothing in the world at all. He strips himself clean, throws away the only thing he has left.'

'He looks like a soldier,' said the sergeant, 'but he speaks like a philosopher. I believe him.'

The lieutenant suddenly nodded. 'So do I. Listen, stranger, we do not have "regiments" in the Carthagan army. We have pavilions. As many soldiers as can fit into a pavilion – that is the number which fights together under the same banner. This is Captain Montecute's pavilion, the Eagle Pavilion. That's our eagle on the pennon there. When we're on the move or go into battle it flies from our standard.'

'Eagles fly, others die!' chanted a grinning warrior close to his shoulder.

'Can I join the Eagle Pavilion?' asked Soldier. 'I would deem it a great honour.'

'I'll speak with the captain,' said the lieutenant, 'but anyone who has ridden on the back of Garnash I'm sure will not be turned away without good reason.'

'Idiot!' snapped the raven, before flying off.

The Carthagan sergeant's eyes went round. 'Did that bird speak?'

'Naw,' said Soldier. 'I think it just squawked.'

The captain was duly consulted and agreed that someone – even a blue-eyed stranger – who had ridden Garnash like a bull or a wild horse would be an asset to his pavilion. Soldier went into the city and managed, after a great deal of trouble, to retrieve his warhammer. Then he joined his pavilion as a common foot-warrior. He helped the other warriors finish striking camp. Before the day had advanced beyond noon they were on the march, towards some mountain passes in the north-west. It was here that the Kermer Pass lay between Guthrum and Falyum, the land of the beast-people. It was through this pass that the raiders came to prey on helpless farmers in the outlying regions of Guthrum.

'We seem to be moving up in great numbers,' said Soldier to one of his comrades, looking back at the long winding column of warriors in their cloaks of burnt-sienna-red and their pack mules carrying their red-ochre tents. 'Just for raiding parties?'

'Their raiding parties are huge,' came the reply. 'Upwards of a thousand riders along with two or three thousand foot-soldiers. And they can fight.'

'As well as the Hannacks?'

'They're more savage than the Hannacks – much fiercer.'

Which told Soldier a lot about the enemy he was going to fight, even though he had met just a single Hannack in his life.

The column of warriors, with foreriders and outriders to prevent any surprise attack, was like a lazy, drifting rusty snake moving over the landscape. There were few trees on the central plain of Guthrum. It was an area covered in wild-flowers and herbs. Soldier was surprised to realise he recognised some of them. There was yellow loosestrife and mugwort in profusion. Here and there grew patches of orris iris which the local farmers used to patch their wickerwork chairs and thatched roofs. Soldier also noticed lavender stickadove and mullein, and some sweet woodruff. Where trees were seen they tended to be quinces and mulberry trees, probably planted by farmers. There were no great live oaks out here, or beeches, or green elms.

On the evening of the third day they came to a volcanic mountain which rose out of the plain like a giant. It was high enough to have snow on its peak, though the pale sun was warm on the backs of the marchers. The army camped at the foot of this mountain, which was called Mount Kkamaramm, after a dragon which had once had its eyrie in the crags some way up. Eagles were seen circling the sky. When the campfires had been lit and the warriors were eating their evening stew, Soldier settled down to talk with a warrior named Velion, whom he had partially befriended on the march. Unlike most of the warriors in the Eagle Pavilion, she was sympathetic to his newness. Soldier always seemed to get on better with women than he did men.

Soldier did not know the ways, the nuances, of the army he was in. He made mistakes, such as referring to the lieutenant's sword as a sword.

'She's from the Jundra region of Carthaga, that one, and Jundran officers call their swords "scissors",' explained Velion. 'You will notice that unlike other Carthagan warriors they wear two blades, one on either side? When we go into battle they draw both blades and employ a scissoring action with them, slicing at the enemy from both sides at once. The victim finds it hard to parry strokes coming from two directions.'

'I imagine so,' replied Soldier, unfolding the worn secondhand blanket someone had given him out of pity. 'It sounds a good tactic.'

'Oh, we have many good tactics,' said Velion, puffing out her chest. 'The Carthagans are great warriors. We put the fear of the gods into our enemy. A Carthagan can't leave the field of battle until the enemy has been defeated. You will hear others talk of Carthagan massacres and these are true. We have been massacred in the past because we fight until the last warrior falls. There are tactical retreats, of course – we fall back like any army when we are overwhelmed by superior numbers – but we never run away. Any fall-back is always followed by a counter-attack. Our courage is second to none.'

'It sounds as if I've joined the right side in this war,' said Soldier, smiling at her earnestness.

He had already experienced two nights around the camp-fires, where the Carthagans sang songs of past victories; held forth with poems and stories of acts of valour; fought mock battles in the spaces between the fires; settled differences with single-stick in front of jeering and encouraging comrades; witnessed punishments by superiors for infringements of rules and laws and orated martial prayers to war gods before retiring for the night.

Wherever they halted and camped Soldier was impressed by the vigilance of the sentries that were posted in layers around the site. He saw how carefully a site for the night was chosen by the officers responsible for fortifying the encampment, how temporary earthworks were thrown up, ditches were dug and staked and any local flora such as thorn bushes were cut and used to make protective walls. It was an impressive display of both discipline and attention to detail. No Carthagan commander was going to lose his pavilions to a savage foe through negligence or indifference, even though he would not be there to defend himself at the subsequent enquiry, since he would without question have fallen with his warriors on the field.

While Soldier was speaking to Velion the other warriors of the Eagle Pavilion suddenly rose and silently gathered around his bed space, staring down at him. The light inside the pavilion was strange, since the sun had not yet gone down and shone through the walls of the tent creating a crimson interior. The skins of the warriors, most of them stripped for bed except for a loincloth, shone a dusty red in the weird light.

Everyone was exhausted by the day's march, but there was a lively look in the eyes of these warriors. There was a sense of expectation in the air which caused a knot in the pit of Soldier's stomach. He had no idea what was going on, but he knew it involved either him or Velion and his female warrior companion did not look overly concerned.

'What do you want of me?' he asked, looking round for officers and finding none. 'What's this?'

He recalled enough of his hazy soldiering past to know that this was some kind of vigilante gathering. If they had been carrying knotted clouts, or sticks, or something of that nature, he would have known he was in for a beating. If the officers were out of the way it was because the warriors were going to subject him to some kind of initiation ceremony. Running the gauntlet? A ducking in an ice-cold lake? Some humiliating sexual or functional act to perform in front of sneering comrades? None of these was out of the question. He had to prove his worth to these fighters, who wanted someone they trusted by their side when they faced death in battle.

'Right, what is it?' he asked, standing up to face them. 'What do I have to do?'

'An eagle's egg,' said Velion. She had of course known all the time that this moment was coming, but it would not have been right to warn him. 'We are camped by a mountain. This is the Eagle Pavilion. You have to climb Kkamaramm, find an eagle's nest and bring us back an egg.'

When she named the mountain she sounded the double consonants at both ends very clearly.

Soldier's eyes went from face to face. 'In the dark?' he cried.

'In the dark,' confirmed Velion, grimly. 'That's the whole point. Anyone can do it in the daylight.'

Can they? thought Soldier, who had never been good with heights.

'Are — are you sure this is the breeding season?'

'The eagles here breed all the year round.'

'Wonderful,' murmured Soldier.

'So, you'd better be on your way,' remarked a grinning male warrior. 'Up and at 'em, so to speak.'

The others laughed softly. There was no spite in their demeanour. Everyone had to do this. It was best to get it done.

'What about the sentries?' asked Soldier. 'Won't they think I'm deserting and cut me down?'

'Yes, if they see you going out. And they'll try to kill you coming back in again, thinking you're an assassin. They're pretty quick on the bowstring, our sentries. Shoot first, ask questions later.'

'No password?' asked Soldier, hopefully.

'No one's supposed to be out there,' said the same man. 'What would they want a password for?'

Soldier acknowledged this point with a nod of his head. He saw there was nothing for it but to get going. The sooner he started his quest, the quicker it would be over.

'Velion,' he said, unbuckling the belt bearing his precious magical scabbard, 'would you look after this for me while I'm gone? Don't let it out of your possession. It's a family heir-loom. I keep it for sentimental reasons.'

He handed her his bent and battered scabbard, which she took. If he were climbing crags in the dark it would only get in the way. It was best he went unencumbered by such objects.

She held the broken sword sheath at arm's length and said, 'I won't let this very valuable possession out of my sight. And Soldier?'

'Yes?'

'Try not to fall.' She gave him a grim smile.

'I'll do my best.'

He turned to the rest of the warriors and with an attempt at humour, said wryly, 'I suppose I should be glad I didn't join another pavilion. I might be going out now to steal cobra eggs, or cut the unborn foetus from a she-wolf's womb.'

'You don't know the half of it,' replied a warrior. 'There's a Shark Pavilion too . . .'

They held the hem of the pavilion up for him and he slipped underneath. Soon he was belly-crawling across rocky ground in the darkness. It was a slow painful business. This was going to take all night. There would be no sleep for Soldier. Should he even make a success of his mission, tomorrow was going to be hell, marching double-pace over the landscape with no sleep.

There were sentries everywhere. He managed to dig a tunnel with his fingers under the thorn hedge which circled the camp. Then he slipped down the trench and up and over the temporary dyke. The fires had since died down and revealed only a blush, so he had shadowy regions to keep to between their glowing embers. Once, in his gradual and painstaking journey outwards, a sentinel came so close to him as to tread on his hand. He bit his lip to stop from crying out. He almost allowed himself to be found, thinking that he would rather take his chances with the sentries than with the crags of Kkamaramm. His comrades could not censure him for being discovered by the sentries, could they? But then he thought, what about next time? They'll make me do it again until I bring that damn eagle's egg and shove it under their demanding noses.

It took an hour to get far enough beyond the sentries to be able to stand up and stretch his limbs. Soldier was already fatigued and the main part of the task still lay ahead of him. Fortunately the stars were out in force and their light was sufficient for him to see vague outlines of the rock face. He had no idea where to start looking for eagle nests, but guessed they would be high up. He found what looked to be a goat track and began climbing, stumbling occasionally on loose scree, and once feeling something with a brittle carapace scuttle away from under his palm when he steadied himself against a boulder.

When he reached the end of the goat track he began climbing alpine style. It was arduous and terrifying. Once, after scaling a rock chimney, he looked down and saw the camp-fires far below. They looked dizzyingly distant. He realised there was nothing between him and ground at that point. If he fell it would be to plunge to his death. He managed to swing himself onto the top of a stack and cling there while he got his breath and courage back. This was his worst nightmare come true. To be standing on a windy pinnacle at a great height in the darkness of a lonely night. Often it was the battlements of a castle or some tall tower that dominated his dreams, but a needle stack on a mountain did the job well enough.

'If I get down from here alive,' he told himself, miserably, 'I'll never take two feet off the ground at once again.'

His ordeal continued, as he climbed ever higher, searching caves and ledges for signs of eagles' nests. At one point he began to think he had been duped. Perhaps those below knew there were no eagle's nests up here in Kkamaramm? Maybe he'd been sent on a wild eagle-egg chase? No doubt they were laughing into their blankets down there in the pavilion, telling each other what a stupid new recruit they had got and how it was unlikely he would ever return alive. It was all most disconcerting and unsatisfactory from his point of view. He was going to die for nothing, some stupid prank, and uselessly too.

'I'll haunt them,' he said, thoughts of revenge keeping his anger sparked. 'I'll make them pay somehow.'

Then suddenly and miraculously — he did believe he was blessed by the gods — he came across a nest. Actually it was not so much a nest as a few twigs and bits of grass scattered on a wide ledge. But even more incredibly, this excuse for a nest had two eggs nestling on its twigs. There was no sign of any occupant, even though when he felt the eggs, they proved to be warm.

'Magic,' he murmured to himself. 'Someone is looking after me — there's no other explanation.'

He took one of the raptor's eggs, feeling guilty about stealing life from a mother, even if it was just a predatory bird. He put the egg inside his tunic, next to his heart, to keep it warm. Then he began retracing his climb, finding the best and easiest path down the mountain.

It was even more difficult going down that it had been going up. And there was the added problem of keeping the egg whole. Part of the way down he realised something else. There was movement inside the egg. He could feel that the creature within the egg was ready to come out. Soldier just hoped it would wait until he got to the pavilion before breaking through the shell. He was not sure his comrades would accept pieces of eggshell and he certainly did not want to do the same quest again.

He did reach level ground, finally. Then he had the same problem as before, only in reverse. He had to get past the sentries to get into the camp. This time the dawn was coming up in the east. Sharp fingers of light were clawing their way across the sky. Dawn is not a good time to be moving over the landscape. At dawn the light is so poor sentries have to be doubly alert. Shadows chase each other over a grey world and those on the last watch of the night are keen to inspect every movement between them and the horizon. Soldier dug deep into a time of training he did not remember on the surface of his mind, but which lay in abundance below his conscious thought.

Navigating thorn trees, he crawled along ditches and furrows, some of them so badly situated that they seemed to be taking him *out* of the camp, though in fact they led to others travelling in a more central direction. Each few yards were taken slowly and with great care. It actually worried him that he was able to gradually work himself along towards the middle of the sentries, be they ever so keen, because if he could do it, so could an assassin with a knife between his or her teeth. Soldier would not sleep so easily in camp again, never mind the sentinels were of the highest quality and state of readiness.

By the time he was inside the ring of guards, the sun was well up. His pavilion had arisen and were washing in their portable leather bowls. He could see Velion, looking for him, as he made his way towards his fellows. Captain Montecute noticed him and looked the other way. Of course the officers were aware of the initiation. They simply ignored it.

Velion looked up from washing and gave him a broad smile.

'I knew you could do it,' she said, as the others clustered round too. 'You *did* get it, didn't you?'

'I got it,' replied Soldier, 'but we'd better be quick. I think it's ready to hatch. Maybe we can put the infant somewhere where the mother can see it and return it to the nest? Down by the stream perhaps? Eagles have to drink too, don't they?'

'Never mind that,' grumbled a man, 'let's see the egg.'

Soldier reached inside his tunic and then brought out his hand with the egg resting on his palm.

The other warriors stared at it, then looked at Soldier.

Velion raised her eyebrows.

'What's the matter?' asked Soldier. 'Is there something wrong?'

There was *obviously* something wrong.

Velion said, 'That's no eagle's egg.'

Soldier began to panic. 'How would you know?' he said, quickly.

One of the other warriors said, 'Of course we know, Soldier. This is the Eagle Pavilion.'

Soldier's heart sank. Not an eagle's egg? What was it then? However, they would soon find out because the shell was cracking in his hand, opening to reveal its live contents. He brought his other hand round, keeping the egg confined within his two palms. It had to be some sort of bird, or giant insect – or perhaps it was a snake? Suddenly he decided to put the egg on the ground. He had remembered that the young of poisonous snakes came out of the egg with venom just as virulent as that of their parents, even though they were not mature in any other respect.

A hole appeared and a little green snout poked through.

Gradually the bits of shell fell away, from the top, from the sides, then out wriggled a short green reptile.

'A crocodile?' said Soldier, amazed. 'How in the name of the gods did it get up there on the mountain? Was it carried by an eagle or something? There were two of them. Surely a raptor wouldn't go collecting the eggs of a crocodile?'

'Quiet!' said Velion. 'Look!'

Under their gaze the creature began licking away the slime from its body. It was a tiny green wonder of nature, with a red underside and red frills around its nostrils. Bright red. The red of good wine or a certain kind of rose. It had a lizardy, long, flicking tail, two tiny legs with sharp claws and an elongated head. The long tongue reached its back, where it spent a relatively long time in licking and preening itself. Then something magical began to happen. Its back began to open like a flower.

They watched in wonder as two tissue-thin wings began to unfold and stretch themselves to dry in the morning sun. At this stage these wings were so translucent the sun shone through them, creating rainbow patterns on the infant's back. Then the tiny creature let out a screech, as it looked up to see it was being observed. The volume of the sound was quite out of proportion to its size: it could no doubt be heard miles away.

The group around Soldier had begun to back away, and had gone pale as fire-ash and deathly quiet.

'What?' asked Soldier.

'Dragon,' came the reply from one of the warriors. 'From a minor species admittedly. This is a two-legged red-bellied green dragon. They're very good at hovering, like dragon-flies. They grow to be about the size of a bear, no more.

'Oh, just the size of a bear?' said Soldier.

Velion grasped his arm. 'It's calling for its mother . . .'

But the rest of her sentence was drowned by the infant's terrible screech, as its eyes fixed on Soldier.

'Actually,' said Velion, following its adoring gaze, full of love and appetite, 'right at this minute it thinks *you're* its mother – and it probably wants milk.'

Another horrible screech.

'Keep it here a minute,' said Soldier, and he ran back to where the field kitchen stood.

He was back within half a minute carrying a big slab of pig's liver, dripping with blood. He fed it to the baby dragon, a sliver at a time. It crooned, and regarded him with wide anxious eyes as he put pieces of soft meat in its mouth.

'Time to move!' yelled a sergeant, from the tents. 'Let's strike the pavilion – *now*!'

Soldier reluctantly left his charge, having first cut the liver into small chunks.

The Eagle Pavilion quickly struck their tent and had their mules packed and ready to go within a few minutes. They had shooed the baby dragon into a rat hole in the ground, where it would have shade. Its cries were muffled by the rock they had placed over the hole. The Pavilion's officers were surprised but pleased by how quickly their warriors had got ready for the march that morning and took a new place in the front of the army.

Anxious warriors scoured the sky with their eyes, expecting that at any moment a huge and terrifying beast would descend from the heavens and rip them asunder. They were never so anxious to to be on the march.

Soldier removed the rock from the hole before they left. He believed the mother would go for its young rather than chase this gang of humans across the landscape. The infant dragon had crawled out of the hole with a look of indignation and hurt on its green features, but on seeing Soldier it had mewled.

'Kerroww,' it had said. 'Kerroww, kerroww.'

Soldier left a wineskin full of goat's milk for the tiny mouth with its rows of needle teeth to pierce and suckle on once he had gone.

'Listen infant,' said Soldier, wagging his finger. 'You look after yourself, you little rascal.'

He then scurried off to join his pavilion on the march.

Chapter Ten

The Carthagan mercenaries circumnavigated Mount Kkamaramm and fetched up on the edge of a desert. During the march and the encampments Soldier got to know his fellow warriors. They were for the most part a simple bunch. Not in any sense ignorant, but with fairly simple needs and a simple life-style. They wanted for little except the respect of their peers. If they did not make him entirely welcome it was not through malice, but because they were unused to strangers. They were reserved with Soldier because they did not know him. It seemed that they had all been children together, had grown up in each other's company, and knew each other inside and out. Soldier did not help his situation by showing an equal amount of reserve and by expecting everyone in the pavilion to respect his desire for privacy.

Velion told him, 'You can't expect them to simply accept you for a good fellow when you've done nothing to earn their esteem.'

'I don't want their esteem. I want their comradeship.'

'But,' she rightly pointed out, 'you're not very friendly yourself.'

This was true. He allowed Velion behind his protective outer shell occasionally, but no one else. What did he expect then? That they should return his coldness with great warmth? Soldier realised that would be unreasonable. He had no right to expect anything except their support during a battle. They did not have to give him their friendship, only their professional backing. They were mercenary warriors.

The truth was he was afraid that if he did open his soul and mind to them they – and he – might discover something unsavoury. Already he was having flashbacks, of being in some place – he knew not where – in which there was a fiery conflict between him and another man. It was as if there were a door in Soldier's mind which had opened a little and provided a chink for him to peer through. The other man had the appearance of a fellow warrior. Soldier sensed that he had done this man a great wrong. Perhaps he had even killed someone in anger.

Could he have done such a thing? Murder a man?

There were blurred images burned into Soldier's brain, of him burying his sword in another man's heart.

Was that why his scabbard had been empty? Was the weapon that fitted that sheath piercing the heart of a blameless man? If these nightmare scenes thrown up by his subconscious were true he did not want to know more about them. A soldier's spirit had to be bright and shining, without the stain of cowardice or military malfeasance. If he had murdered someone, not on the battlefield, perhaps even in the dead of the night, then he was damned indeed. It were better not to remember more.

One night, when he had stripped to wash himself, Captain Montecute had walked by. The captain had stopped and studied Soldier, before saying to him, 'You have the scars of the lash upon your back. They're faint, but in a certain light you can see the white streaks where the whip has left its mark.'

'I have?' said Soldier, wiping his dripping chest with towelling. 'I didn't know.'

'You don't remember being whipped?' asked the officer, surprised and disbelieving. 'A flogging is not something a man forgets very easily.'

The dark door in Soldier's brain suddenly slammed shut again. He felt grim and forbidding. He resented this questioning of his former character.

'No, I don't recall that happening.'

'I have punished enough warriors myself to know the marks of flogging when I see them. Still, if you behave yourself in my pavilion I will have no reason to hold anything against you. But I'll be watching you a little more closely in future. I want no trouble amongst my warriors. They are good fighters.'

'*I* am a good fighter, captain.'

'We don't know that yet — we'll see, won't we?'

Soldier began to wonder if he had been wholly wicked, in his life before finding himself on that hill where he had first met the blue hunter. He would not have been whipped for murder, he would have been executed. The flogging must have been for something else. Thieving? Looting? Disobeying an order? Or possibly for simply striking an officer? His body bore the signs of him being a bad soldier. His mind was trying to send him images bearing the same message. Might it be better not to try to discover his original self, but to settle for who he was now? If he was true to the present he might save himself.

But a man does not let go of his past so easily, and in

unguarded moments Soldier still found himself probing deeply in search of his true identity and his previous life.

Velion had befriended Soldier for a number of reasons. At first the main one was of course that her lieutenant had asked her to keep an eye on the new recruit. Not *spy* on him, exactly, but watch him closely. Carthagans were a naturally untrusting race who were careful about their relationships with other peoples. They did not easily allow others, be they friends or enemies, to see below the surface of their culture. However, once she had come to know him the first reason faded a little into the background. She genuinely came to like the mysterious stranger. She didn't *understand* him, exactly, but he seemed sincere and basically honest, and there was a warmth that developed between them which is hard to explain to anyone who has not felt real friendship for another person. What was more, Soldier seemed to become fond of *her*, and this is always hard to resist, even if one begins by disliking a person.

She did sense that Soldier had a dark side, but this only made him more attractive to a warrior who had joined the army because she enjoyed the heat of a battle.

Velion had been the right person to ask to take on the semi-official role as Soldier-watcher, because she was also an inquisitive woman, interested in all things that made up the known world. She had grown up in a society where feats of strength and endurance were considered the prime virtues of a good citizen. The Carthagans were a martial race. They had fought their own wars, of course, but now there was not a country in the world which would attack them and try to subdue them. Thus they hired out their skills at warfare to those who would pay for them. The only stipulation they made was that they would not fight against their own kind. If two countries both hired Carthagan mercenaries, then those mercenaries would only pit themselves against the foreigners on the field.

Velion's upbringing was strict and harsh. Carthaga was not a rich country. It lay across the Cerulean Sea on a vast southern continent known as Gwandoland. Its immediate neighbour was Uan Muhuggiag, where certain desert tribes dwelt. Carthagans lived in adobe huts made from local clay and practised war sports with as much earnestness as they did their academic studies. It was said that Carthagan youths and maidens would run fifty miles with a mouthful of water and not swallow a drop. They hunted the winged lions of Gwandoland in groups of not more than three, armed only with spears.

They were not allowed the full rights of citizenship – to vote, to marry, to follow an independent career – until they reached the age of thirty years. Before that time, even if they were not in the army, they lived in communes and ate, worked and slept with other youths or maidens. Those who were too sensitive for war or physical exploits went into administration, helping to run the country, teaching the young, and writing those books which needed to be written, including the manuals of war.

Soldier was a different type of man to Velion's Carthagan peers. His looks were more delicate, but there was strength and hardness in him. His eyes were a vivid blue – she was used to the more earthy colours of an umber land – and at first glance looked as if their owner was capable of great kindness. However, the more she looked into those eyes the more she discovered a depth of violence there which astonished her. It was as if the owner of those eyes were restraining himself much of the time. His ideas were sharper and less muddled than those she was used to, his approach to things fresher. And he did not sit on his pride. If he was wrong, he said so, and was not afraid to admit to being ignorant of facts. These things she liked in him.

She did not like his reserve in strange company, and his habit of eating with a forked twig. These things were unbecoming in a tough warrior. One held oneself back in the presence of people one did not know, and one ate with one's fingers to show a proper lack of regard for food.

'You said you've fought in many battles? Where was that?'

They were having a conversation, sitting around the central fire in the pavilion of a calm evening.

Soldier said, truthfully, 'I don't know. That is, I have a hazy recollection of a place of green hills and valleys, with broad rivers running through them, but nothing definite.'

'You have several battle scars, it's true.'

Soldier nodded. 'Yes – and I have the skills of a warrior. They are *all* I have.'

'Show me one of these skills.'

Soldier suddenly whipped out the warhammer from his belt and swiftly threw it at a nearby tent pole illuminated by the firelight. The warhammer thudded into the wood, spike first, at about the height of an enemy's heart. Several heads turned to study the warrior who had thrown the weapon, surprised at the force and accuracy of the throw. There were one or two murmurs and noddings of heads before the warriors went back to their own tasks or conversations.

'Very good,' said Velion, impressed. 'And you just have these abilities in you?'

'I didn't even know I had that one until I did it, just now,' admitted Soldier.

She regarded him thoughtfully. 'You're a great mystery to

me,' she said at last. 'You have these skills, as you say, yet you seem to disapprove of them. A Carthagan would glory in the fact that he or she had such talent. They wouldn't necessarily *brag*, but they wouldn't apologise either. You don't apologise in so many words, but it's implied by your manner.'

'Should one be proud of killing skills?'

'Why not? A baker is proud of his ability to make bread, a wheelwright pleased when he makes a good wagon wheel, why not a warrior proud of his talent for battle?'

'Because the two skills you mention are creative skills — ours is destructive.'

'A bad wizard has creative skills, yet I would not be proud of achievements that further only evil. A tree surgeon has destructive skills, yet I would be proud to own his talents. War is inevitable. It's the autumn for humans, the pruning of the races, the culling of the herds. The old flower has to die for the new flower to bloom in its place.'

Soldier smiled and shook his head. 'No, no — I don't believe in the inevitability of war. There are plenty of other ways to replace decayed wood with live saplings. Natural disasters do that job very well, without any help from us. Floods, earthquakes, eruptions, avalanches. We don't need any help from professional killers.'

'Then why join the army, if you disapprove of its aims?'

'It's the only thing I know how to do well.'

Velion left it at that. She did not want to probe deeply too early. One could lose a friend like that. Better to wait and draw him out little by little. Perhaps she could help him discover things about himself? He seemed genuinely not to know where he came from or who he was. She would be quite happy to assist him unravelling these mysteries.

One morning they were camped by an oasis. They had

arrived the previous evening, just as the dusk was settling. Velion woke Soldier and motioned for him to come with her. He blinked and shook himself completely awake, before following her out of the huge three-poled tent and into the dawn. There were sentries posted outside the camp, which sprawled around the small lake where a forceful stream bubbled up from the bedrock, and came out of the ground as a white fount, falling in cascades to fill a natural stone basin with crystal water. Velion led him within the encampment to a place where the officers had their tent at the far end of the lake. Here there was a water-meadow where wildflowers grew in abundance.

'What is it?' asked Soldier, able to speak at last now that they were out of earshot of sleeping warriors.

'I want to show you something,' said Velion. 'Something very beautiful. This is a magical oasis, placed here by a wixard many centuries ago.'

'It's not natural?'

'The rock bowl was shaped by the wind and sand, but the stream did not arrive due to the course of nature.'

'What's a wixard? You don't mean *wizard*?'

Velion shook her head. 'No, I don't mean wizard, I mean wixard. Watch those large irises when the sun hits them and warms them. They're just about to bloom.'

Soldier did as he was told. He kept his eyes on the patch of flags growing in the corner of the lake. As the minutes went by the sun grew warmer and warmer. Finally he saw the blossoms begin to shiver. Gradually they began to unfold, their petals opening. They were a strong yellow in colour and seemed to have four main petals which gradually uncurled and lay in stretched pairs on either side of the stem. Then, as Soldier watched, the shape of a sharp-pointed head began to appear from within the cup of the flower. There was a crest of stamens sprouting from the back of this strange protrusion. The bird-head shook itself, opened two eyes and stared about it. Then the creature, for that is what it had become, stretched its petal-wings, detached its legs from the stem of the plant, and flew up into the air.

'It's changed into a bird,' gasped Soldier. 'Or was it a bird all the time? Just roosting on top of the plant?'

'No, your first guess was right. As the flower bloomed it became a flying creature. Now watch the others.'

More warriors had come from the camp, creeping up next to Velion and Soldier, to watch this phenomenon. It was one of the entertainments of the march, to stop at such a place and witness its magic. Some had seen it all before, but they came anyway, to see it a second or subsequent time.

All around the water-meadows large wildflowers of various sorts were blooming now, and at the last moment of their unravelling they loosed exotic birds which took to the skies. Purple, red, yellow, white, green – every bright or softened hue. These creatures rose in singles or in flocks, depending upon the plant which grew them, filling the morning sky with colour. No sound came from their beaks, which made it all the more an eerie sight. Like mute parrots they drifted away on the air.

From the smaller plants came bright insects – wasps, hornets, shiny beetles, bees, long-tailed flies, green crickets, butterflies, moths, damselflies – a glimmering swarm of multi-toned flying creatures. They showered upwards, the only sound that of hard-carapaced beetles clacking their shells together in their efforts to find space.

It was a fizzing, effervescent dawn above the water-meadows. A pyrotechnical show of new life. Soldier was entranced by the show which went on for almost an hour. Then gradually the last bird, the last insect, found its way up to a wind or thermal, and went floating away over the pink sands of the desert.

'That was some display,' said Soldier, as they walked back towards their pavilion. 'You've seen it before?'

Velion nodded. 'On another campaign.'

'So tell me, what's a wixard?'

Velion laughed. 'Oh, yes. Well, once in a while a tree grows in such a place. Like the flowers the tree eventually produces a living being – a creature of human appearance – out of its fruit. The head grows first, like a large nut or plum, then the twiggy limbs and torso twist out of the branch on which the fruit hangs.'

'This is the wixard?'

'Yes, a wizard born of a magical plant, with braided limbs and skewed body. It grows upside down and eventually corks off its hands and feet from the mother tree and drops to the ground on its head. When it recovers from its fall, it sets off, going where it pleases, doing as it must, like any other creature with mobility and a walnut-sized brain to help it. There's a kind of waxy dullness about a wixard. It never attains the full intellect of a human being. They never touch solid food, relying on osmosis through the soles of their feet to provide them with any sustenance – and of course rely upon the sunlight on their barky skin. A wixard never gets rid of that greeny complexion and fibrous appearance. You can spot one from a hundred yards, even ignoring the corkscrew arms and legs.

'They're not hostile creatures though. Quite the opposite. They're willing to help anyone in distress and will spend time teaching a white witch the best uses for herbs and healing plants. A wixard might live ten, a hundred years, but there comes a time when it uses its powers to create one more magical oasis out of a desert place like this, then it dies, like a salmon which has fought its way upriver from the sea to breed.'

'Fascinating,' said Soldier. 'You think we'll meet one here?'

'Oh, I doubt it. They're as rare as dragons.'

Soldier pointed out that they had already met at least one dragon on their travels to the country of the beast-people.

'Well, there you are,' replied Velion, smiling. 'Who knows? Perhaps we'll meet a whole clutch of wixards.'

Chapter Eleven

The day finally came when the Carthagan pavilions were approaching the mountain range which separated Guthrum from Falyum. There in front of them was the Kermer Pass, through which the beast-people raiders came. Soldier had a visit from the raven, who told him he was off his head.

'You haven't seen these tribes, these terrible clans,' said the raven. 'They're enough to frighten a blackbird out of his feathers. If I were you I'd turn round and go back to the castle, before you lose one of your limbs.'

'I can't go back now. I'd be looked on as a coward.'

'Better a live coward than a crippled hero – but I suppose you're right. They would hang you as a deserter now that you're so close to battle. Look, here they come! The beast-people! Good luck, Soldier. You're going to need it.'

Almost at once the trumpets and bullroarers sounded all along the Carthagan column. The baggage train, taking up the rear, halted. The line broke and the warriors began to muster up their pavilions. Drum rolls were sounding now, as rallying calls for the Eagles, the Wolves, the Snakes, the Dragons, the Hawks, the Barracudas sounded over the field.

Warriors of these pavilions gathered at their own particular marshalling points, supervised by sergeants-at-arms. Once they were there, they settled into their own personal battle positions, and the officers took their place in the line, captains and above on horseback, lieutenants on foot with the rest of the warriors.

There was cavalry out on the flanks, and archers just to the rear, ready to fire over the heads of their own warriors.

Soldier, as he had requested, was in the front and centre, forming part of the vanguard which would be the first to hit the enemy. The Forlorn Hope was formed from members of all pavilions who volunteered to stand in its ranks. Shaped like an arrowhead, this group of warriors was at least a hundred yards in front of the main line. It looked lonely. It *felt* lonely. Their job was to try to pierce the front ranks of the enemy, using their shape like a wedge, and drive through to create a gap.

Most of these men and women would die.

Soldier felt someone at his shoulder. He turned to find Velion there, grinning down at him. Pe, another warrior from his pavilion, was also there. Unlike Velion he was not smiling.

'What are you doing here?' cried Soldier. 'The pair of you? Don't you know this is suicide?'

'If it's so dangerous, what's a fancy-face like you doing here then, tell me that?' said Pe.

'I'm here *because* it's dangerous. I need the promotion. You two seemed quite happy as common warriors.'

'Well, we just got *un*happy,' replied Velion.

Pe, who had been persuaded to join the Forlorn Hope by Velion, suddenly changed his mind.

'I'm going back to join my pavilion,' he told them. 'You're right, Soldier. This is just inviting death.'

'Go back with him, Velion,' ordered Soldier.

Velion sneered. 'Save your breath. Don't you know my soul is waiting for its release?'

'What do you mean?'

'We believe our spirits sit on our shoulders, their legs crossed around our throats, the whole of our lives. Only at the point of death can they unlock their limbs and leave us. Only then can they drift up to the tops of the mountains, to spend eternity in bliss. My soul will thank my killer.'

'That's outrageous. Your soul is *you*.'

'No,' Pe confirmed what his comrade was saying. 'You see all these Carthagan warriors? They all have their spirits sitting on their shoulders. We are the jails and jailers of our own souls. They sit there, separate entities, waiting patiently for our deaths. We can see them, but unbelievers like yourself can't. I'm told by Guthrumites that they can be heard thanking those who set them free with sword or mace. Listen carefully during the battle. The air will be full of grateful souls, voicing their appreciation of the actions of the foe.'

Pe ran back to his comrades, joining them in the main line.

Soldier, seeing he was not going to change Velion's mind, turned to face the enemy. He received a great shock. He felt the blood drain from his face, and his skin tingled as if charged with electricity as he saw the foe just coming up over the crest of a rise in front. At first he thought they were two-headed horses. Then he saw the subtle lines where horse and rider separated and became two entities. The chargers themselves were just ordinary mounts, though a lot stronger-looking and slower than the sleek warhorses ridden by Carthagans. On their backs were creatures covered only in short hair who had the bodies of humans but the heads of horses. These horse-headed warriors carried weapons of various kinds, including swords, axes and warhammers, which they swung around their heads as they screamed obscenities in human language, though with high, whinnying voices which sometimes reached the pitch of a squeal.

'Great gods!' whispered Soldier, his legs going weak. 'What are they?'

'Beast-people. The stallion clans are always first into the fight. You didn't expect them?'

'I don't know. I suppose I should have. But they're monstrous. Look at the size of their heads!'

The muscled horse-heads of the shrieking warriors were indeed large, bearing long snapping jaws that gleamed along the bone with natural oils and wayward flecks of white saliva. Each head owned a pair of red, fiery eyes large as a man's fists. These monsters looked as if they could *bite* Soldier's own head from his shoulders as their mouths opened wide to reveal rows of large yellow teeth which clashed together like stones. They snorted and tossed their long manes, shaking the hair from side to side in real or feigned anger: some fair and silky, others dark and coarse. They flattened their ears against their skulls, peeled their lips back over their gums, and screamed into the wind, 'Eat their children! Rape their dead! Destroy their godheads!' Then dilated their nostrils to spout steam.

The cavalry parted and moved to the flanks to reveal the foot-warriors who marched up behind them, each looking charged with fury. There was warpaint on their long noses, and warfeathers were flying from their manes. They shook their heavy heads in like fashion to the riders and drummed their weapons against their bark shields. Behind the Horse-people came the Dog-people, with the heads of hounds, followed by the Fox-people and then the Stag-people bearing huge branches of wicked-looking antlers. It was a formidable force, even Velion had to admit. The foe massed on the rise on the other side of the valley, milling around, hooting, barking, shrieking, yelling, stamping their feet and spitting their disdain.

'I don't think our warlords expected the beast-people clans to join with each other. They're usually so busy fighting amongst themselves they can't create a united front. There are more than four clans, of course, but I would say there's upward of fifteen thousand warriors facing us today.'

'How many are we?' asked Soldier.

'Two thousand? But of course, we're more disciplined and better fighters than those we face.'

'Of course,' repeated Soldier, but his sarcasm was lost on Velion, whose flushed face was an indication of the nervous excitement she was feeling. She was armed with a sword and shield, while Soldier still had only his warhammer. It was a formidable weapon, but he wondered what would happen if it somehow left his grasp during the battle. He made up his mind to grab a weapon from the nearest dead warrior if that should happen.

Invocations to the gods were now going up from both armies, whose war priests chanted the names of favourite deities, the names being picked up by the general rank and file. The Carthagans appealed to the seven gods for victory in the coming fight, while the beast-people droned the names of more sinister divinities: cave gods, and goddesses of the foul marshlands beyond the civilized world. These were divinities whose interest was in terrorising humankind from beneath the ground, deities whose domain was under the roots of trees and the foundations of cities, who controlled and destroyed from below.

The chanting grew louder and louder. The trumpets and bullroarers grew in volume, and the log and skin drums. The screaming of the Carthagan war priests spiralled into hysteria. Horses grew wild-eyed and pawed the ground with their hooves. The beast-people on the other side of the shallow valley were ascending into madness with their cries for blood and death.

In spite of himself Soldier felt his blood heat rising. He found himself chanting along with the rest, screaming obscenities at the enemy, his mind rolling with thought of violence.

'Kill! Kill! Kill!' rose the shrieks.

There is a point at which the engendered fury is counterproductive, when berserkers are at the peak of their insanity and in danger of falling on the ground in a useless fit. Soldier was aware that the cavalry of both sides were milling restlessly around the flanks of the two armies, ready to break. One or two undisciplined riders actually did, riding straight at the enemy, hoping for individual glory.

Carthagan commanders, sensing a general breakdown into unrestrained chaos, gave the order to charge. Soldier found himself flying down the slope, yelling and screeching, swinging his warhammer first at air, then at flesh, when the two sides came together as two shock waves along the whole ridge, smashing into each other with a clash of metal on metal. The sudden impact of bodies sent a ripple down both lines.

The arrowhead column known as the Forlorn Hope penetrated the front ranks of the beast-warriors and into the heart of the enemy army. There they were meant to cause internal havoc, to disrupt the enemy, confuse it, make it falter from within. Their job was to worry the enemy front-line warriors, cause them to wonder what was going on behind it and so look over their shoulders. Thus they would lose concentration and fail in their task to break through the Carthagan lines. A small force *inside* the ranks of the foe could create immeasurable confusion.

Soldier found himself ringed by coarse-haired warriors with the heads of horses. Frantically, he swung this way and that with his warhammer, striking bone and flesh with almost every blow. Swords skimmed his body, spears went by him from several directions. Somehow he remained on his feet. His wounds were not fatal, nor immobilising. The points had penetrated his skin but no vital muscles, tendons or sinews had been severed. His bones were intact. Hideous horse heads with rows of clashing teeth snapped at him. One bit him in the shoulder. Another on the left forearm. Each time he was approached from the rear his singing scabbard warned him of a sneak attack. Soldier now knew its song. The warnings were timely. He could swing round and strike his unseen opponent without glancing first. Velion, noticing Soldier's extra help, stuck by his side, also taking advantage of the benefits of his magical sword sheath.

Around these two their Carthagan comrades were going down under welters of blows from the more numerous enemy. Carthagan spirits drifted heavenward from the shoulders of their hosts. They floated upwards now that they were free.

'*Thank you.*'

'*Thank you.*'

'*Thank you.*'

Soon their numbers were down to just three: Soldier, Velion and a warrior from the Wolf Pavilion. This trio of resolute warriors stood with their backs to each other, fending off attack after attack, until suddenly there was a break in the ring of Horse-people and they were able to dash through a hole in the ranks of their foes to be back in their own lines.

'Well done!' shouted Captain Montecute, on seeing his two Eagles return to the fold. 'Rally to me! Rally to me!'

The battle was bloody and awful, but lasted only just over an hour. At the end of this time the Carthagans had marshalled their forces and had formed into disciplined columns once again. The beast-people had retreated to the top of their slope and were gathering breath. There were corpses lying all over the battlefield. Wounded men and beast-people were sitting up or crawling or simply lying twitching, waiting for assistance. Some were without a limb, or set of limbs. Others had been pierced through the body, neck or head. Their moans and groans were pitiful to hear. A severed horse head lay near Soldier's feet, but whether from a real horse or a beast-person he had no idea.

By mutual consent, unarmed warriors from both sides went down in small groups to help the wounded and to dispatch injured horses, brushing shoulders with the enemy in this gory task.

Up on the ridge those warriors who remained from the Horse-people had retired. Dog-people had come forward, to form the second wave of the beast-people's attack. They were supported by the red-headed Fox-people. The Stag-people were held in the rear, presumably for use as reinforcements should the second wave falter or fall into difficulties. These fresh troops looked across at a weary, tattered army of Carthagans. It was true the red pavilions had lost only one warrior for every three of the enemy, but the disparity in numbers was against them.

'What now?' asked Soldier, of Velion.

She shrugged. 'A second attack. But the Dogs are not such formidable opponents as the Horses. They make good gladiators, but poor soldiers. We're in bad shape, but they know we've come back from such a position before and won the battle. They'll be very wary.'

However, the Carthagan commanders decided their troops needed a longer rest between attacks. Men were still straightening inferior swords which had been bent or twisted in the battle. They were yet counting their hands and feet. They were continuing to suck in oxygen. So the commanders played an old card. They asked for a volunteer to step out and issue a challenge to the beast-people. Single combat. Two warriors, one from either side, battling it out on the ground between the opposing armies. A big man from the Barracuda Pavilion – big for a Carthagan at least – stepped forward. Carrying a sword and shield he marched down into the valley. There he called up to the Dogs to send a warrior down, if they dare.

The Carthagan commanders had guessed the Dogs would not be able to resist a single-combat call. They considered themselves the best individual fighters on the face of the planet. They also enjoyed the spectacle and entertainment of gladiatorial combat. A Dog-warrior duly came forth, a fierce-looking canine with a face full of teeth. His hackles were up and his eyes glinted with wicked glee. He strode down the slope while his comrades behind him yelled his name.

'VAU! SLAYER OF MEN! VAU, KILLER OF THE WEAK AND STRONG! VAU, DEALER OF DEATH!' came the cries from the hill.

'What did they call him?' Soldier asked Velion.

'Vau – his name is Vau. He's their best single combat warrior. I've seen him fight before.'

'He is the one who savaged Princess Layana.'

Velion nodded. 'So they say.'

Soldier's eyes narrowed as he studied the figure striding down to meet its Carthagan adversary. Vau's muscles stood proud underneath the dog-hair which covered his body. Truly he was a magnificent specimen. There was great strength and litheness in his walk. Just by looking at him Soldier could tell that here was a warrior with superior skills. What was more, Vau seemed completely unafraid, unlike his opponent, who appeared agitated and anxious. The Dog-warrior's calm face was pointed, his ears pricked, his eyes bright. The mouth below the long nose was half-open, the tongue lolling out. Soldier felt the anger and hatred rise within him. Here was the creature who had disfigured his wife, turned her face into a hideous map of scars.

Vau had no shield, only a two-handed battle-axe.

The combat on that shabby patch of turf was brief and mercifully simple. Vau clove the head of the Carthagan in two after only six strokes had been exchanged.

'*Thank you.*'

Soldier heard the words distinctly in the silence which had followed the encounter. His eyes followed a faint wisp of nothing, rising upwards towards the clouds. Or perhaps it was just a whirl of fine dust raised by the wind? He was unsure.

Vau suffered no injuries whatsoever.

On the point of victory the Dog-warrior raised his head and howled blindly at the sun. His comrades behind him barked and yapped and howled their delight. They moved to the edge of the slope, drumming their shields with their weapons, ready to charge down on the Carthagan army. They knew they had a psychological advantage and they meant to follow it up before the Carthagans found their courage again.

The defeat of a warrior in single combat can have devastating effects on the fallen man's army. That their champion had been dispatched so quickly and effectively depressed the

Carthagans and made them doubt themselves. There were groans amongst them and some had despair written in the slope of their shoulders as well as in their facial expressions. At that point, had the beast-people charged, the Carthagans might have actually been routed. Some might have run despite the strict code of warfare (there are always some who run away) and though others would have stayed and fought to the bitter end they would not have prevailed. The heart had gone out of them.

Fortunately for the Carthagans, the beast-people hesitated, perhaps to savour the moment of victory.

In this prideful second, during which had they charged they might have ensured a successful outcome of the battle for the beast-people, a second combatant went running down the slope towards Vau the victorious Dog-warrior.

A red haze had come down over Soldier's eyes. It was he who had gone flying down the incline, his foaming mouth roaring his fury. He fell straight down on the vanquisher, Vau. There was such an explosive rage, such a lava of loathing in Soldier's breast, he was like a volcano which has contained the earth's magma for so long that when it's finally released it fountains from the ground in a white hot spray of molten hatred.

The mildly-surprised Vau, having beheaded his victim, stood up with reeking, smoking sword. He was undaunted by this show of temper. Narrowing his eyes he regarded the charging man and decided he did not know him. Vau had tasted blood and was not afraid of some maniac who had broken ranks and was falling on him with blind vengeance. Vau believed his attacker to be the dead man's father, brother or dearest friend. There was no other reason for such a wrathful onslaught. Such an intemperate assault was to the

Dog-warrior's advantage. Rage is not always the best companion of skill. Vau intended to coolly stand his ground and chop his blood-maddened opponent down.

But Soldier was not to be halted. He was like an oncoming natural force – a great wind or a meteor hurtling through space – and his path was through the Dog-warrior. Too late Vau realised that he was facing a tornado. He swung at Soldier with his sword, as he had intended, but Soldier was travelling much too fast to present a good target. Vau's blade struck him on the rump, but he continued to hurtle into his antagonist with such savagery it petrified the Dog-warrior.

Struck by this irresistible force, Vau went flying backwards. His last vision was of the hideously distorted features of his attacker, whose absolute fury had turned his face into a crimson, ridged mask under which the old Soldier was unrecognisable. The reversed warhammer came down with terrible power, the squared metal spike going through the right eye and going on to crush the whole canine skull. Several more strikes went into the chest and abdomen, even though Vau had died instantly from that initial blow. Finally the head was literally hammered off the body, the flat of the Hannack's weapon repeatedly beating down on the neck and spine, using a rock as an anvil, until body and head broke away from each other.

Soldier held up the canine head with his free hand.

'Hhhhaaaa!' he cried. 'Dead! Dead!'

He stood there blood and gore running down his arm from the severed head, his face now suffused with triumph, while two silent armies looked on in stunned shock. He turned in the direction of the beast-people and worked Vau's upper and lower jawbones with his hands. He howled, as Vau had howled, just a short while earlier, holding open the mouth of his victim.

'Oooooowwwwwooooo!' he cried, using the head like a puppet. 'Oooooowwwwooooo! Ooooowwwwooooooooooooooo!'

The front ranks of the beast-people reeled back against their comrades in disgust and utter horror.

It was a few seconds before a Carthagan commander regained his senses enough to sound the charge. Now it was the Carthagans who held the psychological advantage. Their warrior had dispatched the beast-people's champion with ease. They were a superior army, better trained, better drilled, better soldiers. They went roaring down the hill in a waterfall of joyous confidence. They poured up the slope on the other side to drive into the stupefied beast-people, and began hacking them down where they stood. Dog-heads, Horse-heads, Stag-heads, Fox-heads. All began to retreat, striding at first, then breaking into a run, until it was a full-scale rout. The victorious army raced after them, cutting them down as they fled in terror. The day belonged to the Carthagans, whose hearts were indomitable.

Soldier was sent for by Captain Montecute. Soldier had washed and cleaned himself. He was now calm and in control of his thoughts and actions. A milder man you could not find in the halls of the clerics. As such, he stood in front of the captain, who regarded him with some distaste as well as awe. 'You have a terrible demon inside you, warrior.'

Soldier hung his head, ashamed now of his actions.

'I know it. I know it.'

'Such an ugly display of frenzied violence. Had he done you some wrong, this Vau?'

Soldier looked up, the shame gone.

'He bit my wife on the face. He destroyed her beauty.'

Light came to the captain's eyes.

'Ah, yes, of course – I keep forgetting – the, er, lovely Princess Layana. Such a mystery, why she married again, and to a common man such as yourself. Still, that's none of my business. What is my business is the fact that I've been ordered to promote you to lieutenant. Normally, you could have expected only sergeant-at-arms, after surviving a charge with the Forlorn Hope – that's the rank Velion has refused. But the killing of Vau helped us win the battle. So, welcome to the officer class, Soldier. You will replace one of my previous lieutenants, who died in the battle – may her spirit be with the gods.'

Soldier accepted the promotion gracefully.

Chapter Twelve

Soldier returned to the Eagle Pavilion to move his kit down to the far end of the great tent where the officers slept. He gathered his things together into a bundle. He did not have a great deal to take to the privacy of the officers' compartments. Once he had it all together he turned to his comrades. So far no one had spoken to him since after the battle.

'It's been a privilege serving with you,' he said, quietly. 'I hope I shall remain with this pavilion, even though I've been promoted. I would like us to still fight together.'

There was a marked silence. Small men with square muscular bodies, and tallish wiry women, turned away from him and busied themselves with small domestic tasks. Others whispered to their neighbours, holding a conversation with a friend, but ignoring Soldier. He felt shunned.

'What?' he said. 'Now that I'm a lieutenant you can't talk to me?'

Velion suddenly stood up and took his arm, leading from the pavilion into the open air and out of earshot of the rest of the warriors.

'They're worried about you,' she said, when she could not be overheard. 'The way you killed that Wild-dog-warrior . . .'

'Oh, that. But I've explained it to people. He violated my wife, ravaged her beauty. This was a personal score.'

'Yes – but – the fact is, they're afraid of you now. It'll take time for them to trust you. We took you for a professional soldier – someone who knew the business of fighting, someone with experience – but no one guessed there was such a hellion inside you. They're worried about saying the wrong thing, or making a mistake in front of you. Every one of them dreads coming under your command.'

'Do they?' asked Soldier. 'What about you, Velion? Surely you still trust my judgement.'

She looked doubtful. 'I don't know. You went berserk. Yet, at the same time, you killed your opponent with superb efficiency, given the weapon you had. *That's* what's so frightening about you.'

Soldier shook his head, wonderingly. 'Well, I did what I had to do.'

He did not add that he had terrified *himself* with this Soldier he had let out of himself during the battle. He did not know this man any better than his comrades did. *That* Soldier had come from somewhere deep within the recesses of his soul, from another world, from another life.

Velion pointed to a bloody flour sack in Soldier's grasp.

'What's that?' she asked.

He glanced down at it. 'This? Vau's head.'

'You're keeping it?'

'Just until I've shown it to my wife. I want her to see that the creature who bit her has paid for it with his life. She may want to burn it. I don't know.'

'I heard it said that the queen decreed no one should mention the incident again in Princess Layana's hearing.'

'Well, that was before I killed him. Now, I'm sure it will

be all right to discuss it with her. I want to exorcise the terror of that attack from her mind. It may help her to sleep better at nights, now that she knows he is dead.'

Velion shrugged. 'Don't say I didn't warn you. Now, you'd better go off and join your officer friends.'

'They're not my friends. You are.'

She shook her head. 'You've given that up now.'

'Is that why you've refused to accept your promotion to sergeant?' asked Soldier, with a trace of bitterness in his tone. 'You want to remain one of the common warriors?'

She looked down at the ground. 'I didn't accept promotion because I didn't earn it. You earned it for me, with that singing scabbard you have slung from your belt. Without that, I'd be dead. We'd both be dead – struck down from behind.'

Soldier glanced down at the sheath. 'So what? So you had an advantage. It's only like having the sun behind you, or the wind blowing grit into the eyes of your foe! One takes what one can get on the battlefield. There's plenty of hard luck stories too. You could be the one blinded by the sun or sand.'

'Well, I have to feel I deserve it, before I take it.' She was suddenly warm again. 'You – you're doing the right thing. I know you want promotion so that you can feel worthy enough to have a princess for a wife. You have to increase your status for this reason. I understand that.'

'Thank you, Velion.' He stared at the sunset. It was not spectacular: a washy shade of yellow. It seemed as if the natural world were growing sicker and sicker, along with the dying King Magus. 'Well, I'd better get on.'

She slapped him heartily on the back with the flat of her hand, almost winding him.

'I'll be watching out for you on the battlefield. You do the same for me.'

He grinned. 'I will. You can be sure of it.'

They parted and Soldier took his belongings to his new quarters, a private room inside the great tent, separated from others by walls of hanging goatskin. Depositing his kit in the bedspace, where previously the lieutenant to whom he had first spoken on approaching the red pavilions had slept, he then went to see Captain Montecute.

'What will be my new duties?' asked Soldier of his commanding officer.

'You will be taking over the archery squadron of the Eagle Pavilion,' said the captain. 'Normally a warrior promoted from the ranks is sent to another pavilion. It's better for discipline that he's separated from those who regarded him – or her – as a comrade. It's difficult to give orders to former friends and for them to take them from someone they know intimately.'

'But I'm staying with the Eagles.'

'Yes, no one else wants you.'

Soldier blinked. 'What?'

'No other pavilion will take you,' said Montecute. The stocky little man's eyes remained fixed on a point just to the right of Soldier's chest. 'Even the colonel was dubious about promoting you, but I persuaded him it was the right thing to do.'

'You did? Thank you, captain.'

'Don't thank me. I have reservations too – but I'm a stickler for the rules. The rules say bravery in action is rewarded. The rules say that those who volunteer themselves for single combat and prevail should be elevated. The way in which you killed that Dog-warrior sickened me to my stomach. Heroes are made of cleaner, brighter material than the stuff from which you're fashioned. You draw your courage from some dark, hellish place – some pit of savage violence not accessible to ordinary Carthagans like myself.'

Soldier gritted his teeth. 'I see.'

'However, there's no doubt you saved the day for us and because of that you should receive what's due to you.'

Soldier's eyes were hard. 'Thank you, Captain – now, is there anything I should be doing now?'

'You could go and help the physicians with the wounded.'

'You mean, use my dark magic to raise the dead?'

Captain Montecute shook his head slowly. 'Don't throw sarcasm at me, Lieutenant. I can still have you stamped into the dust whenever you displease me.'

Soldier drew a deep breath and kept his silence. After Montecute had stridden away, Soldier went to the hospital tent. There were men and women there with horrible wounds. Some would not live. He helped the physicians with binding woundwort and other medicinal herbs, including some mosses and clay, around open cuts to stop them festering. The important thing was to keep gangrene and other poisons at bay. Infusions of yarrow and honey with hot water were made and administered to prevent runaway fevers and rising temperatures. Those who saw Soldier's gentle hands minister to the injured thought he did so with great tenderness and compassion. They could not equate this Soldier with the one they had seen out on the battlefield. The two did not appear compatible.

Several of those in the tent were mortally wounded. They often passed away with a sigh on their lips. But souls released here did not thank anyone, unless it was a physician who had bungled.

Seven hours later Soldier left the hospital tent. He staggered out into the early morning, just as the mists were curling around the guy ropes. Exhausted, he went straight back to the pavilion to sleep, not even going to the field kitchens for food. That day, as he remained in a fatigued state, there was skirmishing with the beast-people, but no fully-fledged battle. At the end of the second day's fighting the beast-people capitulated. Those who could be taken into captivity were rounded up. The rest of the defeated enemy ran for the passes and eventually took goat tracks up into the hills.

Another campaign was over for the red pavilions.

When Princess Layana learned that Soldier had joined the red pavilions she had sent for a Carthagan she knew and asked him to keep her informed of events. This secret messenger carried word of the red pavilions' victory to the Green Tower in the Palace of Wildflowers. The messenger had rushed away straight after the battle and had few details, but Princess Layana learned that her new husband had led the Forlorn Hope into the battle and had been responsible for seizing the day when he volunteered for single combat and won his contest. Nothing was said to her about Soldier's state of mind when he did do, nor about the race and name of his victim. The messenger did not think these important. She simply understood that her husband was the hero of the hour and it pleased her immensely. She told herself she had no real feelings for this man, but it did her no harm to have a husband who was a great warrior.

'But of course,' she told herself, as she fed her fan-tailed doves in the cupola of the tall green tower, 'he is only my husband in name. He has no feelings for me. I was simply the method by which he was able to escape execution.'

She warned herself not to become a fool. If this Soldier learned she looked upon him fondly he might take advantage

of the power it could give him over others. Indeed, should he
wish to manipulate her he might pretend to be in love with
her in order to feather his nest. Layana told herself to be on
her guard, not to reveal any tender feelings for this handsome
stranger, nor to give him any kind of signal which would make
him think he was well regarded. It would be best, she thought,
to show him nothing but contempt and hauteur. That way
she could never be hurt. A cold front. That was the answer.

At that moment Drissila came into the room.

'Captain Kaff wishes to see you, my lady.'

A small frown formed on Layana's brow. She was aware
that Kaff's attentions were well-meant, and her friendship
with him was valuable to both of them in many ways, but
she knew why he was here today. The news that Soldier had
been promoted to lieutenant would not please the captain.
He was jealous of the new marriage and would not have been
unhappy to hear of the death in battle of the stranger. She
wondered why he had come to speak to her of the matter,
when he must be aware she would not accept any criticism
of Soldier from other men, even though she had doubts
herself. Soldier was her husband and that put him beyond
condemnation in earshot of the princess.

'Send him in, Drissila, but warn him to mind his manners.'

'I shall, my lady.' The maid-servant was gone in a rustle of
silks and chiffon.

Layana went to a tansu in the corner of the room, opened
one of its drawers, and withdrew a black velvet hood. She
pulled the hood over her head. This garment, and others like
it, had been specially made by a seamstress whose job it was
to hide the ugly side of the princess as well as possible. One
side of the hood came down over the marred half of Layana's
face, cleverly leaving the beautiful half with its soft,

unblemished skin revealed. The genius of the hood was that it allowed Layana to see through both eyes. In this garment she was able to meet the captain without feeling hideously exposed. It helped her confidence.

Kaff came marching in a few moments later wearing armour and carrying his helmet under his arm. According to the code of good manners his sword hilt was tied against his thigh showing that he knew he was aware of being in the house of a friend. He had obviously come straight from duty on the walls.

'So good to see you looking so healthy, my lady,' he said, giving her a sweeping bow. 'You know I pray nightly for your recovery.'

'You waste your time and that of the gods, if you do, Captain. You know my affliction is incurable.'

Kaff shook his head firmly. 'No one has said that. It might be that one day the spell will lift and you will be well again.'

'What is it you want?'

He looked a little nervous.

'I wondered if my lady would like a walk around the blue lake today? The weather is fair and would seem likely to remain so. A breath of fresh air would do you no harm whatsoever and might put some colour into your . . .' he paused, awkwardly, but having gone thus far had to finish, '. . . cheeks.'

'My one unblemished *cheek*, you mean,' she murmured. 'Captain Kaff, you don't displease me with your attentions, but you must know I am now once again a married woman.'

'I cannot look upon it as a permanent state.'

'You must. Are you waiting for me to murder my latest spouse?'

The large man looked embarrassed and shifted uneasily and awkwardly in his armour.

'Oh, I wouldn't call it *murder*, my lady. These are accidents, due to your unfortunate condition.'

'Be careful one of these accidents do not befall *you*, one of these days, Captain Kaff.'

He made a dismissive gesture as if the thought had never occurred to him and now that it had, he was prepared to risk it for the pleasure of her company.

'You are a brute, you know,' she said with sudden frankness. 'I could never love you.'

Kaff looked taken aback, as well he might. She had never spoken to him in this manner before. Nor had she used the word *love* in his presence. He presumed she was only able to do so now because he was no longer a threat in that respect.

'Brute?' he looked hurt. 'How so? Have I ever given you cause to think I'm less than gentle towards you?'

'I'm sorry, I don't mean it that way.'

Kaff's face hardened. 'You know he's just using your position to get what he wants.'

Layana raised her eyebrows. 'And what does he want?'

Kaff was careful not to cross too far over the invisible line.

'I don't know, but I guarantee it's for his own ends and we shall all end up regretting that we didn't chop off his damned head the moment he stepped into the castle. I still think he's a spy, probably for the Hannacks. How did he defeat that Hannack horseman on foot? There's not a man in Guthrum who could have done that. The Hannack pretended to attack the soldier to give him some credibility in our eyes.'

Layana shook her head in disbelief. 'It may have escaped your notice, but Soldier is not bald.'

'A wizard could have disguised him.'

'You'll have to do better than that, Captain. If I hadn't

chanced along he would be dead by now. That doesn't sound a very successful Hannack plot to me.'

Kaff left the Green Tower in an ugly mood, heading for Marshal Crushkite's quarters. Layana then decided she needed fresh air and freedom. She told her house servants she wanted to go to the textile market. A sedan chair and carrying slaves were arranged for her. She would, as always, be accompanied by six palace guards. The man in charge of the six guards was Corporal Tranganda. She had a long-standing arrangement with the corporal, whose fortunes had increased a great deal because of it. Layana paid Tranganda in gold to allow her to go hunting while she was supposed to be shopping. Tranganda settled with his soldiers, so everyone was happy, but the corporal knew he was taking a terrible risk. If Chancellor Humbold ever discovered the arrangement Tranganda would be cooked alive in his armour, very, very slowly, over a charcoal fire.

'Take me to the blacksmith today,' she told Tranganda, as he marched beside her sedan chair. 'I need some time.'

'Yes, my lady.'

He directed the chair carriers, who all came from the island of Amekni, a residue of the empire which still provided slaves for the Queen of Guthrum and her family. The Amekni slaves were not ill-treated (or they would run away) and were well-provided for in the way of food, shelter and rest. They were slaves in name only and were often better off than house-servants in this foreign land. However, much is in a name, and most of them simmered with a passion for their island home and its inhabitants to be free of the Guthrum yoke.

After a while Tranganda said, 'Forgive me for asking, my lady, but – but what would happen if you became ill while out hunting?'

She smiled at him gently. He was now in his late thirties and the years were passing. Very young men care little for risks, being devil-may-care and wild-thinking, but as they grow older they tend to take better care of themselves, especially if by that time they have enough money to buy a small farm and live comfortably in the country. Tranganda was a good man, but he was beginning to grow nervous. Layana might soon have to begin training someone to take Corporal Tranganda's place.

'You are referring to my madness. It only comes upon me in the middle of the night, never during the day. It may *last* over days, but the first attack is in the night hours.'

He nodded. 'I did not mean to be impertinent.'

'You're risking your life for me, Corporal. You're entitled to all the information that is needed to judge that risk.'

'Thank you, my lady. See, here we are at the blacksmith's.'

They approached the forge from a back alley. There Layana alighted and went inside. Butro-batan was called from his forge by a middle-aged woman who kept house for him. He met the princess in his own rooms.

'Forgive the shabby look to my humble home.' Butro-batan always made the same apology and Layana had long since ceased to tell him it did not matter. 'If you care to wait here I'll get the boy to fetch your palfrey from the stable down the street.'

'Thank you, Butro-batan,' she told him. 'In the meantime, I'll change into my hunting clothes. I'll need my hawk, too.'

The horse was duly brought. Most princesses would have settled only for a golden-maned palomino, or at least a pure white mare, but Layana was not so fickle. She was going hunting and her mount required some camouflage. Layana's little mare was a piebald, a creature of black-and-white patches that could melt into the shadows. Her name was Wychhazel.

Once more the princess was anonymous, under her swathes of indigo hunting calico. She too was like a blue shadow, with nothing but her eyes visible. With her crossbow and her goshawk, Windwalker, on her gloved fist the princess set forth.

The guards on the city gates knew her by sight. That is, they knew her as a youth of a great family who loved hunting, even if they did not know her exact identity. They knew her horse and hawk, they knew her voice, and many of them were in love with her deep brown eyes which always looked kindly upon them. They had been told (a rumour carefully spread amongst the soldiery by Corporal Tranganda) that she was the son of an elderly lord, a cleric, who despised hunting. Since almost all Guthrumites loved hunting there was much sympathy for a boy who wished to follow his favourite pastime.

Once out of the castle Layana rode south towards the Ancient Forest, her favourite hunting grounds.

Windwalker had been well cared for, by Butro-batan's apprentice, the twelve-year-old Cim. Cim adored animals and he lovingly greased Windwalker's buckskin jesses – the leather straps attached to a hawk's legs by which the hunter held her – whenever they were in his care. Jesses have to be kept soft and supple and Cim made sure they were kept in this state. The jesses need to be long, so that the hunter can grip them and hold the bird without hurting it and the hawk can scratch itself when it wishes, but not too long as to restrict the bird in flight. Cim also spent a great deal of his free time – not in abundance as a busy blacksmith's apprentice – in making Windwalker's hoods, so that her eyes were covered while on the fist. This prevented her from panicking when fast-moving creatures broke the forest pale, or the horse jolted and bumped. The hood Windwalker was wearing at the present had a little spray of scarlet feathers sprouting from its peak.

Once out on the downs and riding, Layana talked to her animals all the time.

'So, Wychhazel, have you been getting enough exercise lately? Has the boy been trotting you in the exercise yards? And you Windwalker, my fine feathered hunter, have you been flying up around the turrets of Guthrum's city, showing off your skills to an admiring audience of market traders?'

Of course, the creatures did not answer her, but as a lonely old woman talks to her cat, so a lonely young woman held conference with her hawk and her horse. There were replies of sorts. They knew her voice and the mare whinnied gently while the hawk warbled, which involved stretching her wings above her head until they nearly touched. They were three companions out for some good hunting, and they were one with the world.

The landscape was not all Layana would have wished it to be. But it would be restored, so it was said, once HoulluoH died and his successor took his place. How they hung on to life, these wizards, even when they had seven times the span of an ordinary man! Seven hundred years and still HoulluoH would not let go of this mortal coil. Things would get worse before they got better. She crossed a stream where there were dead trout floating on the surface; went through a brake where the ferns were brown and dying from lack of rain; skirted a spinney which was thick with spiders' webs, over-run with fungi and smothered in too much lichen and moss.

A stag broke cover at one point and had Layana not had the hawk on her fist it might have resulted in an exciting chase, or race, pitting her mount against a creature of the wind.

On the edge of the Ancient Forest, near where Layana had first met Soldier, a pair of pheasants took off, their wings whirring.

Layana let slip her accipiter. The bird was in yarak – keen to hunt – and she raked away from the princess to climb above the two pheasants. The game birds had heard the bells attached to the hawk's legs and they were wise enough to know there was death in the air, but there was little they could do about it. When the hawk stooped and raked, and the first bird fell, the other knew it was safe. It flew down to a grassy ditch.

The struck pheasant fell out of the sky, stone dead with the raking it had received: just one blow from the goshawk's talons on the back of the neck. It was the cleanest, quickest way to kill a game bird. A hunter could try shooting partridges and pheasant out of the sky with a bow, but the likelihood of actually hitting flying quarry with an arrow was almost negligible. More often than not they were snared on the ground, resulting in a lingering, painful death. At least with the hawk death was swift and relatively painless.

The pheasant was the first kill of the day. There were more as the hours went by, including a hare shot with the crossbow.

Finally, Layana was ready to return to the castle. The afternoon was drawing on and there were people who would be wondering about her. Whirling the lure she enticed Windwalker back to her fist, hooded her, secured the game on her saddle, then rode back towards Zamerkand. As she neared the walled city she saw in the distance a long line of marching men. They were carrying scarlet banners bearing representations of animals and birds in black-and-white. The campaign was over. The Carthagan red pavilions were returning victorious.

A flutter of excitement went through her breast as she saw that the leading pavilion was the Eagles.

She quickly suppressed this feeling, certain that it was all so worthless.

Chapter Thirteen

On arrival back at the main Carthagan pavilions, outside the walls of Queen Vanda's castle, Soldier was given a hero's welcome. The warlords and generals there were not concerned about his blind, barbaric and brutal killing of the Dog-warrior, Vau. Any vivid discriptions on the subject they put down to exaggeration and embellishment, knowing that battle-heat fired imaginations. They took the colonel's report into account, of course, but so far as the generals were concerned, the single-combat slaying had been necessary and had resulted in the battle turning to favour the red pavilions.

Soldier was presented with a new breastplate bearing the embossed crest of a lieutenant over the heart. He was also given a sword, a straight-bladed weapon with an elaborate hand guard. This was an ancient sword, recently refurbished by one of the armourers of the red pavilions, an artist in weapons.

'This blade has been fashioned from sixty bundles of iron rods,' he was told by the Carthagan weaponsmith. 'Each of those rods has a different carbon content, to give it flexibility as well as strength and sharpness. You must treat your sword like a brother or sister, give it a name. It is a work of art. This particular blade belonged to the captain of the Bear Pavilion, who died just two weeks ago.'

Soldier appreciated the worth of a flexible blade. He had watched the beast-people straightening bent and twisted bronze swords after the battle. He had seen the ordinary iron swords of the Carthagan warriors, shattered and broken by impacting against shield and armour. Only a blade made with bundles of iron rods with different carbon contents could withstand the clashing and hammering a sharp-edged sword would receive in battle.

Soldier held it up so that the light caught and flashed along the honed edge. Sharp. Very sharp. He made one or two strokes in the air with it. It was a well-balanced weapon.

'This warrior from the Bears, he knew his swords,' said Soldier. 'I shall call it *Xanandra*.'

The weaponsmith frowned. 'Isn't your wife's name Princess Layana?'

Soldier stared at the artisan. 'A thoughtful warrior never names his sword after his beloved. This blade will go into the entrails of some foul beast or hated enemy. Do you think I want to use my wife's name on an instrument for gutting those I fear and despise?'

'I see your point.'

'No,' Soldier said, swishing the blade through the air, 'if you want a sword to be special, you name it after a goddess.'

'You're lucky this weapon's available at this time,' said the weaponsmith. 'Its owner wouldn't have given it up willingly.'

'What happened to the captain?'

The weaponsmith grinned. 'Went for a crap in the middle of the night without his sword. While he was squatting he came arse to face with a monster. It was a giant snake, who swallowed him whole. He didn't even try to run, not with his leathers down and being his size. He was not good at running, that one. A rather ignoble end for an officer of the pavilions. They found the snake and killed it of course. It couldn't go anywhere with the Bear captain inside it. Too late then, though, for him.'

'He must have been either old or overweight, not to attempt escape?'

'Fat as a pig,' said the armourer with another wide grin. 'You couldn't squeeze him into a barn.'

Armed with his new sword and carrying the head of Vau, Soldier went towards the city. Unfortunately the sword would not fit into his old scabbard, so he wore Kutrama on his right side, still empty, and the new sword in its own sheath on his left side. He was aware how ridiculous this looked, to be carrying an empty scabbard as well as a full one, but he cared nothing for the curious looks of passersby.

As he strode along a black bird suddenly landed on his shoulder, making him start.

'Where d'you think you're going, Soldier?'

'Oh, it's you, raven. To see my wife of course.'

The raven clucked in disapproval. 'She'll throw you out. You know you're only married in name. She doesn't give a Hannack's bald pate for you. Don't make a fool of yourself. Is that why you joined the army, to impress her?'

Soldier said, 'I don't have to listen to you.' He tried to brush the bird from his shoulder, but the raven simply jumped over his hand and landed back on his moving perch again.

'Ha! Struck a chord, did I?'

'No,' replied Soldier, smarting underneath.

'Look, why don't you give all this up? Leave this ungrateful army and embrace freedom. They don't like you anyway.

You'll never fit in. You'll always be an outsider and resented, no matter how many Vaus you kill in single combat. You and me, why, we could live. the life of a royal bastard if we went out into the wilds. We'd want for nothing. You could kill things and eat them, and I could scavenge on the remains. You could have the nice joint and I could pick out the eyes.'

'Go away.'

'I'm making sense, aren't I?' said the raven, fluttering its wings as it fought to stay on his shoulder. 'That's why you're so angry, isn't it? You know I'm right.'

Soldier stopped dead. He said very slowly and deliberately, 'If you don't get off my shoulder, I swear I'll bite off your head and spit it into the moat.'

'Touchy!' muttered the bird, but at last it flew away, up into the turrets and cupolas of the city.

Soldier heaved a huge sigh of relief and entered the city gateway.

The guards at the gate saluted him smartly as he went in. This gave Soldier childish satisfaction. A short while ago they would have stopped him, poked fun at him (then in his iron collar), asked him to authenticate his right to be out alone, and generally given him a bad time. Now they saw a man in a lieutenant's armour, came smartly to attention and ordered arms.

Soldier had to go through the market-place in order to reach the Palace of Wildflowers, his destination. He deliberately made a detour in order to pass by a certain stall. Spagg was there, touting for business with that gin-ravaged throat he owned, his cracked and husky voice carrying over the heads of the crowd.

'Hanged men's hands! Hands-of-Glory! Good for all sorts of spells and witchcraft. Once you've had your use out of 'em you can feed your familiars on the rotten flesh.'

'You're an ugly old liar, Spagg – that's why the gods gave you all those warts.'

The market trader whirled, a righteous look on his face, but when he saw who was speaking to him, he went white.

'Soldier? You're – you're an officer?'

'An officer indeed.'

Spagg managed a smile, his knotty head going down inside his pointed shoulders. 'Good to see you, friend. I'm always glad when one of my apprentices does well for hisself. Officer, eh? Must be because I put in a word for you, with that imperial guardsman, what's-'is-name, Captain Kaff.'

'I seem to remember you asked for first dibs on my eyes when they were going to execute me.'

The smile weakened. 'Well, what d'you expect – they're remarkable eyes. I could get a good bit for them if they was pickled in white vinegar wine. I can see 'em standin' on the mantel of some nobleman's house . . .'

'Can you now?' There was menace in Soldier's voice. 'You could have stood surety for me and saved my life. I ought to cut your head off now. People in this market-place would stand around and cheer if I did.'

Spagg had gone pale again. 'Now, now, Soldier – don't get too hasty. Look, look what happened afterwards. If I'd've stood surety, you wouldn't have met the lovely princess – well, lovely except for her,' he touched his cheek, 'you know, the marks and what not. Look,' he repeated in desperation, 'why don't you take a set of these magic hands for free. Any pair. Your choice. Just to show there's no hard feelings.'

Soldier wagged finger in the market trader's face. 'Spagg,' he said, 'you'd better be my friend in future. Don't make the same mistake again, because I always land on my feet. You understand me?'

'Yes, yes, of course, Soldier. We're pals, we are. Best of comrades. I won't let you down again, you see.'

Soldier nodded and went on his way, astonished by the simmering fury inside him. What appalled him was he had been serious about cutting off Spagg's head. Once he had calmed down again, Soldier was once more ashamed that he had almost lost control. He was appalled by the unfathomable depths of wrath he found inside his own soul. It would have been unforgivable to have killed Spagg, yet he had been a hair's breadth away from drawing his sword. Spagg had sensed that and knew that he had barely escaped death.

On his way down the wide tree-lined avenue to the Palace of Wildflowers, Soldier suddenly came face-to-face with Captain Kaff.

Soldier instantly forgot his promise to himself, saying in barely-disguised vexation, 'Have you just been to see my wife?'

Captain Kaff was accompanied by several astonished imperial guard officers, who looked first at Kaff, then at this upstart Carthagan lieutenant who dared to address one of their number in such arrogant tones.

'What if I have?' snarled Kaff. 'What's it to you? She won't even want to see you.'

'We'll see about that. In the meantime, perhaps you would care to meet me at dawn tomorrow outside the walls of the castle, accompanied by two brother officers, your seconds.'

Kaff's head went back and something resembling a smile came to his features.

'You're *challenging* me? To a duel?'

'That's the general idea.'

'Forget it. And what are you doing in the uniform of an officer? Impersonating a lieutenant, even in the inferior Carthagan army, is a capital offence.'

'I earned my promotion.'

'From slave to lieutenant? I don't think so.'

One of the other officers snatched the flour sack out of Soldier's hand.

'Let's see what he's got in here – ho! – the head of a dog? What's this, slave? Packed lunch?'

The man's friends laughed at this and crowded in on Soldier.

'Wait,' said one, 'that's not just a *dog's* head. That's the head of a beast-warrior. Look at the eyes! What did you do, slave, sneak up behind him while he was asleep?'

'I fought him in single combat.'

A cavalry lieutenant said, 'A likely tale. Admit it. You found him drugged on toadthtoolth and decapitated him – hacked through hith neck while he wath unconthiouth, unable to defend himthelf.'

'If you weren't so stupid,' Soldier said, 'you lisping fool, you'd notice that the cut is clean.'

The smile went from the cavalry officer's face. 'Thtupid? I'll thow you how thtupid I am.' He drew his sabre and slapped Soldier on the face with the flat of the blade. Nonetheless the blow brought a thin line of blood down Soldier's cheek.

Soldier said, evenly, 'You'll regret that . . .' but now others had grabbed his arms and held him fast. Kaff had backed away and was watching from a distance, saying nothing.

One of the other officers said, 'I think we ought to teach this slave a lesson. What do you say to crucifixion? We could nail him to that tree over there.'

Kaff spoke up quickly from the background. 'Not in view of the palace. Take him down a side alley.'

There were murmurs of agreement and they dragged Soldier along the avenue and down a cobbled alley. Kaff slipped away during this abduction and was not present for the short trial which followed in the shadows of a hovel. Here the officers were unable to find a suitable place to crucify him, but there was a wagon parked in the street, full of rotting vegetables. They tied him to the wheel of this vehicle, ripped his tunic from his back, and then the cavalry officer gave him thirty-five lashes with his whip. They drew blood, laying open the flesh to the bone. Soldier began silently enough, but after a time he couldn't prevent the groans from passing his lips and this delighted his tormentors. They left him hanging from the wheel, the head of Vau tied around his neck.

None of the citizens who passed him by would even look in his face, let alone set him loose. They were afraid. If someone had done this monstrous thing, they must have been people who did not fear reprisals. It was better not to become involved, to leave well enough alone, to mind one's own business and hurry on by. He was there an hour or more, just hanging from the wheel. Even the wagonmaster came back and then left again when he saw what was decorating his cart. Better not to have seen and return when the decoration had been taken down. People in the houses round about closed their shutters and peeked through holes in the woodwork.

Eventually, the raven found him. 'What a mess!'

Soldier was hanging from the wheel by his strapped elbows. Blood was running down his arms and dripping onto the cobbled street. His mouth was flecked with foam and bleeding where he had bitten his tongue. His clothes were soaked with sweat and hung from his body. He was indeed a mess.

'Never mind the crowing,' gasped Soldier, barely able to remain conscious, 'if you can't undo these knots with your beak, go and get a Carthagan warrior named Velion – a woman – get her to me.'

'Did I hear the magic word?' asked the raven.

'Damn you, bird – this is not the time.'

'Well, it doesn't take *very* much more effort to say *please*, now does it? I think I can manage those knots. If I can undo locks I can certainly undo bits of rawhide.'

The bird went to work and had him free within a few minutes. Soldier staggered away from the wheel, removing the flour sack with the head in it as he went. There was a public fountain and drinking water not far from the wagon. He went to this and washed himself, splashing the cold water over his head, shoulders and back, swilling away the blood. After a while he began to feel a little better. He pulled his tunic back on, covering the cuts on his shoulders and back. A good, long drink and he felt able to walk again, without reeling or falling over.

'Thank you, raven.'

'You're welcome,' said the bird, hopping onto the fountain and taking a drink himself. 'I take it you had a visit from friends?'

'A friend of my wife.'

'She keeps bad company.'

'Yes, she does, doesn't she.'

Soldier once again made his way towards the Palace of Wildflowers. He reached the gardens which surrounded the palace and rested on a camomile seat there, allowing the fragrance of the crushed herb to waft over him and revive his strength. A guard approached him and questioned him, asking him for identification. Soldier said who he was, and told the guard that a man-servant called Ofao could vouch for him. The guard went away and later Soldier felt he was being observed from a window in the palace. The guard returned and indicated that Soldier should follow him into the palace.

'It's the princess I wish to see,' said Soldier. 'I'm her husband.'

The guard said nothing in reply, taking Soldier to a courtyard, where he left him.

Soldier looked about him. The courtyard was quite beautiful. There was a fountain in the middle guarded by four stone lions with a pool at their feet. The pillars and walls surrounding the courtyard were scrolled with writings in a language Soldier did not know. The stonework was grey, pink and pale blue, the colours of a winter sunset, and there were tall windows at the far end which overlooked gardens of stately cypress trees and tear-shaped yews. Apart from the sound of the running water and the cooing of doves, it was a peaceful spot.

'You look very weary.'

Her voice came to him as if out of a dream. He turned to see her standing beneath an arch. She wore a hood which covered half her face, leaving the unblemished side to catch the light. Soldier's heart almost stopped in mid-beat, but he hid his feelings under a rigid mask. She had married him out of pity only and he did not want to betray his true emotions.

'I've brought you a present,' he told her. 'In this sack.'

'It looks to be a very bloody gift.'

He nodded. 'The head of Vau, the Dog-warrior who took away your beauty. I killed him in single combat. Some said I was unnecessarily vicious, but considering his crime I thought my actions were just and called for. Do you wish to look on his face for the last time, before I burn him?'

Princess Layana shuddered and turned away.

'I have no wish to see him. I didn't ask you to avenge me. I have no interest in such matters.'

Soldier was disappointed. He tossed the head into the far corner of the courtyard.

'I had forgotten that day. You have reminded me.'

He said angrily, 'How could you forget? You surely look in the mirror occasionally.'

'What I see in the mirror belongs to the present, not to the past.'

Clearly she was not grateful at all for his actions. He might just as well have let Vau live, for all she cared. Bitterness crept into his soul for a moment, but he managed to banish it firmly. This was not the place to show rancour. Here he was supposed to be master. Here he had to remain in control of his wild emotions.

'I have come to claim my rights,' he said, 'as a husband.'

Her head came up then, her chin tilted, defiantly.

'Oh? You will have such rights as I choose to give you.'

'I am your husband,' he said, simply and without any heat in his voice. 'You are my wife.'

She was silent for a while, then she said. 'You want me? Ugly as I am?'

He sighed, revealing his yearning. 'I find you – irresistible.'

'You are a warrior, returned from the wars. You have fought and killed. The lust is high in your blood. This is why soldiers rape the women of the enemy. You don't want me, you want *any* woman.'

Her chin was still tilted upwards, the light in her eyes strangely both defiant and vulnerable.

'I don't want *any* woman,' he said, huskily, the words coming from deep within him, he knew not where. 'I want *you*. I have lain awake under the stars, dreaming of the first time we make love. There are images burned in my brain. Other women are nothing to me. Every picture of a woman in my brain melts into a likeness of you. You have filled my whole being with your spirit, now I want to complete it with your body. I love every part of you, mind, spirit and body, every single hair on your head, every fold, every rise of your form. Even now your fragrance drives my senses into battle with themselves. I want to breathe you, drink you, swallow you whole.'

She was trembling now, under the onslaught of his softly-spoken words.

'This is so?' she whispered. 'You – love – me?'

'You are my prayer for life itself.'

Without another word she walked towards a room off the courtyard. In this room there was a bed. It was not her bed, it was the sleeping place of a maid-servant. Soldier followed her in and closed the door. They both removed their garments without looking at one another. Both were shaking violently. When they turned towards one another again, they clasped each other . The sudden touch of body against body took the breath from them and they simply stood there, holding one another, staring into each other's eyes.

Soldier then lifted her up and placed her on the bed. She still wore her hood. He began, gently, to remove it.

'No,' she whispered. 'Please?'

'Yes,' he said, firmly.

When he had unwound the velvet cloth and removed the hood, revealing her hideous scars, he bent down and kissed that part of her face on which the skin was puckered and twisted.

'Every fold, every crease, every part of your body,' he confirmed with in a murmur. 'They are all one to me, every pore more precious than myrrh, gold or frankincense.'

They made love and the tears flowed down her cheeks, wetting his face. She was wearing a particular kind of perfume which he finally decided was a combination of ambergris, sandalwood and deer musk. It helped to drive his senses crazy.

When they had finished their first gentle passion, followed by a more furious onslaught on each other's bodies, she felt the open wounds and weals on his back. There was blood on her hands, on the sheets, on his tunic hanging over a chair.

'What has happened to you?' she cried, sitting upright, feeling guilty for not noticing his hurt before now. 'Has the army punished you?'

'Not the army,' he said, wryly. 'Someone else. It happened in the street just a short while ago, not far from the palace gates. But don't worry, they'll pay.'

'Are you hurting? Are you in pain? I shall send for Ofao and tell him to bring ointments and balms.'

Soldier sat up himself now. 'If you call that man I shall have to dress. I think he wants my body as much as I desire yours.'

She laughed at this: a laugh that contained no madness in its tone. It was a sound the palace had not heard in years. It echoed throughout the courtyards and Drissila came running, bursting into the room.

'My lady, what is the matter?'

'What is the matter?' cried Layana, her eyes sparkling, 'Why, I'm *happy*, that's what is the matter.'

Drissila's hand went to her mouth in horror as she noticed the naked man lying next to her mistress.

'Forgive me,' said Soldier, gathering a sheet about his loins. 'I hadn't realised this was your room.'

'It's not my room. Oh, what have you done to my mistress? You're a sorcerer, that's what it is. You've turned her into a simpering idiot. You've – you've stolen her mind.'

'I can assure you,' said Soldier, as Layana lay back, giggling into her pillow, 'that it was certainly *not* her mind I stole.'

Layana hit him with the pillow. Then she turned to Drissila.

'We must have feasting. We must have merriment in the palace. Open up the great hall. Light a fire in the hearth. Roast an ox, or at least a lamb. I want music. Send for the pipers and the flautists and other musicians. I want *dancing*. Yes, dancing in the palace hall. Everyone must dance, even you Drissila. We'll find a man for you. And another for Ofao, in case he can't take his eyes off my husband!'

The maid-servant could see that Soldier had awakened the spirit of her mistress, that her lady was in love for the very first time.

She turned to Soldier and said, 'You didn't need to go to war, you know. She would have accepted you as you were.'

Soldier raised his eyebrows at his beloved.

'Is this true?'

'I don't know, but Drissila often knows me better than I know myself.'

Soldier shrugged.

Later, while the feasting, music and dancing was going on, Drissila drew Soldier to one side.

'You must be careful,' she said. 'My mistress . . .' Drissila checked herself, wrung her hands in distress, and then continued with what she had been about to say, '. . . my lady is subject to changes of mood. She can – she can be very violent, my lord.'

To his rather uncertain knowledge this was the first time Soldier had been called 'my lord' by anyone and it did not seem to fit well on him.

'I'm only a lieutenant,' he told the maid-servant gently. 'You don't have to call me lord. As to your mistress, I am aware that she is ill. I know that she murdered her first two husbands. But then, I also know that she did not love them. You have seen her face, her demeanour, her eyes. She *does* love me and I thank the gods for it, because I fell in love with her the instant I first saw her.'

'It's more in the nature of a family curse, than an illness. You know her sister, Queen Vanda, is also subject to bouts of madness. Their mother, the former queen, imprisoned a wizard and and a spell was put on the family for eternity. My lady is the sweetest-natured creature in all the world, except . . .'

'Except when she is not?' he offered.

'All I'm asking you to do is be very careful.'

'I shall take the utmost care, Drissila, and I thank you for your concern, albeit misplaced.'

Afterwards, while the tumblers were leapfrogging and building pyramids, Layana came to his side again.

'What were you and my maid-servant hatching?' she asked, laughingly. 'It's not my birthday for months yet.'

Soldier turned to his new bride and replied calmly, 'She said your family had been cursed and that you were subject to fits of violent madness.'

Layana's face clouded over. 'You tell me this in such a bald way? Were you not consigned to secrecy by Drissila?'

'I will keep no secrets from you, my love. I have no identity, no past, no knowledge of my real self. For all we both know I could be a criminal of the worst kind. We are both sadly inadequate. We shall have to be honest with one another until the day comes when I know who I am – and you are quite sane.'

For one moment he thought she was going to fly into a temper, but after a few seconds she smiled.

'How wise you are, my new husband. Listen, perhaps we should give you a name until you find your real self?'

'No, Soldier feels right. Just plain Soldier will be fine. Now, would you like to dance? I didn't know I could dance, but my feet seem to be jigging around to that lively air the flutes are playing. Will you take my arm, my lovely wife?'

'Gladly.'

She placed her hand in his and they went out amongst the dancers, who made space for the bride and her man.

Chapter Fourteen

Layana insisted, despite Soldier's protests, that they sleep in separate rooms.

'It's deep in the night that my madness comes upon me,' she told him, weeping, 'and I don't wish to harm you.'

'I think we love each other too much for that,' he argued. But the whipping he had received from Kaff was beginning to tell on his strength. So far the heady excitement of the day had helped to bolster him, but now the violence visited on his body was overcoming that exhilaration. He needed rest, especially if he was to arise before dawn and be outside the city walls to meet Kaff in single combat. Even if Kaff did not turn up, Soldier wanted to be there, just in case. The worst thing in the world would be to be called a coward by Kaff.

So he agreed to separate rooms. Ofao came and ministered to him, with more ointments and balms, and also gave Soldier a potion which he said would help him sleep. Soldier thanked the body-servant and fell instantly asleep on the soft bed. Ofao went out of the room, locked the door from the outside, and pushed the key under the space below the door. Both he and Drissila were of the same mind: Soldier had to be protected from his mad wife.

The knight, Valechor, was in a misty woodland below an oak tree.

He was in full body armour, a sword in one hand, a mace in the other. Around him were the shapes of lesser knights in dark armour. No faces were visible and the insignias on their shields and helmets were vague as shadows. They clustered round Valechor, their armour clanking, the leather straps creaking. There was the smell of urine and faeces in the air. He decided they had been in this woodland for some hours. Men had relieved themselves in their armour, it not being deemed safe to relax alertness. Only he alone had been permitted to rest. In fact he had not been asleep, but deep in the vigil that knighthood demanded before a battle. He had called upon the angels to cluster by his side in the coming fight.

He had consigned his soul to his Lord.

'Sire,' said a knight close by him, 'the Drummond clan are gathered in the glen beyond the brook. It's close to dawn. If we're to be successful in our attack, we must gather on the kneb before the day breaks.'

'You are right,' Valechor said. 'Let us move to the kneb.'

He stood up and strode out onto the spongy meadow, stepping over a beck which trickled down to a rockhang on the moor below, making deep dents in the mossy ground in his heavy armour. There the chargers were corralled with their handlers, protecting the horses against the chill winds which swept across the peat hags. The Drummonds had suffered a great beating the day before and now they were trapped against a steep escarpment which rose straight out of the peat and formed a barrier behind them. He and his knights had the enemy at their mercy. There was to be a massacre which would rid the world of Drummonds forever.

Through the heather came a shadowy figure, cloaked against the cold, hooded against the early morning fog. This figure carried a crooked staff flying a ragged cow-hide pennon. Burned into the hair of the hide was the crest of the Drummond clan. Here was a messenger.

The man in the thick woollen cloak stopped on the dew-soaked ground just twenty yards from the knights.

'I come as an envoy,' said the man, 'from a defeated people.'

'Let us hear the words,' he said.

The man hesitated to reply for a moment, but finally he spoke in a cracked voice.

'I am empowered to offer you our unconditional surren-der,' said the envoy, clearly racked with emotion. 'If you will spare us and our families, we will submit to your commands.'

Valechor stood there, angered by this capitulation. What, was he to be denied final blood? Was his slaughtered bride worth only a few of the hated weasels who had killed her? He wanted every Drummond life to be draining onto the moor by the time the sun warmed the lavender flowers into opening their petals.

'I cannot hear you,' Valechor cried. 'The wind howls into my ears and makes me deaf. What is it you want? A battle to the last man standing?'

The envoy staggered backwards several paces onto a turf-covered knoll. From the top of the knoll a hare broke from its form and curved out across the heather. This creature in turn disturbed two grouse, which rattled up into the misty regions above the heads of envoy and knights. There was the clink of spurs on stone, as one of his own knights stepped forward onto the stepping stones over the beck. He made a motion with the back of his hand for that knight to remain where he was and not to interfere in the negotiations.

'You do not understand,' said the envoy, 'you have won. There is no need for any more killing.'

'No,' Valechor shouted, 'I still cannot hear you. The wind is too loud. Come back at noon, when the moor is calmer.'

The envoy stared at him, knowing that all was lost.

'You bloodthirsty bastard,' the envoy said, before turning to walk back into the mists.

'No more bloodthirsty than a Drummond.'

The envoy stopped and called over his shoulder, 'You heard that all right!'

Some short while later the knights charged down on horseback and the slaughter began. No Drummond escaped the field that day. Their bodies lay draped over tuft and root, the precious Drummond blood sucked away by a thirsty moor. Their wives and sweethearts were raped to ensure that the next generation would only ever be half-Drummond and would be bastards to boot. The children were gathered in and would know their parents no more. They would be adopted by families on border farms, who would work them on the land. It was a massacre which would have sickened the heart of the most bloody of tyrants.

He sat on his horse and watched it happen, never once curbing the excesses of his battle-maddened knights. One old woman, a ragged witch, rushed up to his mount and screamed up at him.

'Curse ye, Valechor! Curse yer kith and kin and their progeny! May yer soul reek in hell, ye murtherin' swine. Curse yer dead bride, may she . . .'

He chopped her down with his mace before she could

utter the final words which would make her hex complete.

Finally, when it was all over, the knights rode away, leaving the dead in a great pile beneath some standing stones. The Drummonds had been slaughtered. Wolves came in to gnaw the flesh from the bones, corbies came in to pick the eyes. But before noon these scavengers scattered in all directions as the bodies moved, pushed from beneath. Not all the Drummonds were dead. There was one survivor, one man who had been struck on the head by a club and who had now regained consciousness.

From beneath the heap of dead Drummonds crawled this soul, bloodied, filthy with gore, sickened to his heart. He screamed for vengeance into the wind on the moor. He promised the gods of earth, sea and sky that the foe would rue this day. Then he began walking, deep into the heart of the moor, his expression rapt, his soul heavy as lead inside him. But the fire within him would not now be quenched until his sword had tasted the blood of that one hated leader of the enemy knights. The killer of his clan would pay, and this Drummond was the man to make him pay, for he was, above all, a professional soldier.

Soldier woke with his magic scabbard singing a warning in his ears.

A shadowy shape flew as light as a bat from the windowsill to his bed, a dagger in its hand. Soldier grasped the wrist of the assassin, wrenching it sideways. There was a scream but his attacker had the strength to hold on to the knife. Soldier struck out with his fist, knocking his assailant against the padded walls. The attacker's head struck the padding hard and the figure fell to the floor and lay still.

With trembling hands Soldier found a tinder box and lit a

taper, transferring the flame to a candle. With the tallow in hand he examined the body on the floor. He recognised her instantly, and cried out.

It was Layana, her face not only disfigured with her old scars but now bearing an ugly bruise where he had struck her. Full of remorse Soldier bent down and lifted her up.

She woke as he was carrying her to the bed and her features twisted into a horrible image of hate and fury. She tried to rake his face with her nails, but he managed to throw her onto the bed. While she was scrambling around, trying to find the dagger, he sought the key for the door. It was not in the lock. Then he saw it on the floor, picked it up and undid the lock.

'Help here!' he cried down the passageway.

Servants came running from their rooms, pulling on their clothes. Guards ascended the staircase. Soldier went back into the room. When he had disarmed Layana he had heard the knife go skidding under a wardrobe. She was still frantically trying to find it amongst the bedclothes. He took her by her wrists again and she kicked out at him viciously, trying to break his nose and smash his lips against his teeth. He held her firmly until the servants had her, screaming her wrath at all and sundry, and dragged her from the room.

'How did she get in here?' asked Drissila. 'We left her safe in her room. 'We always lock her door.'

Soldier said, 'She must have climbed up the chimney and across the roof, to enter this room by my window.'

Soldier had believed that his love for Layana – and indeed her love for him – was having a curative effect. Clearly he had been deluding himself. If it had not been for his scabbard he would be dead by her hand. He conveyed all this to Drissila, who shook her head.

'My mistress is *cursed*, my lord. Were it but an illness we would all be striving for a cure, but unfortunately it is witchcraft.'

'Then we must find some way of fighting this evil spell with the magic that was responsible for it in the first place.'

The dawn rays were striking the windows. Soldier said he had to go. There was someone to meet. He dressed, strapped on his new sword, and set off. He went through the empty streets, crossing the city. When he approached the exit gates the sleepy guards on the graveyard watch looked at him suspiciously, but on seeing his lieutenant's insignia they came reluctantly to attention and let him pass without a word.

Outside the walls there were more guards, this time posted around the red pavilions. Soldier went to the Eagle Pavilion. There he found the bedspace of Velion and woke his female friend.

'I need you,' he whispered.

'What, *now*?' she murmured, sitting up and rubbing her eyes. 'We could have slept together while we were on campaign. That would have been much more exciting.'

'No – no, not that. I'm a married man.'

'I've slept with lots of married men.'

'Look, I need you as a second in a duel. I need you to watch my back. I'm to fight the Captain of the Imperial Guard at dawn.'

Velion looked towards the tent flap. 'It's dawn now.'

'That's why we have to hurry.'

'All right.' She whipped off her shift. Naked, she went to a bowl of water and splashed it in her face. Soldier noticed how tall and stately she was, but also how slow. He hopped from one foot to the other in agitation.

'Can't you hurry,' he whispered.

She looked at him indignantly. 'I'm not going to a duel looking as if I'm out of the rag-bag.'

Finally Velion was dressed and ready to go. They slipped out under the flaps and she followed him towards the castle walls.

'What's this all about?' she asked.

'There's a man who hates me. Captain Kaff. He's in love with my wife. Yesterday I challenged him to a duel.'

'Because he's in love with your wife?'

'No, because he tied me to a wagon wheel and had me flogged in a public street.'

Velion nodded in approval. 'A *much* better reason for a duel. I would kill any man who tried that with me.'

A raven landed on Soldier's shoulder.

'Not you – not *now*,' he said. 'I haven't got time.'

The raven flew off, seemingly in a huff. Velion looked askance at Soldier but said nothing. Eventually the pair came to a place under the walls where some officers were standing. Soldier recognised the cavalry officer who had administered the lashes yesterday. He glared at him.

Kaff was standing a little way off, stripped to the waist, swishing his sword through the air, testing its balance. His hair was tied back in a horse's tail, presumably to keep it out of his eyes. Soldier noticed how muscular were his chest and arms - and how thin his calves and thighs. He had a powerful upper body which was not matched by the lower half of him.

Kaff obviously worked with stone weights, but paid scant attention to his legs.

'We had jutht about given you up,' said the cavalry officer. 'Are you alwayth tho tardy?'

Soldier replied, 'You're lucky I came at all. From what I

remember, Captain Kaff rejected my challenge. I seem to recall that he did not believe I was now an officer and a worthy opponent for the Captain of the Imperial Guard.'

'Oh,' said the cavalry officer, 'we had that checked out of courth. Thinth you *have* been promoted – though only wizardth know how or why – then you are eligible to be thkewered. Afterwardth we'll thend your thkin to the Hannackth.'

Kaff came over to speak now. 'It was my belief that you were flat on your stomach and couldn't get up. That's why you're late.'

Soldier raised his eyebrows. 'You mean that little whipping yesterday? Why, that was nothing. My wife soon soothed away any slight pain I might have felt from that minor drubbing.'

A thunderous look came to Kaff's eyes. 'Your wife?'

'Yes. Princess Layana and I had a belated wedding celebration yesterday evening – a matrimonial feast – didn't you get an invitation? How remiss of us. I do apologise.'

The captain ground his teeth.

'I have just come from a warm nuptial bed,' added Soldier, provocatively. 'I was, I must admit, tempted to remain, but my bride insisted that I go out and defend my honour against that – how did she put it? – that po-faced hog.'

'Are you calling me a pig?'

'I'm merely repeating my wife's words.'

Kaff shook his head. 'She would never say that. I don't believe you've come from her bed. May those words turn to ashes in your mouth and choke you. She told me she never wanted to set eyes on you again. Her only reason for marrying you and saving you from death was *pity*. Compassion for a poor pathetic animal trapped by circumstances. You could just as well have been a sparrow caught in a blizzard, or a wild hare with a wire noose around its neck. She has a benevolent nature when it comes to wretched creatures. Men of my stamp do not. We would just as soon put such creatures out of their misery.'

'Musk, sandalwood and ambergris,' replied Soldier, infuriated by this man's arrogance. 'I'm sure the mix of those three together remind you of someone dear to both of us.'

Absolute fury swept across Kaff's features.

'I'm going to gut you like a fish,' he hissed.

Velion spoke at last. 'You will not, captain. You will observe the duelling code. That's what *I'm* here for.'

Kaff looked irritated. 'Who is this person?' he demanded.

'My second,' replied Soldier. 'She's a warrior with the red pavilions.'

'I can see that. She's not an officer.'

'Is that essential?' Soldier asked. 'I think not.'

'Come on, come on!' cried the cavalry officer. 'Let'th get to it. The thun is climbing the heaventh.'

'Thow it ith,' Velion agreed.

She received a glare from the cavalry officer and threw a smirk in return.

A red kerchief was dropped on the green turf and the duel began. At first both combatants were tentative with one another, circling and feinting. Gradually, as they believed they got the measure of their foe, they began more serious attacks at the body and head. It was clear to all who watched that Kaff would not be content with wounding his opponent. The imperial guard officer was going for the head. Soldier, on the other hand, was attacking the bigger target of the torso.

At one point in the silent but furious double-onslaught, Kaff tripped in a rat hole on the bank. He went sprawling backwards. There was a gasp from his fellow officers as they saw he was at the mercy of his opponent. A groan came from Velion however, as Soldier stepped back, dropping his guard, and allowed the other officer to get to his feet again.

'What's this,' hissed Velion. 'You had him!'

Soldier gave a brief shake of his head.

Blades clashed again noisily in the dawn, interrupting the songs of the birds. The fight continued, swaying back and forth, until Kaff thought he saw a real opening. Abandoning his guard he stepped forward to decapitate Soldier. His blade came swishing across horizontally, just above the level of Soldier's shoulders. There was a sharp intake of breath from the watchers as they anticipated the kill. It seemed, in that frozen moment, that Soldier had no chance of parrying the blow.

But Soldier had untapped skills learned in another life. Instinctively he skipped sideways. His sword moved with the speed of a snake. The blade came up, vertically, to protect the side of his neck under attack. Honed metal edge met flesh, but it was something slimmer than a neck. Instead of a beheading, there was a clean slice through a limb joint. Kaff's arm suddenly felt very light. His momentum made him swing right through, so that he spun on his feet.

Losing his balance Kaff toppled drunkenly down onto the turf. He landed heavily right next to another object which had dropped to the ground just a moment before. Kaff blinked as he stared at this grotesque thing, which he saw was a hand severed at the wrist, still gripping the hilt of a sword. It was a few seconds before he recognised the jewellery on the third finger of the hand to be his own signet ring. Still in a kind of daze he raised his right arm up to see that the hand was missing. Blood spurted from the raw wound at the end. Then his comrades came to life, rushed in on him, staunched the blood with a towel.

Pale and unsteady Kaff was helped to his feet. He stared at Soldier. 'You bastard,' he croaked. 'My sword arm.'

'Better your sword arm than my head,' replied the unrepentant Soldier. 'Perhaps you'll think better of having a man whipped publicly in the street next time.'

The cavalry officer stepped forward and slapped Soldier across the jaw, clearly issuing another challenge. The blow stung but Soldier was not going to be goaded.

'No, no, I'm not going to fight every damn one of you, until finally you *do* have my head. Go and find someone else to bully. I've had my fill of all of you.'

The officer's hand came up to strike him again, but this time Soldier caught it and slammed his fist into the cavalry officer's face. The man went reeling back, his nose spouting almost as much blood as Kaff's wrist.

'You thwine!' screamed the cavalry officer, almost choking on his own juices. 'I thould kill you now!'

But there was a sense of honour amongst his comrades, who held him back. They saw the need to get their wounded friend to a physician. Someone picked up the hand and the sword, wrapped them in a cloak, and then they assisted Kaff towards the castle gates.

Velion heaved a sigh of relief. She had been gripping her own sword, expecting the group of Guthrumite officers to turn on them.

'Well, I thought we'd have to fight our way out of that one. Now what are you going to do? He's the Captain of the Imperial Guard!'

'And I'm the husband of the queen's sister. Now that my marriage has been consummated I shall be taken more seriously. He won't dare move against me here again. If he's going to kill me now he'll have to do it surreptitiously, or out on some remote battlefield, away from witnesses.'

'Well, watch your back, Soldier.'

Soldier smiled and clamped a hand on Velion's shoulder, looking straight into her eyes.

'Thank you for coming today, Velion.'

'Well, it was short notice,' she said, 'but it was worth the effort of getting out of bed early. Now I've got to get back. I'm on duty later. You look after yourself, Soldier.'

'I intend to.'

They parted, he walking towards the city and she going back to the red pavilions.

The raven came down to mock Soldier.

'Well, I hope you're happy with yourself. I saw that. You nearly lost your topknot.'

'Yes, but I didn't, did I?'

'Next time I'll be picking out your bonny blue eyes with my beak, reluctantly of course, but why let them go to waste?'

'There won't be a next time, if I can help it.'

'He'll practise with his left hand and then challenge you again.'

Soldier grimaced. 'He can challenge all he wants, I shan't bite. I've had enough of this rivalry. Now, what have you heard of the witchboy and his mother Uthellen? Are they safe?'

The raven wiped his beak on Soldier's tunic and then said, 'Nothing. They seem to have disappeared off the face of the earth.'

Soldier nodded. 'No doubt she's in hiding again. Her son is still vulnerable. Once he's fully grown and a wizard in his own right he'll be able to defend himself, but until then those who hunt him will find him easy prey.'

'If the woman is to be believed.'

'What do you mean by that, raven?'

'I mean, perhaps there isn't anyone hunting the boy? Perhaps she has other reasons for remaining out of sight?'

Soldier shrugged. 'And what might they be?'

'If I knew I wouldn't be placing doubts in your mind, would I? I'd be giving you the facts.'

'Well, I think you're wrong, raven. There's nothing sinister about Uthellen.'

The raven was not so sure. 'Everyone distrusts witchboys, even if they are about to grow into wizards. And by extension that means you should not trust a witchboy's mum. She would sell her soul for her only child, any mother would.'

'What do you know, you're a bird!'

The raven clicked its beak. 'I'm only a bird on the outside. Inside I'm a boy too. But a *real* boy. A human, not like that creature which Uthellen gave birth to. Let's face it, wizards are a different kind of creature from men altogether. You can never fully trust them. There's no real heart in their chests: just a piece of rock. The King Magus is not there to ensure that the world is a happy place to live in, but to maintain the right *balance* between good and evil. If he's so concerned about us all, why doesn't he wipe out wickedness for good so everyone can live in peace and harmony?'

Soldier said, 'If you don't have evil, you can't have good, it's as simple as that. Without one the other is meaningless. Do you want to live in a meaningless world? There will always be wickedness, it's a law of the universe. What we have to ensure is that it doesn't grow beyond certain limits. We have to keep it bottled, be ever vigilant. Without evil you can't have heroes, or philanthropists, or knights in shining armour.'

'Who needs 'em? Why not just graze on the delights of a

life with no worries? In any case, there's enough world disasters for anyone who wants to be a hero. Earthquakes, floods,
fires: they're all out there. Go and be a hero by saving someone
from a fire. But that's not what satisfies, is it, Soldier. What
satisfies is pitting yourself against another man – or woman
– and winning. It's the competitor in you that would suffer
with universal peace. That's what you wouldn't be able to
stomach: having no mortal enemies, no rivals.'

'Nonsense,' said Soldier, uncomfortably. 'The world needs
divergence. Our spirits need legends and myths to feast on.
Without wickedness to combat there can be neither. It is *inside*
us we must conquer. There are the vast tracts of land, chasms
and mountains within us which must be crossed. Without
unreachable goals, without insurmountable tasks, how can
the men and women make that journey within themselves,
find their true worth, reach the destination which is their
soul?'

'You're very eloquent today, for a military footslogger.'

'So are you,' said Soldier, suspiciously. 'Are you sure you're
my raven and not a wizard in disguise?'

'Just because I was a street urchin, it doesn't make me
ignorant. As a raven I can sit in on the counsel of sages,
priests and scholars. What's your excuse?'

The raven made a raspberry noise with its tongue, before
flying off. Its sudden departure was partly because Soldier
was being approached by two men. They were members of
the imperial guard. Soldier's hand immediately went to his
sword, thinking that another fight was imminent. The two
guards blocked his path and one acted as spokesmen for both.

'Queen Vanda wishes to see you.'

Soldier was startled. 'See *me*?'

'Yes. You must come with us,' said the second guard.

'Whoa, wait a minute. How do I know you're from the queen? This morning I duelled with your captain and cut off his hand. You could be trying to lure me into a trap.'

The news of their captain was so profoundly shocking it registered on their faces. Soldier knew the news was a surprise to them. Still, he had to be very careful.

'What does the queen want with me?'

'How would we know?' said the first guard. 'We're not privy to the queen's secrets.'

'All right. I'll come with you. But you walk in front.'

The two guards turned and marched towards the Palace of Birds. Soldier followed. One the guards said over his shoulder, 'Did you really duel with Captain Kaff?'

'Yes.'

'And you sliced off his hand?'

'Yes.'

The guards did not pursue the matter any further. Once they were outside the room in which the queen sat, they left him without giving him their opinion on the incident. He might have guessed, reasonably accurately, what their thoughts were on the subject. However, there was little he could do to gather men like these on his side. They were Kaff's men, through and through, and would always be so.

The doors to the court opened. There stood before Soldier a small pasty-faced man in silken robes. He had large hands poking through the mandarin sleeves. With one of these he beckoned, the other he held palm up, indicating that Soldier should remain standing where he was. Soldier did not know whether to step forward or turn and go.

'I am Humbold, the queen's chancellor,' said the man in soft, deep tones. 'The queen wishes to speak to you. Come in, fall on your face, and allow the queen to address you without interrupting her. If you attempt to move or speak before you are told otherwise, you will be executed on the spot. If she asks you a question, you are bound to reply. You will address the queen as "Your Highness". Am I understood?'

Chapter Fifteen

Suddenly there was a white wind.

A blast hit the side wall of the palace. Cold air howled through the open windows on the landing outside the court to freeze those inside. Soldier gasped for breath. The guards outside the court and those visible just inside the doorway all reeled with the shock of the wind. The doors to the court slammed shut with the force of the squall, separating Soldier and Chancellor Humbold from those still inside. Torches in the dark hallways were instantly snuffed. Some robes hanging on hooks were swept away like ghosts along the passageway. The slamming sounds continued, throughout the palace, as open doors crashed shut. One or two startled screams were heard.

Outside, the air was a whirlwind of crashing ice. In the courtyard below, Soldier could see that the leaves were frozen on the branches of their trees as if they were made of thin glass. Plants stood as stiff as stone, glittering in the fading light with white crystals of frost. The fountain and its cascades were frozen in movement: water had become marble. Fish caught in the pools were locked inside blocks of ice.

They were still alive and stared out with wide eyes at the wintry world. Icicles grew like quick beards from sill and gutter. Snow began to fall in large soft flakes to cover the palace grounds.

'What was that?' cried Soldier, transfixed with fear. 'Has the world exploded?'

Darkness was now creeping across the land. It swept in like a cloud of fine soot to fill the heavens. Within a few minutes the landscape was white below a dark, heavy sky. This was not the darkness of night, but the darkness of winter days. It was a darkness with soft edges which faded into whiteness where it met the snow. Birds fell from the roof, past the windows, as they were chilled to near death. They dropped like stones to the courtyard below and, wounded by the fall, remained there as fluttering balls of feather. A whole swarm of starlings caught flying over the palace met a wall of sleet moving across the landscape and were hammered out of the air. They rained past the windows to join those who had dropped from the roof. The snow was pockmarked where iced-over bees and wasps zipped into it like small pebbles flung from a slingshot.

'What is it?' asked Soldier, shivering in his thin clothes and plate armour. 'What's happened?'

'Winter,' said Humbold. 'It comes suddenly these days.'

'But why?'

'For the same reason that unnatural things are happening in the world – the King Magus is dying. It's a slow business, the death of a wizard. Someone who has lived seven hundred years is not going to leave the world quickly.'

Soldier huddled, wrapping his arms around himself, trying to keep warm.

'Why doesn't he hurry up and get it over with?'

'Who amongst us does not want as many more seconds of life as we can possibly grasp? He doesn't want to die and will cling on to this world as long as possible. The death of a wizard is a shocking thing. There is no afterlife. Dust and bones are all that remain, the spirit having withered with the body. This is all he has and he won't let it go without a struggle.'

Humbold suddenly remembered the queen. 'We must go in,' he said. 'Don't forget my previous instructions.' Looking at Soldier's weapon the chancellor confirmed, 'Is your sword hilt tied to your thigh?'

'Yes.'

'Good.'

Humbold then ordered the doors to be opened. He entered first, followed by Soldier, who immediately fell on his face.

The queen, sitting on her throne a long way down the room, called to him.

'Where are you from, Soldier?'

'I know not, your majesty,' said Soldier into the cold tiles of the floor.

'What is your real name?'

'My true identity is a secret even to me.'

'Have you come here from another country – or another place altogether?'

'Your majesty, I wish I could answer these questions, but I cannot. I am as ignorant as anyone else on these matters. I desperately wish to know who and what I am, where I come from, who was my father and mother, where my country lies . . .'

The queen interrupted with, 'Come closer, Soldier.'

'You may rise,' hissed Humbold, 'and move to within three body lengths of the queen. There you will again prostrate yourself.'

Soldier did as he was told.

He was left lying there on the frozen mosaic floor for an age, while he heard courtiers and others talking with the queen around him. He seemed to be the only one kissing marble. Finally the queen ordered him to his feet. He rose and kept what he felt was a deferential pose before the throne.

'You may look up, into my face.'

He did so, and beheld a woman whose features resembled those of his wife, Layana. Queen Vanda's looks were more severe and plainer than those of Layana, but they were clearly close blood relatives. She seemed less yielding in nature than Layana – more formal and stern – as befitted a queen, the ruler of a country which had once had an empire. Soldier decided she could be cruel and unfeeling if required, and he was worried now, wondering why he had been summoned.

The queen was dressed simply. There were no crowns or jewels dripping from her form. She carried no mace or orb or any gem-encrusted symbol of her office. A purple dress with a white fur-lined cloak was what clothed her. Soldier suspected that before the winter blast had hit the palace the cloak had been hanging on some hook in a wardrobe. Other courtiers and soldiers in the room had also been supplied with cloaks. Only he and Humbold were without some sort of overcovering.

'Are you a rogue wizard?'

'Your majesty, if I were I would not be in so much trouble, unable to enchant my way out of it. I have never met a rogue wizard, but I'm sure he would have more power of personality that I own. He would have great magnetism. He would have unfathomable charisma. You see before you a humble mortal, with no pretensions to wizardry.'

'Having met you at last, I believe you. I hear you have

become my sister's third husband,' said the queen. 'That makes me your sister-in-law.'

He had not thought of this and his mind raced. He was about to say something when he suddenly remembered Humbold's warning about not speaking unless he was answering a question. Had there been a question? Or was it simply a statement? Soldier glanced towards Humbold, hoping to find some encouragement, or otherwise. There was nothing. The chancellor's face was bland.

'Soldier, do you love your wife?'

Definitely a question. 'More than my own life.'

Humbold rolled his eyes heavenward, not because he was nauseated by Soldier's declaration of ardour, but because Soldier had forgotten to use the formal address to the queen. Soldier made a mental note to ensure it did not happen again.

'Yet you have only known her some few hours. I hear you consummated your marriage last night. Then my sister lost her reason in the early hours. Is that correct?'

News obviously travelled fast in Guthrum.

'Yes, your majesty.'

'Do you not find my sister ugly?'

'Her scars, your majesty? They mean nothing to me. In my eyes Layana is the most beautiful woman in the world.'

There was a raising of royal eyebrows. 'Even more beautiful than her sister, the queen?'

A hush came over the court and the rustling of clothes, all other sounds, ceased as the queen waited for his answer.

'In my eyes,' Soldier said, firmly, 'the queen's beauty is unsurpassed . . .' a relieved sigh went through the room '. . . except by that of my dear wife.'

The sigh turned to a moan of horror.

The queen pursed her lips and narrowed her eyes.

'What kind of man . . .' began Soldier, but Humbold whispered to him, 'Be quiet, you fool! You have been asked no question.' Soldier would not be put off. 'What kind of man would I be if love did not blind me? I am a new husband, still caught in the heat of fresh love. Would you have a husband for your sister who was not completely enthralled by everything about her, including her beauty, your majesty?'

'Are you saying she has put you under some kind of spell?'

'I am under her spell,' Soldier admitted, 'and will be to the end of my days. She has bewitched me, not with magic, but with love. Would it be right for me to yearn after my wife's sister's beauty? I think not, even were such beauty attainable for a common man such as myself. It would be entirely inappropriate. Therefore, your majesty, I *must* consider my wife to be incomparable, for hidden dangers lie elsewhere.'

'You believe her to be more beautiful than me because it is expedient to do so.'

'No – because it is impossible for me to do otherwise. I am overwhelmed by passion and blinded to all other women, be they queens or maid-servants. I am totally in love with my wife, who has me in her thrall every waking hour. Every other citizen in the land believes you to be the most beautiful woman in the world, your majesty. I stand alone in my opinion and therefore in the great scheme of things my opinion is worthless.'

Queen Vanda smiled at this. 'You have a silver tongue, Soldier. Apparently not just a brute who kills and maims other warriors in war. Not just a skilled swordsman who cripples my Imperial Guard Captains.'

Was that what all this was about? If the queen had taken against him because of Kaff, he was lost.

'I have summoned you here,' continued the queen, 'to ask

of you a favour. I give you a quest. To go out into the world and seek the cure of my sister's madness, which I also share. We do not always fall out of reason at the same time, my sister and I, but our illnesses have the same root. Our mother was cursed by a wizard and that curse has come down to us. I would ask you to go out and seek the wizard who placed the curse, make him remove it. What say you, Soldier? Will you accept?'

'With all my heart and head, your majesty.'

'Good. I have already sent a message to the Carthagans. They will release you from their army for an indefinite period. You have our blessing. There are wizards in the western mountains. Go and seek one of them, and force or persuade him to lift the spell which has been placed on my father's line. You may take an assistant with you, as your squire and helpmate. Do you have anyone you trust?'

Soldier considered first Uthellen, then Velion, but finally settled on Spagg. He would not trust Spagg as far as he could throw the queen's palace, but he did not want to put the others in danger. Uthellen, even if he could find her, had her son to look after. Velion was a better choice, but the unworthy Spagg was much more expendable than the Carthagan warrior. No, Spagg it had to be, and with the queen's commission behind him, the market trader would not be able to refuse.

'I have someone in mind, your majesty.'

'Then go, Soldier, and good luck.'

Soldier backed out of the court with his head lowered, followed by Humbold. Once he was outside the Palace of Birds, Soldier hurried through the snow to the Palace of Wildflowers. There he discovered his wife was still rapt in madness and he was advised not to see her. He was given a thick cloak to wear and, after telling Drissila and Oafo about the task the queen had given him, he went forth to seek the market trader, Spagg.

In the market-place the people were huddled together, trying to clear the snow from their stalls. The sudden onslaught of midwinter had caught them unawares. They were frozen to the marrow, bad-tempered, and not inclined to answer questions. However, one woman finally turned her red nose towards her questioner, and told him where Spagg was residing.

'As soon as winter comes,' she sniffed, 'he scuttles away, to the Temple of Theg, to become an apprentice priest, a learner.'

'A novitiate?'

'Yes, one of them things. They take 'im in every winter, whether it comes once, twice or three times a year, the fools, thinkin' he's going to go all the way and become a proper priest. It lasts 'im until spring comes, then he waves goodbye to 'em and comes out here and starts his stall up again. He's a fickle one, that Spagg, but he's not daft. They have coal braziers in the temple, always lit, and he's kept warm by 'em until the winter snow and ice has gone.'

'You have more than one winter a year?' queried Soldier in surprise.

'Spaddle me stressups, yes. We've 'ad as many as six. Three years ago, it was, we 'ad six. Bit unusual that, though. Normally it's two or three. Course, they don't last long. A month or two, sometimes three. Sudden they come, sudden they go. We've got a sayin' in Guthrum – if you don't like the weather, wait a minute.'

Soldier took his leave from the hag and, after obtaining directions, made his way to the Temple of Theg. When he got there the priests at the entrance wouldn't let him in. They told him ordinary citizens could only enter on religious feast days – and then only holidays to do with Theg. He was told that there were maidens inside who had to be protected, or the corn would wither on the stalk and the apples would shrivel on the tree.

'The harvest is dependent upon their virginity. For every virgin lost a field of turnips will rot. For every maiden who goes astray an almond tree will die. For every chaste girl who falls a grape vine will choke at the roots. A soldier like you might think to slake his lust on the nubile young women behind these pillars, for they are most comely.'

The priest licked his lips as if anticipating a very tasty meal once this stranger was out of sight.

'And you let men like Spagg enter?' he questioned.

These temple priests all wore green robes, tall green hats and green sandals made from raffia, and this one was no exception. Green was Theg's colour. He was the agrarian god and was responsible for all things to do with plants and the soil. He was also very passionate about racing horses, and so equestrian activities came under him rather than under Kist, the goddess who loved all animals except human beings, whom she despised.

'Spagg? I don't think we have a Spagg here.'

'I'm told he is here. He's a novitiate.'

'Oh,' the priest's face clouded over. 'The market trader who sells hanged men's hands. We are just about at the end of our tether with that one. It seems to us that he's using us, simply to escape the winter. And between me and you, I don't altogether trust him with the temple virgins.'

'No, really?'

'Yes indeed. Have you come to arrest him for something? It wouldn't surprise me in the least.'

'I need him for the queen's business.'

'Ah,' nodded the priest, as if this confirmed his ideas on the subject. 'I'll send for him.'

Another, younger, priest was despatched. He disappeared into the dark portals of the Temple of Theg, where timid young women roamed in herds, their guardians ever watchful for the wolf that might descend on the fold. He soon returned with a green-garbed Spagg in tow. As soon as Spagg saw that it was Soldier who was waiting, he attempted to retreat back into the temple. However, the priests were not about to let this man have sanctuary. They dragged him back out again and threw him at Soldier's feet.

'Spare me, Soldier!' cried Spagg, throwing his arms over his head to protect it. 'I'm sorry I betrayed you.'

'Get up,' ordered Soldier, embarrassed by this unseemly display. 'You are to accompany me on a quest. I need someone to handle the horses and do the chores.'

Spagg's face took on a crafty expression and his tone changed immediately to one of defiance.

'Go outside Zamerkand? I won't do it.'

'The queen herself orders it.'

Spagg climbed to his feet and dusted himself off. His expression was miserable now. He seemed to be able to change character at a moment's notice.

'The queen? Where are we going then? Not north? I couldn't go north. The beast-people would kill us before we got further than ten leagues.'

'No, not north.'

'Nor east, I hope, because that's where the Hannack tribes live. The Hannacks would have our skins in ten seconds if we showed up there. Please say it's not east.'

'It's not east.'

'Oh! Oh!' cried Spagg. 'It's south, isn't it? We're going to have to take a boat over the Cerulean Sea, to Gwandoland, aren't we? I shall die. I get sea-sick near to death. Please say we're not going on a boat.'

'We're not going on a boat.'

The priests were enjoying this interchange and one or two of the braver vestal virgins were poking their heads around the pillars of the inner temple, enjoying the entertainment.

Soldier said, 'We're going west.'

'West?' wailed Spagg. 'To the holy mountains? To the hallowed valleys? The Sacred Seven will have us on toast. Oh, please say we're not going west.'

'We're going west.'

The priests stood with folded arms and laughed.

Spagg began to fall into a rage.

'I won't go, I tell you, even if the queen orders it. I *refuse* to go. Find somebody else. I'll just fall on the ground, here, in a fit. You can't drag away a sick man. I'll get the populace to rise up against you. They'll lynch you from the eves of the nearest house. I have some standing in the community, you know, the market-traders' guild will support me . . .'

Soldier was growing weary. He drew his sword. The sound of it sliding from its sheath startled the priests and they backed away quickly.

'Be quiet, Spagg,' ordered Soldier in a soft, menacing voice. 'If you say another word, I'll cut off your head. Just follow me through the streets.'

Spagg did as he was told, scuttling after Soldier, who strode out.

Unknown to the queen, in Humbold's private employ was a magician by the name of Pugorchoff. In truth, Pugorchoff was more of a poisoner than a magician. He did indulge in a little magic, on odd occasions, but his real talents lay with virulent plants and their effects on the human nervous system. Pugorchoff could paralyse a man for two minutes, an hour, a day, forever. He could learn the truth from a reluctant man's lips within quarter of an hour, as that man lay dying. He could lock a man in his own body, make it appear as if that man were dead, and have him buried alive. Pugorchoff could kill a man stone dead within seconds by scratching his skin with a treated thorn. In short, his knowledge of poisonous plants and fungi meant that he could kill with ease, from near, or from far off, depending upon the wishes of his client.

At the very time Soldier was visiting the Temple of Theg, Humbold was in Pugorchoff's chambers. They were sitting on a silk-cushioned couch which had been a gift to the magician.

The chancellor told his magician, 'I need to ensure that a man never returns from a hunt.'

'A hunt?'

'Well, from his travels.'

The magician asked, 'Where is this man going?'

'Perhaps beyond the mountains.'

Pugorchoff's figure followed the same contours as his nose: long, thin and arrogant.

'Then why worry, Chancellor? He won't come back anyway.'

Humbold nodded. 'It's true he's going into perilous country, but this particular person seems to have several lives. Can you find me a deadly poison and devise a way to administer it, which would kill him when he's many leagues from the city? I don't want him dying on our doorstep. I'd rather he was in some dark, dank forest where his bones will sink into the mire and be lost and forgotten forever.'

'Is he really as dangerous as all that?'

'I don't know. He's appeared out of nowhere and already has the ear of the queen. I have certain plans which I would prefer not to be disturbed.'

The magician nodded. He went to the wall behind the couch and lifted an agate lamp standing in a window niche. A stone door suddenly swung open in the wall. Pugorchoff stepped through this into the room beyond, which Humbold knew was full of bottles of poison, darts, knives, needles, and a multitude of devices for injecting the concoctions produced in that room. Some poisons, of course, simply needed to be breathed, their perfumes lethal gases. Others could be administered by smearing on the skin and would kill through the pores in one's body. One could sniff a rose, or take a bath, and be dead within the hour.

Pugorchoff had murdered men with envelopes, the glue (when licked) releasing a fatal toxin which after several days peeled a person's skin from their flesh, allowing them to die in terrible raw-nerved pain. He had killed a husband, yet kept the wife alive, by lacing the woman's rouge, the poison only taking effect when the victim kissed her cheek and orally imbibed the venom. Wearing gloves he had shaken hands with men who had died of a fatal dose of ratsbane a short while afterwards. One of his favourites was a pillow which, once the head warmed it, killed a man in his sleep with the noxious fumes it released. Another was a seemingly harmless marsh mist which burned into a man's eyes, the toxicant raising the temperature of his blood to such a heat that he literally boiled from inside his own body.

'Will this do?' asked the magician, returning to the

chambers after quite a long time, during which the chancellor had become increasingly impatient.

He held up a very handsome armoured tunic, the iron plates being sewn into the lining of a red velvet vest.

'How does it work?'

Pugorchoff explained that the brigandine was lined with thousands of needles, each as fine as a hair.

'Every needle has enough poison to kill a horse. The hairs will penetrate a shirt beneath like coarse wool. The wearer will be irritated by an itching, but by that time it will be too late. The tiny needles will have done the task. I made the whole thing myself, including the plates and the tunic.'

The chancellor admired the magician's handiwork. 'It's certainly a beautiful garment, one I wouldn't shun myself if I didn't know its deadly secret. That emblem, on the right breast?'

'Princess Layana's wildflower, her personal crest – a *white rock-rose* – I've just sewn it on. I'm sorry it took so long.'

'No, no, I quite understand,' replied the admiring chancellor. 'A brilliant touch. Brilliant. How can he refuse a gift bearing the crest of his wife? Personally, I've always thought her flower should be the *wild madder*.'

The magician let out a raucous laugh.

'Famous! Absolutely famous. Now let me tell you the scheme I've devised to ensure he only puts on the brigandine when he's out in hazardous country . . .'

Chapter Sixteen

Soldier spent three days preparing for his expedition, helped in part by Velion. Now that he was a paid mercenary he had money in his pocket. The campaign against the beast-people had provided him with enough to purchase two horses, one for himself and one for Spagg. He also bought a pack-mule which would be led by Spagg, the non-combatant, so that Soldier had his hands free in case they were ambushed. Soldier bought supplies for the pair of them and the animals. He seemed to know instinctively how to plan for an expedition.

Velion wanted to come with him, but Soldier wouldn't hear of it.

'You have your duties here,' said Soldier, now wearing a thick fur cloak and hat to protect him against the vicious Guthrum winter. 'There's no telling when I'll be back. Perhaps never. I don't want to be responsible for anyone but myself.'

'And Spagg?'

'He's expendable. He betrayed me.'

Velion shook her head. 'You're not of a very forgiving nature, are you, Soldier?'

'No.'

On the third day, the raven appeared, bringing news of Uthellen.

'She's in the dungeons,' said the raven. 'Below the gardens which separate the Palace of Wildflowers from the Palace of Birds.'

'Dungeons below a garden! What, do the prisoners gnaw on daffodil bulbs?'

'They gnaw on stale crusts and drink the water that runs down the walls,' replied the raven. 'They're starved. I barely escaped with my life. I would be roast raven now if I were a little slower on the wing.'

'How did you find them?'

'I heard something on the wind, in the rustling of the trees, and found a way in through the graveyard catacombs. I flew through the bars of a mausoleum, down through a crypt, and crawled through a rat hole in the wall between the vaults and the dungeons. It wasn't difficult. I can do it again, any time, if need be.'

Soldier left the horses and mule in Spagg's hands, first warning him that if he tried to abscond Soldier would hunt him down and kill him without a second thought.

'I have no interest in you except as a servant,' said Soldier. 'It would cause me no grief to stab you through the heart and then to quarter the body.'

Spagg, sullen and moody, said he understood the situation perfectly.

Soldier then went to the Lord of Thieftakers and obtained permission to visit the dungeons. His position as the husband of the queen's sister was opening all doors now. The entrance was in a gatehouse between the two palaces. Soldier went down into the depths of the earth with the raven on his shoulder. A jailer, a young woman with shifty eyes, led him through a maze of dark tunnels and passageways to the cell where Uthellen was being kept. The witchboy was with her. Soldier spoke to her through the barred window in the door.

'Are you all right?'

'Yes,' replied Uthellen.

'What crime did you commit? Why are you here?'

Uthellen shook her head. 'I had myself arrested on a minor charge. We no longer felt safe in the woods. Here at least we are protected by strong, windowless walls and an iron door.'

'On purpose?' He felt despair enter his heart for this young woman. 'How long will you stay here?'

'Until it's safe to leave. My son is growing stronger every day. He needs to be able to protect himself.'

The raven said, 'What if they're forgotten and are left to rot here forever? It happens all the time. Unless there are people on the outside to constantly petition the Lord of Thieftakers, no one will even bother to release them.'

Soldier repeated this to Uthellen and the boy.

The boy said, '*You* know we're here.'

'But something may happen to me. I might never return from my quest. You can't rely on someone like me. Look,' Soldier glanced about him, 'this raven can pick locks with its beak. I can send it to let you out if you wish. He gets in through the crypt which lies alongside these cells.'

'No,' answered the boy. 'We need to stay hidden.'

Then the strange young man stared around him at the walls and the floor. 'I wondered where that stinking fluid was coming from. I thought we were next to a sewer, but it's obviously bodily juices, seeping through the ceiling and walls from the dead in their graves. Mother, you'll get some foul dread disease down here, in these conditions. The kind of filthy sludge oozing corpses leak carries all sorts of plagues. I'll be all right on my own, I promise you.'

Uthellen shook her head. 'I've been in worse places. I'm staying with you, my son. There's no more to be said.'

Soldier shrugged. There was nothing more he could do for them.

'Goodbye to you both. I'll have some decent food sent down to you, before I leave.'

'Thank you, Soldier,' said Uthellen. 'You're a good man.'

'I don't think so.'

Turning to go Soldier saw that his jailer had left him to find his own way back to the upper world of the castle. With the raven on his shoulder he walked back in the direction he thought was the right one, along slippery-flagged passageways dimly lit by sputtering brands. Once or twice he accidentally touched the walls to find them running with slimy water. He recalled what the boy had said and shuddered, trying to remember not to put his fingers anywhere near his mouth.

'Are we going the right way?' he murmured.

'You're asking me? I'm a bird. Ask me the way around the treetops and I'll tell you at which bough to turn right and at which branch to turn left. What you want down here is a talking mole.'

'You came down here earlier, on your own.'

'Yes, but I made sure I kept strict note of the turns I made. I left that up to you, this time.'

Soldier grumbled, 'I thought the jailer would stay with us. When did she sneak away? I didn't notice her go.'

'That's because you were too busy making eyes at the woman.'

'That's not true. I have no interest in Uthellen. Not that kind of interest, anyway.'

Soldier wandered down tunnels which seemed to have no end, suddenly coming up against a stone wall, or a locked door, and having to go back, take yet another turning, until somehow they found themselves in a part of the dungeons which seemed older than the rest. Here the ancient brickwork was crumbling. There was rotting masonry at the base of the walls. Everything smelled dank and musty, as if the air had not been changed in half a century. The brands on the walls had gone. Soldier had to light some emergency tapers that he kept in his pocket in case he was ever caught in a dark street or room and needed light. They burned poorly in the bad air. Finally, he came up against a huge stone pillar.

He walked all the way around this pillar, some sixty paces, thinking it might be a circular room, but there were no doors or windows.

'What is this place?' Soldier questioned. 'We seem to be in the heart of the dungeons.'

'A circular cell,' answered the raven. 'A hollow stone.'

Soldier shook his head. 'How do you know?'

'Look closely. Can't you see the keyhole in the stone? There. *There*. In front of your nose. And if you look even closer you'll see a crack that goes off at right angles just above the height of your head. I'd say that was a door, wouldn't you?'

Under the light of his taper Soldier studied the rockface of the pillar and found the bird was right. There was a fine fissure which went too vertically straight, and then sharply off at too neat an angle, to be a natural crack in the rock. Also there was, as the raven had said, a strange hole cut into the pillar just waist high from the floor. It certainly looked as if it might be a round room with an entrance.

There was something about this circular cell which worried Soldier. He sensed a presence behind the door. In his mind's

eye a dark shape stood waiting for the door to open. It seemed
to Soldier this shape, this being, had been waiting a long time
for someone to come and release it. An unspoken command
was in Soldier's head, urging him to take some action. Soldier
was confused. He looked down at his hands and then searched
his pockets, looking for what he thought might be a key. The
urging grew stronger, firmer, with an underlying threat of
menace. Then Soldier remembered what the raven had told
him. He was just about to ask the bird to pick the lock with
its beak, when he heard scuffling and murmurs behind him.
Out of the gloom of one of the tunnels came two jailers.

'What are you doing here?' grumbled the woman who had
led them down into the catacombs. 'Leave you for a minute
and you disappear. You should have waited. It's taken ages
to find you again. Wasting our valuable time like this.'

'Sorry,' Soldier said. 'Who's in this cell, by the way?'

The male jailer held up his flaming brand and inspected
the pillar.

'Cell? Who said it was a cell? Don't look like one to me.
Looks just like a crosspaths.'

'Then what's it here for, this great thick pillar at the centre
of it all?'

'Holding the roof up?' suggested the man in a sarcastic
tone. 'I'm no engineer, but somethin's got to be there at the
junction of a crossways.'

'I suppose you're right,' answered Soldier.

'We're not supposed to be in this part of the dungeons,'
said the woman. She shivered, it seemed involuntarily. 'I don't
like it here. I get queer things happenin' in me head when I
come too close to these parts. Best to stay out, I say.'

She was reaching for her keys as she was talking and trying
them in the keyhole, one by one.

'What're you doing?' asked the male jailer.

The woman stopped and blinked several times. 'I dunno. Now, that's what I mean. It's a queer place. Let's get away from here. Come on, Soldier. You've no right to be here in the first place. Let's be gettin' you outside.'

Soldier went meekly enough, though there was a strong voice inside him, telling him to stay. The male jailer was becoming affected too, at this point, because he kept looking over his shoulder as they walked down the tunnels, away from the circular cell. The raven said nothing in the presence of these two jailers, but once he and Soldier were outside, he too confessed to a strong, silent call from within the stone pillar.

'Something's in there,' he said to Soldier, as they trudged through the snow. 'Something wants to get out.'

'Maybe we're just imagining things,' replied Soldier, unsure of the validity of his former concern now that they were out of the dungeons. 'I mean, nothing could live inside a sealed room, could it? There'd be no air to breathe, and how would they eat and drink?'

The raven said, 'There's such things as oubliettes, places where the Forgotten Ones are put — and forgotten.'

'Yes, but oubliettes are usually in the floors of feasting rooms, with grille covers, so that scraps of food can fall down to the prisoners below. It seemed to me that place was completely walled in. No one could live in a cell without light, air and succour. I think we're the victims of some sort of trick of the mind.'

They were passing under a gibbet at the time Soldier said this — an iron cage with the rotting remains of some criminal or unfortunate innocent hanging from a high arch above the cobbled street — and this had immediately attracted the attention of the fickle bird. The raven's empty stomach was more important than a puzzle. He could smell the delicious aroma of decomposing flesh and instead of answering he flew off, upwards, to enjoy a meal. Soldier walked off in disgust as the raven pulled at the rags covered the skeleton to uncover more of the meat on the bones.

Soldier first arranged with Ofao to have food and drink sent down to Uthellen and the witchboy.

'Make sure some goes down every few days,' he ordered the man-servant. 'They're friends of mine. I don't want them to starve while I'm away.'

Ofao assured Soldier he would do as he was asked.

Soldier then went looking for Spagg. He found him in a tavern. Spagg was half-drunk.

'I thought you'd gone an' lost yourself,' said the hand-seller. 'I *hoped* you had.'

'I'm sure you did. Sorry to disappoint you. Well, that still might happen. I'm going to try to see my wife for the last time, and if she doesn't manage to kill me then we're leaving the city at dawn. You'd better get a good night's sleep in a bed. You won't be seeing another one for a very long time.'

'Bastard,' muttered Spagg.

'Who knows?' replied Soldier, reflectively. 'Perhaps I am.'

Soldier went to the Palace of Wildflowers and was delighted to be told that his wife was out of her madness.

'It usually goes away within two or three days,' Drissila told him. 'She's waiting in the yellow room.'

Soldier was shown the way and he entered a large room with a great fireplace in which logs were burning. Layana stood with her good side to the door. A stranger walking in on her would not know that her other profile was ghastly to see.

When the princess saw that it was Soldier, she turned full-face, and Soldier winced, then cursed himself for doing so.

'You find me repulsive,' she said. 'I saw it in your expression.'

He saw no good in denying it. 'Forgive me. It was involuntary and unintentional. I hurt for you, my darling, that's all. I don't find you repulsive in any sense. How can I, when I love you so much?'

Layana was wearing a beautiful scarlet dress, which revealed her ivory shoulders and the swell of her breasts. There was a gold locket on a chain around her neck, which she fingered, as if enjoying its smooth feel. Her small white feet were bare on the cold stone floor. The princess, his wife, then gave him a strange wave of her free hand, as if dismissing what he said as so much fickle flattery.

'As to that,' she said, turning back to look in the fire, 'why, we've been through it all without any advantage.'

Soldier frowned and went forward, to try to take her in his arms, but she avoided him, deftly.

'What? What's that you said just a moment ago?' he asked. 'What did it all mean?'

She turned to face him again with pinched lips and hollow cheeks. Her eyes were surprising cold. 'It means we had our night of passion. Now it's over. Ah, I can see that troubles you? Well, don't let it. I don't love you in the least. It's over now. You may leave the city and go on your expedition in the knowledge that I don't care whether you live or die.'

He reeled on receiving these words. He felt sick to the very pit of his stomach.

'You can't mean that. You're still in the afterthroes of your madness. There is some foul residue of lunacy still clinging to your mind, making you say these things.'

She stared at him with clear eyes. 'I am perfectly sane.'

'But . . .'

'You must understand,' she said, giving him a grimace made to look even more sinister by her scarred features, 'I fall in and out of love all the time. I drop my heart at men's feet more times than my hunting hawk stoops after prey. That's the way it is with me. You're yesterday's meal – cold and very unappetising. I suggest you go on your quest and forget you ever knew me.'

If he were wearing armour with steel barbs inside the suit he could not have been more hurt.

'But – but the quest is *for* you – and your sister.'

'Then do it for my sister, but not for me. I couldn't care less. I probably won't be here when you return. I'm thinking of leaving myself. I don't know where to. Now, go.'

'You can't be so hard.'

'I can be as hard as I am, which is like stone, when I'm not interested in a man.'

Soldier was about to protest some more when the door opened and someone came in.

'You sent for me . . .' the person began to say, then stopped dead, halfway through his sentence.

Soldier turned to see Captain Kaff standing there. The man was clothed in outdoor furs, but Soldier could see that the stump of his right wrist was bound in bandages. The captain made a step forward, his face grim with hatred. Soldier's hand automatically went to his sword hilt, and then he remembered he had tied it back. Both men then stood, glaring at one another, until finally Soldier was the first to speak.

'What's *he* doing here?'

'I – I sent for him,' faltered Layana. Then she seemed to gather herself together. 'I don't have to answer to you, even if you are still my husband. If I feel like doing something, I do it.'

'This man is my enemy.'

She shrugged. 'That's nothing to me.'

Soldier was rigid with anger and hurt. He stared at her for a few moments more, then walked stiffly from the room, brushing past Kaff, who had a thin smile on his lips.

What Soldier did not see, as he strode out, was that Layana took a step towards him, her hand half-raised to stop him. Her eyes were full of hot, stinging tears and her mouth was open as if she was about to call to him. Then she changed her mind and let her hand fall to her side, her mouth closing. She walked back to the fireplace, and kicked at a red, flaming log in the grate with her bare foot, wincing as she was burnt. Her petulant action sent out a shower of sparks onto her dress.

They smouldered there, smoke rising, making tiny black holes in the scarlet fabric, until Kaff came to his senses and stepped forward quickly. He knelt before her to brush away the burning slivers of wood with his good left hand, which patted at her thighs and lower legs. She allowed him to do this service for her, though his touch was not welcome.

By the time he looked up, into her face, she was composed again, ready to issue orders to the captain.

Soldier and Spagg set off on their horses the next morning. Spagg had slept like the dead in his bed until Soldier had come noisily in and had begun flinging his armour and clothes about the room as he took them off. Even once Soldier was abed he had tossed and turned all night long, keeping the hand-seller awake as well. They clopped through the snow, Spagg leading the pack-mule towards the main gates. The breakfast of dried fish and corn meal had not been to Spagg's liking. His preferred fare in the morning was six rashers of grilled bacon and five fried eggs. The dried fish had caught in his throat and the corn meal porridge had been weak and watery.

'What was the matter with you last night?' grumbled Spagg. 'Banging and crashing in that bed of yours.'

'You keep a civil tongue in your head.'

'Grouchy, eh? What's all that about?'

Soldier said nothing for a few minutes, then he asked a question.

'What's the hardest rock in the world?'

Spagg shrugged. 'I don't know. Gneiss?'

'A woman's heart,' said Soldier, bitterly.

'Oh, so that's it? Wife trouble.'

Soldier reined in his mount and put his hand on his sword hilt.

'I swear your head will part with your shoulders before we go another mile.'

'Keep your hair on, keep your hair on,' cried Spagg. 'Excuse me for breathin'.'

But the hand-seller said no more and they continued on their way through the gates. Here the churned snow was a virulent yellow with animal dung and piss. Beyond lay the red pavilions like hot beacons on the white ground. Past the red pavilions were the slopes leading to the western mountains, covered in a crisp, white, untouched snow. The only things on these downs were wild animal and bird tracks which marked the snow like ciphers.

'Lieutenant!'

Soldier halted his mount and turned to see a man scurrying towards him from the direction of the two palaces. Hope leapt like a deer within him for a moment. Perhaps his wife, the Princess Layana, had had a change of heart? Perhaps she had been appalled by her treatment of him?

'Lieutenant,' the man said breathlessly, catching up with the two horsemen. 'I have a parcel for you!'

Indeed, to Soldier's disappointment, the man held out a bundle wrapped in calico and tied with ribbon.

'What is it? Who sent it?'

'The Princess Layana,' gasped the runner, gulping down more air. 'I am to give you the message that everyone, including the queen, wishes you to return safely. Under this calico wrapping is a brigandine of the finest red velvet with strong iron plates between the layers. It's an *enchanted* brigandine, which will protect you from all harm and will render you invulnerable when you wear it. However, there are specific instructions. The spell on this brigandine does not last forever, nor is it unlimited. Whenever you wear the armoured garment you will be using up the magic. Think of it as a candle burning down! It's best to wear it only in an emergency, when trouble is immediately at hand, that way the magic will last longer.'

Soldier untied the ribbon and let the calico fall away. Indeed, inside was the handsomest claret brigandine he had ever beheld, with his wife's flower sewn on the breast.

'The princess sent this?'

'Yes, Lieutenant.'

Soldier frowned. 'Was there no other message?'

The carrier stared for a moment as if lost.

'She is still of the same mind?' Soldier asked.

The errand-man nodded slowly. 'Yes,' he said.

'Then I don't want her damned present,' snapped Soldier, flinging the brigandine down in the snow.

The nervous messenger was horrified by this action.

'But – but – it was a gift.'

'A *parting* gift,' snarled Soldier.

Soldier realised how churlish he looked, flinging his wife's gifts onto the ground. He dismounted, picked it up and wrapped it once again. Then he tied the bundle to the pack-mule.

'Thank my wife very much,' said Soldier through clenched teeth, 'and tell her not to worry about me.'

'Oh, I don't think she'll worry,' said the ingenuous messenger, thinking to reassure the lieutenant, so that he would not go back and thank his wife personally, thus exploding the whole plot. 'I'm sure she's not worried about you at all.'

'I'm sure she isn't,' said Soldier, evenly.

With that, he remounted and spurred his charger, out through the gates of Guthrum castle. Once they were outside, the raven came to bid Soldier goodbye. 'I'll bring you news, if you like,' said the bird. 'News of what's going on in the castle.'

'Can you cover the distances? Can you fly that far?'

'I could fly into the maw of nowhere and back again, if I felt like it. Don't expect me, though. I'll come when I'm able, but I can't promise to be dependable. Birds aren't like that. We obey a whim, an impulse, but not a command. I'm season-able, but not timely. Some day, when the air feels right and the scent of the mountain pine is light enough to be carried on the back of the wind, I'll land on your shoulder.'

Chapter Seventeen

Soldier rode out across the snow with bitter feelings in his heart. It was a winter world outside and a winter world within. He set his face against the freezing wind. So, he had been nothing but a plaything to her! Well, he could be strong, he could withstand rejection and go on. One day she would suffer as he was suffering now – he hoped – and have her heart broken like a glass bowl. Right at this moment, he hated her. If she had been within sword's length, he told himself, he would have no hesitation in running her through with Xanandra.

Then he let out a terrible sigh. His heart fell like a heavy stone into some deep, deep well-shaft within him, to which there seemed no bottom. Of course he could not hurt her. Of course he loved her. How could he deny these feelings by trying to coat them with a shell of hate? He knew, deep down, that he would always love her.

'If you're not going to use that enchanted brigandine, why don't you let me have it,' said Spagg. 'I couldn't care less whether you get killed, but I'm a bit more partic'lar about me.'

Soldier flung the parcel at his companion.

'Here, take it. It's tainted.'

Spagg caught the bundle, which nearly took him off his saddle with its weight.

'Cor, you really have got it bad, ain't you?'

Soldier did not reply. He walked his horse on, the sound of the hooves muffled by the thick snow. This was still falling in large, soft flakes, drifting down from some cold heaven no longer visible to the riders. Aloft the sky was a low, hazy slab of marble. Beneath the landscape had been covered by white calico, had hidden its face as if it had something of which to be ashamed.

They rode all day, without a break, much to Spagg's disgust. He kept complaining that he was hungry, but Soldier took no notice of him at first. Finally, after many protestations, Soldier shouted at him, 'You'll eat when you're told you can.'

'All right, all right, I didn't realise I was riding with an emperor.'

In the evening they stopped at a wood, finding shelter amongst the trees. Soldier made a bivouac for the pair of the them, laid birch twigs over the snow beneath until they were protected from the cold ground. In the meantime Spagg cleared a patch in the meadow opposite the wood, so that the horses could graze on the grass beneath. When that was done he made a fire and put some water on to boil. All the while he was looking around him, nervously, as if he expected an attack. Then he began searching amongst the rotten logs which lay on the greenwood floor, beneath the trees.

'What's the matter with you?' asked Soldier, with some irritation. 'There're no Hannacks in this direction, are there? What are you looking for?'

'Hannacks is everywhere, but I'm not worried about them.'

'What then?'

'Drots,' answered Spagg. 'I hate 'em. There's a fungus you can rub on your skin, to repel 'em, but I can't find none.'

'Then none we shall have and the drots will come.'

And come they did, after the darkness fell, and the fire had died to embers. Soldier swatted the tiny winged creatures with his hands, trying to knock them off his shoulders. He kept hearing crunching sounds, followed by a crackle and hiss from the fire. He looked to where Spagg was fighting his own battle with the parasites. He was disgusted to see that Spagg was snatching the miniature human-shaped creatures from his body and biting off their heads, throwing the fluttering-winged bodies into the glowing logs. The fire grew brilliant as the gossamer wings flared. Spagg spat the heads into the coals too. He seemed to gain great satisfaction from his efforts.

'That's repulsive,' said Soldier.

'No more repulsive than blood-suckin',' argued his companion with some rationality. 'You see, they're not on me no more. They're all on you.'

It was true, Soldier was crawling with the creatures. He grabbed one and held it close to view it. In the light of the flames from the fire he could see a little human face with burning eyes like fiery pinpricks. The creature looked quite charming, just as a fairy should, until it opened its mouth and revealed the triple row of tiny sharp teeth. Soldier threw it away, quickly, and it took to the air, flying back immediately to sink its teeth in his neck.

'Damn it!' cried Soldier.

He began biting the heads off the creatures now, realising it was the only way to deter them.

'Mind they don't bite your tongue, when they're in your gob,' advised Spagg. 'You'll never get 'em off.'

When Soldier had disposed of a dozen of them, the others left. As with the last time Soldier had encountered the small creatures, there were one or two bloated ones which could not fly because they were so distended with blood. Spagg stepped on them and popped them, the blood showering the snow.

'We must get some of that fungus,' said Soldier. 'We can't have this every time we want to sleep in a woodland.'

When they were bedded down for the night, Soldier found he was uncomfortably close to the hand-seller, who stank of stale sweat and whose breath was rank. Still, there was nothing else for it, if they were to stay warm. He realised he was going to have to put up with these inconveniences.

'Aren't there any *good* fairies in Guthrum?' asked Soldier, irritably. 'Are these drots the only ones?'

'Why, no, there's good 'uns too, but you don't see 'em very often. Why should you? There's nothin' we've got that they want. Fairies is essentially selfish creatures. They ain't interested in anythin' that's not to their advantage.'

'A bit like market sellers, eh?'

'Uncalled for, Soldier. Uncalled for.'

In the middle of the night the darkness was the deepest. Soldier found some comfort in this. He had never been afraid of the dark as some people were. He found its velvety cloak warm and comforting. He was safer in the blackness than he was in the light or twilight, when monsters were abroad. Black was good. Black was not just one colour, it was all the colours of an artist's paintbox mixed together. He knew this, having tried it once when he was a child, stirring up red, blue, yellow, green, pink, mauve, brown, purple, to a thick paste. Black. Black had always given good service, was dependable, reliable.

Sometime, while he was half-awake, half-asleep, Soldier heard the wolves howling a word. The sound was distorted by the distance and the echoing hills, but somehow he knew they were calling his real name. Sadly, and painfully, their hollow cries mingled with the sound of the wind in the trees, and he could not quite understand what they were saying.

In the morning it was Soldier who woke first, the heavy lumpy form of Spagg still snoring into the dawn.

Soldier rose, and in his underwear (though wearing his sword) went in search of water. He trod through the snow, his clothed feet getting wetter and wetter. His breath came out as sprigs of steam. Overhead the branches of the trees were heavily-laden with last night's snowfall, ready to drop on his shoulders. Deer tracks were everywhere. He actually saw one, skipping between tree trunks, and wished he had brought a weapon with him. Spagg would not have complained at venison for breakfast.

Soldier found a pond deep in a thicket not far from their bivouac. It was beset with dwarf elders standing like crooked old men around the edge of the ice. The ice layer was not especially thick. There were white air pockets in it, along with clusters of twigs and leaves which had fallen from above. Soldier smashed the ice with a broken branch, only to find the water unsuitable to drink. It would do for the horses though.

As he broke more of the surface ice with his makeshift club, Soldier thought he saw something at the bottom of the green water beneath. It looked like two gold coins shining. Fascinated, as any man is with finding gold, he began poking about with the branch. It was not long enough, so he found a willow pole and began stirring with that. He thought, still in his underwear and shivering hard, if there were two gold coins, there might be more. What he did not wonder about was the fact that the two coins remained the same distance apart, no matter how he churned up the bottom of that pond.

Suddenly, something massive and squamous rose roaring from the depths of the pond. It was a monster which seemed all mouth and teeth. It smashed through the remainder of the ice like a whale crashing through the ice of northern seas. Water streamed from its bulbous form. Weed hung from its cavernous nostrils and from the many rod-like feelers which protruded from its brow. Two great speckled gold eyes shone amidst the warty greyness of its slimy head. There was a stink of primeval mud accompanying its ascent into the world of air and light.

Before Soldier could leap out of its reach, the monster had his foot and was dragging him down to the icy depths of the pond.

Soldier had managed to take a single breath before he was pulled into the water. The icy coldness of the pond gripped his chest like a giant hand and squeezed that breath from him. With his foot caught in the corner of the monster's mouth he went down, down, down, until the monster reached its cave at the bottom of the pond. Soldier was then swept along this passage. All the while he fought to unsheathe his sword. Finally, when the cave opened up into a cavern, Soldier had his sword in his hand. At his first thrust he managed to plunge the blade between those golden eyes he had first mistaken for coins. These eyes had of course been the bait, to draw unwary travellers closer to the edge of the stagnant waters of the magic pool.

The monster's flesh yielded to the sword, but it seemed to have no effect. There did not seem to be a vital organ beneath that fleshy-fat brow. Certainly no heart or liver, but no brain either. It was a spongy mass of cells and nothing more. Soldier might as well have thrust the blade through the creature's tail fin, for all the harm it did. Withdrawing his weapon, Soldier stabbed again, and again, all to no avail. His chest was ready to explode now. There was pain rushing from his lungs to his limbs. In his head there were bright, white, dancing lights, which he knew were the harbingers of unconsciousness. Finally, and mercifully – for the pain had reached an unbearable level – he blacked out.

Soldier woke just a few minutes later. He was lying on the rocky side of an underground lake. In fact he was still in the cavern at the end of the cave, but this was no watery world. He had been taken to the surface and deposited on the stone shore. There was a dim green light to this place. It shone on the stone walls, on the stalactites and stalagmites. The source of this light was a mystery, for it seemed to throw shadows in every direction. Turning his head, Soldier saw a horrible sight, which chilled him to the very core of his being.

The ceiling and walls of the cavern looked like that of a butcher's shop, with poles and lines covered in hanging hooks. Dangling from the hooks were joints of meat in various cuts. The more Soldier studied these lumps of meat the more he was convinced they were all from human beings. Indeed there were whole arms and legs, still with the hands and feet attached. Sides of torso hung in slabs, the red raw flesh exposed to the air. There were human entrails swinging from some of the hooks, and on rock shelves around the cavern were hearts, livers, kidneys, and other offal. Worse still, heads were hanging pierced through with a hook by their ears, as if they had once belonged to pigs, the eyes milky and glazed, the tongues lolling long and floppy or snipped at the root.

The horrifying part of it all was that most of the body parts he was looking at had once belonged to children.

Soldier heard a thump and spun round, to see the ugliest hag he had ever beheld. She was in the act of raising a meat cleaver to chop an arm into small rolling joints. By her side was a large knife and what appeared to be buttocks, from which rashers had been cut and laid neatly in a pile. *Thwack*, the chopper came down again and a piece of arm flew towards Soldier. The hag turned to watch it and saw that he was awake.

'With us again, eh?' she cackled. 'Not for long.'

Soldier's sword lay just a few feet away. He tried to get up but found he was tied hand and foot. The freezing water had numbed his limbs and he had not felt the ropes until now. This horrible crone had bound him to render him helpless.

'What are you?' he croaked. 'Some sort of witch?'

She laughed again. The sound was like feet sliding on gravel. 'A witch? Yes, a witch. My little hound brought you to me. He's a good pointer, that hound. Fetches in the game every time. Thought you'd found riches at the bottom of the pond, did you? Shiny gold. Stupid mortal. *You're* the riches. You make me a fortune, you greedy travellers.'

'Hound? Oh, the monster. You call that a hound, do you?'

'He's a good hunting dog, that one.'

Soldier watched as the witch began cutting up some guts and lights and placing the bits in muslin. She chatted as she worked, just as any butcher might. Strangely, there was a buzzing sound in the cavern. It seemed to be coming from the witch, though Soldier could not be sure. The noise interfered with his ability to think straight. It was as if the sound was there deliberately to interrupt his thought patterns.

'I like little boys and girls, really. They're my best sellers. Plump children. Easy to cut up and they taste delicious.

Didn't your grandmother ever warn you not to go near stagnant ponds? Most grandmas do. So they should, because we drag 'em down and cut 'em up. Lovely chubby little waifs, sent into the forest to look for firewood, or mushrooms, or blackberries, or wild herbs. Drowned, they say. Gone to their green watery death at the bottom of the pond. Later, I send 'em back to their mums and dads – at a price of course. The children return to the place from whence they came, along with a few truffles, into the bodies of their parents.'

Soldier felt he had to ask, though he believed he already knew the answer.

'How – how do they get them back?'

She looked up, her grisly face breaking into a grin. There was hair spouting like water from her nostrils and ears, grey and grizzled, curled like a beard. Bristles covered her chin and upper cheeks. Her skin was like a wart-hog's, grey and wrinkled. There were no eyebrows or eyelashes, just half-moon creased lids that closed with a single reptilian shutter coming up from below. Most shocking, though, were her eyes. They were clear and beautiful, like that of a baby: a deep, enchanting green.

She raised a bony hand and pointed, at the same time the buzzing increased in volume.

'You've already guessed, haven't you? I sell my meat to human butchers, who in turn sell in the market-place. Of course, I have to render it unrecognisable. Don't want anyone identifying their son or daughter. Got to watch for fingernails and teeth. Mustn't get tempted to sell the heads, though they'd look fine coming out of the roasting oven with a crab-apple in their mouths, wouldn't they? A few cuts here, a few snips there, and they look like animal carcasses. Lots of nice chopped liver. Kidneys resembling goats'. Who looks too close anyway? Stick a sprig of parsley between some podgy little fingers – snipped off at the second joint – and you've got an animal's paw.'

Soldier felt sick. Perhaps he had unwittingly eaten one of these children himself at one time? The thought was so horrible to him he actually wretched. The witch tutted.

'The thought of cannibalism a little too strong to stomach? Never mind, you're next Sunday's joint, so you won't ever have to worry about it after that.'

Soldier saw no reason to argue with the witch, but he wanted to become more than just a Sunday joint to her, so he engaged her in conversation.

'I don't understand,' he said, 'how you manage to get all that meat from one pond. Surely visitors to that particular woodland backwater are few? I can't imagine that you'd get anything but the odd goatherd or child collecting firewood.'

The witch laughed. 'Oh, there's a whole network of ponds, the caves from them all leading here.'

The buzzing noise was driving Soldier crazy. He wanted to scream. He had to force himself to think clearly,

'That's clever. And you have a monster in each?'

'The monsters come from my imagination. I create them from nothing. I'm no ordinary witch. I have special powers.'

'I can see that. I might even feel honoured if I were not in the position of prey. The hare can admire the intricate mechanism of the gin trap, I suppose, once he's been caught and is at leisure to do so. Once all hope is gone a kind of peaceful acceptance settles in. No more earthly worries. Simply sit and wait for the inevitable. You *will* make it quick?'

The meat cleaver came down on leg-bone and chopped it clean through to the block underneath.

'As quick as that!' said the witch. 'I'll do you in a minute.'

'You don't mind me talking so much?'

'It's refreshing. Usually there's just wailing or screaming. People don't seem to realise I have need for society too. I get lonely down here. It's pleasant to have a conversation with someone from the outside world. What's your name?'

She continued hacking away as Soldier told her.

'They call me, Soldier, but I don't know who or what I am, or where I've come from. I'm on a quest to find a wizard who'll cure my wife of her madness.'

'I'm not interested. You won't be set free on that account. Now if you said you were a barbarian out to slaughter innocents, then you might stand the faintest chance of being let loose. So, you're an outlander are you? Come from the outside? I might have guessed by the blue eyes. There have been one or two like you, in the past. They usually die very quickly . . .'

As the witch was speaking Soldier saw an insect crawl drunkenly out of her hairy left nostril like a winter wasp overfed on honey. It was long but bulbous, of a dull yellow colour, and it had transluscent wings folded down its back. Its head, however, was a pale white. It took off and buzzed into the air but the witch's neck stretched as long as one of her arms. Her head shot out with open mouth. She snapped at the escaping insect and swallowed it quickly. Then retracted her head.

During this eerie episode the witch had not once paused in her chopping or her conversation.

She did so now, awaiting an answer. Soldier gave her one.

'I've managed to stay alive all right.'

She snorted. 'Until today, that is. Now you're in the deepest trouble you've ever known. You're going to end up in the gut of your mad wife, if I have anything to do with it, and I seem to have everything to do with it at the moment. You knight errants. You think you're chosen of the gods, don't you? Well down here there's nothing can help you. I rule under the roots of the trees. There's no one down here who can stop me, mole, badger or snake. This is the last you'll see of this world, you poor lost soul, before going to quite a different one.'

Soldier could see he had not aroused her curiosity in the least with his confession that he had come from somewhere else. Her arrogance was in full flood. She believed herself to be both ingenious and invulnerable.

'What's your name?' asked Soldier.

'What do you care?'

'I'm interested. Let's say I want to take something new to the afterlife with me.'

'They call me Wwssxxyynn.'

It was a kind of hissing sound which Soldier did not think he could repeat with any confidence. He was silent for a while and she cackled. 'Can't say it, eh?'

Soldier suddenly decided rage might help him.

'You think you're so clever?'

'I do. I am.'

'How come I'm the only one here then, if you're such a brilliant trapper? What about the rest of my party, my pavilion of Carthagan warriors? I'm a lieutenant in the Eagle Pavilion, you know. My warriors are all waiting on the edge of the wood and you won't get a single one of them, because when I fail to come out, they'll know there's something magical about the place and leave quickly.'

'They'll send someone looking for you.'

'Ha! A lot you know about the red pavilions. One lost lieutenant is enough. Why send in precious troops where an officer has vanished off the face of the earth? It's bound to be magic. The army doesn't like magic. The army is very practical and prefers to fight its battles with ordinary men.'

Soldier didn't elaborate on this, not knowing what to say next. He was making it all up on the spur of the moment and his inventiveness was seriously hampered by the speed at which he was supposed to be thinking.

'Now, a really clever witch would have caught one fish and used it as bait to draw the others into the net.'

Wwssxxyynn's eyes narrowed and the droning sound grew monstrously loud.

'I've done that before. I've thought of that. I just didn't know there were warriors camped outside the wood. I'm still not sure. You could be lying.'

'You could go and look.'

She nodded slowly, then a crafty expression came over her features.

'And while I'm gone, you'll find a way to get out of those bonds? You think I'm stupid, Soldier? Anyway, I'll need you for bait. If you call those warriors into the wood, have them search the area around the pond, I'll let you go.'

With that, she picked up his sword and then grabbed him by the collar. With amazing strength for a frail-looking being, she dragged him to the edge of the underground lake, prodding him with the point of his own weapon. He might have been a cow or a pig considering the way she goaded him. Still gripping him with one hand the witch plunged into the water and went down swimming with her legs and feet, back along the waterways, to the pond.

Soldier's brain was working rapidly. He knew there was only the ghost of a chance, the faintest of hopes, that he could still escape Wwssxxyynn's clutches. They both emerged dripping and breathless from the stagnant waters of the pond, having passed a rather docile-looking monster resting in the mud at the bottom of the pond. The witch spoke to it as she passed and the monster roused itself to follow her. She dragged the bound Soldier to the far side of the wood. Here she ordered him to call his troops to rescue him from an attack by a bear.

In theory, to reach him any searchers would have to pass by the area of the pond, where the monster would be waiting. The monster could then leap and pluck several tangled bodies off the bank with one jump. The wide-mouthed beast was certainly capable of snatching a whole bunch of gesturing people clustered together.

'Call them,' hissed Wwssxxyynn. 'No tricks, or I'll stab you through the heart with your own sword.'

Soldier did not know what to do now. He had been playing for time, hoping something would occur to him. Still with his hands tied behind his back and his ankles bound with the same cord, he could not even hope to overpower the witch. Then again, if he called Spagg into the forest, the two of them could end up on butcher's hooks.

On the other hand, Spagg was his only hope. The market-trader knew this world better than Soldier. Whatever else he was, Spagg was a wily, cunning man, who knew the art of survival in Guthrum as well as anyone. Perhaps he would guess what had happened and come riding in armed and ready to fight?

'Sergeant Spagg,' called Soldier. 'Can you hear me? Bring some men into the wood. I'm – I'm trapped here. I've caught my leg in a root and can't free it.'

The witch hissed, 'I told you to say it was a bear.'

'You don't know Spagg,' murmured Soldier, knowing that

if the hand-seller thought there was a savage bear in the forest, he'd be halfway back to Zamerkand.

They waited but there was no answer from outside the wood.

'Did you hear me, Spagg?' called Soldier.

After another short period of silence, there came the answer.

'What's all this "sergeant" business? And what men? What's to do? I'm not comin' in there with you actin' so strange. I'll wait out here. If you're not out by noon, I'm going home.'

'Spagg, I order you . . .'

'Save your breath, I ain't comin' in.'

Spagg was indeed a survivor, but he stayed alive and well by not getting into situations, rather than fighting his way out of them. Soldier was in despair. He tried to think of something else, but merely ended up wrestling with his bonds. Wwssxxyynn was disgusted with him and herself. She took him by the collar again, ready to drag him back into the water.

'There's no warriors out there. There's only one man. A coward by the sound of him. You're chopped meat . . .'

She raised the sword but at the last moment Soldier threw himself to one side, so that only the flat of the blade struck him on the temple. He lost consciousness immediately.

Before the witch could finish her work, there came the sound of hooves pounding on the mast of the greenwood floor. She turned her head in time to see a shadowy blue rider coming out of the tangled thicket to the north of the wood. There was the flash of a drawn sword in the shafts from a winter sun. The horse, a piebald, was fleet of foot. Its rider seemed a slight but determined figure in the saddle. Before the witch could cry out, horse and warrior were upon her. A blade whirled and sang in the stillness. It sliced through the witch's neck. Wwssxxyynn's head flew off and struck a tree, to burst like a dried, hollow pumpkin.

Except that it was not like a pumpkin *inside*, but honey-combed, like the interior of a wild bee hive.

Out of the shattered head flew a swarm of buzzing yellow insects, similar to the insect one that appeared from the witch's nose down in the cavern. Once these detestable creatures hit the freezing air of winter, however, they only managed to fly a few yards before they died, dropping down into the snow. Each of the tiny flying things had its own human head. Their complexions were as white as ant's eggs and as wrinkled as the faces of newly-born babes.

Brains. Each little piece with a life of its own. An evil swarm of witch's brains.

Wwssxxyynn's body lay twitching amongst the acorns and leaves churned up from beneath the snow. While Soldier was having his bonds cut by his rescuer, whose face was hidden by a helm, the body of the hag gradually turned into rotten wood. Finally, it lay like an old tree trunk, still with one or two crumbling branches attached, covered in moss and fungi. The rescuer touched the sodden decayed log with his boot and it broke away, revealing nests of woodlice larvae beneath.

The rider now mounted and left the forest, charging past a gaping Spagg on the edge of the tree line.

'What a coward you are, hand-seller!'

Then he was gone, his mount's hooves pounding on the baked turf of the fields.

Soldier came to. He stared around him, realising he was now free. He looked around for the witch, but she was nowhere to be seen. Picking up his sword, Soldier could just see a rider through the trees, disappearing over the next ridge. This must have been his saviour. It certainly hadn't been Spagg.

Soldier walked slowly back to the campsite on the edge of the wood, carefully avoiding the bank of the pond. Spagg was there, the horses saddled and ready to leave. He stared at Soldier as if he was the last person he hoped to see.

'Bad luck, Spagg. I survived.'

'Survived what? Bein' eaten by an elm?'

Soldier remembered he had called out that he was trapped by the roots of a tree.

'I was in the hands of a witch! I thought you might come and set me free.'

Spagg let out a hollow laugh. 'The end of the world would come first. Why should I come and risk my life for you? I didn't ask to be here. You made me come. By the way, we had a visitor, a rider. Wouldn't say his name but he was a stripling. Nothin' to him, really. All swathed-up in blue cloth. Weedy sort. Voice not even broke, yet.'

The hunter! thought Soldier. The blue hunter who had first carried him to the castle? What was he doing, following Soldier and Spagg out into the wilderness? Or was it just coincidence? Once again Soldier was beholden to this young man.

'Did you send him into the wood after me?'

'I didn't *send* him,' replied Spagg. 'He heard you callin' me and came in by hisself.'

'Well, I owe him my life.'

'That's not much,' remarked Spagg. 'Pocket full of change, really. Now *my* life, that's worth a quite lot. Gold and jewels wouldn't buy it, nor a grandmother's love. If the stranger had saved me from death, that'd be worth talkin' about, but *you*? Why, it's unimportant really . . .'

'Sometimes, Spagg,' said Soldier, mounting his horse, 'you just leave me breathless with your rhetoric.'

Chapter Eighteen

The two horsemen continued their journey through the snowy wastes leading into the fastnesses of the west. Wrapped in warm furs they were bent in their saddles against the fierce winds which came from between the distant mountains. During the day they were cold. A blood-red sun occasionally appeared through the misty regions of the upper sky, but there was no warmth in it. At night they were colder, sleeping under an indigo moon beneath trees from which icicles hung in glittering clusters, some a full three feet in length. There were freezing mists curling around them when they rested and the air hurt their lungs when they were active. The chests of their horses creaked with the effort of plodding through the snow. Water was hard to find: most of it lay under six feet of surface ice. Unlike the march to fight the beast-people, where the landscape had been studded with farmhouses and isolated crofts, there were no dwellings to the west. It was cold, lonely country, with little comfort to offer.

'If I was a god,' grumbled Spagg, 'I would set the world on fire, open a few chasms in the ground, let off one or two volcanoes – anythin' to get rid of this winter.'

'If *you* were a god,' replied Soldier, 'the world would be in a tangled mess.'

His encounter with the witch had left Soldier feeling morose and uncertain. It seemed now like a dark dream, unreal, and there were occasions when he wondered if he had either dreamt it or had been subject to one of nature's apothecary tricks. There were plants and fungi which, when ingested, invented such tales in one's head. Or perhaps he had breathed some marsh gas which had a similar effect on the mind? Certainly, when he came to consider it carefully, he could not in all truth decide whether it had actually come to pass. It was as if he had been through some illness which caused a high fever, and his state of mind as well as his body had been affected.

'Good comp'ny, you are,' Spagg told him in sarcasm. 'You're a miserable toad much of the time.'

Soldier could not help but agree with this observation.

One morning they came to a low valley with steaming springs and places where hot mud had bubbled through cracks in the earth's surface to warm the ground. Here, for a change, they could see green grass and wildflowers which seemed to thrive on sulphur fumes. Here they stopped to camp for a while, thankful to be able to wash in hot water. They collected birds' eggs and boiled them in the mud. After the freezing reaches of the foothills, this valley was a blessing.

The deeper into the country of the gods they ventured, the stranger the sights became. In this shallow rift valley Soldier witnessed a similar phenomenon to the sight he had seen while with the red pavilions. Birds whose camouflage had developed beyond simply melting into their backgrounds. They became the vegetation they hid amongst.

These were colourful creatures, about the size of a thrush,

which actually changed into flowers when they sensed danger. Once the danger had passed, they transformed back into birds again. He saw some of these birds amongst some red flamboyant flowers with tall, sharp petals. When Soldier walked slowly towards the birds, pecking at the moss on the edge of a hot beck at the time, they changed instantly into the same short scarlet blooms amongst which they were feeding. Their legs became the stem and their bodies and heads the flower itself.

Again, when those same birds were wading between yellow flag lilies at the edge of a pool, a similar approach had them blossoming into yellow flags. On inspection they proved to be 'real' flowers, not just birds pretending to have petals where they had wings, and stalks where they had legs.

Once Soldier was at a safe distance they reformed into birds again and flew into some stunted trees at the end of the valley. Soldier was fascinated by the process, several times walking up to a group of these feathered creatures, only to witness them folding like paper into themselves, their feathers becoming petals, their beaks opening into glorious, coloured bells or trumpets, their yellow tongues becoming pollen-budded stamens, and their legs turning into green-leaved stalks. Any wildcat or eagle would be left tripping amongst the daisies, wondering where their quarry had disappeared to just like that.

So 'real' were these flowers transfigured from birds, the bees and other insects instantly descended on the blooms and found rich harvest.

The strangenesses of this hinterland did not confine itself to witches and bird-blooms. Soldier saw a mammal – something like a cross between a mole and a badger – whose whole family fitted into her like boxes of decreasing size. The female

– he knew her by her milk teats – opened her back. Her spine parted from neck to the base of her tail. The male then climbed inside her. His back then opened and the largest of the brood climbed inside him, and so on, until all six of this family of mammals were one.

The mother then proceeded to produce a huge array of weapons: teeth and claws. An impressive forest of thick spikes with a ferocious attitude to go with them. Far from running, she then stood her ground ready to fight off any attack, be it from human, from predator, or from an enemy amongst her own species.

The whole process took less than two or three seconds to perform. Soldier had to see it happen several times, before he could see into the speed of the action.

'You goin' to spend your life watchin' nature, are you?' asked Spagg, who refused to be captivated or intrigued by these wonders. 'I can't be bothered with nature and such. It's there and it's there. Can't do anythin' with it, can't do anythin' about it. Just forget it, that's what I say.'

'Your philosophy never fails to absorb me,' Soldier said, drily.

It was noon and they were boiling some greens in a vessel over the fire, when Soldier's scabbard sang out. He spent precious minutes searching the skyline and eventually saw some riders in the east. They came over the misty-white horizon like five ghost horsemen, all in a line. At first the snow-haze distorted their shapes, made them ripple like a mirage, until they hit a patch of cold, clear air. At the same time as the horsemen themselves became visible enough to be perceived as a real threat, they themselves saw the pair of travellers. The riders then came on at such a pace there was no time for Spagg and Soldier to mount, let alone escape.

Soldier had time to draw his sword, put his back against a friendly rock, and wait for any attack that was likely to come. Spagg rushed to his side, drew a dagger from his leggings, and uttered one fearful word.

'Hannacks!'

There were five of them: big, brutish fellows. Because it was cold they were wearing animal furs, instead of their preferred skirts, jackets and cloaks of human skin. Only one of them wore anything on his head: the jawbone of some luckless bearded man whose body had relinquished its mandible to become the adornment of a Hannack. Spagg pronounced this person to be the warlord. The man had fearsome features. His own jaw, plus his cheekbone, had been crushed on the right, so that his face looked lopsided. Part of his lip had been torn away, revealing teeth to their roots. That he had actually survived after receiving such a terrible blow testified to his strength.

Now he was faced by a definite danger, Soldier felt he had been rather rash in giving Spagg the enchanted brigandine.

'Here they come,' muttered Soldier. 'Are you wearing that brigandine? The one that's supposed to be enchanted and will protect a man from death?'

'No. I'm wearing my jack. I forgot about the magic brigandine. It's over there, on the mule.'

Soldier thought about it for a moment, then decided against running for the brigandine. He too had on only a jack: a quilted coat with protective padding. His chain-mail vest was draped over the front of his saddle. It was too heavy to wear all the time and his fingers stuck to the iron links out in the frozen air of the countryside. The pair of them would have to face the Hannacks in their jacks and nothing else.

The Hannacks arrived in a thumping of hooves.

They crashed through the camp-fire, the hooves of the warlord scattering the pot and its contents. Soldier's and Spagg's mounts were tethered to a sapling nearby. They reared and whinnied when the small, stocky Hannack ponies — painted with ochre colours on face and flanks — stamped around them. Big-boned faces stared silently at the two men with their backs against a granite cliff. The warlord went forward first, walking his mount slowly, and Soldier went into a crouched position, making his intent of defending himself obvious.

The Hannack warlord said something in very loud harsh tones to his accompanying warriors. There was a coarse laugh from one of them. The others smiled. These were not the smiles of a mother for her child, or that given by friend to friend. They were smiles overlaid with ugly, vicious sneers. They yelled at one another as they kicked over the objects around the camp.

'Why are they shouting?' hissed Soldier to Spagg.

Spagg muttered, 'They have very small ears.'

Soldier stared. It was true. Their ears were like tiny cockle-shells.

When the warlord was within range Spagg suddenly threw his knife. Soldier was amazed at how quick Spagg was. The arm flashed up and down, the dagger sped through the air as a spinning wheel of light. It was next seen transfixed in the Hannack's throat. The leader of the group had a wide-eyed expression on his face, as if he had been surprised by an audacious act. Then his hands flew to his throat. He whipped out the knife. Blood spurted and gushed from the wound. When he reached for his sword he was already weak. Finally, in view of the silent audience, he slipped from the back of his horse and crashed down onto the smouldering remains of the fire.

There he lay dying, his fur cloak burning crisply in the midday air, exuding the horrible stench of singed hair.

There was havoc amongst his followers, who prepared to ride at the pair against the rockface, once they had ceased shouting at one another and at the foe.

'Now you've done it,' muttered Soldier. 'I was about to bargain with them.'

'With what?' asked Spagg, producing another dagger from somewhere in the folds of his clothing and testing its balance in his right hand. 'They can take anythin' we've got, after they've done us in.'

'With something I have in my saddle bags. I brought them specially. No good now. We've killed one of their number. They won't leave until they've revenged him.'

'Huh, you don't know Hannacks. They probably hate the bastard. They're not like us. Revenge ain't their first priority. Rape and pillage is what they're most fond of – plunderin', lootin', all that sort of stuff.'

'But they're vain too, aren't they?'

'It's their finest sin.' He produced yet another knife from a hidden pocket and balanced it in his left hand.

'How many more of those have you got?' asked Soldier, glancing down.

'As many as I need,' came the reply.

The Hannacks began to come forward, but Soldier held up his hand.

'Do you speak their language?' he hissed at Spagg.

'A bit.'

'Well, tell them I have a bargain for them.'

Spagg shrugged and croaked something at the Hannacks.

The horsemen still came forward, swinging warhammers and maces as if they were itching to use them.

'Tell them their hairless scalps will never be seen bare again, if they allow us to go on our way.'

Spagg sighed and shrugged but passed the message on.

The four horsemen stopped now and looked intrigued.

'All right,' Spagg said, 'you've got their attention.'

'Tell them I will cure their baldness, but they have to promise to let us live.'

Spagg whispered, 'You better be tellin' the truth, otherwise they'll cut us up into little pieces and eat us. What are you, a wizard?' But he did as he was told and conveyed the information to the raiders.

There was some discussion amongst them now. It was not conducted with any reserve. The Hannacks shouted and yelled at one another, waved their weapons in each other's faces, pointed at the two men they had trapped, spat on the ground. Finally, one of them screamed at Spagg with great menace in his tone. Spagg smiled and nodded.

'He wants to do business. But he says if you're lyin' he'll cut you open slowly, make you a scarf of your own guts and walk you till you drop.'

'Fair enough,' replied Soldier. 'Can we trust them – to let us go?'

'I dunno. We ain't got much choice, have we?'

'No.'

Soldier sheathed Xanandra and walked slowly towards his horse. The Hannacks studied him closely, warily, ready for any trick. Soldier undid his saddle-bag and began pulling out hairy objects he had purchased just before leaving the castle. The Hannacks watched, their interest growing. When Soldier had four of these items he went to the Hannacks.

'Wigs!' cried Spagg. 'That's what you've bin carryin', is it?'

There were four wigs, two of black hair, two of brown. The

Hannacks looked at them curiously. One of them took a wig and put it the wrong way round on his head, so the long hair hung over his eyes. Soldier indicated that he should bend down. His friends shouted at him. He did so. Soldier then straightened the wig for him. Then Soldier held up a mirror he had taken from the same saddle-bag. The Hannack stared at himself in the glass, then hooted with delight. He preened himself before his friends, rode up and down with the wig hair lifting gently in the valley breeze, and generally paraded himself.

The other three quickly demanded their wigs and were given them. They pointed at each other, hooted and yelled, walked their ponies back and forth. Already they were arguing over the colours. It seemed that they like the brown hair wigs better than the black hair, though the quarrel did not seem serious. There was just a slight preference as they each tried on the others' wigs and murmured in satisfaction at the results.

While this show was going on, Soldier and Spagg quietly gathered together their stuff and made ready to depart. Soldier was still painfully aware that there was a dead man amongst them, still lying on the embers of the fire. It was true that the warlord's warriors had taken little notice of him, except that one of them had bent down and lifted up the decorative jawbone and hooked it into his horse's bridle. This did not mean that they were not considering avenging their leader's death. It just meant they were preoccupied for the moment.

When their horses were ready Soldier and Spagg mounted and began to quietly ride away from the camp. The Hannacks took no notice of them. They were still enthralled with their new hairpieces. When Soldier and Spagg were about fifty yards away, one of the Hannacks yelled and pointed at them with his mace. The other three stared hard for a moment. Then all four them re-engaged each other in a shouting match, seemingly forgetting all about the two men who had killed their warlord.

Soldier was pleased to get away so easily, but he was appalled by the Hannacks' lack of regard for their leader.

'It's almost as if he were just a piece of meat now,' he said to Spagg.

'That's exactly it,' replied the Guthrumite. 'Just a lump of flesh. I told you, they ain't interested in revenge. Only in booty. They had a good, crafty look at our stuff, while they was arguin' away and we was packin'. I watched 'em out of the corner of my eye. If they'd have seen anythin' else they wanted, they'd have taken it quick enough. Still, we're lucky to get off so light. It's only a whim with them. Another time they're as like to chop us to bits and to hang with any promises of freedom.'

They put as much distance between themselves and the Hannacks as the daylight hours would allow. When nightfall came, which was much too soon, they found themselves outside a village on stilts. There was marshy ground beneath, now frozen solid and hard enough to ride on. Frozen rats and mice littered the frosted turf and iced-over reed beds. No doubt they had starved to death now that winter had hit the land so suddenly. They had had no warning of the coming harsh weather and had not fattened themselves in preparation, nor stored any food to carry them over the unexpected lean period which had come upon them.

Behind the village of huts was a sheer face of obsidian rock, which looked so smooth as to be unclimbable. The rockface rose to the height of two hundred feet and ran forever on either side. Soldier wondered how on earth, since they

obviously could not go around it, they were going to sur-
mount this obstacle. It looked an impossible task. However,
that was for the morning. When he wasn't so tired and could
think more clearly. Soldier was determined to figure out a
way to get over this glass cliff.

'What is this place?' asked Soldier, pointing to the huts.
'Are there people here?'

'No. It's a ghost village. Used to be a people called the
Beerites — marsh men — but they've all up an' gone. They
moved out, reluctantly, when the gods took up residence in
the nearby mountains. They didn't speak about why they was
moving of course, because they didn't believe in the existence
of their new neighbours. One day they just got everything
ready and travelled inland, into Guthrum proper. Once there
they fell away in numbers until they finally all died out, every
blasted one of them still utterly convinced there weren't no
such thing as a god, or a spirit, or an afterlife to go to once
you were dead. O' course, they went to the worst part of the
Otherworld, as punishment. Some say you could hear them
cursing each other on their way to hell.'

Soldier studied the village in the dusk. It was true that
most of the thatched rooftops of the stilted huts were in a
state of disrepair. They were full of holes and covered with
nests. Some of the wooden walls of the huts were holed and
broken too. There was an air of decay about the place.
However, huts meant shelter, even if they were dilapidated.
Soldier prepared to spend the night in the best of the high
dwellings.

Against the very rockface itself they found a hut which
seemed more or less whole. The cliff had protected it from
the worst of the weather. Scratched on the lintel above the
doorway was a crude picture of a stork.

'Waylander's hut,' Spagg said. 'This is where we're s'posed to stay, anyway. It's for travellers. That's the mark of a way-lander, that stork.'

The horses were stabled below, in a battered tithe barn. The two men climbed a rickety ladder to the hut above. On entering they found it quite cosy inside. There was a strong smell of methane gas coming from the bog below, but apart from that the place was dry and wholesome. No dead rats, not even a cobweb. This should have put them on their guard, but it did not. They made a fire in the stone and metal hearth, in the centre of the hut, where there was a hole in the roof for the smoke.

Spagg had killed a white hare with a slingshot from the saddle: a feat which had impressed Soldier a great deal. All Soldier had seen was a piece of snow detaching itself from the rest of the white landscape. Spagg had swiftly whirled a slingshot around his head and let loose the smooth pebble found in a stream. The missile hummed through the air, struck something soft, and then a small scarlet sunrise took place on the snow. Now they had dinner. Soldier was learn-ing there were more skills to the market trader than he had first supposed.

Late in the evening the raven arrived, with news from the now distant Zamerkand.

'I thought you'd like to know,' said the raven, 'that your wife is having lots of visits from Captain Kaff. He seems to hang around the Palace of Wildflowers until all hours of the night and morning. Of course, she's been out of her head most of the time, but not all of it. Some say she went away with the captain for a few days, but there's no proof of that.'

'I need to know all this gossip, do I?' snapped Soldier, not at all pleased by the news. 'I should have killed that captain when I had the chance. I wish I'd run him through when I had him at my mercy.'

Soldier was quiet for a moment, but clearly still ruffled. He turned on the raven.

'You enjoy this role, don't you? The unwelcome messenger? Sometimes I get the idea you make most of it up, just to upset me. You're a malicious tattle-tale.'

The raven ruffled its feathers. 'Please yourself. I won't tell you about her in future.'

Soldier calmed his thoughts and sighed deeply, knowing that he had to know, even if the news was bad.

'I'm sorry. Of course you must tell me.'

Spagg was looking open-mouthed, back and forth from one speaker to the other. He was obviously astounded by the conversation, or rather, by one of the speakers. He finally fixed his stare on the black-feathered raven.

He said, 'What's this? A gabby bird?'

Soldier said, 'He's my raven.'

The raven said, 'I'm not anybody's raven. We met on a cold hillside when he awoke from a bad dream. He killed a snake that was about to eat me and I've been looking after him ever since. *Somebody* has to. Without me, he'd perish.'

'Witchcraft!' muttered Spagg, darkly, turning his back on the pair to stoke the fire. 'Don't have anythin' to do with witchcraft.'

'That's it,' cried the raven, contemptuously, 'put your head in a box, don't confront what you don't understand.'

'I understand it all right. I just don't want to have nothin' to do with it.'

The raven left them after a while, flying out through the open window into the winter night. Soldier watched him go. Once he was in the blackness he vanished amongst the stars.

It was a clear night in the heavens, encrusted with constellations Soldier did not recognise. Surely, he thought to himself, my poor memory would not hide such things. I know what a tree is. I can recognise an oak from an elm and the names sit comfortably on my tongue. Why don't I know the star patterns then? Are they new to me? Is this not my world at all? Perhaps some things here are familiar and others are strangers to me?

'What are you dreamin' about?' asked Spagg. 'Your little princess?'

Soldier turned on him. 'Don't you ever mention my wife in that tone of voice again. I'll slice out your heart without a second thought . . .'

He was cut short by a song coming from his scabbard. Once more the magical scabbard was warning its master of a possible threat. Spagg looked startled. Soldier had the presence of mind to draw his sword and face the door, ready to fight.

At that moment a figure appeared in the doorway to the hut. Soldier jumped back and Spagg gave out a little cry. It was a little old man, wizened and bent, supporting himself on a crooked staff. He glared at the two occupants of the room, before taking a few faltering steps inside.

The old man was dressed from head to toe in a long, dark, ragged cloak, filthy at the hem where it dragged on the ground. When his toes poked out from underneath as he stepped across the room, Soldier saw that he had thick red socks on under his sandals. They looked stiff and damp from walking in the snow. On his head was a floppy broad-brimmed hat of the kind temple monks wore when they went travelling abroad. The hand which grasped the staff was thin and claw-like, with silver rings around the joints of the fingers. His other hand clutched at his gown, as if he were supporting his weight on it.

The old man stared at Soldier, as he grasped and twisted the end of a long white beard which looked frozen stiff. It seemed he was trying to warm the icy beard by working it back and forth. Still he said nothing. Then the end of the brittle beard snapped off in his fingers. He looked down at the goatee in disgust. He threw the broken end in the fire, where it sizzled and sent out that unmistakable smell of singeing fibres.

'Cut his heart out will you?' he chimed in the metallic accents of a mechanical clock. 'You might regret that remark, a little later on.'

He shuffled across the floor and sat in the corner of the room, well away from the fire, while the other two men simply stared at him.

Finally, still with sword in hand, Soldier asked, 'Who are you? Why are you hostile?'

'Hostile?' came the chimed reply. 'Ah, you have some magical device which warns you of potential harm. I had one myself once, when I needed it. In answer to your question, I am hostile by nature. The whole world is a dangerous place. I must be prepared for conflict. My attitude is to strike first.'

The old man laid down his staff and rubbed his hands, making a clicking sound with the rings.

'How are you called?' asked Soldier.

'Call me the Weatherteller. I go in and out, you know, through doors in the sky. I have no influence, of course, but I can direct men to a safer haven when a storm is brewing. I'm a sage, forespeaker, a soothsayer if you will. Trees talk to me. Grasses sing to me. I hear their voices. You'll find me in the lull before the great wind tears down your house.'

'A wind is coming?' said Spagg. 'Here? Tonight?'

'Not now,' chimed the old man, with some contempt in his ringing tones. 'When necessary.'

'You said there's a storm coming,' Soldier told him.

'No. I said I *knew* when one might be coming. I feel it in my bones. Oppression fills my head. My scalp tingles with electricity. I have thunder in my ears, lightning in my eyes, gales in my lungs. Chaos courses through my veins. I have secret ways I keep and turn and pass again. I read the cryptic messages in the heavens. To study the blizzards of space, the storms of the milky galaxies, the clinking of stars and comets as they strike each other in the great cauldron of the sky! Then the blast, as they fly from the pot like sparks from a farrier's hammer striking a white-hot horseshoe. It's all one, to me. The natural cycles, the spinning swirls of the universe, the heave and roll of the majestic oceans, the lurching of a subterranean quake, the cascading flood, the toppling mountain . . .'

'You're a male witch!' cried Spagg in great fear. 'Don't let him stay here, Soldier. He speaks in riddles. He *must* be a wizard. We'll wake up as toads if he stays.'

Soldier was confused. 'Is this true? Are you a witch? Or a temple priest? A monk? What are you?'

'I am what I am, I can be no more, can I?'

Spagg wrung his hands anxiously and looked to Soldier for some guidance.

Soldier did not know what to do. How could he turn an old man out into a winter night? Yet Spagg might be right. If they allowed him to stay, who could say that he might not take advantage of their hospitality? Their quest was too important to be jeopardised by a witch in disguise. Perhaps this was really a young man before him, in the guise of an ancient? One who could brave the night without failing? There were plenty of other huts. Let him stay in one of those.

'You must leave us,' he told the old man. 'Go to one of the other houses.'

The old man said nothing in reply. Instead he reached into the folds of his cloak and took out a paper bag. The bag was heavy, with moving contents. At first Soldier thought there might be a small animal inside, a furry rodent perhaps? But then, as he watched, the movement in the bag seemed to have a regular rhythm. It was pulsing. What was more the bag began to stain with red at the bottom, as if the thing inside was leaking. Soldier could not imagine what the old man had in there.

'You heard me,' he said. 'I asked you to leave. I know this is the waylander's hut, but I don't trust you.'

'I have to stay here,' said the sage. 'You don't understand, do you, how these things work?'

'I don't care how they work. You must go, now.'

Soldier drew his sword and held it in a threatening manner, not intending to hurt the old man, but trying to show menace in order to get rid of him.

Holding the paper bag open with his left hand the ancient of days reached inside with his right. He appeared to grasp what was inside the bag and squeeze it. Soldier dropped his sword instantly. It clattered on the wooden floor. His hand flew to his own chest as he felt the shock of a terrible pain within. It was enough to have him gasping, his eyes starting from his head. Another squeeze and the pain was even worse. It creased through him. Soldier went down on his knees and groaned in agony.

Spagg stood up as if ready to run.

'I can destroy you now, if you like,' chimed the old man, pleasantly. 'Look!'

He reached forward and showed the racked Soldier the contents of the bag. It was a live human heart, pumping rhythmically. The old man squeezed it as Soldier watched and the pain that shot through Soldier's chest was excruciating. Soldier let out an agonized scream and fell back on the floor, at Spagg's feet. He rolled over and over, trying to ease the terrible cramp in his chest.

The sage had Soldier's heart in the bag, kneading it, squeezing it, squashing it with his strong bony fingers until the muscled walls of the organ ballooned between the old man's ringed knuckles.

Having given Soldier pain for a few minutes the ancient of days put the bag on the floor and carefully placed his foot on it.

Soldier was horrified. He felt he was about to die.

'No,' he gasped. 'Don't burst it!'

'Just a little pressure from my sole.'

In his mind's eye Soldier witnessed his heart bursting, the blood spraying and sloshing inside the paper bag. He saw the consequent useless, flattened, flapping skin of the punctured organ as the old man tossed it away. These were very real images in his head. It was as if it had been done already.

'Don't do it. I'm sorry. You can stay.'

The chimes rang out in merriment. 'Of course I can stay. I know I can stay. The question is, do I let you live? You insulted an old man. You lack hospitality. Such behaviour has to be punished. Surely you can see that? You can't be allowed to get away with such things. Are you sorry?'

'*I* am!' shouted Spagg, dropping to his knees as he stared at the heart in horror. 'I'm *very* sorry.'

'That's because you know you're next. I've reserved a very special torture for you. I thought we might draw your liver out through your nostrils? How does that sound?'

'I – I think you should be satisfied with what you've already done.'

The old man nodded. 'I might be at that.'

He took his foot from the paper bag and sat in the corner of the hut. Soldier eventually got to his feet. He picked the bag up and looked inside. There was nothing in there but a large soft aubergine. Surely the old man must have been squeezing his heart? He took off his jack and the shirt beneath to inspect his chest. There were no visible marks there. So how had the old man accomplished his torture?

Hypnotism? That was possible.

Or perhaps everything had been real up to the point where the old man took his foot off the paper bag, but was no longer real now, nor ever had been. Soldier was convinced he would have died had the sage crushed the paper bag.

The old man was asleep now, snoring softly. Soldier resolved to be a little more careful, show a little more kindness to strangers. He also wondered about their safety, not because something might get in – it wouldn't last long against the sage – but because the old man himself might have a change of mind during the night and settle his death dust upon them.

Just before Soldier went to sleep, he thought about the enchanted brigandine. Should he get up and put it on, to protect himself during the night? But then Spagg might be the first to be killed. Soldier thought it was not fair to protect himself and leave Spagg vulnerable. While he debated with himself he resolved the matter by falling asleep.

Chapter Nineteen

When they woke in the morning Soldier rose and went to the doorway of the hut, and almost fell two hundred feet down to the ground. He managed to clutch at the two doorposts and prevented himself. It seemed that the stilts which supported the hut had grown in the night. They were now level with the top of the cliff face and could step out of the back way onto the plateau. This was the magic of the waylander's hut.

Soldier turned to see that the old man was still asleep in his corner. He had not murdered them in their beds after all. No wonder the sage had wanted to stay in this particular hut. He must have known about the night growth. It was probably the only way to get to the plateau.

Spagg sat up, coughed, hawked and then spat through the open window.

Soldier winced. 'Do you have to do that?'

'Yes,' came the reply from the bleary-eyed market trader.

Spagg rose and went to the window, only to exclaim in terror at the drop he saw below.

'What's happened?' he cried.

'We've come up in the world.'

'What about the horses – they're down below.'

Soldier hadn't thought about this.

'We'll have to walk from here on in,' he said, grimly. 'Don't worry about the animals. When they get hungry they'll soon kick their way out of that flimsy stable and graze. So long as no one steals them, they should be around when we come back this way.'

'That's wishful thinking,' grunted Spagg. 'Damnation, the food's down there, on the pack-mule.'

'You've got your sling, haven't you? And we've got a few things – blankets, a backpack containing the brigandine and a few other essentials, like the tinder box. We'll be all right, I think.'

At that moment the ancient of days stirred and then sat up.

'Are we up?' he asked.

'Yes – does it always happen?' questioned Soldier.

'No. Not always.'

The old man rose and went out through the back door of the hut, stepping onto the plateau. There was a misty river nearby which fell as a bridal veil waterfall over the edge of the cliff. The water steamed and smelled of sulphur. The old man washed himself. Soldier and Spagg did the same, finding the water extremely hot. Soldier guessed the source was deep underground, probably close to some liquefied lava bed. Spagg made a great show of washing himself, but very little water touched his skin, and when challenged by Soldier about his dirty habits Spagg grew defensive. He addressed his remarks to the old man, knowing that Soldier would poo-poo his reasoning.

'I really like to gather the dew from rose petals,' he

explained to the old man. 'It's much better for your complexion. My dear departed mother used to bathe me in dewdrops when I was little. Look, here's some on this spider's web. So much gentler on one's skin, don't you think?'

He got no more sympathy from the old man than he would have done from Soldier.

'If you want to be a filthy hog, then be brave enough to admit it.'

'All right,' said Spagg, simply. 'I like dirt. It keeps you warm. Why should I pretend otherwise?'

'Because you're a sly and consistent liar,' the old man said.

Spagg took exception to this remark, but he let it pass, knowing that the sage could cripple him.

'Are you travelling on westwards?' asked the ancient of Soldier. 'Shall we go together?'

Soldier replied, 'I've been thinking of using the hot river – making a raft. What do you say to that?'

The old man nodded. 'A good idea. You'll be travelling upstream, but away from the falls the flow isn't fast.' The old man's eyes narrowed as he stared over the winter landscape of the upper world. Here the trees and hedgerows were dwarfs, the features of the land miniature in aspect. 'We're entering a strange region though. We have to be careful not to run into hostile creatures.'

'What kind of creatures?'

'Faery folk, giants, those kind,' he replied, vaguely.

Soldier nodded. 'But you've been this way before? You can guide us?'

'I've been this far and no further. Last time I had to turn back when a giant toad swallowed my companion, right here on the cliff-top. Tongue flashed out. Took him down whole, no trouble at all. I could see my friend wriggling as the toad made off with him inside its stomach. It upset me a great deal.'

He took off his hat and wiped his face with a kerchief.

'I hope we don't run into the same amphibian.'

Spagg looked about him, hoping the same thing.

'Couldn't you save your friend?' asked Soldier. 'You seem to have special powers.'

'They don't work on the kind of creatures you find up here – this is Faeryland, traveller, not the real world.'

Soldier, who wondered whether there was a 'real world' at all, did not reply to this. Instead he began to gather wood for a fire. Spagg helped him, but the old man sat down and waited for the fire to appear. He was clearly not used to manual work, nor did he intend to get used to it. Once they had a roaring fire going, Spagg went off and found some edible bracket fungus growing from the dwarf oaks. He dug at the roots of the trees and found some kind of onions, which went into the pot with the mushrooms. This vegetable stew was enough to fill their bellies while they built a raft to carry them on the river.

Soldier wondered about his two companions. Spagg was growing on him a little. Once you understood the crafty market trader it was easier to abide him. Watching them move against a snowy background brought images to Soldier's mind. Loyalty. One virtue Soldier prized, venerated above all, was loyalty. He could not stand betrayal, despised it. Once, in some dim and distant past, separated from him not by time but by space, Soldier had been betrayed. He felt a memory pang, the loss of someone very dear to him, snatched from his breast by a foul enemy who had been led to his side by a traitor.

The fury, the anger, the hatred simmered inside Soldier

these detached but recognisable memories came to him out of the smog of some dimly-lit well deep with him. They came as phantoms, ghost feelings, which he could not fully grasp but which flitted through his head. He saw a shape, a woman in a bridal dress, snatched from the arms of her lover and protector, thrown across a horse, ridden out into snowy wastes. He followed tracks in that snow, until he came upon the white maiden in her blood-soaked gown, lying on the whiter snow, a halo of seeping red surrounding her broken form. These images came as flashes in his brain, causing him great mental anguish. Betrayal. He could never allow betrayal to go unpunished again. Spagg was now his companion. The market trader now had obligations. Woe betide him if he ever betrayed Soldier in any way. He would die a horrible death.

'What you lookin' at me like that for?'

Spagg was speaking to Soldier, who realised he was glaring at the man across the fire.

'I – nothing – just be careful.'

'Careful? What 'ave I got to be careful about?' asked Spagg, indignantly. 'I ain't done nothin' wrong.'

'Not today,' replied Soldier.

The old man was staring curiously at Soldier.

'Ah,' he said, 'there are other countries in that head of yours, aren't there? Other times? Other men and women? You must be careful you remain in control. I've heard of you. Yours was the hand that slayed the dog-warrior, Vau. Be careful of yourself. Don't let the beast out too often.'

'You mind your own,' said Spagg, for some inexplicable reason feeling he had to defend Soldier. 'What's in his head belongs to him and nobody else. Anyhow, I can stick up for meself. I don't need you to protect me. I can vanquish the worst of 'em, I can. Faery folk don't bother me none, either. Goblins, boggarts, trows, you name it, I've killed it.'

Once they had finished eating they doused the flames of the fire with snow. Spagg then told Soldier it was not feasible to make a heavy raft. There were no thick timbers around and they didn't have the tools for such a job in any event. He suggested instead that they fashion a rough coracle.

'I've made a few in my time,' he told Soldier. 'They're not difficult if you've got clay.'

There was indeed clay on the banks of the river. It was frozen ground, there being thin ice on the edges of the torrent, but Spagg showed Soldier how to make the clay pliable in such conditions by stamping up and down on it. With such manipulation repeated the clay soon softened.

Nearby there was a small copse of downy oaks, not much larger than big shrubs. Soldier and Spagg cut branches from these with Soldier's sword and wove a coracle. Spagg had the basket-weaving skills, while Soldier provided the muscle. The old man stayed aloof from these two, humming a tune and staring at the distant mountains. He seemed not to care that he was a useless third of the group.

Once the framework was complete they lined it with moss and then caulked the whole with yellow clay from the bank. By noon they had a serviceable boat which would carry the three of them. Soldier made three paddles and informed the old man that they were not carrying passengers. If he wanted to come with them, it had to be as a member of the crew.

'You will paddle along with us, or you don't come.'

'I'm an old man. I have no strength left.'

Soldier said, 'You had enough strength to squeeze my heart until my brain jangled in agony.'

The ancient smiled at Soldier. 'Yes, I did, didn't I? And I'll do it again, if you refuse to take me along with you.'

'All right,' murmured Soldier, 'I can't be bothered to argue, but you've made an enemy of me.'

'I'll manage.'

Soldier and Spagg carried the coracle along the water's edge for about half a mile, until they deemed it safe to launch it. The river had several bends here and was a lot slower in its flow. Climbing aboard the flimsy craft they set off along the river's edge, just outside the ice rim. It was hard going at first, paddling against the current, but the pair of rowers kept at it, gradually making progress, until the river widened and slowed down even more and their advancement became easier.

Along the banks of the river there were elder and alder, and all kinds of water trees, such as goat willow. Everything was layered with snow and glistened under a bronze sun. At one spot they passed a tree with birds and animals – mostly squirrels, tree martens and polecats – dangling from nooses. They swayed in the wind, their shadows cast against the snow.

'Hanging tree,' murmured the old man, by way of explanation. 'The branches create tendrils on their tips, which form into loops that strangle living creatures. Once they've rotted, the branches feed the bole. You see that hole in the bark? That's one of the hanging tree's mouths. It's a flesh eater. I find it very decorative, like a festive tree hung with baubles.'

'You would,' muttered Spagg.

At another point they reached a freezing plain. There were thumps on the landscape which caused ripples in the steaming surface of the water before they reached the flatlands. As they wound through and across the wide plain they saw the reason for the dull noises and subsequent vibrations. Two great human giants were tossing stones as large as houses.

They were a long way off but the tremors the stones caused when they hit ground reverberated. It seemed the giants were trying to beat each other, each trying to put their boulder further than their opponent's. To Soldier it was fascinating. It was like watching some huge beasts battling for a mate, except there was no cow giant here, only two great bulls more intent on impressing each other than any female. The massive boulders went hurtling through the air, to land jarringly on the snow-covered mud, crushing trees, flattening hills, and all for the sport of two bad-tempered giants.

After a long and tedious journey over the plain they reached some mountainous country. The river followed a valley between two outcrops of rock which rose to about five hundred feet on both sides. Between the river bank and the cliffs was about a hundred yards of flat land. Underneath the snow it was probably meadow-land. When the boat rounded a bend in the river, they suddenly saw a barrier coming up. It was a log with rocks hanging from it on ropes. It had clearly been placed across the river to stop any traffic. Since the current was against them it was simple for Soldier and Spagg to come to a halt and make for the bank.

'We'll have to resort to portage,' said Soldier. 'Spagg and I will carry the coracle. You, old man, can manage the paddles.'

'I can't carry anything.'

'You'll carry the paddles.'

They stared at each other, young and old, and eventually old gave way.

'All right, I'll carry the paddles,' said the ancient.

With the coracle on their heads Spagg and Soldier made their way along the left bank of the river. The old man stepped out in front, the paddles in his arms. When they reached the barrier across the river the old man started looking nervously around him. There were marks in the snow at this point, hundreds of footprints, all around the weighted log. But they were the small prints of children, not of grown men.

'Kids, all the way out here,' grumbled Spagg. 'You get enough of them at in Zamerkand. Haven't they got anything better to do than annoy innocent travellers . . .'

Soldier's scabbard sang out, loud and clear in the snowy wastes beside the river.

The old man had turned around with a worried expression on his face. He seemed about to say something. Then there was gentle swishing sound of air being parted. Something shot out either side of the old man's throat. His eyes bulged. His lips pursed. There was an annoyed look on his face for a second, then he slid to the ground.

Spagg let out a yell and tossed away the boat.

He could see now that what he thought had sprung from within the old man, had actually come from some nearby trees. It was a black iron bolt from a crossbow. It had penetrated the neck of the ancient and now it was lodged halfway through. The four-vaned head of the bolt was covered in stringy strips of flesh. No doubt the sage's spinal column had been shattered, his windpipe pierced, and his voice box punctured.

All things taken into account he had received a mortal wound, and now lay dying in the snow at their feet.

Soldier instinctively dropped to the ground. Spagg was not far behind him. More bolts swished over the places where they had been standing, landing on the river-edge ice beyond and skidding into the water. Soldier remained huddled on the cold breast of mother earth, hugging her, until he sensed figures around him. When he looked up he saw gnarled and knobbled faces peering down at him with hard expressions.

He stayed where he was, hoping he would not get a bolt in the back of the head.

'Trolls,' muttered Spagg. 'Don't move.'

Soldier had no intention of moving until someone told him he could do so without being harmed. He could see the small feet around him, some of them wrapped in rags, others with boots. He felt himself being prodded by the hunched, large-headed creatures around him.

Eventually something was barked at him in coarse, guttural tones.

'Better get up,' said Spagg. 'They want us to go with them, up to their mountain fortress above.'

Soldier got to his feet and was prodded on by a pike held in the small hands of thick-set troll.

'Gaaahhhh!' said the troll. 'Oop! Oop!'

Soldier felt like snatching the pike and ramming it down the troll's windpipe, but there were far too many of the creatures to attempt any escape. They looked strong, too. For their size they had huge shoulders and backs, and deep boat-shaped chests with a ridge from chin to waist. Their big heads rocked on very short necks, but for the most part they were muscular individuals. One of them ran ahead, blowing a cow-horn, the hollow notes of the instrument floating up the cliff-side. High above came the excited sounds of celebration. The raiders were returning with victims and perhaps treasure.

Soldier and Spagg were forced up a narrow path not much wider than a goat track. Once they reached the top of the escarpment they found themselves on the walls of a fortress. The natural curve and shape of the rock was given to a defensive position, but this had been enhanced by walls built between rock towers and stacks, thus ensuring that the river raiders' hide-out on the shelves above the valley was virtually impregnable.

Looking around him, Soldier assessed that it would take an army to breach these defences, with sangars large enough for a single archer to hide behind; rope bridges – which could be withdrawn at a moment's notice – from one high vantage point to another; natural towers and inaccessible turrets. A huge horde of river-raiding trolls garrisoned the fort: they looked well-armed and ready to fight any foe sent against them. An invading force would pay a dear price to capture this place.

'Very impressive,' he told his troll captors. 'Not an easy fort to overrun. I see you have deep wells too! And goats and other livestock. A seige would be difficult. I congratulate you on your choice of position.'

'Me speak you same tongue,' grunted a troll. The creature was now wearing one of the murdered old man's red socks on his head as a loose, dangling hat. Ears as ugly as dried figs poked out from beneath the rolled-up sock bottom. He was also wearing a grimy, grey vest which hung on him like the shift of a country milking wench. Soldier assumed this was one of the old man's undergarments. 'You shut mouth.'

'Ah, you have a command of human tongue . . .' began Soldier, but he was immediately silenced by the butt end of a spear in his stomach. When he had recovered his breath, he was forced through the grounds of the fortress, until he stood before a troll with a long, dark, wispy beard, which trailed in the dust at his feet. He stared at Soldier with obvious displeasure. Spagg he did not even waste a glance on.

The troll who had spoken before, a fat fellow about two-and-a-half-feet tall, was obviously the intermediary. The bearded troll said something in what was almost the growl of a wolf. The intermediary nodded and turned to Soldier.

'He want know if you rich?'

'I'm not wealthy,' replied Soldier. 'I haven't two bronze miadores to rub together.'

This appeared to be a mistake, this honesty, because immediately three or four trolls stepped forward with battle axes in their hands and would have felled the hapless Soldier like a tree, starting with his legs, if Spagg had not yelled at them that the man was lying, that he was rich.

'Take no notice of him,' cried Spagg. 'He's got more courage than sense. His wife is Princess Layana of Zamerkand. The lady of the Wildflowers. If you ransom him she'll pay a fortune to get him back. Me too. I'm his lifetime servant and friend. She'll pay to get us both home safely.'

'Don't pander to them,' snarled Soldier. 'I'm not afraid of these short people.'

'You ought to be,' Spagg said. 'If they think you're useless they'll kill you without a second thought. This is their trade. They're river pirates. They stop everything that comes along this waterway and charge a toll. Since we haven't got the price of a crust between us they'll either ransom us or kill us and eat us tonight. Did I mention they're cannibals?'

The trolls looked suspiciously at their prisoners. Whether they believed they had a prisoner worth ransoming or not the pair did not learn. Soldier and Spagg were manacled in chains attached to the wall of the fort. They were in full view of all who passed by them. It seemed that most trolls, especially the females, felt it necessary to give either one or both of them a kick or a punch. They became the butt of ribald jokes and the target for throwers of vegetables and, occasionally, stones.

'Now we're in trouble,' groaned Spagg. 'We'll never get out of this.'

Even as he spoke one of the trolls was leading a giant owl out of a stable. A troll, smaller than the rest, climbed onto this creature's back. The handlers released the lines tethering the bird to the ground and it took off, with its rider, into the afternoon sky. Soon it became a mere speck in the heavens. It was heading towards Zamerkand, in the east.

The sock-wearing troll came to them shortly.

'He go on horse of air to find money.'

'I hope he finds a spear of fire,' replied Soldier, grimly. 'I hope they send up a falcon to greet him.'

Spagg cried, 'No, no, he don't mean that. He speaks without thinkin', this man.'

The troll grimaced. 'He no speak no thinking. He hate troll people.'

'Not all troll people,' said Soldier, pleasantly, 'only those murdering thieves and brigands who stop legitimate river traffic to kill and rob. I am a lieutenant in the red pavilions. When I return to Zamerkand I shall take the Eagle Pavilion and return here and wipe out this colony of misguided, malicious little assassins as I would a nest of scorpions.'

Spagg let out a false laugh, as if he thought Soldier a jolly fellow.

'You shut up,' snarled the troll, at Spagg. 'I roast you firstly. I eat you eyes. I eat you heart.'

Spagg winced on hearing this. When he saw it was useless to try to get on the troll's good side, he too became angry.

'See those 'orrible horny appendages,' he nodded at the troll's hands and feet, which looked too big for his body size, 'I'll cut them off meself and sell 'em cheap to some dollmaker. He'll put 'em on a clay doll with a painted face and sell the doll to hang on doors to scare away demons.'

Nothing could have enraged the troll more than to speak of his feet and hands. Trolls were very sensitive about their overlarge appendages. Otherworld creatures – fairies, elves, goblins and the like – all made fun of the size of the hands and feet of trolls.

'Me eat you liver!' he screamed in Spagg's face, his bad breath mingling with the equally foul breath coming from the mouth of Spagg with its gums full of rotten teeth. 'Me eat you tongues.'

'Me eat you brains,' retorted Spagg, with some spirit, 'if me can find a small enough biscuit to put 'em on.'

The troll whipped the old man's sock off his head and began to flay Spagg with it. Spagg laughed and jeered. The troll kicked him. Spagg yelled at the troll, then laughed again. Finally the troll spat in Spagg's face and walked away, screaming threats over his shoulder, saying that even if the ransom came he would still kill both his captives and eat them.

'Now you've done it,' said Soldier.

Spagg snorted in indignation. 'Me? You started it.'

'Yes, but my insults were reasonable. You had to go and mention his hands and feet. We'll never get out of here now.'

The pair were kept chained to the wall for three days with very little food. On the second day they smelled roast meat and Soldier's saliva juices were running. They were famished. It was agony being within the odour of that roast and not being able to join in the feasting. Finally Redsock brought Spagg and Soldier some rashers of cooked meat. They both gobbled these morsels down. The roast meat, running with hot greasy fat, tasted delicious. It had obviously been basted for hours as it cooked over a slow fire.

Redsock laughed at their eagerness.

'You eat you friend,' he screamed, as other trolls gathered round and laughed. 'You eat him buttocks.'

'What?' asked Spagg.

'You eat old man on boat. We cook him, eat him liver, eat him heart, eat him brains. He very tasty.'

Redsock licked his lips and rubbed his tummy as he grinned at them with blackened teeth.

'You silly men. You *cannibal*.'

'You're the cannibals,' roared Spagg. 'You're the ones who cooked him to eat.'

Redsock looked superior and shook his head. 'We no cannibal. We *trolls*. We no eat trolls. We eat *peoples*. You peoples are peoples. You eat old man. *You* cannibal.'

'He's got us there,' muttered Soldier, feeling queasy. 'We're the cannibals all right.'

It rained once in three days and they were able to lap puddle water from the ground to quench their thirst and try to wash away the taste of animal fat from their mouths. At the end of this period the troll owl-rider returned. He seemed upset and annoyed. Redsock came to see the prisoners a little later. He was none too happy either.

'Princess no can be found. Troll can no speak with queen. Only with queen's man. Man say no money. Man say kill you dead and riddance.'

'Queen's man?' queried Soldier. 'Now who would that be?'

'No care less,' said Redsock, turning away. 'We eat you breakfast.'

It seemed that the trolls cared little that no money had arrived. They celebrated the fact that there was to be a meat feast in the morning. They enjoyed a brew of fermented pine-sap and proceeded to get drunk on it. All afternoon they swigged from wooden bowls, their behaviour becoming more and more outrageous as the day wore on. There were horrible fights in which they clawed at each other with hands and feet, trying to blind their opponents. There were displays of idiocy, where some of them tried to jump a wide chasm, until one drunken troll fell two hundred feet and his crumpled body sobered those others who felt they could make the leap. They were sick where they stood, their vomit freezing to ice. They came and spat on the prisoners when they felt a mind to, saying it would lubricate the meat and was a precursor to basting.

Finally they were all so drunk they fell upon the ground in a stupor and lost consciousness.

Evening came, then night followed. It was bitterly cold. Soldier studied the stars as he sat with his back against the wall, the manacles chafing his wrists and ankles. Spagg had fallen into an exhausted, fitful sleep by his side. Had it come to this? To die at the hands of some mean, little, unscrupulous river pirates? Surely he had a higher purpose than this deserved? But perhaps all men on the point of death think that? Perhaps we all believe that our place in the great plan – our mission in life – deserves more than a foreshortening of our natural span, especially when the executors are less than worthy themselves. But was a death in some fusty bed where the greasy linen clings to a body which has already begun decomposing – was that any better than dying in the open air, with the scents and sounds of nature stimulating our senses? Soldier thought not – but still – still he regretted having to die.

'A fine pickle you're in.'

Soldier stared at a piece of darkness. There was a shape there as black as the night itself. Only the stars shining on its shiny feathers told Soldier who it was.

'Raven,' he whispered, in some relief.

'When I saw that owl coming over the castle, I knew it was you that was in trouble. So I followed it back. I suppose you want me to pick the locks on those manacles?'

'Can you do that?' asked Soldier, hopefully.

Without replying the raven flew down and settled on Soldier's wrist. Immediately he began pecking at the lock, getting the point of his beak inside the keyhole and working it around. It seemed to be taking an age and Soldier was afraid there was a problem. Finally, after a lot of scratching and scraping, the lock snapped open.

'Bit rusty,' said the bird, 'but we'll get them done.'

The raven worked on the manacles one by one, until Soldier was free. Spagg remained asleep all throughout this operation. Soldier woke him by clamping a hand over his mouth. The hand-seller's eyes bulged in fear, probably thinking his time had come. Then Soldier whispered in his ear, telling him to remain quiet. The raven then worked on Spagg's manacles and eventually freed him too. By this time it was nearly dawn. All around the snow-covered battlements of the trolls' fort were little creatures lying asleep, snoring away as if the temperature were not several degrees below zero. Many of them remained drunk on the fermented pine sap. There were still pools of frozen vomit everywhere.

'I see there's been a wassail,' the raven muttered. 'No one invited *me*.'

'Not so much a wassail as a race to break all the seven deadly sins in one fell swoop,' replied Spagg.

'Let's get out of here,' whispered Soldier. 'We need to be well away before daylight wakes them.'

Chapter Twenty

Much to the consternation of Spagg, Soldier crept around and through the troll bodies to locate his sword and sheath. The weapon was hanging from the spur of a rock where it had been placed by one of the trolls. At the foot of the spur was the backpack containing, among other things, the enchanted brigandine. Once he was armed again Soldier was tempted to put on the brigandine for protection and begin slaying the owners of the fort. Such was his anger at these monsters who had kept him prisoner for so long without nourishment. He resisted the urge, however, and after putting the pack on his back, he rejoined Spagg at the wall.

The two men climbed over the wall and began descending the steep path leading down the cliff-face. They passed several troll sentries who had fallen asleep. The raven flew ahead of them, his dark winged form stark against the snow of the valley below. It did not take the party long to reach the bottom of the escarpment. They then began to run along the river bank, travelling westwards. Before they had gone half a mile however they heard the sound of a cow-horn carrying over the snow. The trolls had woken and discovered their captives were missing.

The raven landed in the snow and urged the humans forward.

'Get a move on! Those hairy little beasts will be on you before you know it. Don't you value your lives? Quickly, quickly.'

The two men went as fast as they could, but they were weak from hunger. Spagg, whose fear was a wonderful spur, was actually faster than Soldier, who had to carry the pack. But neither man was making great progress through the deep snow. When they reached a black-branched, tangled spinney on top of a rise, they paused to gulp down breath. Soldier felt he could run no more. He turned to face his pursuers, sword in hand, ready to fight and die if that was what it had come to.

The trolls had swarmed out of the hillside fort and down the steep slopes to the river. Now they were battling through the same deep snow towards their quarry, waving their thick clubs.

'Here,' said Soldier, taking his warhammer out of the backpack, 'you take this, Spagg.'

'I'm no hand-to-hand fighter,' said Spagg, looking at the weapon he had been given. 'I've never killed anyone like that. I can throw a knife, that's all.'

'Good for you,' said the raven.

Soldier growled. 'If you don't fight here and now you'll be beaten to death. There's a time to contemplate the niceties of life and a time to disregard them.'

'You're both going to die anyway,' the raven said cheerfully. 'Look how many are coming! You'll be overwhelmed in a few minutes. Well, goodbye Soldier, it was a pleasure knowing you. I think I'll leave you now. I can't do anything to help and I don't wish to watch you both being slaughtered.'

In the vanguard of the trolls was Redsock. He looked enraged. It seemed he took the escape as a personal affront to his hospitality, because he was shouting, 'You peoples *bad* guests. You no say thank you. I bash you head full with thank yous . . .'

Spagg looked down at the warhammer in his right hand.

'Well,' he said with a resigned sigh, 'I ain't goin' to go out whimperin' like a beaten dog. I suppose killing a troll ain't like killin' a person. More like killing a rat. Lord Theg, give me strength. I was a novice priest, remember? I did my duty, my service to the Sacred Seven. Don't let me die like a dog in the snow. Save your faithful apprentice to worship you again in the temples of the land. Gifts I will bring you. Orisons I will intone. Liturgies, litanies, what you like, only don't let 'em get me, Theg. That's not too much to ask, is it?'

Like most atheists, Spagg was not above appealing to the gods, once death stared him in the face.

The trolls swarmed towards them, indeed looking very much like clothed rats.

Just then, the raven returned and landed on the branch of a tree nearby.

'Something's coming,' the raven said. 'I got out of the sky just in time.'

The two men, about to be engulfed by trolls, looked up into the blue and saw a red-and-green winged shape descending towards them.

'What is it?' cried Spagg. 'It's not a bird. It's not a bat either. It's massive. Oh, goddess Kist, I know you hate humans, but what is this flying beast you've sent?'

The shape grew larger and more definable in the morning

air. It was green with a bright red underside. Its head was larger than its shoulders. It had long jaws full of white, pointed teeth and its black talons flashed in the icy daylight.

Spagg cried, 'It's a dragon!'

'One of those things could swallow me whole,' said the raven, hunching himself smaller on the branch, and adding, 'Of course, I'm just a tid-bit. There's other food running around on two legs which would satisfy a dragon's hunger.'

The dragon landed in the snow just a few yards away, just as the trolls reached the two runaway prisoners.

'SLAHGGUS,' it said.

It was a muscular creature, about as large as an average-sized bear. Its green ears, sprouting stamen-like bunches of yellow hair, stood tall and straight as spires on the back of its head. Cavernous nostrils breathed blasts of hot air which melted the snow in front of the creature, now standing on its back legs. On its small front limbs were its lesser claws, which it clicked together like a man flicking the fingernails of his two hands against each other. Lesser claws these pairs might be, but they could disembowel a man with a single slash.

There was a lightning streak down the dragon's nose, which was its own personal mark – its name if you like – by which it was known in the world of dragons. Every dragon of every type had one of these marks on its nose and they were unique, differing slightly in their jaggedness, colour or size.

This was a young male dragon which had just reached puberty. Its purple eyes regarded the prey around it. There were men and there were trolls. A choice had to be made.

These men and these trolls regarded the dragon with some trepidation. Both knew they were facing one of the world's most savage predators. A dragon, like a shark, thinks of filling its stomach before considering anything else. All the warm-blooded creatures stood like statues, waiting for the dragon to make its move, so the survivors could run. Some would undoubtedly escape while the dragon was devouring friends, but one thing was certain from the moment the creature landed – it *would* eat.

Redsock imparted some intelligence, though he did not move a muscle in case he attracted attention to himself.

'He go eat you,' said Redsock to Soldier and Spagg. 'He eat fat juicy man, not stringy troll.'

'We're not so fat and juicy after you starved us,' reminded Soldier.

'You still fatter than troll.'

This was undoubtedly true. The trolls were so short they were up to their armpits in snow, while Soldier and Spagg were only up to their thighs. The dragon could see most of what was available to it on the men, could mentally joint them. Even half-starved the humans were obviously the more succulent, tasty items on the menu. Soldier waited hopefully for the armoured hunter to come out of the white wilderness and save him – the same who had rescued him from the witch – but his saviour did not appear and the dragon suddenly lurched forward.

Redsock was unafraid now. He was convinced the dragon would eat the men first. There would be time to run away.

Redsock screamed.

One moment he had been standing there, a smug expression on his face, the next he was in the dragon's jaws. There was a crunch of skull-bone and his body went floppy. A hand opened in reflex and a club fell with a soft plop into the snow.

Trolls began running now, back to their fortress home. Redsock was dropped and a second one was snatched up, just as he thought he was heading for safety. The dragon bit off his head and swallowed it, leaving the limbs jerking on a raw-necked torso, so that it thrashed in the snow. The dragon quickly ate his way through the available meat, surprisingly bird-like in its table manners. It hardly used its forepaws, preferring instead to draw the body into its mouth with its back teeth.

When it had finished, it turned and stared at the two men, frozen to the spot in exhaustion and horror.

'KKKERRRROOOW,' cried the dragon, sending out a long hot tongue to lick Soldier's hair. 'KKKERRROOOW.'

It was a kind of whine – the sort of noise a cat might make when it wanted petting – only much louder of course.

'Go and pat it,' croaked the raven.

'What?' cried Soldier, his hair standing on end. 'Not on your life.'

'Do it. Do it now.'

There was something in the raven's tone which made Soldier step a few paces forward and pat the dragon's head. The skin was surprising silky to the touch. The dragon made a mewling sound. Soldier patted it again. The dragon dropped on all fours for a moment, licked Soldier's legs with his rough tongue, then stood up again and swiftly rose into the air. All the way across the sky, until it was a small dot in the heavens, it kept calling that same sound, 'KERROWW. KERROWW.'

Spagg fell backwards in the snow as if he had been felled by an axe.

'Theg's legwarmers,' he murmured in sweet relief, 'we're still alive. I was sure we was in for it there. Oh, you lovely snow and ice, so cold on my face. I can still feel you. I'm still alive and warm, and alive, and, yes,' he pinched himself, 'alive and warm. Oh gracious gods of the seven mountains. Will I ever doubt you again?'

'What happened there?' asked Soldier, puzzled, as he rested in the snow before going on. 'Why didn't it attack us? I could have sworn it sized us up and down, and then it attacked the trolls instead. Surely we were more of a meal than those hard-muscled creatures?'

Spagg sat up, before replying.

'I don't know why – for reasons known only to the dragon itself, I suppose – but I'm very, very glad.'

'Wrong.'

The two men stared at a tree branch. It had been the raven who spoke.

'What's wrong?' asked Soldier.

'As well as the dragon itself, I too know the reasons why it didn't attack you. Did you hear that sound it kept repeating? I happen to be very familiar with male dragons and I speak their language. I'm not bragging, it's not a hard tongue to learn and understand. Male dragons speak only five words from eggshell to the grave. Food, mother, mine, fight and yes.'

'Don't they have a word for "no"?' asked Spagg.

'During their long, eventful lives male dragons only get asked one question by fellow male dragons. *Fight?* To which they always answer "Yes" since invariably the conflict is over mating rights with a female dragon or dragons.'

'And what about female dragons?'

'Oh, they have a large, comprehensive vocabulary, full of diphthongs, and upper and lower plate clicks, to differentiate between gerunds and subjunctive nouns, with rolling verbs and exploding adjectives. Don't stand too close when they're describing something because you get sprayed with warm spittle. Their sentences tend to be looping, the last word fitting into the first word as a kind of locking belt-buckle.

For instance if the first word is VALUCUME – meaning *sovereign-lord* – the last word will be something like GNAS-VALU – meaning *dead-fish*, the beginning and the end syllables fitting each other exactly. I don't speak a lot of female dragon-language. It has far too many nuances and is spoken very fast. There's a kind of etiquette which says that the reply must always be faster than the question. Since many conversations involve questions and answers the speech gets quicker and quicker, until the whole thing is just a varying drone, like a bee buzz, or cricket song.'

'I only asked,' grumbled Spagg.

Soldier was fascinated, though still not sure that the raven was not inventing the whole idea of dragon-language, just to fool the two men.

'So – why do the males only speak five words and the females thousands?'

'Hundreds of thousands. Well, the females have more to talk about. They're actually fussier about what they eat and prefer herbs and vegetables to meat. They not only have names for all the plants, but each individual plant has several names which carry a description, to denote texture, colour, age . . . A TANAL might be a dark green dock leaf with a rough underside, while a TANIL might be a light green dock leaf with a sharp edge to it. Do you see what I mean? Subtleties.'

Soldier was sure now that the raven was being facetious.

'So, when the dragon – our dragon, the one that ate the two trolls – when it shouted "SLAHGGUS" that meant . . .?'

'Food.'

Soldier nodded, sagely. 'Of course. And KERROWW?'

'Mother.'

Soldier frowned, losing his superiority for a moment.

'What?'

'The word means "mother". That's what it called you. Mother. That's why it didn't eat you. Or rather *us*. Because you were its mother and we were under your protection.'

A light suddenly dawned in Soldier's mind. 'The egg I found on Mount Kkamaramm!' he exclaimed. 'I was the first thing the baby dragon saw when it hatched. I fed it.'

'There you are,' said the raven, 'problem solved. You're blue-eyed and therefore instantly recognisable, my two-legged friend. So, you're the mother of a dragon? I suppose we're lucky it wasn't the real mother. Egg-stealing is a very serious crime amongst dragons. So is posing as a dragon-mother. If I were you I'd tread very carefully around large mountain nests.'

The raven left them about noon. Soldier and Spagg continued battling through the snowdrifts, fighting their way westwards towards the mountains of the Sacred Seven. It was in the mid-levels of these mountains that wizards dwelt in larger numbers than anywhere else in Guthrum. Large numbers in wizard terms being around a baker's dozen. Wizards are happier living in the shadow of the gods, where the air is charged with mystery and superstition. They rarely seek neighbours of mortal hue.

It was in these mountains Soldier hoped to find a wizard who would cure his wife of her madness and possibly solve the mystery of his loss of memory.

The following morning, they hunted a hind, tracking it across the snow. Their hunger was their spur. Once they had the beast cornered in a dark copse which crowned a smooth hill, it was Spagg's job to flush the creature out. Soldier had made himself a longbow out of yew, with ash-wand arrows, and waited on the far side of the trees for the animal to bolt, so that he could shoot it down on the run. Soldier was not as proficient with the longbow as he was with the crossbow, but he hoped to get in a good shot at close range.

The hind broke from the trees after Spagg had gone in clattering a dagger-blade against a drinking cup.

Soldier went down on one knee as the frightened hind sped by him, nimble despite the deep snow. He loosed the arrow. The haft struck the hind behind the left shoulder and brought the beast down into the snow.

'I got it – we got it!' shouted Soldier.

Another creature, a dwarf, suddenly appeared from a blasted hollow oak trunk, whose cavity was large enough for the dwarf to shelter from any blizzard or winter storm.

'Mine!' shouted the dwarf. 'I shot it!'

Spagg came up behind the dwarf and clouted him a backhander around the ear.

'You ain't even got a bow, you little sniveller. Get away, before I lose my temper.'

The chunky dwarf went roaring off, into the wood, yelling insults over his shoulder.

In the meantime Soldier was running as fast as he could through the drifts. When he reached the wounded hind it was still alive. It lay there, its red blood blotting the white snow. Its big brown eyes looked up at him. They were full of terror. It tried to get to its feet again, scrambling, scrabbling, churning up ice crystals from below the light fluffy topcoat which had fallen that morning, but its hooves could not grip and the arrow, sticking out, remained an awkward obstacle, its flight stuck in the drift.

'You poor creature,' murmured Soldier, pitying it, 'how beautiful you are.'

He did not so much regret killing the beast, for he and

Spagg were close to starving, but he could still appreciate the fear and distress the animal was going through. He knelt down with his hunting knife, to cut the hind's throat, when he noticed it had a black velvet collar studded with jewels. The collar bore a silver plate on which were etched some words:

'Touch me not, for Caezor's I am.'

'What? What's this?' cried Soldier. 'A tame hind? If it belongs to someone, what's the creature doing out here in the wilds?'

He reached over and pulled the arrow from its wound. Since the barb had been hastily fashioned, with inadequate tools, it was not severe. The arrow came out fairly easily. Once it was removed the hind leapt to its feet and was running across the snow, towards a distant hill.

Spagg arrived just as the hind darted away.

'Oh, ye deadly plagues and 'orrible diseases,' cried Spagg in consternation and disappointment, 'take me now, 'cause I can't hunt another one of them things.'

He fell down beside Soldier, who was still kneeling in the snow, and tears coursed down his cheeks.

'What happened?' he wailed. 'I thought you had it in your hands?'

'I did, I did,' replied Soldier, still staring after the hind. 'But it – it was a tame creature. It had a collar with a phrase on it. *Touch me not*, it said.'

'They taste just as good, you know,' shouted Spagg, still desperately upset. 'Tame or wild, the meat would have settled nicely on my stomach, which is now complaining so loudly they can hear it back in Zamerkand.'

'Let's follow it,' replied Soldier, seeing that beside the creature's prints was a blood trail. 'Let's track the spoor. I'm sure it'll drop before it gets a mile. We might still yet have our venison lunch if we can find that fawn.'

Spagg climbed wearily to his feet and followed after Soldier into the wilderness.

They plodded through the deep snow to the top of the next rise. It took them an hour. When they reached there they were met by a heavy-set bulky man on horseback. His beard was thick, curly and black, and covered most of his face. He wore a velvet cap with a beautiful golden brooch pinned on it. His robes were fit for a king, being made of velvet and ermine. Around his neck dangled a thick gold chain with a gold pendant. His leggings were of chewed deerskin and looked soft. They were held in place by rawhide crisscrossed straps coming up from leather boots that were so pliable they gathered in elegant folds at his ankles. His horse was a magnificent white charger, strong-looking, with a maroon saddle rich in the workmanship of an expert.

'Have you seen a . . .?' began Spagg, accusingly, but Soldier stopped him with a wave of his hand.

'Who are you, sir?' asked Soldier of the rider. 'Is this your land?'

'I am Caezor, the alchemist, and this is indeed my land,' said the deep-throated rider. 'You are poaching.'

'Poaching what? We haven't killed anything,' replied Soldier, warily.

'You carry a hunting-bow. You look starved. You are tracking blood in the snow.'

'I confess we are hungry,' replied Soldier, 'but we are not conscious thieves.'

'The woodland dwarves steal half my game already. They

use snares to trap them. Snares kill very slowly. They are cruel devices. I trust you do not use snares?'

'Nope,' replied Spagg, 'nor gin traps neither. We hunt on the fair and square, with bow and arrow.'

'Then follow me to my house, gentlemen, where you shall find warmth and succour. My wife is at this moment cooking a supper which will soon fill out those limbs of yours and put some heat in your blood.'

With that the big man led the way on his horse.

Over the next rise they came upon a large single-storey dwelling by a lake, with trees to the back. It was a rambling lodge with about twenty high chimneys that reached up into the white swirling sky. On each end of the lodge were squat, round turrets with peaked roofs. The windows were narrow and mean, the sort to keep out harsh winters and help to make the interior cool in hot weather. There was the smell of woodsmoke in the air – hickory and pine – coming from the many chimneys.

'This is my abode,' called Caezor the Alchemist. 'Welcome, gentlemen. Come inside.'

The big man dismounted and led his horse through a wide archway into a coaching yard. There he handed the reins to a dwarf groom who took the wonderful beast to its stable. The three men then trailed through horse dung to a back door and entered a steaming kitchen which smelled like heaven to the two famished travellers.

'This way, this way,' called Caezor, leading them through to a door at the far end, 'into the hall.'

They found themselves in a great hall, the walls covered with shields and weapons, some of them for hunting, others for war. The floor was tiled with slate and the walls and ceiling were of red hardwood. There was a great dining table, scarred with the marks of many knives, down at the end, with tall-backed oak chairs around it. Magnificent hides hung on the walls as tapestries, to keep in the warmth. In a wide open fireplace a fire roared happily, sending woodsparks up the chimney. There was an ox roasting on a spit over its flames. A pretty young woman in a velvet dress was basting the carcass.

The woman looked up and smiled. She had large, soft, brown eyes. Her shoulder, below the green velvet dress, revealed a bandage which bore a small patch of red stain the size of a pedlar's coin. She looked about a third of Caezor's age, was petite and slim, and her heart-shaped face, with its small nose and bow-cherry lips, was that of one of the prettiest females Soldier had ever seen. Her hair, falling from a small green cap, was a tumble of shining brown waves.

Soldier could not help noticing that her bodice was laced in a criss-cross fashion.

'My dear,' said Caezor, 'these men are hungry. I have invited them to share our meal.'

'Quite right, husband,' came the reply. 'Hospitality is the first rule of our household.'

Soldier stepped forward. 'But you are hurt, my lady. Your shoulder . . .'

She shrugged her dress over the wound.

'It is nothing. Please do not concern yourself, sir. I caught it on a rose briar.'

A rose briar? What was she doing near a rose briar in this weather? He stepped closer and then stopped dead.

The young lady! She had on a velvet choker with a silver plate. He could not read the words from where he stood but Soldier knew what they said. *'Touch me not, for Caezor's I am.'* He felt guilty and upset for what he had done to the hind, but he was also alarmed at the magic in this household. If he had wounded the woman as a hind, what was she doing running over the countryside? Where had she been when they came across her in the copse?

'Sit at the table,' ordered their host, 'while I carve you some pieces of this ox. Cresside, will you fetch some bread from the kitchen? Bring also some cooked vegetables and of course some jugs of malmsey and mead. See if you can warm the malmsey before pouring into the drinking vessels: hot malmsey is so much more satisfying on a cold day, don't you think?'

'I do – I do indeed, husband.'

Cresside left them and went into the kitchen.

'Your – your wife,' said Soldier, coughing a little in embarrassment. 'She's hurt.'

The lord of the house looked after his wife and nodded.

'Ah, yes, poor lady. She went out riding this morning and returned with that wound. She says a briar, but I suspect some dwarf poachers shot her by accident. She will protect these creatures. I shall deal with them in due course. They deserve to be hung from the old oak, but I suspect my anger will have cooled somewhat before I have them in my grasp, and I predict they shall get away with a mere whipping. But do not concern yourselves with my affairs! Please! Feast yourselves! Do not stand on ceremony.'

Soldier coughed again, feeling awkward. 'I – we – that is, we were hunting too, you know. The gods forbid, but I hope it was not one of our stray arrows . . .'

The alchemist shook his head emphatically, his black beard swishing on his chest.

'No, no, no. I think not.'

'But we might have . . .'

Caezor seemed to be getting angry. 'I said you did not, sir. Please do not argue with me over my own lady. I know what happened. I am informed.'

'I'm sorry,' replied Soldier. 'I don't mean to upset you or doubt your word. I would just hate to be sitting here at your table when I'm responsible for an injury. It would be better to get it out of the way, to beg your forgiveness and that of your lady, and to have my apologies accepted, before indulging in the fare you offer . . . but,' it seemed that the alchemist was getting angry again, 'if we were not responsible, then of course there is no need to go into this any further.'

'Quite, quite. Ah, here's the bread and wine.' His voice was back to being cheerful and hearty again. 'And some good green vegetables I managed to freeze in my icehouse. This will turn you back into a lusty young man again.'

'And me?' inquired Spagg.

'And you into a whatever you were before you became a frozen corpse,' laughed the alchemist. 'Eat, eat, both of you. And drink your fill. Let us praise the gods that I found you before you both fell and died from exposure. Later I will show you the room where I make gold out of pig lead. You will be amazed, sirs, I guarantee. It's a process I brought back with me from far eastern shores, from twin cities called Sadon and Targe, situated on the two nesses of the great Aegisonian rivers of Ellprates and Isgan. There are only two people in the world who know the secret – the Thag of Isgan – and myself.

'But I am stopping you eating. Please. Pick up your forks. Let us hear your story while we dine.'

Chapter Twenty-One

Soldier told his host and hostess that they were on a quest to find a wizard who would cure his wife and the queen of their madness. Cresside said it was commendable that he should take on such a quest, when there were such dangers to travellers in these dark times of a dying King Magus. Caezor added his praise to hers, saying he hoped he would do the same for his wife, should she ever come under a similar spell.

'But eat, eat,' Caezor encouraged them. 'And you, Spagg, what is it you do . . .?'

Try as they could the two guests could not get food into their mouths. Each time they raised the fork to their lips they were asked yet another question, which they felt bound by politeness and etiquette to answer. Yet it seemed that their hosts were feeding themselves very well. The meat and vegetables were disappearing from the plates on the table at a very fast rate. Finally, Spagg could stand it no longer and he ignored Caezor's latest question in order to fill his mouth full of meat, potatoes and bread. He crammed as much in as his cheeks would hold, much to the consternation of his disapproving hosts, who stared at him in revulsion.

'Sir!' cried the lady.

Soldier was glad of the interruption. He too managed to chew and swallow a few bites, while the lord and his lady were engaged with being offended by Spagg's manners. The meal progressed but it was hard work feeding himself while trying to answer an endless stream of questions, and at the end of it all Soldier did not feel satisfied. Spagg too confessed under his breath to be inadequately fed. However, they could hardly complain, even though the wine jugs had passed them by two or three times while their cups remained empty, going between husband and wife, but failing to halt or even pause in front of the guests. The hosts seemed oblivious of this poor behaviour and the guests were too embarrassed to be outraged.

'Come and see my gold room,' cried Caezor, as the pair tried to wipe their trenchers with some bread to get the last few drops of dripping fat. 'Come – come – don't stand on ceremony. Follow me.'

They were urged to their feet by a hostess who practically pulled the chairs out from under them. Hurried along passageways and past other rooms, they were finally pushed into a chamber full of glass bottles, brass instruments and measuring sticks of all kinds. Their host gave them a passing acquaintance with the art of alchemy, but said that of course he could not tell them how to turn base metals into gold, because the secret had to remain with the few.

'What's this in 'ere?' said Spagg, picking up a dark green bottle and staring at the contents.

'Hemlock.'

Spagg put it down and picked up another more viscous, rolling fluid. 'And this one?'

'Quicksilver.'

'And what about this?' Spagg held up a medium-sized bottle.

Clearly Caezor was becoming impatient with Spagg. The alchemist was wanting to impress his visitors, but he wanted to ask the questions as well as answer them. He waved an irritated hand in front of Spagg's face.

'Pure alcohol,' he snapped. 'Nothing exotic. Now this *is* very rare,' he said, picking up a bottle made of lapis lazuli and showing it to Soldier. 'It's musk oil.'

'What do you do with it?' asked Soldier.

'Why, I use it as a perfume,' replied Caezor, uncorking the bottle and sprinkling a few drops in his beard. 'It helps attract the deer during the hunt.'

Spagg had been quietly sniffing and examining the bottle of alcohol behind his host's back. Soldier saw him in a bronze mirror in the act of replacing the stopper. Soldier could not help noticing that when Spagg put back the bottle on its shelf there was less in it than when he had picked it up. Considerably less.

'Look, I'm done in,' said Spagg, staggering down the passageway afterwards. 'So tired I can't walk straight.'

Caezor frowned, clearly suspecting something, but not being able to guess what had occurred.

'Perhaps you'd both better get some sleep in a proper bed with sheets and blankets,' he told them. 'I'll ask my wife to show you to your rooms.'

Although the house had looked like a one-storey building from the outside, it was indeed two. Spagg was given a room on the first landing, where everyone tramped by on their way to the wooden garderobe at the head of the timber staircase. Soldier was shown to a fine chamber in the middle of the house while Spagg was left to his rest. The lady smoothed down

Soldier's sheets for him, then stared at him with doe eyes as he shuffled his feet and wondered when she was going to go.

'My lady,' he said, after a long while, 'I would like to rest my head, if you would be so kind.'

'Yes,' she replied, simply, still standing there.

'But – but I cannot if you remain in the room.'

She raised her eyebrows. 'Why not?'

'It would be improper.'

'I can't think why,' she replied, brusquely. 'However, if it upsets you to look upon me . . .'

'No, no, your form is divine. I have seen no lovelier lady since I left my wife behind in Zamerkand. It's just that – well, I don't think she would approve. Nor, I imagine, would your husband. We are bare acquaintances, my lady, and not even close friends. Please, I would prefer to wash myself in that bowl over there without being scrutinized.'

She shrugged, either mystified or put out. 'If you insist.'

Then she left the room. There lingered in the air the tantalising scent of musk. He remembered that he had first met this lady as a hind. Soldier sighed. He went to the basin on the bench and poured some water from a jug. This he splashed on his face with his hands. Then, after carefully locking the door, he undressed and climbed into the bed. Soon he was warm and snug and fell fast asleep.

He awoke some time later to the singing of his scabbard and sat bolt upright in bed, wondering where he had put his sword. The lord of the manor was entering the room. There was also someone lying asleep beside Soldier. He turned, alarmed to see the lord's wife, Cresside, curled up with her head on the pillow next to his. He quickly threw the blankets over her sleeping form and sat up to hide that side of the bed from view.

'Time you were up,' cried the alchemist from the doorway. 'I shall take you hunting stag tonight! I'll see you in the hall in one hour.'

Soldier sat there, stupefied, as Caezor marched off again, along the passageway.

Soldier pulled back the covers again. Brown locks cascaded over the pillows at the top of the bed, framing a pretty countenance. A slim, pale arm, at the shoulder of which was a bandage, lay across Soldier's lap. A soft, white breast was half-exposed above the sheets, while its twin companion rose and fell beside it to the rhythm of Cresside's soft breathing. Something silky with a leg inside it pressed against Soldier's thigh.

He was mortified. Had his host had seen him in bed with his wife? Thank the gods he had not done anything.

'What are you thinking of?'

He looked down at where the words came from. She was awake. Her large moist eyes regarded him with some puzzlement.

'My wife.'

'How sweet of you.'

She sat up and yawned coquettishly, allowing her silk nightdress to fall forward and expose her upper body. Soldier groaned and looked away.

'Did we?' he began. 'That is – how did you get into my bed without my scabbard warning me?'

'Oh, your singing scabbard? I heard its song. You must have been so fast asleep it could not wake you.'

'So fast asleep,' he said, thankfully, 'therefore we merely lay side by side, without – without engaging?'

'Without engaging what?'

'Each other – each other's affections, that is.'

She pouted. 'I was displeased about that. There's no need to sound so proud. You did me a disservice. I could not wake you. Your manners are wanting, sir.' She waved an admonishing finger playfully in his face.

'I'm sorry,' he said, jumping out of bed, happier to learn that his fidelity was intact. 'I did not mean to seem ungrateful for your hospitality.'

Spagg appeared in the doorway, watched Soldier trying to put on his hose, took in the fact that the bed was occupied by a female in a state of undress, and shook his head sadly.

'Trust you,' he said. 'Can't resist a pretty face, can you? You must be mad.'

'It's not what it seems,' explained Soldier.

'So you say.'

'I mean it. The lady came to my bed after I fell asleep. I had no part in it.'

'I should be so fortunate.'

'Perhaps one day, you will be, Spagg. Until then you've got to learn to trust me. Nothing happened between this lady and me. We were merely – merely bed companions. By the way,' he said, coming closer to Spagg's ear, 'her husband knows nothing of this and I think he should continue in his ignorance.'

'I'm going back to my room,' said Spagg, loftily. 'Goodnight.'

Soldier went down to the great hall and found his host pacing up and down.

'Ah, here you are.' cried the big, bearded man, impatiently. 'Come, come, let us go. The moon is full. I have two mounts ready for the hunt. By the by, have you seen my wife?'

'The lady Cresside?'

'I only have *one* wife.'

Soldier coughed. 'Yes, yes, of course. Now when did I last lay eyes on her . . .' He stalled, as if trying to recall the incident, until Caezor's impatience overtook him.

'Well, well, never mind. Tonight we shall find ourselves a magnificent stag, what say you? Put on these furs I have for you – there, you must keep warm in these midwinter conditions.'

With that the lord of the house strode towards the doors at the end of the hall and flung them open. Outside, under a clear sky showing a heaven rich with stars, stood a dwarf groom holding two black horses. Another dwarf stood nearby, with two crossbows in his hands. Soldier mounted one of the horses and was handed a crossbow. Caezor was already riding out, across the snow, towards a distant woodland. Soldier followed him, under the moonlight, his breath coming out as steam.

It was indeed a glorious night. Foxes barked deep and hollow across the winter wastes. The ermine and his kin were out hunting voles and mice. White hares were blanks against the snowy background, only their eyes glinting in the moonlight. The air was fresh and clean. Beneath surface ice brooks bubbled and tumbled across otherwise silent moors. Ancient stones stood as snow-capped guardians of the landscape, some with symbols carved upon their faces, others virgin to man's art. Tangled trees were stark against the moon, their dark tracery like veins.

Caezor rode out in front, blowing on his hunting horn.

When they came up over a rise they saw a bonfire burning in the middle of a snow-covered meadow. Around this fire danced a hundred dwarfs, men and women, with children running hither and thither. The dancers wore leather caps with loose ear-flaps which slapped against the sides of their heads in a rhythmic accompaniment to their fife and log-drum musicians. Rough-looking woollen shirts covered their backs and their leggings were of the same leather as their caps. On their feet they wore enormous wooden clogs.

'A dwarf wedding,' grunted Caezor. 'I hope they haven't panicked the deer.'

The dwarfs had set up a long wooden table in the snow and this was spread with fare. Dwarfs in long aprons were hurrying to and fro with trays and platters of food and drink. At either end of the table sat a male and a female. She was dressed in a dress made of fir branches, with cones dangling from her hair, breasts and knees. He had on a stiff suit of armour which appeared to be fashioned from tree bark. Oaken branches, like antlers, protruded from the bridegroom's head. The pair had no eyes except for each other, like any bridal couple.

'Ho!' cried Caezor, riding up.

The dwarfs stopped in mid-note, in mid-dance, and looked ready to scatter. Their eyes revealed a suppressed panic. They had obviously been so busy having a good time they had not seen the riders approach.

'Stay, stay,' Caezor ordered, 'dwarfs are not the quarry tonight.' He let out a laugh which told Soldier that other nights were different. 'Tonight we're after the stag. Have you seen any tracks, any spoor? Tell us and we'll be on our way and leave you to your cavorting and feasting.'

An elderly dwarf stepped forward. He had on a coat made of flour sacks with roughly-carved wooden toggles for buttons. His arm went up and he pointed with his finger.

'Yonder, Lord – in Mistlemus Wood. I observed with my own eyes the marks of a king stag just this very morn.'

'I see you have one of my hares cooking on your fire amongst the platters of roasting chestnuts.'

The elderly dwarf glanced quickly in that direction and smiled nervously.

'Only a rabbit, my lord, not one of your grace's hares.'

'Ah, a rabbit! With such long ears? Well, never mind, a wedding is a wedding. Tonight you dance, tomorrow we shall hunt poachers and run them to ground. Enjoy your feast.'

'Mistlemus Wood, my lord.'

'I heard you.'

With that, Caezor rode on. Soldier stared about him at the dwarfs, who seemed to have had all the joy taken out of them. 'I shall do my best to persuade him it is a rabbit,' he told the dwarfs. 'You may rest easy in your beds.'

They stared back at him as if he were mad.

'Who are you?' asked the elderly dwarf.

'My name is Soldier. I am the lord's guest.'

'Be careful, Soldier. You know not the ways he keeps and turns and turns again. His moods are no less cryptic than his actions. He may find you for a friend now, but tomorrow may be different. Try not to give him an excuse.'

'An excuse for what?'

'To assuage any guilt he may feel in hunting you down.'

Soldier caught up with Caezor on the edge of a great dark woodland.

'This is Mistlemus Wood,' murmured the lord. 'Come, let us find the tracks of the stag.'

'The meat on the fire,' said Soldier, 'I inspected it more closely. I do believe it to be a rabbit, not a hare. Perhaps the ears were stretched in the skinning?'

Caezor looked at Soldier with narrowed eyes, but said nothing on the subject.

Soldier, having done his best, walked his horse along the edge of the wood and eventually found the marks. He called to the alchemist, who came at the trot. Together they followed the stag's spoor, which led them up and behind the wood, past a dew-pond on the crest of a shallow hill, through a brake, and finally onto the edge of a moorland. Here they saw the mighty stag feeding on saxifrage. For a few moments both men sat in their saddles, admiring the creature's beauty. Soldier, as always, felt a pang. It seemed a great pity to kill such a fine animal. The world would be poorer, he knew, for its sudden loss.

'This one is mine,' whispered Caezor. 'You may have tomorrow's kill.'

'HO! HO!' yelled Caezor, galloping forward and startling the grazing deer. 'Up, up, up!'

Then the stag was off, over the moor. They gave chase in great delight. Despite not wishing to kill the beast, Soldier always got a thrill from the chase. He loved going at the gallop, with the wind rushing through his hair. There was great danger in night riding: at any moment the mount might step in a rabbit hole and throw the rider to his death. It was this danger mixed with the exhilaration of the chase that filled Soldier with excitement. Gradually they gained on the stag, until Caezor saw a chance to shoot it as it leapt high over a beck.

He raised the crossbow to his shoulder and released the bolt.

The missile struck the stag under the front haunch. A despairing bellow went out from the red beast, as his front legs gave way. Then slowly, he keeled sideways and dropped on his flank into the snow. There he lay, panting, the black metal bolt protruding from his breast. Then the lord rode up quickly, dismounted, and cut its throat with one slash of the hunting knife he carried in his belt.

Soldier rode up. The moonlight gleamed on the red coat

of the stag. Its eyes were already glazing. Caezor was busy cutting around the base of the antlers, removing them from the deer's head. Finally, he had them free, the bloody stumps at the bottom dripping red spots onto the snow.

'Fine branches, eh?' cried Caezor. 'These are the only things worth hunting for. We'll leave the carcass here and collect it in the morning. No harm will come to it. The dwarfs will not dare to touch it and the night is freezing, so the meat will not spoil.'

'What about wolves?' said Soldier. 'Won't they eat it?'

'There are no wolves in this region.'

'No wolves?'

'I've killed them all.'

Soldier blinked. To kill all the wolves! They were not the most endearing of species, wolves, but to exterminate them was an act of great stupidity. Wolves had their place in nature's scheme, just as did green woodpeckers and coachman beetles. To remove a species entirely was to cut holes in the fabric of the world. Soldier determined to leave the man's lodge as soon as it was reasonable to do so.

'Those dwarfs,' said Soldier, as they rode back to the rambling dwelling. 'I'm sure they did not mean to hunt your hares. I would be grateful if you would grant me a boon. Let them have the hare for their wedding feast, with no retribution? You will be better for it, I'm sure.'

The lord stopped his horse. 'You said you believed it to be a rabbit.'

'So I do, but you clearly do not.'

'Have a care, sir,' said Caezor, in a low threatening voice. 'I will not be lectured.'

'Indeed, I do not mean to lecture you. I simply request a favour.'

'You have had enough favours from me. Next you will be asking to sleep with my wife.'

Soldier drew in a breath, sharply. 'Indeed, I will not.'

'Will you not?' asked the lord, in a lofty voice. 'We shall see. In the meantime, we are coming closer to the lodge. Here, you will take my horse the rest of the way. I shall remain out here for a while, in the night snow.'

Without another word the lord dismounted and handed the reins of his hunter to Soldier. Then taking the antlers, Caezor walked back, to stand underneath an old oak. Soldier glanced back at him, then walked his horse on, taking the other mount with him. He made his way towards the stables. A groom took the horses and bade Soldier goodnight. Soldier then made his way wearily into the house and up the stairs.

When he passed a window on the landing he felt compelled to look out.

There, in the moonlight, he saw an extraordinary sight. There was a man. At least, he *began* as a man. But there were antlers sprouting from his temples and as Soldier watched he was transformed into a stag. And there was a woman. At least, she *began* as a woman, running across the outer gardens. But even as Soldier watched, her form melted into the shape of a hind. The stag was after the hind, his hooves thundering on the hard earth, and when he reached her somewhere out in the snows of the night there was a frenzied act of mating. The heavy smell of musk wafted over the outer gardens of the lodge, up to the landing windows, choking, cloying, filling Soldier's head with thick, hazy thoughts of tangled bodies and quivering limbs.

Soldier could not help noticing that the hind had a velvet collar around her neck.

Much disturbed he went to his bed, hoping to dream of

his beloved Layana. Once again he locked the door securely, but wondered how effective this would be.

In the middle of the night, when the owl was crying havoc at the moon, he woke. Straddled across his chest was a naked Cresside. She had two sets of antlers, one in each hand. As he sat up with a start she rammed the antlers onto his temples. They fused there, the ends joining with his flesh.

'Ahhhggg!' he cried. 'What have you done?'

He pushed her pale form from him and grasped the roots of the antlers, trying to wrench them from his head.

They refused to budge. They had grown into his skull.

Cresside laughed.

Soldier could see the choker around her throat, the silver plate which read, 'Touch me not . . .' He tried to resist.

To no avail. There began to surge through his body, from the antlers, a strange mixture of unusual feelings. Foremost was strength and knowledge in nature, sensation which overwhelmed him. He seemed drugged, yet at the same time, fantastically alive. Then there was a sense of his intellect slipping from him, to be replaced by an earthy insight to the raw world of wild things. There was the taste of fungi in his mouth, and tree bark, and moss, and many other plants of woodland and meadow. The sound of his own heart pounded in his head, his senses were quickened, he was on the edge of fear, yet outwardly calm. Blood rushed through the muscles of his legs, arms, shoulders, torso, and filled his loins and thighs to the point of bursting. An overpowering lust swelled in him.

'Yes!' he said, lurching for the woman. 'Now! Yes!'

His breath was thick with the smell of the lewdness that washed like a torrent through his body. He could not help himself. He was bewitched by a carnal need which had to be satisfied. Then he was on her, thrusting, thrusting, burying himself deep in her mossy form. She encouraged his insane passion with cries of satisfaction that he was unlocking her soul with his key. She was his, but then he was hers. He knew he was losing himself inside this lovely young woman. She was wrapping him, enveloping him, swallowing him, imprisoning him. Yet still his eyes blazed for more of her, his hands finding every mound, every crevice in her. Deeper and deeper he plunged, careless of what he was losing, intent only in gratifying this terrible fathomless craving within him. Then finally he spent himself, just as she split the night with a shrill sound that must have startled the dead in their mouldy graves below the turf.

There was silence for a moment while they lay in their own sweat, still tangled, locked together.

'Yes,' she said in satisfaction, 'at last.'

Then a sudden roaring went through the manor, which Soldier knew was the sound of anger. Her husband, the lord, had heard her cry of ecstasy and knew what it meant. There was a crashing on the stairs, the sound of running feet, and Soldier knew that death was hurtling towards him. With the antlers still on his head he leapt from the bed and through the open window, dropping several feet into the deep snow beneath. Even as his bare feet touched the ground he was running, wild-eyed and naked through the night, with the roaring following in his wake.

Halfway across the fields he looked back, to the see the lord on his horse, racing after him. It was to be a hunt after all, and Soldier was the quarry. A black crossbow in Caezor's right hand signalled the intent. Soldier gulped down breath. Although he had not been fully transformed into a stag, and in fact had only the antlers to identify with that beast, he still had the strength and power of the creature. He ran swift as any deer, over the snow-covered meadows, through hedgerows, down gullies to bottomland, over brooks and brakes, and up towards the woods where lived the dwarfs.

Still the fast horse and rider behind him were gaining. Suddenly, Soldier's strength began to wane. When he entered the wood the antlers abruptly fell from his head. The energy drained from him rapidly. Soon he was standing in the moonlight, the object of curious foxes and wide-eyed owls, looking desperately for some place to hide. Caezor was thundering up the hill, blowing his hunting horn, going in for the kill. There was a loud halloo, a crashing of branches as horse and rider entered the wood, and the snorting of man and beast. Bushes were swept aside, snow flurries flew into the air from the hooves of the hunter, and a rhythmic drumming on the forest mast.

'Pssst. In here!'

Soldier, almost resigned to death, stared about him.

'Over here,' came an irritated whisper. 'Quickly. In here. Come on, come on.'

Then he saw, in the moonlight, the open mouth of an oak tree. A dwarf stood inside the cave-like entrance in the oak's trunk. Soldier stumbled over to him and stepped inside the bole of the tree. He found himself scrambling down a dark slope, aware of roots and stones, down into the darker earth beneath. The dwarf scrambled ahead of him. Soldier simply followed. They were in earth tunnels which honeycombed the countryside under the woods and fields of the land belonging to Caezor.

'Not much further,' said the dwarf.

Finally they came out in a huge cavern, with earth walls and a tangled-root ceiling. There were bugs and beetles everywhere in this huge dark space lit by soft-glowing lanterns. Soldier saw worms and snakes and all manner of underground creatures. In the corners great spiders lurked. On the rooty ceiling hung live centipedes and millipedes.

There were also many more dwarfs here. They were crouched down, about a hundred of them, in the middle of the cavern.

'Go,' said the dwarf who had fetched Soldier. 'Get down there with them.'

'Why, what's the danger?'

'Caezor. He will try to smoke us out. The best place to breathe is low on the floor.'

Sure enough, within a few minutes, smoke began to fill the cavern, coming from the entrance.

'He's treating us like badgers,' said Soldier, angrily. 'Why doesn't he come down here and fight?'

'Because he knows this is our territory,' replied a dwarf lying nearby. 'It would be more than his life's worth. What did you do to upset him, anyway? Yesterday you were good friends.'

'Ah me,' groaned Soldier. 'His wife and I . . .'

He was now feeling great remorse for his actions. Not because of Caezor's anger, but because he was now an infidel, having betrayed his wife's trust.

'You made love to his wife? The games you mortals play. Well, you can't go back to his manor now. We'll have to find some way of stealing your clothes from the lodge and getting your servant to you. It can be done, don't worry, so long as we survive this smoking.'

'Why are you doing this?' asked Soldier. 'Why are you helping me?'

'Any enemy of Caezor is a friend of ours. He treats us like

serfs and has killed many poachers amongst us. We enjoy any revenge we can get. If we help you escape it will hurt him badly, because he believes himself to be untouchable. We want to see him squirm with frustration. That will be worth the effort of assisting you to get away from this region.'

Soldier felt badly about this.

'I've brought great trouble upon you.'

'Not at all,' said the dwarf, cheerfully. 'You've given us great entertainment.'

Chapter Twenty-Two

Layana woke after several days of suffering the terrible effects of prickly tares and thorny weeds growing in her head. She knew the moment she opened her eyes that Soldier had been unfaithful to her and hurt pierced her heart like the point of a spear. Sitting up, she found her bed surrounded by servants, who had been holding her down during one of her mad fits, in case she injured herself.

She looked in the mirror. The ravages of madness were taking their toll on her beauty. She decided that in a very few years she would look like a hag anyway, and her scars would be neither here nor there.

'How long has it been?' she asked.

Ofao replied, 'Three days.'

Her servant-friends looked exhausted.

'Thank you,' she told them, 'once again.'

She sent most of them away, all except Drissila and Ofao, who would not have gone anyway. Then she bathed, dressed in fresh clean clothes, and made her way down the spiral staircase to the library below. There she tried to read poetry, to take her mind off Soldier's indiscretion. But it was impossible.

Images haunted her head. She saw the laughing lady astride her husband under a lunar heaven. His unbounded lust had his horned head jerking and shaking, the moon caught in the tangle of his antlers, whilst he was thrusting into her.

'Am I thus forgot?' groaned Layana, laying down the volume of poems. 'Am I so soon put aside?'

The scenes in her mind were impossible to dismiss and tortured Layana unceasingly. Of course, she had not known from whence Soldier had come, who had been his previous lovers, if any, and whether he was constant or not, but Layana had fallen in love with him the moment he had come down from the hill and asked her about a battle. All his previous history was of no consequence to her. His blue eyes, his open candid face, his apparent vulnerability combined with a strength of character, these were what had attracted her. No matter had he come from hell.

This was different. Now he was her husband. She was entitled to his faithfulness. He had deliberately forsaken her.

'Oh, Drissila,' said Layana, breaking down and weeping, 'I've had the most horrible dream, yet the worst part is I know it to be true. I feel it, here in my heart . . .'

She proceeded to tell the story of Soldier's betrayal to her two most trusted servants, knowing it would go no further. It was something that had to be told, she had to unburden herself of the knowledge, yet she would have died a thousand deaths rather than have such information ever reach others, like Captain Kaff. When she had finished she dried her eyes.

Drissila's lips were pursed. 'He should not have done this to you, my lady.'

Ofao nodded, as if in agreement, but then said, 'Yet, you know, my lady, perhaps it was not entirely his fault? This creature, the wife of a local lord, she enticed him, did she not? She tricked him into wearing the horns. Some of the blame must lie with her also. Without her connivance Soldier never would have betrayed you.'

'Must it always be the woman's fault?' asked Drissila, severely. 'Why is it when men go astray it is because they are given no choice?'

'No, no, you mistake me. He *must* bear some of the blame. And I'm sure he would say so himself. I have no doubt he is going through agonies of remorse at this very moment. But my mistress here is contemplating something final, is that not so, my lady? You are thinking it would be better to sever the relationship now and marry someone else?'

Layana gave them no sign that this was the case, either with her mouth or her eyes, but they knew from her silence that it was so.

'Oh, my lady,' whispered Drissila, clearly distressed by this thought. 'But he has only just yet become your husband. Two husbands have gone already. A third loss would harden your heart to stone. You would never feel love for any man again.'

'Would that be such a bad thing?' asked Layana, with some asperity in her tone. 'For my heart to shrivel to a dried and bitter kernel?'

'It would be terrible,' said Ofao, speaking for both servants, 'for you have so much love to give. To stem the flow of that love now, in the prime of life? It does not bear thinking about. That torrent of love would turn in on itself and destroy you. Please, my dear mistress, please think of forgiveness, for your own sake if not for his.'

'I am ugly,' she murmured, 'but there is one other man in this land who would have me for his wife.'

'Do not even think about it,' groaned Drissila. 'He is a cruel and ambitious man.'

'He loves me. I know it.'

"But will he *always* love you? After a while he may grow tired of you and put you aside, perhaps even imprison you in some bedlam. It would be easy for him to say it was for your own good, my lady. He'll dismiss us, your friends, and during one of your bouts of madness he'll put you away in some dark hole and you'll never again see the light of day.

'Soldier, you know, would never do anything like that. He loves you to distraction. Yes, he has hurt you badly, but his love has not wavered.'

'There is no excuse for infidelity.'

Ofao agreed. 'But you have the capacity for forgiveness.'

'Yes, I do, but I'm not sure I wish to exercise it.'

They left her later, to her grief. She was feeling a mixture of wrath and hurt. Yes, she saw that Soldier had been the victim of two worldly creatures, but she felt he should have guarded himself against it. He should have been able to do more to stop himself falling in with their schemes. Yet she knew Soldier was this curious mixture of vulnerability and strength. When she had last seen him, the victim of the water witch, he had seemed almost defenceless. Had she, Layana, not decapitated the witch, then Soldier would have been lost and gone to this world. Yet he somehow always survived, even when Layana was not there to protect him. Oh, she thought, if it had not been for my madness I would be with him, to shield him against such creatures as this lord and his wife.

Yet, if it had not been for her madness, then Soldier would never have had to go out into the wildernesses of a magical landscape, into the fastnesses of the high gods, into the waste-lands of monsters and fiends. In fact, if it had not been for her madness, would she have married him at all?

'Captain Kaff, my lady,' sniffed Drissila from the doorway of the library in which Layana was sitting.

Kaff entered the room in full armour, his helmet beneath his arm.

'My lady,' he said, bowing. 'It's good to see you out of your latest sickness.'

'Is the winter still with us?' she asked, looking at the clumps of compacted snow dropping from the soles of his boots. 'Or has the thaw come?'

'There's a blizzard out there. I was about to accompany the red pavilions, on their march to the north. The beast-people again. But the weather has hardened. They say the land will be locked in ice before noon and no progress can be made until a thaw.'

'Oh!' she exclaimed, rising to her feet and going to the window. 'Is it really that bad?'

'Why, were you thinking of a walk?'

She shook her head. She was not thinking of a walk. She was thinking how bad it would be in the mountains of the west. Soldier and Spagg would at this time be attempting the passes in those mountains. A cold death would be everywhere. The intrepid pair might easily starve, or freeze, or fall foul of some ice monster, and so their quest would be at an end. While she had been busy condemning Soldier for his faithlessness, he had been out in the most dangerous, the most hazardous of country, seeking to find a cure for her madness. She could not forgive him yet, but oh, she could not but be fearful for his safety.

'We have had no word from your husband,' said Kaff, unable to keep the satisfied tone out of his voice, 'I would suspect he is dead.'

'He's not dead,' she snapped. 'Not yet.'

'You know this?'

'I feel it in my heart.'

Kaff raised his eyebrows, but he knew better than to argue with the princess when she stated things so emphatically.

'I hope you are right, for your sake. There was a troll here, on the back of an owl. He spoke with Maldrake, Lord of the Locks, and said that Soldier was a prisoner.'

Layana frowned. 'What did Maldrake do?'

'Do? Nothing of course. One cannot deal with trolls.'

She turned on the captain, releasing the pent-up fury she actually felt for Soldier.

'You would not have him come home alive. You would kill him if you could. Let us have no hypocrisy.'

Kaff shook his head. 'There's no hypocrisy. Yes, I want him dead. But you, my lady, wish him alive. I said for your sake, not mine.'

Captain Kaff left the library in the Palace of Wildflowers and made his way back to the guardroom. As always after seeing the princess, he was feeling depressed. She would not let go of this idea that she was in love with this intruder, this outsider who called himself Soldier. Kaff could not see the attraction. He put it down to some romantic ideal in her head. She had saved the man from execution by marrying him. This had somehow transformed itself into a feeling that she loved the man she had rescued on the eve of his destruction. Kaff believed it was nothing more than a woman's fancy gone wild.

'Why hasn't that brigandine killed him?' asked Kaff of himself. 'Humbold told me it would poison him the first time he wore it!'

It was infuriating. Kaff knew that Layana had special powers of insight when it came to people close to her. If she said Soldier was still living then Kaff had no doubt he was. But surely the foreigner must have come up against terrible danger by now, on his journey to the western mountains? Why had he not donned the padded armour-jacket and so died foaming at the mouth? None of it made any sense. Soldier appeared to have a dozen lives, for if not the brigandine, then surely some monster should have bitten his head from his shoulders by now?

'I must find other ways to make sure he never returns,' Kaff said to himself. 'I shall despatch Olgath.'

Having made this decision, Kaff felt he should have done this before now. Olgath was a warrior-sorcerer, a half-magician who was more human than sorcerer, but still with powers enough to transform himself into beasts and birds. Olgath could change his shape into some creature more suitable for travelling in this bad weather, catch up with Soldier, and bring about his death. Olgath lived in the slums of Zamerkand, his downfall being drink. This burly, intelligent man had been brought low by frequenting the inns of the city every night, every day, and most hours between. Sober, he was a brilliant combatant. Drunk, his fists caused much damage.

Kaff took some of the guardsmen and found Olgath, as predicted, in a tavern.

'Come, you drunken sot,' said Kaff. 'Outside.'

'Kiss my backside,' growled the inebriated Olgath, bunching his powerful fists.

There followed a scuffle as the guards dragged the drunk from his seat. Olgath began to punch them in their heads and they went down under the blows. But there were too many of them and Kaff waited patiently until they had the man out in the snowy street, where they started to pummel and kick him.

'Enough,' warned Kaff, 'I don't want him damaged.'

The guards reluctantly ceased hitting and kicking their victim. They were smarting under the blows he had handed out in the inn and they wanted their pound of flesh. Holding him by his arms, they bent him backwards round a horse-tethering post, ready and very willing to snap the bones should their captain require it. Olgath snarled and spat at them, muttering drunken obscenities and threatening to break every one of them into small pieces, once he was released from their grasp.

'Why don't you change into a bear,' one the guards mocked him, 'then you can make good your threats.'

They knew he could not transform in his present state. Alcohol in his blood nullified any shape-changing powers, or any magical spells. He would have to be completely sober to reach the depths of his mind needed to work such magic.

Olgath glared up at Kaff. 'What do you want?' he asked.

'I have work for you. Work which will enrich you and enable you to remain drunk for a year. First though, we have to sober you up and get you ready for the task.' He smiled at the baffled Olgath. 'How would you like to be an eagle for a while? Soaring high above the earth?'

'Where would I go?'

'To the mountains in the west.'

'To the home of the gods and every evil spirit and strange beast that ever walked the world? I think I will not go.'

'I think you *will*. We'll see which of us has the most accurate thought in his head, after we've cooled a few hot irons on the surface of your skin.'

Soldier and the dwarfs survived the smoking-out with nothing more than a few lungfuls of bad air. The dwarfs had known that Caezor would get nowhere. They had been through this a hundred times or more. Dwarfs only got caught when they were actually out there, poaching salmon from the lord's stream, or stealing his pheasants. They would have hunted his deer and wild boars too, if they had the weapons. As it was, woodland dwarfs relied on traps to catch the game. Sometimes Caezor caught them emptying the traps and then he hanged them, or dragged them behind his horse, or enslaved them.

'Poaching is the most heinous crime under the sun,' he told them, frequently.

They replied under their breath, 'That's why we hunt under the moon.'

Once the smoke had cleared and Soldier was permitted to see the dwarfs' underground warren, he saw how well they managed for themselves. Deep down below the trees, the temperature remained constant. It wasn't particularly warm, but it wasn't freezing either. From the roots in the ceiling the dwarfs hung smoked meat and fish. Dried apples, many of them tough, shrivelled and wrinkled, were stored in heaps about the place. There were piles of nuts too. Passing dwarfs took from these heaps as they felt the need. There was hay and straw spread throughout the warren on the floors. When the dwarfs wanted to sleep they just lay down where they were and others stepped over them.

Badgers and other subterranean dwellers shared the network of tunnels and chambers with the dwarfs, seemingly in harmony. At least, Soldier saw nothing down there which led him to believe otherwise. It seemed that in the confined quarters dug by the dwarfs they had to behave themselves too, for fox did not chase rabbit, nor weasel attack vole. There seemed to be some kind of truce in force. If the carnivores wanted to eat they had to go above ground and hunt their prey away from the kingdom of the dwarfs.

There were chambers off the tunnels and the main cavern. These were mostly storage areas, but one was a music chamber where talented dwarfs could practise without interfering too much in the daily life of others. Soldier noticed that amongst their instruments they had a kind of miniature fiddle, a soft-stringed lyre which seemed to be played with the tongue, hollow wooden tubes which were used as percussion instruments, a kind of tambourine which was struck with a short stick and a huge deerskin drum which reverberated throughout the colony whenever it was punched or kicked by a heavy-set, knotty-muscled, enthusiastic dwarf.

No matter what time of the day or night, there was always someone practising in the music chamber.

The dwarfs themselves were very rustic looking creatures. Both males and females had roughly-cropped, coarse, short hair which stuck up at all angles from their heads. They all appeared to go prematurely grey, but there were no bald dwarfs anywhere. Their ears were larger than a human's, probably because they relied on their hearing more than any other sense. Muscled, thick arms and legs on a sturdy torso told Soldier that these beings had not always relied on poaching to feed themselves.

He asked Xnople, the elderly dwarf, about this.

Xnople scratched his skull and replied, 'We weren't always reduced to poaching. Once upon a time we were miners. We owned some diamond mines on the other side of the hill. But Caezor forced us away from our rightful heritage. He seized the mines himself, and gave the mining rights to boggarts when we refused to sell our diamonds to him at a cheap rate.'

'Boggarts?'

'Faery folk who normally do the mundane trades like black-smithing and leatherworking. Boggarts, though used to hard work, are not natural miners. They didn't know a lot about the work. They took unshielded candles down the mines instead of safety lamps, and there was a gas explosion.'

'They had an accident?'

'They were buried alive. Every last one of them. And all because the greedy Caezor wanted his diamonds cheaper. Now he gets none at all. And he blames us for this. He says if we had agreed to sell him the gems at a cheap rate in the first place, none of this would have happened.'

'He is not a good man,' said Soldier. 'If he had not a wife and I had not wronged him, I would challenge him to single combat.' He sighed. 'But I was a guest in his house and the laws of chivalry do not permit guests to challenge their hosts.'

'He hunted you!'

'True, but before that he gave me meat when I was starving and a bed when I needed shelter. Men like Caezor always come to a bad end at some time. If not me, then someone else will ride by one day and think it wise to cut off his head. Now, will you help me get Spagg out of his house alive? Is it possible?'

'You mean the man Caezor pinned to an iron gibbet this morning, and hung on his gates?'

Soldier let out a cry. 'He has killed Spagg?'

'No, but the man is dying slowly.'

'Then I must rescue him,' cried Soldier.

'This man, Spagg,' said Xnople. 'He has spikes through his hands and feet and is set upon the iron gibbet like an X. Caezor spreads bird feed on him, and the starlings with their sharp, stabbing beaks cluster upon his chin and peck the seed from his mouth. I believe he is a snare set for you. Caezor wishes you to come and rescue your man-servant. It is a trap baited with man.'

'Poor Spagg,' mused Soldier, 'little did the hand-seller know what this trip had in store for him.'

'Hand-seller?' queried Xnople.

Soldier explained, 'Spagg has a market stall. In better times he sells the hands of hanged men to use as hands-of-glory.'

'A macabre and morbid trade.'

'A lucrative one, Spagg would say.'

Soldier knew he would have to rescue Spagg. He sighed, troubled in his heart. Not for the first time Soldier wondered who he was and what he was doing in this unfamiliar world. Even now, as he looked at the ceiling of the cavern, the roots seemed to spell a name which might be his, except that it was not quite there, not quite comprehensible. The same thing happened with the branches of winter trees, whenever he went into the forest. The tangle of limbs shaped a name, which was changed by the wind rustling the boughs just as he looked up and almost saw it.

'The wolves know who I am,' he moaned. 'Yet I remain ignorant of myself.'

'What's that?' asked the white-bearded Xnople. 'What did you say?'

Soldier sighed again. 'Nothing.'

'You want to know something, don't you?'

'Yes, but no one seems to know the answer.'

Xnople said, 'Possibly because you haven't asked the right questions yet. Ask me. I have certain intuitive powers. Perhaps some images will come into my head? What is it you wish to discover, friend?'

'I was just wishing I knew who I was and what I was here for.'

'No one can tell you who you are. Only you know the answer to that question. But as to your reason for being here? Why, that might be uncovered, if we look at it closely enough.'

Soldier looked up abruptly into the gnarled features of the old dwarf, whose countenance itself resembled a tree root.

'You think?'

Xnople nodded. 'I find that people go to a strange place for two main reasons: to seek someone they wish to find — or to lose themselves.'

'I'm sure I don't want to get lost, but then who is it that I wish to find?' cried Soldier.

'A loved one, or a hated one?'

'How will I ever know?'

Xnople closed his eyes for a few minutes, then spoke again, 'I see a woman not of this world, a bride, in a white dress stained with red. I see a man also not of this world, with sword in hand, the blade running with a virgin's blood. These two are all I have. They are yours.'

Xnople opened his eyes. 'Has that been of any help?'

Soldier cried in anguish, 'What does it mean?'

'I would say you are either here to seek a runaway bride, or to find her murderer.'

Soldier felt the stone in his heart. 'It must be to seek the murderer, then, for if she was slain . . .'

'I did not say she was dead, only that blood stained her wedding gown. Perhaps it was not her blood? Perhaps she was not mortally wounded, and she escaped into this world before the fatal blow could be struck? You must not assume too much.

'Then again, you might have come upon the scene of a murder and the perpetrator escaped your wrath by slipping into this world from your own. You followed. In crossing over, your memories of your own world could have been lost. Neither of you will know who you are, why you are here, and who it is that you fear.'

'Yes, yes, I feel you are right,' Soldier croaked, grasping this explanation. 'I do feel it, deep within me. This would account for all the hate, the fury, that seethes deep within my soul. I am here to hunt a murderer, who does not know who he is or why he is here.'

'Or a frightened bride.'

'No, no. Why would I have fallen in love with the Princess Layana, if I were already in love?'

Xnople shook his head in wonder. 'My poor fool. Can you not be in love with two women at the same time?'

'Not I,' cried Soldier, thinking of Layana. 'I could not, in all honour, be so faithless.'

The elderly dwarf pursed his lips. 'You must know yourself.'

Soldier said, 'Why hasn't anyone told me these things before now?'

'As I have said, perhaps you have not asked the right questions of the right people?'

Soldier nodded, accepting this explanation. He considered the situation very carefully, and decided that it must be that he was hunting the murderer of a bride. Perhaps she, this lady in the blooded gown, had not been his bride? Could it be that the maid in the wedding dress was his sister, or the bride of his best friend? This was less likely, considering the hate he harboured in his soul. Yes, her murderer, it must be. Someone here, in this world, who did not know he was the killer of a young maid Soldier had once loved. Someone who did not know he was being hunted by an avenger from the old world.

Suddenly, Soldier felt the blood drain from his face as yet a third possibility made itself known to him, brought on by a remembrance that there was another emotion seething below the surface of his soul.

Guilt.

A terrible guilt.

'What is it?' asked Xnople, seeing the abrupt change of Soldier's expression. 'Tell me.'

'Something has just occurred to me. Something you did not mention yourself. I could be chasing a murderer . . .'

'Yes,' encouraged the dwarf. 'Go on.'

'Then again,' Soldier said, his voice wavering, 'I could *be* the murderer.'

Chapter Twenty-Three

In the short time that he remained with the dwarfs, Soldier learned of the presence of an Old Man in the forest. Xnople informed him that the Old Man was wise in the ways of wizards, though not one himself.

'Though powerful in his own right, the Old Man is a person of peace. He spends his time turning metal weapons into ploughshares and wooden weapons into ship's masts. There are a young boy and a woman who assist him. It is the boy who goes out and gathers the swords, where he may find them. The child creeps into the encampments of warriors at night and steals their weapons. The woman works the furnace for the Old Man, keeping it hot enough to melt down the tools of destruction and death which he finds so odious, so repugnant, as any man of peace would.'

'You think the Old Man might help me with locating the wizard to cure my wife of her madness?'

'It's possible.'

While in the underground world of the dwarfs Soldier was sewn a new set of clothes. They were not of the best material, of course, for the fabric which the dwarfs were able to trade for was of the cheapest kind. It was the males who sewed and the females who inspected the stitches. Once the garments were completed — a set of jerkin and hose in the style that the dwarfs themselves favoured, this being the only type of raiment they knew how to fashion — Soldier found them to be loose and coarse. They rubbed his skin raw, they itched, but they kept out the cold and would probably last a lifetime. He hoped they wouldn't, but his fears were probably correct. Thus attired he asked Xnople how he should set Spagg free.

'We'll do that. We can take him down tonight. There's no moon, certainly not a hunter's one. You must go and see the Old Man of the forest. Tell him we sent you.'

'What about my things? I left everything behind at Caezor's mansion. There's an enchanted brigandine for a start. And a magic scabbard. Also my sword and warhammer. How will I fight without them?'

'You must learn, or get yourself some new weapons, for you'll not see your sword or any of your possessions again.'

Soldier was extremely troubled to hear this, but he felt he could not waste time arguing with Xnople.

'If you think you can free Spagg tonight, then I am most grateful to you. Please tell me where I can find the Old Man. I think I should speak with him now.'

Soldier was given instructions on the path through the forest. He crawled out through one of the tunnels which opened like a badger's hole from under a set of oak roots. Once out in the winter's chill, biting atmosphere, Soldier followed the signs he had been given. These were mostly trees with scarred trunks, or old rabbit burrows, things of that nature. One sign led to another and by this way Soldier was able to find his way to a mossy cave deep in the heart of the forest. The region he was now in was a place of even more mysterious forces and spirits. Every so often he stopped to look fearfully over his shoulder, convinced he was being followed.

He was, but only by a manifestation of his own inner self. In this place of magic a part of his own spirit freed itself and took on the form of a crooked elf. This elf trod directly in Soldier's footprints, and was inclined to jump smartly behind him when he turned around, so Soldier never quite saw the creature full on. What he saw were darting shadows and almost-shapes. He knew of the elf's presence, but was not quick enough to confirm it. There was nothing Soldier could do about this situation but let it continue as it was, with the elf laughing at him in a low voice, just under the note of the wind, and he becoming more and more furious as he failed to catch the creature.

However, at one point he really was being followed, and not by himself.

'KERROWW!' cried a delighted dragon, as they came across each other in a clearing. 'KERROWW!'

'I'm not your mother,' growled Soldier, as the scaly creature nuzzled his thigh with its large bony head. He kicked it on the rump. 'Go and find your real mother.'

'KERROWW!' shrieked the growing beast, more delighted than ever on being caressed by its parent.

It followed Soldier through the forest, making crooning sounds.

'Go away!' ordered the exasperated Soldier. 'Leave me alone.'

The dragon nuzzled him again, rubbing skin from Soldier's calf with its coarse brow and spiky ears.

They went further, still with Soldier protesting, still with the dragon making mewling noises, until they were forced to part by the density of trees, through which the great beast could not venture without damaging its wings. It flew off, up into the sky, still shouting its affection for its human mother.

Finally, where the forest trees grew thickest, Soldier came upon a land of humps and bumps – great mossy mounds of rugged design – where birds flew backwards and had the faces of men. He saw an owl with a man's visage, staring at him from the upper branches of a white tree. He was pursued by a tiny wren with the minute savage features of a disturbed child, its head turning this way and that as it looked over its shoulder to see where it was going in this topsy-turvy woodland world. Once, a nightjar screeched into his eyes, frightening the life out of him with its hideous human features set upon a body of feathers and claws.

Here Soldier found a real boy, hurrying through the shadow-bars of the forest trees, carrying an armful of weapons. Guessing this was the boy who served the Old Man, Soldier spoke to him.

'Boy!' he called. 'I'm looking for your master.'

The child, wrapped up in tattered women's shawls bound tightly to his body with thongs, stopped at these words and stared in Soldier's direction.

'My master's home lies beyond the forest fence. You'd better follow where I tread,' he shouted back, before hurrying on, 'or you'll lose my trail.'

Soldier did indeed have trouble in keeping the padded boy in sight, as the latter skipped nimbly through the trunks which grew so close together. Soldier was thankful he had not eaten for a while or he would have been too fat to squeeze between them. They left the tree line and entered some sweeping downs upon which was unblemished snow. The landscape was formed of feminine curves and swellings, soft to the eye.

Soldier would have gladly lain down in some hollow, albeit filled with snow, and fallen asleep forever. He was travel-weary and low of spirit, though he he instinctively felt his journey's end was not too far away.

Finally the boy came upon a copse containing one of those ferny, mossy knolls, in which was set a dark cave. On top of this mound was a blackened chimney made of pale clay, through which smoke and black grit issued in puffs. The snow on top of the mound had melted, leaving a green island in an ocean of whiteness. The boy disappeared inside the cave entrance, from which hung long fangs of ice. Soldier followed at rapid pace, in case there were multiple tunnels within and he should lose the child at some fork. Finally, he came out in a forge where the heat was so intense as to drive the air from his lungs for a few seconds. In this place he found the other troglodytes, the Old Man and a woman, who regarded him with mild surprise.

'I found him,' said the boy, dumping the weapons before the furnace with a clatter, 'out in the woods. He was coming from the direction where the dwarfs have their warren. He said he wants to speak to you, grandfather.'

All the three inhabitants of this hot mossy cave were dressed in shabby garments which hung from their bones like sackcloth from a scarecrow. They looked poor, wasted creatures, but Soldier was not surprised at their appearance, considering the sweltering conditions under which they worked. And they seemed busy people, never pausing, always melting, cutting, shaping, pouring, doing what must be done to turn swords to ploughshares and lances to ship masts. The walls of the cave were decorated with them, they hung from rafters set in the ceiling, they gathered in piles around the sides of the dwelling.

'What do you do with them?' he asked. 'These tools and fittings you make.'

'Why, we give them to the poor,' said the woman. 'They use them to grow their harvest, to reap, to catch the bounty of the sea – and more important, poor people do not have the means to turn them back into weapons again.'

'I think your plan is admirable, but a waste of time. Men will fight. Men will kill men. It's in their nature.'

The Old Man looked up. 'Then we must change their nature, forge it into a new shape.' He dunked a red-hot, roughly-shaped tool into a trough of water, which then hissed and bubbled. 'Men are yet infants, to be turned into useful beings.'

'I cannot remember much, if anything, about the world from which I've come, but this world seems to spawn violence at every seam. The half of it seems dedicated to destroying the other half. I have met with beings both strange and weird – creatures I never believed existed, and which probably did not in my old life – all attacking each other, intent on killing and maiming.'

The old man halted his toil for a moment to stare into Soldier's eyes.

'Things may not be exactly as you perceive them.'

'I can't see how they can be otherwise.'

'That's because you view them through eyes which were fashioned elsewhere. What is it you want of me? Did the dwarfs indeed send you?'

Soldier confirmed that he had come from the underground kingdom of the dwarfs, unless of course he had dreamt he was in a place peopled by small gnarled beings with knobbly noses, and explained that he sought a wizard who might cure his wife of her ailment.

'There is a path,' said the Old Man, 'on the far side of a great lake. If you find it and follow it, there is no certainty what you will find at its end. It may be there will be one who can help you. But the path changes its destination, from day to day, hour by hour, minute by minute. It could be that you arrive at the wrong time and find the wrong sorcerer, or indeed, none at all. Perhaps you will nothing but a pile of frozen dead leaves, crackling with frost which tries to turn them to glass.'

'Is that my only chance? Is that what I've endured terrible dangers to find?'

'Nothing is definite. You find only what you earn. Do you think you deserve certainty?'

Soldier shrugged, annoyed with himself as much as with the Old Man.

'I suppose not. I hope for it.'

'Hope is as much as you'll get, and more than any man of violence deserves.'

'You think I'm a man of violence?'

The Old Man continued with his work as he spoke. The woman fed the furnace with charcoal. The boy vanished out of the cave again, presumably to go out to steal more weapons.

'Have you had time to study this world yet, into which you say you have been unwillingly projected? It may look as if it is a world based on evil, with good struggling to gain a place in it. In fact it is neither based on evil, nor good, but on *power*. In a world ruled by evil you would not have survived more than a day or two.'

Soldier felt affronted. 'I came here powerless.'

The Old Man began hammering a piece of hot metal on a great anvil, sparks fountaining from beneath his hammer as a waterfall of light.

'No, you came to us with enough power to keep you alive, or it would not be so. There is a certain power in being an unknown quantity, obviously so with your blue eyes in a place where only brown-eyed beings dwelt. You did not know yourself, but then neither did others know you. You were allowed to live until they found out whether you were a threat to them, or useful in some way, or had some special secret which might empower *them*. There is no profit in destroying what might give one an edge over others. And in the beginning no one knew whether in destroying you they might be arousing the antagonism of some dark force which could, in turn, bring them down themselves.

'Also you had your soldiery to fall back on. You had this instinctive knowledge of warfare and you guessed you had been highly trained in slaughter. Not that I approve of this, of course, but it was yours to draw on, along with the bonus of a scabbard which had gathered magic on its journey between worlds. Gradually, using all these assets, you have gathered more power unto yourself. You seem destined to continue, unless something unforeseen cuts you down without a second thought for your usefulness.'

Soldier considered all this, and decided there was something in what the Old Man said. There was the queen, whose power was derived from her birthright. There was Humbold, whose power was gathered from that reflected from his queen. There was Kaff, who had the power of the military behind him. Some of these people had reached a point where they could not be removed from power.

'We are going through a bad time,' continued the Old Man, 'what with the imminent death of the King Magus. There'll be a struggle after he goes. We must hope that Good wins that struggle, for, in a land where Evil rules unopposed, all

power goes to one pair of hands. That pair of hands dis-
seminates power as it sees fit: gives it out, takes it back, with-
holds it, removes it. We must hope we never see the day
when such a creature rules the magic of the land.'

Soldier agreed and thanked the Old Man and the woman.
They gave him, before he left, a tinder-box, without which
he would have surely died in the coldness of the winter land.
He left the cave. On his way out he stole one of the swords
which lay in heaps about the entrance. Soldier did not feel
guilty about this, since he reasoned they had been stolen from
someone else in the first place, but as he made his way
through the forest he began to feel a little uneasy. The Old
Man had helped him, in more ways than one, and this was
not the way to repay such assistance. Still, he reasoned further,
what choice had he? There would be dangers ahead and he
must be prepared for them.

Already, the further westwards he went, the more oppressive became the presence of the gods. Monstrous creatures
no living man had ever seen, they dwelt apart from each other
in the high citadels of the craggy, misty heights. He felt them
like a great weight pressing down from above. He sensed their
disapproval of all things human

As Soldier was musing thus, shivering, feeling the cold
through his thin garments as he tramped through the snow,
a raven flew by him and settled on a bough.

Soldier stopped. 'Is it you?'

The raven cocked its head and said nothing.

'No – why should it be. There are thousands of ravens in
the world. I can't tell one from the other. You all look alike
to me.'

He passed by the bird.

'That's because you don't look hard enough,' spoke the

raven, with some asperity in his voice. 'We *are* all different you know, just as you lot are. Can't you see the sheen on my feathers is quite superior to that of most of my kind? What about this little greyish feather on my left wing? How about the width of my eyes, the length of my beak, the fact that I keep my claws honed sharper than most ravens?'

Soldier stopped again and grinned. 'So it is you? I'm afraid I'm not keen-sighted enough to notice those fine details.'

'Huh! Anyway, I'm not here to argue or exchange niceties with you. I've come to warn you. There's an eagle on the way.'

'An eagle?'

'An eagle which is not an eagle.'

'You love speaking in riddles, don't you? What does that mean?'

'Kaff has sent a magician, a man called Olgath, to kill you. He's a warrior, as well as a magician. He'll chop you into little bits.'

Soldier nodded. 'Don't sound so pleased with it all.'

'Well, I can't help thinking this is the end of the track for you. Look at you. Dressed in scarecrow's clothes, a rusty old sword in your hand! What have you been up to? And where's that idiot rogue Skagg? Did you run out of food and eat him?'

'At the moment he's probably being taken down from the gates of a tyrant's mansion and feeling very sorry for himself. But never mind him. Where will I meet this Olgath? You say he's a warrior?'

'His mother was a washer-woman and he has her brawn, if his father's brains. Some of those washer-women! Have you seen their meaty arms? Anyway, where? Search me. All I know is he's on his way. I had to fly like mad to keep ahead of him. Just keep your eyes and ears alert. In the meantime, I'm hungry. I've delivered the message. You've been warned.

There's nothing else I can do.' He looked around him. 'There's not much to eat out here, is there? I'm not used to chipping through permafrost with my beak. I must look for some old squirrel caches.'

Once the bird had flown, through the stark network of bare black branches that tangled the sky, Soldier let out a heavy sigh. What a load was on his shoulders. Yet, there was no telling that it would all be for the good. He was here to persuade someone to do a good deed. That was not always rewarded.

He made himself a fire, and thawed and cooked some edible roots which he dug from the ground with the sword. This work caused the weapon to break at the tip, further depressing the wandering man. Fortified, though hardly satisfied, Soldier continued his bleak journey through the woods until he came to the shores of a vast frozen lake ringed by forests. On the other side of the lake he could see a small mountain in the lea of some giant mountains – seven of them – which had their tops somewhere high above the level of the clouds. The shadows of these seven massive and brooding mountains fell across the lake, making it colder and more foreboding than anywhere Soldier had yet seen.

He gathered some firewood, made a bundle, and strapped it to his back. Then he stepped out, onto the frozen surface, into the cold, cold shadow of the homes of the gods. A chill entered his heart, icier than any winter weather he had experienced thus far. That freezing shadow penetrated him as a frozen mist, reaching down into the depths of his spirit and causing him the utmost despair. Would he even see the other side of this white lake, let alone find the path to the wizard who might cure his wife?

He walked.

He walked all day and all night.

In the morning he guessed he was about halfway across, though the mountains seemed no nearer in aspect.

No sun rose. It remained a grey, frozen world with a marble sky, utterly forbidding in every way.

At noon an eagle flew over his head. It landed on the ice in front of him. In a moment it had transformed into the shape of a muscled warrior.

Olgath had arrived, fully armed and armoured.

Soldier blinked with eyelashes glittering with frost. His face and the backs of his hands, and his feet, had gone beyond being painful, into a numbness. He felt the heat of his heart's fury enter them now, warm them into a tingling hurt. His blood rose in temperature. Who was this barbarian, to come flying in over the vast spaces which Soldier had had to conquer on foot?

Soldier parted his lips and he croaked. 'Get out of my way, oaf! I have a hatred in me which heats my brain to the level of activity enough to stun your belief. Have you not heard of my battle with the dog-warrior? I slew him in a great frenzy which had even the red pavilions looking at the ground, a sickness gripping their hearts. I shall unleash that same anger on you, if you do not step aside and let me pass.'

Olgath snorted, swishing his sword. 'You are not even armoured, and that sword looks likely to fall apart after the first blow.'

Soldier looked down at himself. It was true. He was entirely vulnerable. He had no protection. On realizing how unequal the fight was going to be, he retired a hundred yards, removed his pack of kindling and firewood, and thought a little. He was a soldier and had a soldier's brain. It might not be the most intricate instrument in his body, but it did serve him at times like this. A soldier always makes the most of his environment. If he is without weapons in a rocky place, he makes himself a slingshot, or uses heavy stones as missiles. If he is in a wooded place, he makes himself a servicable spear. What did he have about him at this moment? Ice. A whole lake of ice. This had to be of *some* use to him.

With his back to Olgath, who stood waiting for his challenge to be taken up, Soldier went down on his knees. Using the broken sword he began to carve largish plates from the ice. He found that the idea of imminent battle had raised his energy levels. He was full of zeal, full of the fire of combat. This gave him the strength to do what – an hour ago – he would not have been able to do. Within a short while he had cut himself some plates of armour out of the sheet ice. He made thongs from torn hems of his clothing, bored holes in the plates, and hung the frost-fashioned armour from his body. Thus attired, the hero then turned to the villain, and called him out.

'Oaf I called you and oaf you are. You have the brains of a gnat and the testicles of an ant . . .'

Olgath answered in kind. This kind of taunting might go on for some time before any blow was struck. But both warriors were eager to feel sword bite flesh. This was a cold, strange land, this place of the lake in the shadow of the gods, and neither of them had the desire to prolong their presence in the region.

'Let's get it over with,' snarled Olgath.

The first blow was struck by Olgath on that glistening afternoon out on the frozen lake. Chips of ice flew up as the blade creased into Soldier's ice-armour. Birds flew up in the far trees at the sound of Olgath's loud attack-oath, which echoed round the lake, forests and mountains. Bears turned in their sleep. Ermine stopped, startled, on their rabbit-tracking quests. Wolves turned from high crags and wondered. There were eyes on these two dark figures out on the ice. Animal eyes. Perhaps wizard eyes. But no human witnessed this combat.

Soldier's furious blows began to rain on the metal armour of his opponent, causing dents to appear in various places. Olgath staggered back under the onslaught. The magician now admitted to himself that he had not expected such a terrible attack. Soldier, he realised, was a veteran when it came to single combat. His footwork, his eyes, his use of the weapon all served to announce that this was not new territory to him. Olgath now doubted what Captain Kaff had told him, about Soldier's effeteness, his supposed ineptness. Kaff had likened him to a woman.

Olgath gave as good as he got, forcing Soldier back on his heels under a similar furious flurry of blows.

Both men seemed fairly evenly matched. Soldier at one point had an opportunity to stab Olgath in the throat, but failed to make it a killing blow because of the blunt sword end. He cursed to high heaven and beyond, thinking he should have selected a better weapon to steal from the Old Man's pile.

The battle on the ice went on for the rest of the day. In the early evening, the raven arrived, and frustrated both combatants by flying around and between them offering advice and encouragement to Soldier.

Flap, flap. 'Watch it! Watch his left hand, Soldier! He's going to punch you. That's it. Step back, parry, thrust, no, no, *slash*. Oh, you've missed him. Keep your balance on your back foot. Watch his eyes. You can always tell their next move by their eyes . . . ' Flap, flap, flap, flap.

Eventually both men had had enough of the raven's constant chatter. By silent mutual consent they both took a pause in the fighting, while Soldier remonstrated with the bird.

'Look, please go away.'

'But I want to help. He's a crafty one.'

'You're just being a nuisance.'

'Well, there's gratitude for you.'

Soldier shook his head. 'I know you mean well, raven, but you're not helping. You're liable to get me killed . . .'

'Or me,' interjected Olgath.

'. . . and if I'm going to die I'd rather it was my own fault and not yours.'

'All right, all right, I'll just stand over there and watch.'

'I'd rather you went away,' said Soldier.

'That's not fair. I flew a long way to see this fight. I think I'm entitled to spectator's rights.'

'Well – so long as you don't fly around or shout anything.'

'I won't fly around,' said the raven, ruffling his wings. 'but I can't promise not to shout, because I might get carried away. What if he sneaks up behind you while you're not looking? I'll have to warn you. There wouldn't be a choice.'

'I think I can take care of myself.'

'Ha!'

However, they left it at that, and the fight continued into a crystalline night, with the stars providing a frosty heaven, while the world below twinkled just as brilliantly. The wolves came out with the darkness and howled Soldier's name. The sound echoed round the hills. He could not hear the word clearly enough to recognise it, especially above the noise of clashing metal. It got colder as the night went on. The pair were now becoming exhausted and frequently had to pause to gather breath and strength. The length of their intervals was becoming more and more extended with every halt of the fight.

Under the mild glare of a blue moon they battled. Finally, as dawn came up in a grey and forbidding coat to remind them that another day was due to be ushered in, they stopped altogether. Soldier went back and collected his bundle of firewood while the raven flew off and returned with tinder. Olgath changed himself into an eagle, flew around the hills until he spotted a hare, stooped, scooped, and returned with a meal. They made a fire out on the ice and roasted the hare for breakfast. As Olgath chomped away on a haunch, having returned to human shape, he voiced what was in both their minds.

'I think we've fought enough. Clearly we're both evenly matched. We're not going to get anywhere like this.'

Soldier nodded. 'I agree, but then this was not my idea in the first place. What are you going to tell your employers?'

Olgath licked the hot fat running off his fingers and let out a sigh.

'I don't think I'll bother. I'm not going back. I'll fly over to Carthaga, over the Cerulean Sea, and settle there. It's warmer anyway. They don't have winters like these on that coast.' He stretched out a hand. 'Good luck, Soldier. It was an honour to do battle with you. You're a better fighter than you look. When I first saw you, I thought, this skinny runt? I'll cut off his legs and use them to walk home afterwards. But I see how wrong I was.'

The raven whistled. 'Listen to it! Mutual admiration guild. Well, so long as you two have stopped short of kissing and cuddling each other . . .'

But they hadn't. They hugged, kissed each other's rough cheeks, shook hands again. Then Olgath once more transformed himself into an eagle. He took the remains of the carcass of the hare in his talons and went aloft. The last Soldier saw of him was the magnificent raptor with its powerful wings, flying over the dark forests of the morning.

'What a wonderful bird,' murmured Soldier, watching the eagle disappear from sight.

'*What a wonderful bird*,' squeaked the raven, mimicking Soldier in high, sarcastic tones. 'That's the trouble with you humans, you always admire brawn over brain. What does it matter that a bird has a big wing-span, or huge talons, or glides on thermals like a god? There are those of us who are sharp-witted and who could fly circles round those thugs of the sky.'

Soldier turned and grinned again. 'Of course. I owe you a lot, raven. I won't forget. Now, I must continue my quest. Be off with you. I'll see you at the city, when I return.'

'*If* you return.'

'As you wish.'

Soldier got to his feet, removed the ice armour, and wearily continued his journey under the oppressive eyes of the gods.

Chapter Twenty-Four

On the other side of the lake Soldier found the path up the mountain. As quickly as winter had descended, summer arrived. It came in as a hot wind, sweeping down the steep slopes and melting all ice and snow in its way. The sun came out, blazing hot, to parch the hills. He avoided the trees when huge icicles began dropping as giant spikes to bury their points in the ground beneath. There was such a cracking, creaking and groaning from the world around him that it seemed as if the earth was coming apart at the seams. Great slabs of ice slid rumbling down the mountainside, shooting dangerously past him like sledges, to crash into rock pillars and stacks under ledges and rims.

Hissing fissures appeared, from out of which steam and gases rose, filling the air with oppressive fumes and decorating the rocks with yellow-green stains. Tendrils of heat licked from these chasms, and occasionally hideous creatures, neither afraid nor hostile, crawled from the depths to slink away before Soldier's approach. The skin of these creatures was repulsive, as if they had not seen air for a thousand years, and their sad glare as they looked once over their shoulders before vanishing into the morning was reproachful and demanded apology.

Below him the bright blue waters of the lake appeared as the ice melted. Floodwater from the snows raced joyously down rocky stream beds to shoot out from high crags, spilling over into the lake. Everywhere the water was rushing through cracks and creases in the earth, to find its way finally into valleys throughout the whole region. Before the noon sun appeared, blood-red, sizzling above his head, the world had appeared in all its earthy, watery colours, through the snows.

'Just when I had started to climb,' panted Soldier, now with a raging thirst. 'Someone up there doesn't like me.'

He drank from a clear, tumbling stream. Mountain goats scrambled away from his approach. There were beds of garnets at the bottom of the stream. He reached in and grasped a handful, intending at a later date to make a necklace for his beloved Layana. Wild sheep jostled each other on the path as he continued to ascend. Animals and birds had appeared from everywhere to meet the instant summer. It was as if they had waited on sprung heels for the first sign of the wind, then leapt out into the warm air. Lush grass had appeared, sweet new leaves sprouted from bushes, buds popped open. Insects arrived in their millions, most of them gnats and midges. Frogs croaked and sent out long tongues to gather them in. Fish leapt in the rivers and streams, silver bars under the sun. A profusion of mammals rustled in the grasses beside the mountain paths.

At one point where the track faded, he was lost, but he found some talking rocks.

'Where do I go?' he asked them.

'There is a stone called the Needle of Destiny, further up. You must follow the stream now, for it is here the path ends.

Go to the stone and rap on it with your knuckles. Someone will answer.'

Soldier thanked the rocks and did as he was bid.

He found the needle, just as they had said. It was a roughly-hewn obelisk, four-sided, with a blunt point. There were markings and hieroglyphics on three sides of the stone. The fourth was virgin blank, as if waiting for an imprint of some kind: perhaps the biography of some unheard-of king?

He struck the stone with his knuckles.

Instantly the earth opened before him, and Soldier went down some steps into what appeared to be a cellar below the needle.

He could not explain it afterwards – after he had surfaced again – but the cellar was like another country. Once he was standing on the flagstone floor he could not see the walls. They lay beyond some distant horizon. There were seas down there, and mountains, plains and valleys. There were great rivers, and fields of wildflowers. There were bears in the forests, and whales in the ocean that he crossed in a living ship which he knew would bleed if he were to cut it. The ship pulsed and breathed below his feet. He stood on its deck, its three sails swollen and full like the breasts and belly of a pregnant woman, and let the cool wind flow through his hair.

Other vessels passed his own, each carrying a single creature on its deck. Sometimes it was a mortal. Sometimes it was an animal. Less often it was a mythical creature, like a griffin or a basilisk. Always their eyes were on some distant place and they ignored any attempt at communication. Some appeared as if they had been sailing for years, perhaps centuries, seeking something they wished to find. Once or twice the ship which passed him was empty of any passenger and on these occasions the craft bellowed painfully like a wounded beast, its hollow-horn cry ringing faintly over evening isles.

Soldier remained standing on his own deck, his hand on the warm, veined mast which bent and swayed with each new tack they took, until he had been deposited on the white sands of a distant shore, covered with blanched seashells and bleached driftwood, along with the bones of ancient creatures not yet known, not yet born, not yet found anywhere else on the earth. Long lines of surf went booming down the strand, tossing yet more of the ocean's treasures up on the white sands.

Here he met a black-skinned beachcomber in a faded robe. This wise-faced and magical fellow had a long, flowing beard and hair which billowed about his head. There were no sandals on his feet. He carried a staff made of ebony and his eyes were as intelligent and promising as the evening summer skies. His countenance carried peace and good will in its features.

Soldier asked the man if he were a wizard. There was a slow nod in return. Then Soldier explained that he had travelled far and long in search of someone who could cure ills. The beachcomber replied that he had that power. He then asked Soldier for his wish and Soldier, not expecting the question so soon, had to think of the answer very quickly.

'My wife and her sister have a terrible affliction,' he said. 'Can you cure them of it?'

'You are permitted to plead for only one.'

Soldier was tired and confused. 'I don't understand.'

'You can request a cure for your wife, or her sister, but not both. One wish only. Or one question to be answered. The choice is yours. You may think about it.'

Soldier thought about it only briefly. As a citizen of

Guthrum the responsible thing to do would be to ensure the ruler of the land was sane. But Soldier was not a pragmatic man, he was an emotional one. He loved his wife and wanted her well, no matter what the wider consequences were. In his mind there was no choice. The queen would have to wait for her time.

'I wish you to cure my wife, Princess Layana, of the affliction which causes her so much distress.'

'It is already done,' replied the beachcomber, and went on his way, examining the bounty of the ocean which the storm tide had scattered along the beach.

Soldier called after him, 'Can you tell me who I am and where I come from?' but the beachcomber ignored his cries. *One wish only. Or one question.*

Soldier threaded his way through piles of seaweed and driftwood to his living ship. Once again he was taken across high seas, through beautiful malachite islands which called to him in plaintive tones to step on their shores. He ignored their cries, desperate instead to return to his own home. A golden horn appeared in the heavens, his own name etched upon its brilliant surface. Once he had landed again, and climbed the steps back up to the obelisk, he had forgotten the name on the golden horn, and was as before, cursed with a blank mind and an empty memory.

Standing by the obelisk again he was minded to return to the world below, to find his name again. He knocked again on the stone – knocked until his knuckles were raw and running with blood – but no stair appeared the second time. With a heavy heart he began to descend the mountain, down past the talking rocks, to the shores of the lake below. Finding no wood or rope to fashion himself a craft, he looked along the

shore line for some other boat-building material. There he
found a mass of elvers, squirming in sargasso weed. He made
a raft of tangled eels, which took him, writhing and knotting,
over the lake to the far side.

At the end of two weeks he was again in the cavern of the
dwarfs, having unlocked the secret of wizards' mountain.

Spagg was there, feeling very sorry for himself.

'Look at these hands, these feet,' he said to Soldier.
'Stigmata! I'm stigmatised for life.'

He showed Soldier the holes in his extremities.

Soldier nodded. 'We will make Caezor pay for these crimes
to you.'

'Do it for yourself,' said Xnople, 'not this moaning weak-
ling.'

'No, no. I cannot do it for myself. I violated the lord's wife.
I deserved to be hunted down.'

Xnople snorted. 'From what I know of the lady, it was probably the other way around. She is a temptress, that one. There
are not many like her amongst her sex, but that particular
enchantress has brought many a man to his knees. Some say
she is not a mortal lady at all, but a wicked fairy, who seduces
wandering knights without mercy.'

Soldier sighed. 'Well, I must fight this Caezor in any case.
He tortured my servant.'

'I'm not your servant,' retorted Spagg. 'And I think we
should be on our way home, rather than messing around here.
Leave this so-called lord to stew. Let's use shank's pony to
get away from here and back to our own people.'

But Soldier would hear none of this talk. He girded his
loins, took up his broken sword, and went out of the cavern.
He left the wood, and trotted down the meadow which led
to the manor. Spagg followed at a distance.

'Come out and fight, Caezor!' Soldier yelled. 'I want my scabbard and my brigandine returned to me.'

Something then occurred to Soldier, and he turned to speak to Spagg. 'What does Caezor know of the brigandine?'

'Why, everything,' replied Spagg. 'He tortured the truth out of me. I told him that if a man wore the armoured jacket, it would keep him immune from blows. He knows if he puts it on he'll be invulnerable.'

'Thanks,' muttered Soldier, sarcastically. 'Now I shall be fighting an unbeatable foe.'

'You're welcome.'

Soldier remained undaunted. He repeated his challenge. At the third call he saw the lady Cresside appear behind the crenellations on the manor-house's flat roof. She stood there, the muslin from her wimple flying in the breeze, and stared down at Soldier with contempt in her eyes.

'My husband is coming,' she sneered, 'to cut off your head and spike it on the manor's gateposts.'

At that moment the gates of the manor were flung open by unseen hands. Soldier stood, legs apart, and braced himself for battle on the meadow. He was exhausted with his journey, and his previous combat, but there was no help for it. He had to stand his ground and fight an invincible enemy.

The scent of camomile and myrtle wafted from the court-yard within. Medlar trees were visible, growing in circles of earth set amongst the flags. From the interior, Caezor, armoured in the brigandine, with drawn sword and plumed helm, came riding out with the intention of cutting Soldier down.

By the time he reached Soldier, Caezor was already dead. His faithful charger continued to thunder towards the stalwart outlander. The lethal poison in the tips of a thousand tiny needles, each no bigger than a stinging-nettle hair, had penetrated his skin. A fatal dose had entered the lord's bloodstream and caused his heart to seize on contact. Such a bolt of pain had gone through him that Caezor had gripped sword hilt and reins with iron fingers. He sat so stiff and upright in his saddle that his mistress did not know he had departed this life for places unknown. She believed him to be still alive and determined to ride down his treacherous guest.

The charger bolted out of control, past the standing Soldier, who stood and watched its progress, amazed at his good fortune.

'Husband!' shrieked Cresside. 'Where are you going?'

Soldier and Spagg later found the horse wandering at the edge of the forest, its reins dangling in the dirt. Caezor's grey, bloated body was discovered further on in the wood, caught in the fork of a dead hornbeam. Removing the brigandine, they found the inside of the velvet-padded armour covered in small droplets of wet blood, looking not unlike the hips and haws which decorate rose briars and hawthorns in the autumn. Clearly it was this garment which had killed the lord of the manor, with its deadly mass of tiny pricks. Soldier realised that he had had a lucky escape, and his heart was heavy with the knowledge that his wife – or someone using her name – had tried to murder him.

'Would you look at that,' announced Spagg, in horror. 'That could've been you or me, Soldier.'

The poison had caused the corpse of Caezor to swell in death, and it now lay like a huge distended fungus on the floor of the forest. Soldier found his scabbard and his good sword, Xanandra, on the body. He took them. The brigandine he left lying open on the chest of the former lord. Spagg took the dead man's purse, half-full of gold coins, and a jewelled dagger. He even plucked some silver buttons from his under-waistcoat, putting them in the purse with the coins. There was a opal brooch on the man's velvet cap and a pearl earring in his left lobe. Spagg offered these to Soldier, who declined, and thus they too ended up in the purse.

'This will pay for my trip out here into this hell-ground of fairies and monsters,' said Spagg, with some satisfaction, 'and for these holes in my hands and feet.'

Soldier did not blame the market trader for robbing the corpse. Caezor had treated him badly and deserved to lose his treasures. Perhaps they might have gone to the dead man's wife, but she was rich already, not only having her grand house, but all the wealth which lay within.

The dwarfs came out of their holes in the ground and spat on their former master. Some danced a jig around his body. They praised Soldier and Spagg, calling them heroes.

'Be merciful,' said Soldier, feeling contrite. 'Take his remains back to his wife, so that she might give him a proper funeral and burial. Do not desecrate the corpse, nor mutilate it in any way. Even a man such as this needs to be respected in death, and the feelings of his wife taken to account.'

But the dwarfs heeded not his words. They called Cresside a whore and a false wife, and twisted and tore Caezor's arms from their sockets. They hacked away his legs. These limbs they bundled up like firewood gathered from the ground and threw them into a nearby pond. His head they ripped from his body and hung in a the strong net of a fairyland spider's web. They took the torso out into the meadow and sent it rolling, accompanied by a great cheer, down the hill like a giant egg. Cresside stood on the roof of the manor house and watched all this with a grim face, her thin lips like a scarlet scar across her pale features. Then she turned and left, to be seen no more by the two travellers. Soldier went from that place with a heavy heart, took Caezor's horse for his own, and let Spagg mount up behind him. Together they rode homeward.

Captain Kaff was ill. There was an epidemic in Zamerkand. A sudden summer plague was sweeping through the city, carrying off hundreds of people each day. It was not necessarily a killer plague – some victims recovered – but it was highly infectious and it took away two in three of its victims. One only had to be in a room with someone who was falling ill of the plague to succumb oneself. A mere breath was enough.

To protect herself, her courtiers and her advisors, the queen had sealed off the Palace of Birds. Chancellor Humbold was on the inside. When that great man heard that Soldier was close to returning, and would arrive any day, he was incensed but frustrated. There was nothing he could do about it. He certainly was not going to leave the sanctuary of the palace and go abroad in the streets to find an assassin. The virulent disease frightened him as much as it did anyone else. Nor was he going to meet secretly with Kaff, who was at that moment sweating and turning in a fever on his own bed. Besides, the Captain of the Imperial Guard was delirious and utterly useless to him.

How had that infernal Soldier managed to carry out his mission without being killed? Faeryland, the mountains of the gods, the land beyond the hanging valleys: he had traversed all these and still he survived to return? It did not seem possible. And all their plots – those of Humbold himself and of Kaff – had come to nothing. Soldier was indeed a dangerous man. It had been foolish of Humbold not to kill the newcomer the moment he had been brought to the city by the hunter.

'Nothing to be done about it now,' muttered the chancellor to himself, staring out of one of the high windows down on the city streets. 'At least he did not complete his quest. The queen is still as mad as she ever was, and that leaves me in control.'

Down below him there were poor people, staggering around in various stages of the disease. Some had fallen, died, and were rotting in the gutters. In the beginning death-carts had gone through the city, but now there was hardly anyone around now who was well enough to gather up the corpses.

The red pavilions had moved up country, away from the danger. The Carthagans would never have entered the city to do that kind of work anyway. They were warriors, not physicians or morticians.

Across the gardens, on the other side of the tower from which the chancellor viewed the city, was the Palace of Wildflowers. It too was shut tightly up, but for a different reason. The Princess Layana had gone down with the plague just yesterday and to protect her staff she had ordered everyone except her personal maid to leave the main premises. She had sent them to the gazebos and garden rooms below, where they could isolate themselves from her and the outside world. Humbold knew all this because, having seen the yellow plague flag raised above the princess's palace yesterday evening, he had called down to Layana's servants as they came from the building.

'So, the princess may soon be dead, which will remove some of Soldier's protection. The queen will not be so interested in him once Layana is dead. The hero's return might still yet be turned into the hero's funeral.'

Rats were everywhere in the streets below. They had emerged boldly from the sewers, once the population's attention had been diverted by the plague. There was plenty to eat, too. A plethora of rotting corpses supplied the rat population with abundant food. They thrived. They procreated. Humbold had an army of servants killing those creatures which tried to climb the walls of the palace. Since many of the towers were fashioned from obsidian, the surface was very slippery and it was not an easy business for the rats to enter. In any case, the food was below, in the houses and alleyways, not inside the palace. Only the actively curious attempted to scale the walls.

'Well,' mused Humbold, sighing, 'there is nothing to do but wait now. It's galling that the outlander might be entering the city any day now, but he still has to face the plague, which has no favourites.'

It was a comforting thought.

Once the plague had begun Uthellen and the witchboy were forgotten. Their jailer was first among the sick and died within three days, leaving no one to attend to the prisoners. Although they were safe from the plague in the dungeons, they starved. Finally, the bird Uthellen had come to know as 'Soldier's raven' came and picked the lock of their cell with its beak. Uthellen in turn let out the other prisoners and left them to swarm out into the city streets, where many of them caught the plague and died within a week. She and the boy left the city.

They went to the forest and found their old campsite. There they remained. It was a safe place, away from the ghastly stink of death and disease.

'We must remain here,' she told her son, 'until Soldier returns.'

'Yes, Mother.'

The boy regarded Uthellen with eyes devoid of emotion. She was his protectress and he did as she bade him do. There was no love in his expression. She saw this and it grieved her, but she knew that her son was a wizard and did not have human sentiment. There was no harm in him towards her, no malice. She was simply the woman who had carried him for nine months in her womb, and who was now his devoted defender. She knew the world and its ways, while he was still a novice, and she would keep him safe.

Kaff rolled and turned in his bed in the guardhouse, attended by faithful Imperial Guards. His determination to live was apparent by the strong fire in his eyes. Captain Kaff was not about be to carried off like some weak girl by an illness he regarded as an affront to his manhood. He now had a metal hand, a silver one, which flashed in the light every time he moved his right arm. Even in his fever each flash reminded him how much he hated Soldier, and that he had a score to settle with the outlander.

Chapter Twenty-Five

Soldier and Spagg rode through the long avenue of severed heads outside Zamerkand. They were astride the horses they had first set out on. Soldier had found the beasts wandering near the village in the valley of the growing-shrinking huts. Caezor's steed was left on top of the plateau, to find its own way back to the manor. Perhaps it never would? There was plenty of lush grass to eat along the river bank, now that the snow had gone, so the creature would not starve. It might simply run wild.

Now that they had knowledge of them, the two travellers had managed to avoid the trolls on their return journey. They rode north of the river, keeping a wary eye out for hunting-parties. No troll raiders were seen however, and the pair were able to pass through the region without having to run or fight. It was just as well: they were both on the point of exhaustion.

When they arrived at Zamerkand there were no new heads on the stakes. The old ones were skulls now, with little flesh on them. And the gates to the city were wide open. No guards could be seen. The raven was sitting on the rump of Soldier's horse, dispensing his usual wisdom.

'Where are the red pavilions?' asked Soldier, of the raven. 'Have they fled the plague?'

'Wouldn't you?' replied the black bird.

At that point Spagg halted his horse.

'I think I'll go an' stay with my cousin. He's got a farm a little north of here. No sense in riskin' life and limb by going into there while the pestilence is about. Jugg will be pleased to see me, I'm sure, now that I've got a bit o' gold.'

Soldier nodded. 'I can't blame you.'

'Why don't you come?' asked Spagg. 'You don't want to risk gettin' the plague. Jugg'll put us up, both. If he won't let us in the house, we can sleep in the barn.'

'No, you go on, Spagg. I've got to see my wife. I hear she's very ill.'

'That's what I mean. She'll give it to you.'

Soldier still declined. He thanked Spagg for his company on the journey. He said Spagg's services had been invaluable.

'Do me a favour though,' Spagg grunted in reply. 'Don't ask for me next time you want to do somethin' like this?'

The market trader then left.

Soldier spoke with the raven. 'There don't seem to be any guards about.'

'They're all sick – or scared to death.'

'Is everyone indoors?'

'Most of the sensible ones.'

Soldier rode through the gates. The streets were indeed deserted, except for flies. There were flies everywhere. And shadowy shapes which scuttled between the rotting corpses.

'Rats,' murmured Soldier. 'Feasting.'

He rode through the cobbled bailey, then along an alley into a public courtyard. Still he encountered no people.

'If the city were attacked now by an enemy, we wouldn't stand a chance.'

The raven replied, 'What self-preserving nation would want to attack a plague city?'

The bird then bade Soldier farewell for a time and flew off in search of its own food. Soldier did not like to dwell on what the raven was going to eat. He had already guessed.

Soldier dismounted and led his horse through the streets. It defecated, the dung falling on the stones. Soldier noticed that there was no fresh manure stuck between the cobbles. And weeds had begun to grow in grubby corners. The doors of houses he passed were covered in crudely-painted red markings which he guessed were symbols to do with ritual and enchantment: to keep away the plague. Though of course, he told himself, they may have been put there by the city's administrators, to inform others how far the plague had progressed inside each individual house. He, being an outlander, would have no idea.

Soldier reached the Palace of Wildflowers. Again there were no guards outside the building. He took his horse to the stables at the rear, found some hay, and left it in a stall to eat and drink from its trough. Soldier then passed through a bower in the palace gardens and entered the palace by way of the empty kitchens. Once inside he went straight to the main hall and ascended the stairs. Drissila met him halfway up.

'Your lady is sick,' she said to him. 'You had better leave until she is well again. Stay somewhere else. At the inn perhaps? Or better still, outside the city walls.'

'I must go to her,' said Soldier, passing the maid-servant on the stairs. 'She will be in need of company.'

'She is out of her head with fever. She's burning up and I

must keep her cool. The disease is still infectious. In any case, she needs no one. You especially are not welcome.'

He was surprised to hear this. 'Have I done wrong? What have I done?'

'You'll find out.'

Drissila continued to descend the stairs, leaving him staring after her. The maid-servant had a bowl of vomit in her hands and it was beginning to stink the place out. He could see she wanted to get rid of it as soon as possible.

Soldier continued up the stairs. He found the passage to the Green Tower. Once he reached Layana's boudoir he paused outside the doorway. Why was she angry with him? Was she never satisfied? He had surely cured her of her madness? The queen would be none too happy with him, he was well aware, but surely Layana appreciated his efforts? He had been through much – to the very edge of the precipice, and looked over into the valley of death – yet she was still acrimonious?

He then heard a low moan and his true feelings flooded to the fore. 'I want her to live so much.'

He entered the room. On the far side stood the four-poster bed, swathed in black muslin curtains, which wafted back and forth in the cool breeze from the open windows. Soldier strode over to the bed and stared. He could see the pale form of his beloved, stretched out, covered only by a thin cotton sheet. No details were visible to him through this dark diaphanous screen, so he could not tell how far the illness had progressed, or whether she was out of danger or not.

He could smell the rank sweat which soaked the bed and could just make out her hair, brushed into a fan shape over her pillow (Drissila's work, no doubt) but looking damp and lank none the less. The foul stench of bile and vomit pervaded the whole room. Her breath was shallow, faulty. He felt something wrench at his heart. Oh, how thin and wasted she seemed, even through the screen of cloth! He wanted to take her in his arms, tell her he was here and would look after her, make her know that he loved her and wanted her to live more than anything else.

Soldier reached out to draw back the black muslin.

'Don't touch it!'

The command came not from bed, but from behind him.

It was Drissila, back with jar of large black spiders. 'Leave it. It's there for a reason. No direct light must go into her eyes. She will be blinded otherwise. The eyes of plague victims are very sensitive to the light.'

'I'm sorry. I did not know. What are they for?'

'The spiders? They must bite her. Their poison is beneficial in the healing process.'

Soldier shuddered. 'Are you sure?'

Drissila looked at him as if he were a five-year-old.

'This is Guthrum, where I was born. I know a few things. It's taken me a day and a half to collect these spiders.' She added with some pride. 'I knew just where in the cellars to find them. Everyone is after them at the moment.'

'I'll stay and watch.'

'You should not even be here. You will catch it.'

'You are here.'

'I had the plague when I was ten. I am immune. You, on the other hand, are an outsider. If *you* catch it, you'll surely die. You have no natural defence against such pestilence.'

'I shall stay,' said Soldier, determined.

'Captain Kaff did that and look what happened to him. He caught it within three days. Now he's fighting for his own life, and all for nothing really.'

Soldier simmered. 'Kaff was here?'

'He sat over her bedside, administered poultices, wiped her brow with a cool damp cloth, just as you are no doubt thinking of doing, if you're so foolish as to wish to risk disease and death,' replied Drissila. 'But I won't let you. One man has already caught the plague from her. I won't permit another one to do the same.'

Soldier almost envied his rival. Layana and he shared the plague together! So, Kaff had watched over Soldier's beloved as if *he* had been the husband and lover. Was nothing sacred in this land?

'Damn the man,' growled Soldier, in great pain, 'may he rot in some dark, unknown place and may his soul go swiftly and surely to the worst side of the Otherworld.'

'In the meantime,' remarked Drissila, matter-of-factly, 'I must feed your lady some watered soup. If you're staying you can sit over there, on that tall chair. I must slip between the folds of the curtains and assist my mistress.'

Drissila carried out her duties, while Soldier sat and watched. He could not help himself calling to Layana once. She turned her head slowly in his direction, but he could not see her expression through the folds of the dark muslin. Then once more her head was laid back on the pillow and she drifted into sleep.

Soldier sat in the chair all that day, and the following day too. He remained in or near the room for a whole week. Drissila made sure he got fed. When he realised she was doing all the cooking he took his turn in the kitchen, making soup and broth.

'Has she passed the worst?' asked Soldier of Drissila, every hour of every day. 'Will she live?'

One day Drissila was able to nod to this question. Soldier

almost collapsed with relief. The servants were ordered back into the house since the infectious stage was over. Ofao returned. And the guards and cooks. Soldier went to Layana's boudoir. The muslin curtains were drawn. She was sitting up in bed. When he entered the room she turned at the sound of his footsteps and glared at him.

The sight of her face made him stop halfway across the room.

'My dearest lady,' he cried, delighted. 'Your scars have gone! Your face has been healed! Your loveliness has been restored. I am so happy for you.'

'You did this,' she said, in a strangely bitter tone. 'You must have asked for this instead of pleading for my sanity. You preferred the shallow choice of a beautiful wife instead of a sane one. Was that it? Could you not stand the jibes of your fellow warriors in the red pavilions? Did they call me a freak, a deformed creature? And did they call you a fool for marrying me? So, you decided, when you had the wizard at your beck, to smooth the wrinkles in my skin, instead of smoothing the distortions of my mind. How base you are!'

He was stunned by this reply. 'You – you still suffer from your madness?'

'Of course. Just before I fell ill I woke with my face restored, but my head full of demons. I have nothing in my heart but hate for you, Soldier. How foolish I was to trust a blue-eyed outlander, someone who came from nowhere. I should have stuck to my own kind. All you want is a wife you're not ashamed to be seen with, instead of one who would be sane enough to share your life. You're like all men. Why don't you go back into nowhere again. I don't want to see you. Leave my room. Go away from here.'

She covered her face with her hands and began weeping.

'This is partly your fault,' he said, recalling his words to the wizard. 'I asked you to be cured of the affliction which distressed you. You must have been more concerned by your looks than the state of your mind.'

She paled under his words.

'Also,' said Soldier, unhappy beyond measure, 'what of the deadly brigandine, bearing your crest?'

'I know of no brigandine.'

She was telling the truth, he could see that. They stared at each other in frustration, neither able to tell the other that they were relieved to see their loved one alive and out of danger; neither able to declare that the only thing on their minds for the past few months had been the life of that loved one. If one had broken down at that moment, the other would have done too, and they would have fallen into each other's arms sobbing and confessing: but each had an iron will and kept their true thoughts, their true feelings, locked within.

Soldier stamped, distressed and angry, from the room. He wanted to explain that when he had asked for her affliction to be removed, he had not even been thinking of her scars, only the troubles of her mind. He had no idea that the wizard would restore her beauty rather than her sanity. It had not occurred to him to make the distinction. Now his journey had all been in vain. The queen would be angry with him, and Layana believed him to be a false lover. Surely that oaf Kaff would win her from him now?

He shouted, as he crashed down the passageway. 'Have I risked my life, and that of another man, to be shunned like this?'

Drissila came out of another room and stared at him mildly.

'You men,' she said, 'you think all women are only interested in their looks.'

He opened the palms of his hands. 'Drissila, please believe me, I thought I had cured her madness, not rid her of her scars.'

'Well, be that as it may, neither I nor you can convince her of that now. I hear the queen is none too pleased with you, either. You'd better lie low for a while. You can sleep in the North Tower. I won't tell anyone you're there.'

'Thank you, Drissila,' he said, from the depths of his despair. 'You'll tell me when to show myself?'

Shortly after this conversation, however, Layana's madness visited. Still very weak from having suffered the plague, Layana was worse than usual. Drissila made the mistake of telling Soldier of this development, and he left the North Tower.

Soldier insisted on staying in the Green Tower with his wife, to try to assist her at this most distressing time. She rejected him completely. Three times during the first night she crept up to his couch, intent on murdering him. Each time the scabbard's song woke him. He was able to wrest the weapon from her hand. She must have had a dozen daggers concealed about the room and knew exactly where to find them.

'If I don't kill you now,' she hissed, 'I shall poison you later. You'll never be safe near me. You'll die in terrible agony.'

On the third attempt, after putting her back in her bed, he went outside the room. He found the balcony at the end of the passageway and went out into the cool air, to stare at the night stars. Utterly miserable, he noticed that the red pavilions had returned. He could see the ochre tents in the light of the moon. How he yearned for companionship at that moment! Perhaps he should leave, he told himself, and join his friends in the pavilions. Velion would have stories of battles fought to tell him. And he, in his turn, could recount his adventures into the land of gods and fairies.

It was but a fleeting thought, a wish that relieved his feelings for only a short time.

He knew he had to stay with Layana, at least until this bout of lunacy had left her. Poor Layana. How useless he had been as a husband. He had given his best and his efforts had brought him not love, but hatred. A man needs love of some kind. He needs someone who believes him to be best. He needs a sign from the world that there is someone in it that regards him above all others.

While he was standing there, something dark and monstrous moved in the depths of the city. Soldier frowned and gripped the balcony rail. For one instant it seemed the earth had turned over. Then it was over and all was still. He was puzzled, but when no further movements came, no shadow crossed his mind, he decided it must have been an earth tremor.

Moments later a shadow passed over the moon.

He looked up to see a large, winged, reptilian shape gliding across the bright discus in the sky above the city.

'KERROWW!' came the affectionate sound, from the mouth of this creature passing by. 'KERROWW! KERROWW!'

Soldier, the mother of a dragon, allowed himself a smile.

WIZARD'S FUNERAL

Kim Hunter

Kim Hunter's masterful epic of dark sorcery and fierce battle continues . . .

In the troubled kingdom of Zamerkand, the enemies within are as dangerous as those at its borders. For Soldier, the warrior whose influence is already too great for some courtesans' liking, there is no such thing as rest. Death can strike at any moment, and from any direction.

But it is another death that will shake the world to its core: that of the King Magus, whose power alone can keep the forces of good and evil in balance. His successor needs to be found, and the responsibility is given to Soldier. The successor, however, is only a young boy, and there are many who would prefer him – and Soldier – to meet a more bloody fate.

'An absorbing tale of sorcery and strife'

DREAMWATCH

TRANSFORMATION

Carol Berg

Seyonne is a man waiting to die. He has been a slave for sixteen years and has lost everything of meaning to him: his dignity, the people and homeland he loves, and the Warden's power that enables him to step into a human soul and do battle with demons.

But Prince Aleksander, heir to the Derzhi empire, has been possessed by the very demons that Seyonne once fought – demons now allied with the savage Khelid nation. Seyonne must recover his power and cast down the Demon Lords before they destroy both the prince and his empire.